Soul of the South

Bedside Books
An imprint of American Book Publishing
P.O. Box 65624
Salt Lake City, UT 84165
www.american-book.com
Printed in the United States of America on acid-free paper.

Soul of the South

Designed by Chris Krupinski, design@american-book.com

ISBN 1-58982-267-6

Witham, Mike, Soul of the South

Special Sales

These books are available at special discounts for bulk purchases. Special editions, including personalized covers, excerpts of existing books, and corporate imprints, can be created in large quantities for special needs. For more information e-mail info@american-book.com.

Soul of the South

Mike Witham

Dedication

This book is dedicated to the loving memory of Margaret "Penny" Downey, my grandmother, whose love and support helped make me the writer and person that I am.

1

August 28, 1835 greeted Mobile, Alabama, with a warm sun, a calm ripple of Gulf water on its coastal shore, and the sound of common flickers chirping their pleasant melodies. In fact, it was a picturesque Southern summer day. Yet it was only fitting, for future generations of Southerners would look upon the day with happiness, glory, and honor. On August 28, 1835, William Henry Lytham of Mobile, Alabama was born.

William was the eldest child in a family of five. Though the predominant religion of his hometown was Baptist, William's parents, Matthew and Melissa, along with many of the townsfolk, were descendants of the English Catholics who left the persecution in their "Mother Country" and settled in the South. The Lythams were patriotic to the bone, and no one doubted their commitment both to their country and to their faith.

William had a brother and a sister. William's relationship with his brother James, six years his junior, was very close. They loved each other tremendously and were committed to supporting each other in any way possible. They knew that blood was thicker than water, and whatever sibling differences they may have had while growing up, they would, in the end, always position themselves on the same side.

William's relationship with his sister Tara, twelve years his junior, was obviously the relationship of an older brother to a much younger sister. Tara was truly priceless and a bundle of joy. She would always bring a smile to William's face. William wanted nothing but the best for her and was committed to making her life happy any way he could.

William was a child like any other. There was something about him, however, that no one could explain. He was sensitive, caring, yet at the same time he could, if required, demonstrate a ferocity rarely equaled. The townsfolk were unable to explain these polarizing characteristics. Yet both were essential parts of William's character. All who observed it testified that it was meant for something—something significant.

William's dual composition was poignantly demonstrated at the tender age of seven. On his seventh birthday, a boy in his grade school class, Darren McKenny, boasted that he was stronger than William. William knew this to be untrue and kindly told him so. The boy, however, challenged William to a duel, which William promptly accepted. It did not take long for Darren to realize that he was no match for William. William straightaway administered a flurry of lefts and rights to his opponent's stomach and face such that, before Darren could even say his name, he lay defeated on the ground. Those who had witnessed this episode quickly realized that William was no ordinary boy.

William's encounter with Darren would not be his last. For the present, however, William warmly received Darren's subsequent offer of friendship, even though the McKennys were from the North—something Southerners, at the time, did not look highly upon. Moreover, the two remained the best of friends until the eve of the Civil War.

At the age of eighteen, William followed the footsteps of his father and his grandfather before him: The young man entered the army at Mobile Academy. The Lythams were constantly concerned with love of country and of the patriotic duty to defend it against any foe. The only foes William considered a threat to America, however, were the British to the North and the Spanish to the South.

William thrived during his years at Mobile Academy. In fact, he soon gained the distinction as the Academy's best soldier. During the heat of battle, in simulated war games, William continually commanded his troops to victory. Even President Buchanan commended Lytham on his performance, stating that he looked forward to the day when the young man would lead the entire United States Army.

Perhaps William's greatest gift, however, was his acute perception. Time and again, he knew what his opponents were up to and defeated them thoroughly. Some called it a sixth sense. Others, however, were certain that he had spies on the go.

After seven fruitful years in the army, William was made an officer at the age of twenty-five. The year, however, was 1860, and William well knew the nation's tension. Mobile Academy offered an abundant illustration. Although William was able to have his unit operate in concert, when the troops were at ease, the men would continually break into factions according to their place of birth. Such a delicate uniformity could, in fact, recess into a division so great that literally friend against friend would be at arms. William had no better manifestation of such than in his friendship with Darren McKenny.

Seven years at Mobile Academy saw Darren change from a Southern supporter to the most formidable weapon the North could ever muster. In his first six years, however, he was indeed a loyal Southerner. Whenever the troops were at ease, Darren would always sojourn in the Southern camp. But in his seventh year, he became increasingly uneasy of the talk around camp. One such conversation in particular pushed McKenny from Southern allegiance to Northern embrace.

The dialogue was between two soldiers discussing the deepening national crisis—with them being convinced that someone from the Southern camp was ascertaining information and sending it to the Northern camp. Darren considered the men having the discourse, Paul Shen and John Jedd, to be his good friends.

"Thank goodness Lytham is in charge of our unit."

"Thank goodness, indeed," Jedd said. "If we had someone from the North, I think there would be a mutiny."

"You're right. You can never trust a Northerner. They think they're so morally superior because they don't have slavery. But they have made our economy dependent upon slavery as we must grow cotton to be considered economically feasible. Yet they come across as if they are the true moralists of the nation. It makes me sick!"

"What about McKenny, Paul? He tells us that he's originally from the North but that he grew up in the South and favors us rather than them—even though his parents detest Southerners. Do you think he is putting up a front? Do you think he is a spy for the North?"

"I wish I knew. It's hard to say. But I wouldn't put it past him."

"Me neither. I will never trust a Northerner!"

Paul and John's conversation wounded Darren to the soul. Hitherto, he had trusted their friendship. Thus, for them to suspect him as a spy for the North was thoroughly devastating. He even started to believe that William felt the same way.

That evening was the longest in Darren's life. He did not get even an hour of sleep. He kept thinking, *What should I do? Who am I? Will I ever be accepted by the South?* After many restless hours, McKenny became convinced that he would never be accepted as a Southerner. As a result, on the following morning, he went to meet William for the final time—as friends.

"Good morning, William. How are things?"

"Good morning, Darren. Fine. And you?"

"All right," he answered unconvincingly. "William, I am troubled by the tension in the Academy and, in fact, in the entire nation."

"Me, too, Darren," Lytham said sadly. "Here, I constantly strive to have us do all activities together—dividing up only when participating in simulated war games, and then only by drawing lots and not by places of birth. I do believe this course has been very successful, for our unit has not incurred an insurrection in a nation presently embroiled in such. Regarding the nation, I am continually sending letters to the president and to congress beseeching them to resolve the matter peacefully. But can it be resolved peacefully? I personally detest slavery, as do most Southerners. If the North would only help us diversify our economy, we could end this subjugation of human beings. Yet the North continues to refuse our entreaties. Instead, they sit idly by on their high horses and tell us what to do."

"Maybe they have a moral obligation to tell you folks what to do."

"'You folks'?"

"Yes, William. I will never be accepted as a Southerner. Yesterday, I overheard Shen and Jedd talk about me as if I were a spy for the Northern camp. What kind of nonsense is that? The more I think about it, William, the more I am starting to side with the North in all this."

"Darren, Shen and Jedd don't trust anyone. I don't think they even trust their own mothers. They are talking pure nonsense!"

"I wish I could believe that, William. But I don't know anymore."

McKenny abruptly departed and, from that day forward, resided in the Northern camp. In his last month at Mobile Academy—December 1860— he incited an insurrection with the Northern soldiers over William's leadership to assert himself as the new commander and chief of the unit. Darren failed in the attempt, but in the process drew many soldiers from the border states to the Northern side.

The failed insurrection was all William could withstand. Shortly after order was restored, he addressed the soldiers.

"Hitherto we, as a unit, have withstood the nation's tension and division. We are all Americans first and foremost—regardless of where we were born. I myself am from the South. I am honored to be a Southerner. But before anything else, I am an American, and this crisis our country is going through will eventually pass. So, it is up to us to remain united. Thus, due to recent events, I order that from henceforth, when at ease, no one will be permitted to assemble according to his place of birth. This is the law I now make as commanding officer. Any questions?" There were none. "Then as I have said, so it shall be."

Then he turned to McKenny and took him aside.

"Darren, I would like a word with you. I've been informed that you were behind the insurrection. Is this true?"

"No, sir," McKenny lied.

"Don't lie to me, Darren." Lytham was guessing.

"I am not, sir."

"Shall I call in my informants, then?" Lytham was bluffing.

The bluff worked. Darren realized William could be lying, but he also realized that William could very well have had spies in the Northern camp, and if they were brought to prove his guilt, he would be spared no mercy.

"All right, I did it. But only in the best interests of the country."

"Explain."

"William, as you know, our nation will very soon be at war. You, of all people, can perceive this climate. So I decided to take action on the side of the Union, our country—because you and I know the section that will secede from the rest won't be the North."

"Expressing the side you would take in the event of a military conflict is one thing. To actively set about an insurrection while the nation is united is quite another. I have no other course of action but to discharge you from the military. I could do this as a dishonorable discharge but…because and only because of our past friendship, I will not. Yet, you are discharged nonetheless."

With that, Darren left the Academy. Later that day he left for New York where, after explaining the circumstances of his discharge to the New York division, he was readmitted into the army and promoted to lieutenant.

For William, he knew it would only be a matter of weeks before the South would secede. Consequently, he became more and more troubled. He wanted desperately not to take sides in the national dispute. Moreover, his career was already highly impressive. To be promoted to so high a position at so young an age was nothing short of remarkable. Yet, all this prestige and future promise would be lost, William thought, if he had to choose the South. "What an unenviable plight to be in," he sighed to himself.

2

January 1861 brought matters to a head. Alabama, along with Florida, Georgia, Mississippi, and Louisiana, had voted to secede from the Union, following South Carolina's lead in December. William was at an impasse. Must he relinquish all that he had worked for his entire adult life? After much deliberation, he decided to consult with his father on the matter at the family home in February.

After exchanging pleasantries and enjoying a delicious Southern supper with his kinsfolk, William conversed with his father privately in the study.

"So," his father began, "how is army life, William? Are you making our family proud?"

"That is why I'm here, Pa. What am I to do? I want to have a distinguished military career as you and Grandpa did. But it looks as if there will be war between the North and the South. Am I to throw away all that we have worked for and bring disgrace upon our family by siding with the South?"

"Son, you won't bring any disgrace to our family. You are our pride and joy. Your charm, your wit, your sincerity are all attributes people admire. You have before you one of the toughest decisions in your life. I know this is not an enviable position to be in. As for us, we will support the decision of our state legislature. But whatever choice you make, we will understand, support, and love you all the same."

The next day, William took leave of his family and entered St. Mary's On-the-Hill Church to contemplate his sorrow in prayer. "Oh, what am I to do, blessed Lord?" Lytham earnestly entreated. Just then, a stilling silence fell upon the church, and the more William reflected upon his anguish in this silence, the more he felt that he should follow his heart. He was a Southerner. He detested slavery and felt the impending war was but the culmination of the South's continual desire to be free from Northern economic dictates. Hence, once a nation of her own, the South would be empowered to end all forms of slavery in its society. William embraced this resolve—even though he knew it would incur the loss of his prestigious Federal military career. He believed his best course of action in the conflict would be to disappear from the scene and take on a new role as a spy for the Confederacy.

Accordingly, at the beginning of March 1861, Lytham met General Beauregard in Montgomery, Alabama, to discuss these plans.

Brigadier General Pierre Beauregard was among the initial military selections of Confederate President Jefferson Davis. A Louisianan, Beauregard prided himself on his French descent and ardently wanted to bring glory for the South as his hero Napoleon Bonaparte had done for France. Beauregard viewed the Union as the Union had previously viewed Britain—a state trying to force itself upon another with tyranny. Accordingly, Beauregard wanted to throw off the Union yoke as America had done to the British some 90 years earlier.

"General, I have thought long and hard about the stance I should take in our national crisis, and I have come to the conclusion that I should, and thus will, support the South. And I believe that I can best serve the South as a spy. If I could obtain a new name and a new look, I would be able to reside in Washington and uncover Federal strategy, which I will immediately relay for our advantage."

"Do you believe this role would be better than you heading a division in our military, William? After all, you have one of the best reputations in the Federal army. You are well known for your ability to bring about victory, even against formidable odds."

"General, as it stands now, the Union will think I have fled the nation—believing I was not willing to engage in such a civil crisis. Thus, if I reappear, they will still consider me a loyal subject. However, if I emerge as a Southern soldier, they will know for certain my status."

"I respect your decision, William. I will arrange for you a meeting with our best disguise artist—Mittle Tobbs of Charleston, South Carolina. He will give you a new look as well as a new identity. No one will recognize you."

"Thank you, General Beauregard."

"Thank you, William. In fact, after you meet Mittle, you can help us ascertain something we have been earnestly trying to find out."

"Yes, General?"

"Well, at present, we are in the process of overtaking all the Federal military outposts in the South. Up to now, we have incurred no resistance. I fear, however, Fort Sumter in South Carolina may pose a problem. Word has it that the North plans to take a stand at Sumter. Find out if this is true and confirm the matter to me as quickly as possible."

"Yes, General, I will!"

Mittle Tobbs was a highly respected professional in crafting new identity and looks. His celebrity was known not only in America, but also in Europe. Entering Mittle's shop, William realized the man was the best in his field. The plaques and memorabilia from dignitaries such as Napoleon III, Queen Victoria, as well as American presidents Jefferson and Jackson, decorated the store. Mittle was a fourth-generation Tobbs who ran the hundred-year-old family business. As Mittle's great-great-grandfather used to say, "Disguise results in the demise of the foe." The legacy that the first Mittle Tobbs had instilled in his family remained true to the present.

"It is an honor to meet you, Mr. Tobbs."

"Please, call me Mittle. It is an honor to meet you too, William Lytham. Your meritorious fame precedes you. Many here in the South know your name or have at least heard of your success at Mobile Academy," Tobbs warmly expressed. "Anyway, General Beauregard has asked me to provide you with a new look and identity."

"Yes. If you could accomplish this task, Mittle, I would be extremely grateful."

"Well, disguise has been our family's forte for generations. You need not worry."

There was indeed no need to worry. After his time with Mittle, William looked completely different. His short hair was covered with a state-of-the-art long wig. His military clothes were replaced with a type of wealthy business clothing frequently found in Northern circles. He was instructed to grow a moustache. His new name became David Stenner—fully supported with identification papers. Finally, and perhaps most importantly, Tobbs, who previously had many customers from Boston, schooled Lytham on the way they spoke and presented themselves. Hence, with his affluent apparel, long hair, sharp moustache, and Bostonian demeanour, William was a new man—with the documents to prove it.

After two weeks with Mittle, William was ready for Washington. Accordingly, after thanking Mittle for all his help, Lytham made posthaste, via the train, for the Federal capital. In Washington, William found accommodation in a house owned by a widowed Mrs. Edith Smith. Mrs. Smith was kind, elderly, and credulous. Hence, when William stated that he was a traveling salesman seeking a room for lodging, Mrs. Smith accepted him immediately and did not ask any probing questions. "As long as you pay on time and keep your room clean," she said, "it is my pleasure to have you stay here."

During the evenings, William would frequent Washington's many taverns in the attempt to overhear any conversation relating to military operations at Fort Sumter. One such conversation he overheard took place at the Evening Express on April 2. The two Federalists conversing about the garrison were Lieutenant Oliver Duckworth and Officer Ron Steinburt.

"Those Southern bastards!"

"What is the president planning to do, Oliver? We can't just sit here and allow every military outpost in the South to be usurped by those renegades."

"Don't worry, I've been conversing with General McDowell and he says that Lincoln will take a stand at Fort Sumter. If the South attempts to acquire it, they will have to take it by force and thus draw first blood."

"I don't understand. Why don't we just go down there and whip 'em?"

"Don't you see, if we do, the South will have the upper hand. They will say, 'Look, we are being attacked without provocation.' As a result, they will look like the defenders in the public eye, incurring international sympathy and perhaps even international support. This would totally undermine our cause!"

"So, if the South draws first blood, public opinion will be in our favor?"

"Most likely. Or at least more in our favor than if we were to initiate the conflict."

Lincoln will take his stand at Sumter! What should we do? Should we strike and possibly draw first blood? Should we instead wait before attacking the fort? With the conclusion of the Duckworth and Steinburt conversation, William, without delay, sent a dispatch to Beauregard informing him of the discourse.

Receiving the news, Beauregard painstakingly assessed the situation. *So it is true*, he thought, *the North will stand at Sumter*. Upon deliberation, the general, with Confederate president Davis' assent, decided to take Fort Sumter regardless of Lincoln's actions or of how the public would perceive such an event. To Pierre, the events of the last few months had made it obvious, even though it had not been declared, that the South was indeed its own country and that as a sovereign nation, it should conduct its affairs accordingly. Thus, on the morning of April 12, 1861, the South fired upon the garrison, and within two days, Union Major Anderson had surrendered. Cheers of euphoria rang throughout the South.

Learning of the successful strike, William felt the victory was bittersweet. While he was joyous that his country was triumphant in the takeover, he realized that it would likely result in the full mobilization of the United States Army—an army wealthier in men and machinery than its counterpart. William thus realized that his services as a spy were all the more necessary if the South was to have any chance at combating this deficiency.

On April 15, 1861, Lincoln, as William suspected, fully mobilized the United States Army.

For William, his next course of action was to ascertain where the Federalists planned to attack. Weeks passed with him relentlessly seeking this very thing. Finally, in late June, he became aware (through a bar conversation with Union Officer Dean Slasbury) of an impending Federalist offensive. Lytham learned that Union Commander General Irvin McDowell was planning an imminent attack against the Confederates at Bull Run, Virginia. William, as the wealthy Bostonian, stated to Slasbury that he was interested in providing financial assistance to the Federal army and in meeting with McDowell to discuss this. Slasbury warmly received the request and arranged for William the audience with McDowell. The meeting took place at McDowell's headquarters on the morning of June 29.

"Good morning, Mr. Stenner! Officer Slasbury has spoken fondly of you. He has informed me that you would like to assist us financially in the smashing of the secessionist states."

"Indeed, General," Lytham said. "For years, my family has prided itself on its allegiance to the Federalist flag. We believe that any segment of the populace wishing to discard this sacred icon of ours is committing treachery of the worst kind. This matter of secession by the South has wounded my family, and indeed the entire nation, to the soul. It must be stopped! The South must realize that its traitorous undertakings will be met with swift and severe Northern punishment. As it stands now, my sources in Massachusetts inform me that the Union is rather ill-equipped for such an enterprise. As a result, I have come from Boston to financially assist in this deficiency."

"Mr. Stenner, such an action on your part would be greatly appreciated! In fact, if you were to provide us with immediate monetary assistance, I am sure you would see your hard-earned money quickly put to use."

"Oh, is the government planning to employ a contingent for Massachusetts to secure my home state from those despised rebels, General?"

"You have no need to worry about the safety of Massachusetts, Mr. Stenner." McDowell chuckled. "I am talking about the complete crushing of the rebels at Bull Run, Virginia, by the end of next month."

"Oh. But the strength and movements of our army in rebel-usurped territory would have to be well-crafted in order to ensure victory."

"Indeed, Mr. Stenner." McDowell then went on to detail the strength and movements the Union army would employ at the battle.

"Very impressive, General. But the strength and movements that you have most skillfully devised would be such even without my assistance. Would it thus not be fitting if I were to deliberate in the interim upon where in the army my money could best be employed?"

"Certainly, Mr. Stenner," McDowell said, though visibly upset. "Though I recommend giving us the money now, it is, after all, your money and whenever you do give it, it will be greatly appreciated! Perhaps we can rendezvous after we crush those blasted rebels at Bull Run to further discuss your willingness to assist us?"

"I would like that very much, General. Thank you!"

With that, McDowell was consoled that he had at least secured another meeting. *Hopefully at that time*, he thought, *Stenner will provide us with much-needed financial aid.* The general proceeded to shake the man's hand, arranging the date of August 3 for their next meeting—a time when McDowell believed the battle at Bull Run would be well completed.

With the critical information he had uncovered, William's heart beat fast with excitement. *Beauregard must be informed at once! Calm down, William! Calm down.* Lytham labored to collect himself. After partial success, he assessed the situation. How was he to impart the critical facts to Beauregard, while at the same time ensuring that it would not be intercepted? He decided it best to send a dispatch to Beauregard telling him of the "extremely important matter," and asking how he was to transmit it.

Within a week and a half, Beauregard instructed William to meet a widowed Mrs. Rose O'Neal Greenhowe and reveal the information to her.

A Mrs. Greenhowe? he thought. *Beauregard even has female spies? Incredible!*

William met Mrs. Greenhowe at her Washington home on July 9.

"It is an honor to meet you, Mrs. Greenhowe."

"Please, call me Rose. It is also an honor to meet you, William Lytham. I, like the rest of the South, have followed your success at Mobile Academy with the greatest of delights. Yet, when our struggle commenced, we all wondered as to your whereabouts. We had no doubt that you were on our side, even though the Yankees were trying to convince us otherwise. So, when Pierre informed me that you would be coming with paramount, advantageous news, I was overjoyed. Oh, how we need you, William. My informants tell me that the Yankee army increases by the day and that their manpower and ability to furnish weapons is much greater than ours. Consequently, espionage must be our edge, William. We must triumph in this measure if we are to have any chance at achieving our independence!"

Although forty years old, Mrs. Greenhowe was very attractive—a woman who still possessed her Southern beauty. Moreover, her passion for the Southern cause enticed William all the more. *My gosh*, he thought, *to have a woman like this would be absolute paradise! I would trade in all the money in the world for such a woman.* All his life, William had admired the Southern woman. He considered her to be the most beautiful of all women and dreamed of the day when he would have one as his wife.

"You are amazing, Rose. I cannot believe your passion and your beauty, if you don't mind me saying so. Your husband was a very fortunate man."

"Oh, William, thank you." Rose smiled. "I am flattered. But addressing the issue at hand, what important news do you have for me?"

"Yes. Yes, Rose! I have extremely important news!" Lytham declared, visibly shaken.

"Calm down, William. What? What is it?"

"Rose, believe it or not, what I am about to say is the absolute truth. On June 29, I conversed with Union Commander General McDowell, and in our discourse, he informed me of the strength and movements the Yankee army plans to employ against us at Bull Run, Virginia, for the end of this month." Lytham then disclosed the information and the way in which he had discovered it.

"Fantastic, William! Do you know what this means?"

"Truly. We must alert General Beauregard at once!"

"Consider it done. McDowell will soon taste the bitter pill of defeat. William, Pierre would like you to remain here as a spy until further notice. If the situation becomes too volatile, however, you are to leave for our capital, where the General will decide upon your next mission."

"Understood."

William kissed Rose's hand and with a bowed salute, headed home.

"Take care, lovely William," said Rose, seeing him out. "Our hopes ride with you!"

Within two weeks, the battle at Bull Run was on, and thanks to William's vital information, the Union incurred a smashing rout.

The disastrous defeat infuriated Lincoln. When McDowell returned from the Confederate beating, the Union president summoned him for an immediate meeting.

"Good morning, Mr. President."

"Sit down, Irvin!" Lincoln angrily replied, as McDowell apprehensively sat. "What the hell happened at Bull Run?"

"I truly don't know, Mr. President. I had everything thoroughly planned and was sure of victory. I cannot believe what happened. When we were on the battlefield and the campaign was ensuing, it seemed as if the rebels knew what we were up to."

"Well how could that be? This operation was conducted under the strictest of security."

McDowell then recalled his meeting with David Stenner. *No. No! Could he have been a rebel spy? No! He had the accent of a Bostonian. He was appareled in wealth. He possessed unequivocal allegiance to the*

Federalist flag. There is no way he could have been a spy! Such attempts to relieve his mind, however, were quickly failing. *My God, I allowed myself to be deceived. I dare not tell Lincoln.*

"I don't know, Mr. President. I told not a soul."

"Well, I have no other course of action but to relieve you of your command. I will still allow you to retain your rank as general, however. So get back to your post and find out what the hell went wrong! I will not stand for an embarrassment like this again."

"Yes, Mr. President," McDowell answered with head bowed.

With that, McDowell left the Oval Office totally destroyed. Then he thought of David Stenner and the blood in his veins boiled. *I will get that Stenner,* McDowell inwardly screamed to himself, *if it's the last thing I do!*

* * *

The victory at Bull Run was celebrated throughout the South. Davis was hailed as the "prodigious president." Letters came in from Southerners everywhere expressing thanks and gratitude to the Confederate president for the South's first major victory.

Davis himself was ecstatic. He eagerly awaited the arrival of Beauregard to tell him firsthand how the Southerners defeated the Federal army.

Beauregard's entrance into Richmond was met with jubilation. The townsfolk laid flowers on the ground hailing Pierre as the country's best military leader. "Hurray, hurray, General! Way to whip 'em Yankees!" was the continual chorus. The noise was electric.

Witnessing these events, Davis even more eagerly awaited his assembly with the victorious general. Finally, after thirty minutes of shaking hands and signing autographs, Beauregard entered the Confederate White House and proceeded to its Oval Office.

"Congratulations, Pierre. We did it! We showed the Yankees that we are prepared not only to battle, but also to win!"

"Thank you, Mr. President," Beauregard humbly replied. "We did it, indeed! We demonstrated to the enemy that we are just as capable of winning this war as they think they are. In fact, although we may lack their numbers and military strength, we do possess the advantage in terms of terrain and espionage."

"Are you saying a key to our victory was not only our territorial positioning, but also our attainment of enemy strategy from spying?"

"That is exactly what I am saying, Mr. President. Our spies in Washington discerned the Union's military movements and strength for Bull Run in advance, enabling us to formulate successful counterstrategy. In fact, the spy who uncovered this pivotal information, Mr. President, was none other than William Lytham!"

"William? William Lytham? I am overjoyed! I knew he'd never leave us. When he vanished at the outset of our conflict, although I believed he was still for us, I was without proof. And now I have it. This is great, great news, Pierre."

"Absolutely, Mr. President. This past March, William conveyed to me his entreaty to serve the South as a spy. At first I was taken aback, as I believed he would better serve the South as a soldier due to his distinguished military career at Mobile Academy. Yet, after listening to the young man's passion, I started to believe in his supplication. Moreover, when he uncovered the Union's movements and strength for Bull Run, I believed all the more."

"This is excellent news, Pierre. Successful espionage is truly crucial if we are to triumph in our struggle. But what of his appearance?"

"I arranged for him a meeting with Mittle Tobbs, Mr. President— undeniably the best disguise artist in the world."

"Mittle Tobbs? Oh yes. Mittle Tobbs. The fourth-generation Tobbs from South Carolina, correct?"

"Correct, Mr. President."

"I am highly impressed, Pierre! This has been more than welcome news to me this day. Continue to keep me apprised of all activities: both on the war front and on the spy front."

"I will, Mr. President."

With that, the two emerged from the White House to the cheers of the Virginians. "You have no need to worry, my fellow countrymen," proclaimed Davis, with his right hand on Beauregard's left shoulder. "We have the finest commander in the field!"

"Hip, hip, hurray! Hip, hip, hurray! Hip, hip hurray!" the crowd cheered.

Learning of the South's victory, William was overjoyed; but he now had to decide whether or not to attend his meeting with McDowell.

Chapter Two

He realized, on the one hand, that if he did not meet with him, McDowell would most certainly conclude him to be a Confederate spy—resulting in a thorough and immediate search for him. On the other hand, William knew that if he was already deemed to be a spy for the Confederacy, then a meeting would be the end of him. Realizing the risk of a manhunt was preferable to certain capture, William decided it best to avoid McDowell and change his appearance. Consequently, he discarded his Boston apparel and assumed the alias of a pauper.

* * *

On the morning of August 3, McDowell was restless. He paced up and down his office, glaring at his watch every two minutes. *That Stenner better show up!* he kept saying to himself.

The sweat poured down his face after a half hour elapsed from their scheduled meeting time. "Dammit!" he screamed aloud. "He's not going to show. That Southern bastard!"

Fifteen minutes later, with still no sign of the man, McDowell addressed his troops. "Men, he has not showed. This proves beyond any doubt that he is a spy for rebeldom. I want all of you to search the Washington area and show artist Michel Tremblay's sketch of the traitor. Offer them a $500 reward for any information leading to his capture. I want the sketch with the reward affixed to every tavern wall and on every post throughout the capital. I want this done now! We will work around the clock. We will not rest until this villain of villains is captured. Do I make myself clear?"

"Yes, General!" the soldiers answered.

3

On August 4 at 3 a.m., William entered Mrs. Smith's house and headed straight to his room, a continuation of his routine since assuming the apparel of a pauper. William feared that if Mrs. Smith saw him in shabby clothes, although she was credulous, she might nevertheless become suspicious of his traveling-salesman front and inform someone.

Having made it safely to his lodging, the young man contemplated his observations of the past day, and in doing so became greatly concerned. Not only was the David Stenner sketch posted everywhere, but Federal soldiers were also asking individuals if they knew the man in the drawing. William realized Mrs. Smith herself would soon be approached by the troopers, as they were knocking on every door. Although her mind was failing, William knew that she would still know what David looked like, and she would immediately recognize the name. Thus, it would be only a short while before the Federalists would stake out her dwelling and lay in wait for him.

As a result, William decided to leave Mrs. Smith's abode and head to a homeless shelter. The thought of such an action, however, made him sick to his stomach. All his life he had lived in relative luxury, and to have to spend part of his time in such a dwelling was, to him, abhorrent. Yet, he realized that it was necessary if he was to remain in Washington as a spy. Accordingly, William packed his possessions and, with the leaving of a thank-you note on the kitchen table enclosed with the last month's rent, he took leave of the kind lady's house.

Within an hour, William entered the Hope Haven shelter in downtown Washington. The keeper of the shelter was a cordial, energetic Federalist named Herb Tarson. Herb had been in charge of the shelter since 1845. A man fifty-eight years of age, Herb had the stamina of a thirty-four-year-old and would ceaselessly seek employment for his homeless to help them on the road to independence. Hence, when William entered the shelter poised as a jobless, drunken hobo, Herb warmly received him and said, "Young man, in no time at all will I have you employed, earning a steady wage."

Herb had seen many destitutes in his life. In fact, he himself was one in the early 1840s. His weakness for alcohol was all too common in an age when America was slowly emerging from her colonial roots to become a successful, prosperous nation. Thanks to the kindness of the previous owner, Tom Hope, Herb was given the much-needed love and support necessary to overcome his alcohol addiction. Tarson never forgot Hope's clemency, and the two remained the best of friends until the latter's sudden and fatal stroke in July of 1845 at the tender age of sixty-seven. In his will, Tom bestowed the shelter to Herb, beseeching him to maintain its existence as a sanctuary for the homeless. Although wanting to transform the shelter into a saloon—for he had never truly quit his drinking habit—Herb realized it would be only proper to honor Tom's entreaty. Accordingly, he did so, and as the new owner, he renamed the Lonely Abode to Hope Haven in loving memory of Mr. Tom Hope.

With the Civil War, Herb's numbers at the shelter drastically dropped, mainly because many of his homeless enlisted in the Union army. A significant minority, however, enlisted in the Confederate army. Although a Federalist, Herb resented the perceived rough stance by the North toward the South as characterized in the person of Lincoln. He felt sorry for his Southern country folk and felt they had no other course but to secede. However, when the conflict ensued, Herb was committed to keeping the Union preserved.

Consequently, after the Federal defeat at Bull Run, he arranged an audience with McDowell's replacement, General George McClellan, to discuss his desire to serve the Union, even on the battlefield.

Though impressed by Herb's fervor, McClellan was unwilling to allow him to fight due to his age. But he stated that Herb would be performing a vital role for the cause by continuing to operate the shelter and by encouraging all of his homeless to enlist in the Federal army. Additionally, if he could overhear any potential threat to the Union, either at the shelter or anywhere else, and quickly alert the government, Herb would further assist his nation. Tarson graciously accepted his charge, and with a formal salute, enthusiastically went at it.

William's first night in the homeless shelter was about what he expected. Hope Haven lacked all the luxuries of middle-class life. In fact, it was not uncommon to see cockroaches throughout the shelter fighting for leftover crumbs. *What a grotesque sight*, he thought. *But for the South, I must endure!*

With the dawn of morning, William was once again set to search for Federal strategy when, unannounced, Herb entered his room. Now acting sober but still portraying himself as a hobo, William graciously thanked him for his hospitality.

"Thanks very much for taking me in, sir. Appreciate it!"

"My pleasure, young man. What's your name, friend?"

"The name's Brinson, Brett Brinson."

"Well, it's a pleasure to meet you, Brett." Herb shook his hand. "I'm Herb Tarson—keeper of Hope Haven."

"Well, it's a pleasure to meet you, Mr. Tarson, and thanks again."

"Herb is fine, Brett. You're most truly welcome. So, are you from Washington? Do you have a family here or something?"

"Actually, I've come from New York, where I drifted the streets for most of my life. I am an only child, and when my parents died in a mugging when I was twelve, I went from shelter to shelter trying to survive. I hope to make something of myself someday. I thought coming to Washington would bring me plenty of work—you know, with the war on and all."

"Brett, would you like some breakfast?"

"Appreciate it."

Satisfied that the man was telling the truth, Herb decided to entice him into joining the Federal army over bacon and eggs. "How do you like it, Brett?"

"Fantastic! I could eat this all day, but I best go out there and find a job."

"What type of work do you do?"

"Any type that pays."

"I see." He chuckled. "Brett, how would you like a job filled with excitement, adventure, and personal satisfaction?"

"Sure, what is it?"

"A United States soldier destined to destroy those blasted rebels from the South. The Union needs men like you, Brett!"

William became concerned. Hitherto, he had only wanted a shelter where he could reside for some three or four hours a night and be left alone. *Now this Tarson fellow is asking all these questions and even wants me to enlist in his Union.* William started to suspect that Herb was working for the Federal government. He was at an impasse. Although he would never fight for the North, if he even suggested a refusal, Herb might become suspicious. Quickly, he had an idea.

"I would love to, Herb. Could you arrange a meeting for me with an official to see where in the military I would be of best use?" William was hoping to discern the person Herb was working for—if such was indeed the case.

"Why sure, Brett! I happen to know not just an official but General George McClellan—commander of our entire army. I am sure he or one of his auxiliaries would be more than happy to meet with you to discuss your entreaty."

"Well, thank you, Herb. When can I meet such a person?"

"How about tomorrow morning? I will speak with General McClellan today to see if he can arrange something."

"Well, that would be perfect, Herb. Thank you, thank you very much."

"You're more than welcome, Brett." Tarson finished his breakfast. "Well, it's best I leave early to meet with the general. In the interim, please feel free to help yourself to any food or drink. We don't possess any alcohol, however," he said with some regret. "We are a dry establishment."

"I humbly thank you, Herb."

"My pleasure, Brett."

With that, Tarson made for McClellan's office quarters. Unknown to him, however, William followed at a distance.

At his headquarters, McClellan was conversing with Oliver Duckworth on the security of Washington. During their discourse, McClellan's secretary entered the office.

"Excuse me, General. I have a request to relay to you from a Mr. Herb Tarson."

"Oh. What is it?"

"General, Mr. Tarson is at the front foyer and wishes to speak with you. He says that the matter is of an important nature."

Deeming Herb to be in possession of crucial information that might alter military preparations he had been discussing with Duckworth, McClellan thought it best to immediately speak with him. "Yes. Please send him in."

"Yes, General."

Tarson entered. "Good morning, General. I bring good news!"

"Good morning, Herb. What news have you?" Tarson glanced at Duckworth. "Oh, this is Lieutenant Duckworth, Herb. A trusted friend of mine."

Tarson nodded. "General, last night a destitute entered my shelter and this morning, upon meticulous questioning, I discerned him to be free from rebel sway. Moreover, he would like to enlist in our army but would like a meeting with you or one of your auxiliaries to discuss how he could best serve our cause."

"Herb, why did you bother me with such trivial information, especially when I am in an important meeting with the lieutenant? Herb, the man is a hobo, a bum. I have no time or interest to discuss anything with a vagabond. If he wants to enlist, you enlist him. Tell him once he is in the army, the army will determine where he would be best put to use. From now on, I only want you to notify me if you have crucial information—such as the whereabouts of a rebel spy or the uncovering of enemy strategy. Do I make myself clear?"

"Yes, General."

"Good. You may go!"

Tarson left McClellan's office completely humiliated at the scolding. *Perhaps I am trying too hard*, he thought. *I should just take things in stride and not make a mountain out of a molehill.*

Fortunately for William, McClellan's window was left wide open—due to the severity of the August heat. Hiding behind dense shrubs little more than five yards away, William was able to overhear the conversation. Moreover, with Herb's departure, William was privy to even more startling information.

"Sorry about that, Oliver."

"That's all right, General. I must admit, I do admire his ardor for the cause."

"Yes, Herb is a good man with a good heart. It seems that his intensity overwhelms him at times, however. Anyway, what were you saying about the vulnerability of Washington?"

"Yes, General. We must strengthen Washington! Right now, we have neither the fortifications nor the manpower necessary for its defense."

"I know. We have entered upon this conflict in a most unprepared fashion. Fortunately, the rebels are just as unprepared. I'll leave you in charge of getting everything in place, Oliver. Be as swift as you can and keep me posted."

"I will, General."

With the conclusion of the McClellan and Duckworth discourse, William made a quick exit; once safe, he walked the streets of Washington contemplating their conversation. *So, Washington is vulnerable—lacking fortifications and manpower essential for its defense. Incredible! Beauregard must be alerted at once! We must overtake Washington and put a noose around the throat of the Federalists.*

Believing the fastest and safest way to inform Beauregard would be, once again, through Mrs. Greenhowe, William made for Rose's abode.

Being within the vicinity of her residence, William hid in a nearby hedge and waited until nightfall in order to approach her house under the cover of darkness.

With the onset of night, relentless rain ensued. Yet, William decided to stick to his original game plan. He would wait until 2:00 a.m.—a time when the chance of being spotted by a passerby would be slim if not altogether nil. After many shivering hours in the torrential downpour, William, at the chosen hour, was set to approach her lodging when he spotted through the window a male individual. *What's going on?*

An hour later, the man left Rose's house after a kiss on her lips. William could see he was wearing a Federal uniform. In fact, he appeared to be a Union officer. *Has Rose defected from the Southern cause? No, it is not possible.* William tried to console himself. *Don't jump to any conclusions until you know all the facts.* He kept saying this to himself and gradually it started to soothe him. Yet, with the man's departure, William was in a quandary. Should he follow him, or should he proceed to meet with Rose? He decided upon the former. He wanted to find out who this person was in case Rose was hiding something. Yet, just as he was about to do so, a second man emerged, following the first. *What is going on here? Who is this other man?* William's mind was spinning a mile a minute. Again, he tried to calm himself. *Clear your mind. Deal with one thing at a time.* Being better collected, William followed the second individual as well.

Eventually the first man entered a Federal building, while the second was apprehended by the soldiers guarding the building's entrance. *Perhaps the man following the first is a Confederate spy? If so, he was sure careless.* William, however, stopped well short of the building and went undetected by the troopers. *What should I do now?* In the end, he decided to return to

Rose's house to find out what she knew before he would reveal to her what he had observed.

Arriving at her dwelling, William surveyed the premises for other onlookers. Satisfied that there were no others, he made for Rose's back door. After three soft knocks, Greenhowe came to the door, but before opening it, she asked who it was.

"It's me, Rose. William Lytham!"

Always one to recognize a friend's voice, Rose immediately opened the door and was prepared to give William a big hug until she saw this hobo standing in her midst.

"Don't worry, Rose, it's me, William. I had to assume this identity because, as I'm sure you know, my David Stenner alias is posted everywhere."

"Oh, I know, William. This is terrible," Rose said, leading him into the house. "Would it be better to leave for Richmond, William?"

"It's better that I stay, Rose. There is much information still to be obtained in Washington, and thankfully my hobo disguise is working well."

She smiled at his bravery. "True, William. Which reminds me, I have great news! Please, come and sit down while I bring you some fresh tea."

"Oh, fresh at this hour?"

"Yes, William. That is my great news! Earlier this evening, Union Officer Elwood came by to inform me of the location of the Federal fortifications in and around Washington and of the manpower contained in each. He also stated that these fortifications and their manpower are presently ill-equipped for the city's defense against us!"

"Thank goodness, Rose. I observed Officer Elwood leaving your premises earlier tonight and was worried that you had switched sides. Please forgive me, Rose. I should never have suspected that you were even capable of…"

"No, William. That is just part of your careful character. That is why you are our best spy. Your mind is always thinking and that is why you are so successful. You prepare yourself for the worst in case the worst comes about."

"Thank you, Rose."

"So, William, do you have good news for me?"

"Yes, Rose. I have some great news as well! I overheard General McClellan and Lieutenant Duckworth yesterday confirm Elwood's exchange about the Federalists having neither the fortifications nor the manpower necessary for Washington's defense. Oh, Rose, with our information, we have the opportunity to overrun Washington, to which our independence will be immediately secured!"

"Yes, William, truly! Oh, William, I do love your passion. Your heart and mine are the same."

"If my heart could even come close to yours, Rose, I would be most fortunate."

"For the South!" she proclaimed, raising her teacup.

"For the South!" he echoed, raising his and ringing it with hers as both drank.

"I will inform Pierre of our information at once, William."

"Rose, there is something else, which I am not sure what to make of."

"What is it?"

"Well, this evening I also observed a man following Elwood—leaving from your premises."

"Well, Officer Elwood assured me that he came alone, and knowing him and his heart, I believe him."

"Do you think the man is one of our spies?"

"I'm not sure. What did he look like?"

"It was so dark and with the rain blowing as hard as it was, I was unable to see him clearly."

"Well, I have no reason to believe anyone suspects Elwood of his Union front. Thus, anyone who would follow him must be on our side. He must be one of our spies!"

"Maybe so. Tell Beauregard about it anyway, just to be on the safe side. He knows where his spies are situated. Thus, if the man is indeed on our side, Beauregard would know it."

"I will, William."

"It's best that I go."

"Where are you staying?"

"At the Hope Haven shelter. I found out yesterday that the shelter's keeper is a Union spy—Herb Tarson. A nice man. Too bad he's for them."

"Well, you be extra careful then, William. Don't give him a reason to suspect you."

"Of course. You be extra careful as well, Rose. If the man following Elwood is a Union spy, you may be in great danger. I wouldn't be surprised if he overheard you two converse tonight."

Chapter Three

"Not only will I alert Beauregard about this man, William, but I will also inform Elwood. And if the man is a Union spy, I will quickly leave Washington for our capital—to see where I can next serve our beloved cause."

With that, William nodded and bade Rose a good night with a kiss on the cheek.

At breakfast the following morning, Herb conversed with William; yet, after the former's embarrassing meeting with McClellan on the previous day, he was, not surprisingly, in a disheartened frame of mind.

"Good morning, Brett. How are you today?"

"Gee. Ah, I'm fine. You?"

"Well, could be better," Tarson said sadly.

"Ah, what's wrong? Did you talk with the general?"

"Yes, but I think I interrupted him at a bad time," he answered, too embarrassed to reveal what had actually occurred.

"Oh, I'm sorry, Herb."

"Listen, Brett, I would still like you to enlist in the army. Once you enlist, the army will know where you would best be put to use."

"Sure, Herb! Whatever you think is best. I am so glad they will accept a man with heart trouble."

"Heart trouble? You didn't tell me you had any heart trouble."

"Oh, I didn't? I'm sorry, Herb. That was why I was hoping to meet with an official to see where in the military I would be of best use—you know, with my condition and all."

"Ahhh, now I understand. I'm so sorry, Brett. It must be terrible to have to live with that."

"It is, Herb. Throughout my life, I've been restricted from normal activity. But, deep down inside, I realize that my condition, which I've had since birth, is for a reason. So, I never try to look upon it with bitterness."

"You're a remarkable man, Brett." He mused. *Well, Chef Jacques Gagnon does need an assistant.* "Brett, how would you like to work as an assistant cook here at Hope Haven?"

"Why sure, Herb. I would love too."

"Then consider the job yours. The hours circle breakfast, lunch, and dinner—Monday to Friday. I know these may seem like rather long days but at least you'll have your evenings and weekends off."

"Why, that would be fine, Herb. I am truly grateful."

27

"Think nothing of it, Brett. I am glad to have such a brave, impassioned Federalist employed here at Hope Haven!"

* * *

As the search for David Stenner continued in earnest, Federal officers Brent Parker and Luke Carter knocked on Mrs. Smith's door.

"Good morning, ma'am, sorry to bother you, but we're asking residents if they have seen this man," Parker pronounced as he presented her with the sketch of Stenner.

"Let's see," Mrs. Smith said, taking the picture and looking at it closely. "Why, sure I have. He is my tenant David Stenner. Or at least was my tenant," she stated sadly.

"Are you saying this man is…I mean was…your tenant?" asked Carter.

"Why, yes. Up until about two weeks ago."

"What? What happened to him?" Parker rushed.

"Well, I don't know. I thought everything was fine. David would pay his rent on time and would always keep his room clean. That was all I required. Not much you know. Pay on time and keep your room clean. That is not asking a lot, is it, boys?"

"No, no. Please, please go on," they urged.

"I knew David enjoyed the vices of the evening but, all in all, he was a fabulous young man. His sudden departure without a personal good-bye still breaks my heart. But I know it must have been for a good reason. Perhaps he had an urgent sales appointment in another state or something. But at least he did say good-bye to me in his letter enclosed with the last month's rent."

"Where? Where is the letter?" Carter asked.

"Well who, pray tell, are you anyway?"

"Ma'am, we're Federal officers and we desperately need to find this man," Parker answered.

"Why? What has he done? David is a law-abiding citizen."

"Ma'am, this so-called David Stenner is a rebel spy!" Carter said.

"No. Not my David. He is a salesman!"

"Ma'am, this David met General McDowell and stated that he was from Boston willing to help our army financially. They then scheduled another meeting and he never showed up," Parker asserted.

"Well, that doesn't mean he is a rebel spy."

Chapter Three

"Well, General McDowell seems to believe so. And if he does, it must be for a good reason!" declared Carter, with a look questioning her patriotism. "Now we need to get that letter and search your house to see if he left anything else."

"Well, if you must. But I'm sure David is no rebel spy."

With their entrance, Mrs. Smith gave the officers the letter and proceeded to show them his lodging. The room, however, was fully vacated. After searching the room—as well as the entire house—and finding nothing, the officers sought to console themselves.

"At least we have his letter, Luke."

"I know, Brent. Now if we can decipher the writing, the bastard's identity will no longer be a mystery."

"Agreed."

After a second unsuccessful search of the premises, the officers coldly thanked Mrs. Smith and with the letter made straight to McDowell's headquarters.

"General, we've got great news!" Parker proclaimed as he entered.

Still traumatized by his demotion, McDowell could not help but reveal his woe. "No, nobody loves me. I search the seas, cry on my knees, and all to appease my commander. I fought the fight with courage and might and all for the plight of my commander. Hence, now I'm alone with nowhere to roam and all for the home of my commander."

"General," Carter followed, "we have great news. We found out Stenner resided at a Mrs. Smith's house prior to Bull Run, and we have his handwriting here on paper!"

McDowell revived somewhat. "Say again. What have you?"

"General, we have the rebel's handwriting!" Parker exclaimed.

"Bring it here to me," McDowell said as Carter brought the letter. "So, this is the traitor's writing…I will get that bastard if it's the last thing I do! What of his lodgings? Did you find anything else?"

"No, General," Parker sadly said. "He left nothing else."

"Well, at least we've got his handwriting. We must work from here! Have his writing displayed alongside his picture throughout Washington. Inform the others of this new information as well."

"Yes, General," was their uniform response.

With that, Parker and Carter set off on their directive, while McDowell enthusiastically mulled over the recent turn of events. *I'm getting closer, Stenner. I'm getting damn closer!*

4

After weeks of working in the Hope Haven kitchen, William was becoming an expert in cooking. *If only Ma could see me now,* he thought, *she would be highly impressed.* In his childhood and teenage years, William was infamous for his culinary prowess. In fact, everything he cooked turned out burnt. Yet, in spending time with Chef Gagnon, William was slowly acquiring the art of cuisine.

Meanwhile, important events were occupying his mind. He continued to roam Washington, entering as many taverns as would let him in—the sticking point being his hobo appearance—in the attempt to overhear any discourse relating to Federal strategy. Throughout this time, he eagerly awaited the arrival of his compatriots. With the crucial information advanced to Beauregard, William believed the overtaking of Washington would be imminent. Yet, months had passed with no Confederate army. It was now late December 1861. *What is going on? Why the delay?*

William decided to meet with Rose to ascertain the answers, especially as each passing day brought the Federalists closer to having their capital fortified. As he was set to knock on her back door at 2:00 a.m., he suddenly witnessed two Union soldiers through the den window.

Horrified, William advanced closer, hoping to overhear the men's conversation. Though they only whispered, he was able to overhear them because of the stillness of the Washington night.

"He is not going to show."

"You never know, he might."

"Yes, but we've been staking this place out for months and have not seen him. I'm sure he's left Washington by now."

"Well, we'll wait a while longer before calling it a night."

Quickly, William departed the premises with his heart racing a mile a minute. *She is gone. Gone! They are waiting for me! Where did we go wrong? The man the other night. He must have been a Union spy. Oh my God! But what of his apprehension by the Federal guards? It was a trick. All a trick. They set us up. Rose is captured.* All these thoughts haunted William's mind as he returned to Hope Haven. Upon arriving, Herb happened to be awake.

"My gosh, Brett. You look as though you've seen a ghost!"

William was sweating profusely and appeared visibly shaken. "Oh, Herb. Help me. Help me. Help me catch my breath with my bad heart and all."

"Sure. Sit down. Please, Brett, be calm! Everything is going to be all right. What? What happened?"

"I was being chased by a couple of men trying to rob me as I left one of the bars this morning. Did I make it back safe, Herb?"

"Yes. Yes, Brett. My gosh! Here, stay put. I'll get you some coffee."

"Thanks, Herb."

The front worked, but William's mind was still in a state of shock. Ultimately, however, he forced himself to regain his composure. Hence, when Herb returned with some strong black coffee, William had collected himself.

"Here, Brett—try this." Tarson gave him the coffee. "It'll make you feel a lot better."

"Thanks, Herb."

"You're welcome. Brett, I…never mind. I'll tell you in the morning when you are in better spirits."

"What is it, Herb?"

"Don't fret about it, son. It's all right. I'll tell you in the morning."

"Really, Herb. I'm fine. What is it?"

"Well, I got a visit from two of General McDowell's officers today. You know, the unfortunate general who incurred our disastrous defeat at Bull Run?"

"Oh yes. Quite a shame."

"Quite a shame, indeed. Not only did he lose the battle, Brett, but he was also demoted shortly thereafter. From what I hear, he is convinced that he was betrayed by a rebel spy under the alias of David Stenner. The officers want to know if we have seen the man or recognize his handwriting."

Tarson showed him a photo of the sketch and the handwriting. "I told them that I haven't seen him but that I would ask everyone in the shelter and that any information would be sent forthwith. So far, no one in our shelter has seen him. Have you seen him, Brett?"

William looked intently at the sketch and the handwriting and shook inside. "No…no, I don't believe I have, Herb. Do they think he is still in Washington?"

"I guess. They're searching the entire city for him. I hope they find that scoundrel. I would kill him myself if he were in my midst and not bother to wait for the authorities to arrive."

"Well if I do see him, Herb, I will tell you straightaway."

Tarson looked proud and patted him on the back. "That's my soldier boy! Anyway, it's getting late and you definitely should get some rest."

"You're right, Herb," Lytham answered, well aware of what he really went through. "I think I'll do just that."

With that, William finished his coffee and, after wishing Herb good night, went straight to his lodging. Entering his room, William collapsed on the bed. He could not believe what had transpired in the past few hours. Deliberating, he decided to inform Beauregard in a letter about the vulnerability of Washington—in case Rose had indeed been captured before she was able to inform Pierre. While devising it, William was overcome with exhaustion. As a result, after writing the main points of what he wanted to say in semi coded fashion—deciding to rewrite the letter in full-coded fashion at dawn when he was more alert—young William, suffering from total fatigue, fell sound asleep.

At 7:15 a.m., fifteen minutes past his starting time, William was still asleep. At 7:30, Herb decided to wake him. Never before had Lytham been late for work, let alone by a half hour.

As Herb drew near to wake him, he stumbled across a letter that he believed had fallen from the young man's luggage. Intending not to read it, but rather to just return it into the luggage bag, the title irrevocably prevented him.

<u>URGENT!</u>

G[eneral]. B[eauregard]. m[a]n[y]. w[ee]ks. p[assed]. an[d]. s[til]l. no s[ign]. W[ashington]. is vul[nerable]! At[tack]! I s[ta]y. Ho[pe]. Ha[ven].

D[on]'t. wai[t]. Fe[deralists]. attem[pting]. to f[ortify]. Ta[ke]. th[em]. t[wo]. m[ore]. mon[ths].

Yours, S[outh]. O[ver]. U[nion]. L[ytham].

Reading the letter, Herb was unable to discern the abbreviations. At first, he believed it was just scribble the youngster did to pass the time. He decided, however, to report his finding to McClellan in case the letter was something more. Returning the letter to where he found it, Herb proceeded to touch the young man's shoulder; all of a sudden, William leaped from his bed prepared for a fight.

"Relax, Brett. It's just me, Herb. Remember?"

"Oh, hi, Herb. Gee, what time is it?"

"Just after 7:30."

"My gosh! I should have started work over a half hour ago. Please forgive me, Herb. I won't ever be late again."

"Don't worry about it, Brett. Anyway, I thought I'd just come up to see how you were doing, that's all."

"Thanks, Herb. That's good of you. Tell Jacques I'm on my way."

"Will do, son."

With Herb's exit, William could not help but give his head a shake. *You fool! How could you have allowed yourself to slack like that? I can't even give the enemy a reason to suspect me; and here I am, allowing myself to be awakened by a Union informant of all people. What am I, stupid?* William started to worry. *How long was Herb here? Did he see anything?* Quickly, Lytham searched the room to see if there was anything incriminating. There it was: the half-coded message. Although it was in a semicoded state, any half-decent code detector could make out its contents and know that it came from a Confederate spy. Moreover, the message was written in his own handwriting—the same handwriting displayed throughout Washington.

Oh no! What am I to do?! Lytham's heart raced in earnest. *No! Don't allow yourself to be overwhelmed. Think. Think and you'll survive. What am I to do now?* Contemplating, he suspected the worst. He presumed Herb had seen the letter and would surmise that it was from him, a Confederate spy, and would accordingly alert McClellan and McDowell. William also presumed Rose had been taken captive before she had the opportunity to alert Beauregard. He realized it was futile for him to remain

Chapter Four

in Washington while his compatriots were unaware of the opportune time to attack, notwithstanding that his pauper disguise had now no doubt been discovered. Accordingly, he quickly packed his belongings to depart before the assumed arrival of the Federalists.

Heading down the stairs, Herb recalled David Stenner's handwriting shown to him by the Federal officers. *It is Brett. Brett's writing is exactly the same as David's. Brett is David Stenner, the rebel spy!* Walking briskly down the remainder of the stairs with his heart beating like a racehorse, Herb quickly called two of his men and sent one to McDowell and the other to McClellan—with the communiqué stating that the alias David Stenner was at the shelter.

Waiting for William to emerge from his room, Herb was restless. *Perhaps he is planning to jump from the room's window? If so, he might escape and I will look like a fool to McClellan and McDowell.* In addition, Herb remembered his words to the young man: *I would kill him myself if I had him in my midst and not bother to wait for the authorities to arrive.* Although he had previously thought the youngster innocent, he now wanted to shoot him down. *A traitor to America deserves but the surest of deaths!* While mulling these factors, Herb decided to take action.

Adrenalin rushed through the old man's veins as he retrieved the revolver from under his office desk and headed toward the young man's room.

"How are you doing, Brett? Everything all right?" Tarson asked, walking up the stairs.

"Yes, Herb. I'll be right there!"

Lytham, the crafty spy, could hear Tarson's voice coming ever closer. William reached for his own revolver hidden in his belongings and placed it behind his back. He did not want to make the first move; but once he was sure that Herb intended to kill him, William would, without hesitation, reciprocate.

Tarson entered with his revolver behind his back. "Hey, Brett, how are you doing?" Immediately, Herb pointed his revolver squarely at his adversary. "You treacherous David Stenner, Brett Brinson, or whoever you are, rebel spy! What's your real name?"

"Herb, what are you talking about? It's me, Brett Brinson, your assistant cook, remember?"

"Don't give me that! I know you're not Brett Brinson! What do you take me for, a fool? I read your sorry attempt at a coded letter. Not only did I recognize that this was done by a rebel spy, but I also recognized the handwriting: the same handwriting David Stenner used to thank Mrs. Smith for her kindness and lodging."

"So, who do you think you are, anyway? You and your beloved Union are about to be crushed! You will soon taste defeat like your good-for-nothing McDowell at Bull Run."

"I should wait for the Federalists to arrive but I won't. This is my chance to represent my country as a true soldier. Be prepared to die, traitor!" Tarson cocked his gun.

Lytham immediately retrieved his revolver and fired upon a startled Tarson. The bullet struck the left side of Herb's chest with deadly precision. Tarson fell to the floor as William came to his side.

"Forgive me, Herb. I didn't want to have to kill you. So that you know my name, it's Lytham, William Lytham. That is who I am."

"The William Lytham? Commander of our troops at Mobile Academy? You are he, the Soul of the South?" he asked, gasping for breath, recalling the Confederate letter with the signature of S.O.U.L.

"Yes," Lytham answered, taken aback at being called the Soul of the South but recalling the signature.

"But why, William, why did you leave us?"

"It wasn't a question of me leaving, Herb. I loved the Union, but my people crave to have a country to call their own. What else am I to do? Attack my own people?"

"I know, William. I never once blamed the South for the decision it took. I believed Lincoln forced it upon you. But I am from the North and so you can see why I behaved as I did. Forgive me, William. I forgive you."

"All's forgiven, Herb." Then Tarson died. "May God have mercy upon your soul, my friend," Lytham uttered with much admiration and love.

William could hear the advance of horses. Thus, moving at the speed of a gazelle, he grabbed everything he could and jumped out the back window into the dense Washington forest, which led straight to his beloved South.

McDowell's arrival at Hope Haven was followed by McClellan's only seconds later. The sight was impressive. McDowell's force of thirty was only surpassed in splendor by McClellan's contingent of fifty. Neither general was taking a chance at arriving ill-equipped for the job at hand.

Arriving at the shelter, McDowell ordered a search of the premises and of the surrounding vicinity. Now on the second floor, officers Parker and Carter observed the dead body.

"That damn rascal! He has killed a kind, gentle man in cold blood!"

Though he saw that Tarson was armed and perhaps was killed in self-defense, Carter did not bother to correct his friend. "Don't worry, Brent, we'll get that bastard!"

"General McDowell. General, we have something," Parker shouted.

"What? What is it? Did you catch Stenner?" McDowell inquired, running up the stairs. Then he saw the dead body. "That blasted scoundrel! Men, join the others. He can't be that far off. His body is still warm."

Parker and Carter immediately left.

"General McDowell, have you found him?" McClellan called out as he arrived.

"No. The bastard escaped!"

"Men, join General McDowell's troops and search the premises and its environs for the villain."

"Yes, General," the soldiers answered.

McClellan dashed for the second floor and saw Tarson. "Oh my God! Herb! Oh, poor Herb. God bless you, kind man! I'm sorry, Irvin. I realize how much his apprehension means, especially to you."

"That man destroyed my life! I have not slept a good night's sleep since my disaster at Bull Run. I have had my men working around the clock to apprehend this traitor. After we captured Greenhowe and turncoat Elwood, I had Rose's house staked out, all in the hopes that the villain would eventually emerge. Yet, after several weeks, there was still no sign of him. Now we are told that he is here and we are only minutes late. But it may as well be hours. No doubt he has sought refuge in the dense Washington forest and is currently crossing the Potomac River into rebeldom. I am devastated, George. Who is this man? Who is he?"

One of McClellan's soldiers, searching the room, found the coded message accidentally left by Lytham in his rush to escape. "Look, General."

McClellan quickly read it. "A coded message with the signing of S.O.U.L. This is our man, Irvin—the Soul of the South," McClellan said, surprised at his words, as he gave the letter to McDowell.

McDowell, just as surprised, read it. "I will show this message to our best code decipherer—Colonel Brian Togging of the New York division. If anyone can ascertain the letter's contents and identity, it is definitely Brian."

"Good. But I must first bring the letter to the president. All matters relating to the war must be immediately brought to his attention."

"Absolutely, General."

"Men, have you found anything else?" McClellan asked the four soldiers searching the room.

"No, General," they answered, which increased McDowell's woe.

"Don't worry, Irvin," McClellan comforted, "we'll get this guy."

5

Having crossed the Potomac, William knew he was safe. There was little chance the Federalists would risk crossing the river into Confederate territory without a strong brigade. Emerging from the water, William was stopped by Confederate soldiers John Jedd and Steve Jesson.

"Who goes there?" asked Jesson.

"Me, friends, Lytham; William Lytham," Lytham answered with his Southern tongue.

John, who served with William at Mobile Academy, approached and recognized him. "William. William Lytham. Welcome. Welcome home!" Jedd embraced him.

"John. Thank you! It's sure nice to be back home in sweet singing Dixie!" William exclaimed as all were jubilant.

"William, I would like you to meet my patrol partner, Steve Jesson."

Jesson, who had heard of William's fame as an adolescent and had just turned twenty, advanced with much awe. "It is an honor to meet you, Mr. Lytham. Your name here is gold. You are our secret weapon that the North can never match!"

Lytham was touched, yet humble. "Please, call me William. It is an honor to meet you too, Steve. Any man willing to defend his homeland is a friend of mine!"

"What news from the North, William? Are we safe from attack?"

"Absolutely, John." Lytham proceeded to look to the nearby Confederate fort. "Who is our general there?"

"None other than General Joseph E. Johnston, William," Jedd exulted.

"General Johnston? Here?"

"Indeed, William." Jedd smiled.

"Why, this is fantastic news!"

Ever since he was a youngster, William had wanted to meet the esteemed General Johnston. As a highly reputable fighter in the Mexican War, Johnston's name was spoken of with much praise in the Lytham household.

"Please, lead me to him."

"It would be our great pleasure, Mr. Ly…I mean, William," Jesson responded, leading the way.

"General, we have someone who would like to speak with you," Jedd said, knocking on Johnston's office door.

"Sure. Who is it?"

"William Lytham, General!"

Johnston's heart leaped for joy. Never had he met William, but he knew of the man. He closely followed his career at Mobile Academy—proud that such a fine commander was a Southerner. Johnston always believed Southerners were better soldiers and better people than Northerners. Thus when William was thriving at Mobile Academy, the general smiled from ear to ear knowing that his belief was no better personified than in William Lytham. Though somewhat bewildered when Beauregard informed him that William had decided to serve the South as a spy, Johnston's doubts were quickly dispelled when he learned from Pierre that William's crucial information had led to the Confederate victory at Bull Run. Thus, when Johnston finally met William it was, understandably, one of total affection.

Johnston embraced William. "Welcome, son! Please, have a seat."

"Thank you. It is such an honor to finally meet you! So, General, how is the situation?"

"Not bad, William. Since our victory at Bull Run, morale is very high. We firmly believe that it is only a matter of time before we defeat the Yankee menace and gain our independence. How about Washington? Any news?"

"Yes, General. Washington is poorly defended. I overheard General McClellan and Lieutenant Duckworth state this very thing. Moreover, Rose Greenhowe, at the time, ascertained the locations of all the ill-equipped Yankee fortifications in and around Washington and the manpower contained in each."

"I've received no such news!"

"Well, when I last conversed with Rose in August, she informed me that she would immediately alert General Beauregard."

"Oh. That is why then," Johnston said in a most downcast tone.

"What, General? What is it?" Lytham inquired, fearing the worst for Greenhowe.

"Well, our beloved Rose was captured by the Yankees about that time, William. She is currently in the custody of the enemy."

"That would explain it then. I thought that might be why we didn't attack. Well, that is why I have crossed the Potomac, General—to inform the Confederacy of this crucial information. We must attack at once!"

"William, this information is now months old. I am sure the Yankees have since fortified their capital."

"General, throughout these past months, I have been scouring Washington to assess this. Although there have been some reinforcements, the Yankee capital is still relatively weak and with a concerted effort on our part could be overrun."

"Well, tomorrow we'll travel to Richmond to confer with Beauregard and the president on the matter. We'll see what they think."

"Thank you, General."

"Come, William, I'll show you where you can wash up and lodge tonight. In the morning, we will head to our capital."

"Thank you, General. I am most grateful!"

* * *

With his newfound information, McClellan left Hope Haven and made straight to the White House to confer with Lincoln.

"Mr. President, General McDowell and I were informed earlier this morning that the alias David Stenner was lodging at the Hope Haven shelter. We immediately dispatched ourselves there. Yet, upon our arrival, Stenner had vacated the premises—leaving the shelter keeper dead in the process. We are currently searching the area, but in all likelihood, the man has probably crossed the Potomac River and is now in rebeldom. In his rush, however, he left behind a coded letter." McClellan took the message out from his pocket and presented it to Lincoln who, in turn, read it.

"A coded message with the signature of S.O.U.L. So, it's the Soul of the South that we're after…Did you manage to decipher the contents?"

"At this point, Mr. President, we have only been able to discern that it is a message to General Beauregard exhorting the rebels to attack Washington immediately."

"Well, I'm not surprised. Washington is terribly ill-fortified. I have been concerned about its safety from day one. Is Duckworth working on this deficiency?"

"Indeed, Mr. President. He has made tremendous strides in these last months."

"Well, obviously he has not made enough strides or Washington would be secure. Double, even triple, the personnel working on the project. An attack may now come immediately!"

"Yes, Mr. President!"

Lincoln further studied the message as he retrieved the sketch of Stenner on his desk. "What of his identity, George? Do we have anyone who can uncover it from this communiqué?"

"General McDowell claims that if anyone can do so, it is a man by the name of Brian Togging—a colonel in our New York division. The general has, in fact, offered his services to be set upon this assignment."

"Good. Send him promptly upon it then."

"Yes, Mr. President."

"Again, George, I want all means employed for Washington's defense. I cannot stress this enough. Washington must not fall! Do I make myself clear?"

"Absolutely, Mr. President. Absolutely!"

6

In the morning, William awoke refreshed, feeling better than ever. He had not enjoyed a sleep free from the worry of capture for many months. After a warm bath and a close clean shave, William checked his belongings to make sure that everything was accounted for. *Not again! The letter? Where is that bloody letter?* He could not believe it. After checking his belongings yet again, although the rest of his possessions were present, the letter was still missing. *Perhaps it fell out while I was crossing the Potomac?* William tried to console himself. However, such consolation failed. In the end, he presumed the worst—that the letter was in Union hands, being deciphered by a decoder specialist. Yet, William believed that even if the Union knew of his knowledge that Washington was vulnerable, and suspected that he was now informing the Confederacy, it would still take them better than two full months to adequately fortify their capital. *So, if we attack within the next two months, we still have the advantage. Fine. So, relax. It is not as bad as it could be.*

Having emerged from his room, fit with fresh clean clothes provided by Johnston, William made straight to the general's office.

Johnston rose at Lytham's knock. "So, are you ready to head to our capital, William?"

"Very much so, General."

"Good. Let's go, then!" As the two left Johnston's office, the general approached Officer Ken Torring. "Ken, I'll leave you in charge of operations in my absence. I will be gone only a few days. At present, the Yankees are nowhere near to attacking, so I do not expect there to be any trouble while I'm gone. If there is, however, you know what to do. Come, William, let's go to our capital."

"Gladly, General Johnston. Gladly!"

When Richmond was chosen as the Confederate capital, William looked forward to the day when he would finally lay eyes on it. He dreamed of what it would look like: Confederate flags flying everywhere with pretty Southern belles filling the landscape. His heart was filled with joyful anticipation.

"What is Richmond like, General?" Lytham asked during the journey. "Is it beautiful?"

"Beautiful indeed, William. A breathtaking landscape filled with lovely women," Johnston answered, as if he were reading Lytham's mind. "Perhaps you will meet your future wife there, William," added Johnston with a smile.

"You never know, General. But first business, then pleasure, right?"

"Right you are, my boy. Right you are!"

The arrival of Johnston with his entourage was met with joyous enthusiasm by the Richmonders, who were now drawing near them.

Looking at the approaching assembly, as well as the landscape, William was highly impressed. Richmond was as beautiful as he thought. An amazing landscape with amazing Southern belles. *Incredible. Incredible indeed!*

"General, what news have you?" questioned one Richmonder.

"General, did we whip 'em Yankees again?" inquired another.

"General, who's that man in civilian dress?" asked a third.

"William. It's William Lytham," answered a lady from the throng.

"William? William Lytham? Is it true, General? Is he William Lytham?" they asked.

"Yes. Yes, my fellow countrymen! William has returned. William has returned!"

"Hurray! Hurray! Hurray!" was the euphoric response by the crowd.

William's disappearance at the outbreak of the American conflict was met with Southern uncertainty as to his fate. Some thought that he had died of a rare disease. Others professed that he was kidnapped and taken North as a captive. Still others believed that he had turned into a grizzly bear—wreaking havoc on all Northern soldiers. The legend of him was that grand. No one, however, believed that William went North to join the Union army. To Southerners, there was something about him that convinced them beyond any doubt that he would never leave his people. He was a Southerner, through and through. Yet, no one could pinpoint exactly what it was that made them believe this. Some believed it was the way his sparkling blue eyes revealed a love for the South. Others believed that it was the way his blond hair flowed ever so carefree—epitomising the Southern leisurely way of life. Most, however, believed that it was his heart—which possessed kindness and love for all people. Even blacks looked upon William as the one who, after the conclusion of the war and with the South sovereign, would lead them to true freedom—not just in name, but also in action. In the absence of one specific characteristic to identify William's allegiance to the South, Southerners merged all of these characteristics into one and called it his soul. It was William's soul that exemplified his unparalleled love for the South. Hence, to all Southerners, both white and black, William was truly the Soul of the South—someone whom they all cherished.

Lytham slightly smiled, concerned that his spy cover might now be revealed. "Thank you, thank you."

"William, will we see you at the New Year's Eve dance tomorrow night?" asked several ladies. "Please, please say you'll come."

"New Year's Eve dance, General?"

"Yes, I forgot to tell you, William," Johnston answered, as he now addressed the large female crowd. "Ladies, ladies, don't worry. William is looking forward to seeing you all at the dance tomorrow night."

"Woo hoo! Woo hoo!" the women exulted.

"I'll see you there, William," stated one woman.

"My name is Bev, William," began another. "I will be wearing the pink dress with flowers…"

"I'm Debbie, William…" All the ladies crowded in on Lytham.

"Ladies, please! William will see you all at the dance. But until then, please give us some room."

Reluctantly, the women gave them space.

"You are sure popular with the ladies, William!"

Lytham blushed. "If I can find one like Rose Greenhowe, General, I will be a lucky man."

"That you will, William. That you will."

Entering the Confederate White House, Lytham was immediately greeted by General Beauregard, who had been observing William's arrival through one of the house windows.

"Welcome to Richmond, William," Beauregard greeted as he took Lytham aside. "So tell me, what's the situation in Washington?"

"Vulnerable and dangerous, General. I barely made it out of there alive. But the Yankee capital is considerably vulnerable to attack. I tried to send word to you on this through Rose Greenhowe back in August."

Initially enthused, Beauregard was now dejected. "That would explain it then, William. Rose was apprehended by the Yankees around that time."

"That is why I have come to Richmond, General. I presumed Rose had been taken captive before she had the opportunity to reveal to you Washington's vulnerability. There is still time, General. I've been scouring Washington since August, and although the Union is actively addressing their military deficiency, they are still about two months away from adequate fortification. Thus, if we attack now, we can still overrun them."

"Well, let's go meet the president and see what he says."

"General, there is something else."

"What is it?"

"General, prior to my decision to leave Washington, I intended to inform you of my findings via a coded letter. I devised a rough draft in semi coded form, but before I had the chance to complete it, it was discovered by a Union spy. The spy informed the authorities and set upon my elimination. Within seconds of killing him, I could hear the horses of the Yankees approaching. Since I can't locate the letter, we must assume that it is in Union hands—with Lincoln aware of its contents."

"What did the letter say?"

"That we must attack Washington because of its vulnerability. Do you have a pen and paper?"

Beauregard gave him both.

William proceeded to write the letter exactly as he had written it at Hope Haven.

"There it is, General," Lytham said, showing Beauregard the draft message. "The entire letter—word for word."

Beauregard read it and then paused. "Do you think even with the Union aware of this message, it will take them another two months before their capital can be considered sufficiently fortified?"

"Absolutely, General. Without a doubt! Even if they work around the clock on Washington's defense from the day I escaped, it will still take them better than two months, at the very least, before they are able to exhibit any type of successful resistance against us."

Beauregard pondered, and pondered again, and was then confident. "Fine. We'll still inform the president that you have discovered that it is an opportune time to attack the Federal capital. We'll see what he says. I, for one, hope he decides to attack. I trust you and I have no doubt that this is a chance of a lifetime. I have been wanting to attack the Yankee capital, even without your information, for quite some time."

"Did your other spies also inform you of Washington's vulnerability, General?"

"Actually, William, you and Rose were my only spies," Beauregard answered, downcast.

Lytham, not willing to offend, just gave a smile.

"At any rate, with your information, who knows if we will ever get such a chance to attack the Union capital again." Beauregard saw that Lytham was still mad at himself for the mishap. "Don't worry, William. The letter is of no consequence to the Yankees. There is nothing they can do to ensure Washington's protection against us within the next month anyway. So, if we attack now, we can still overrun their capital!"

Lytham was grateful for Beauregard's consolation. "Thank you, General."

"Come, William, let's meet the president."

"Yes, General!"

"Mr. President, I would like you to meet William Lytham," Beauregard pronounced with a proud smile.

"Good afternoon, Mr. President. It is an honor to meet you, sir."

"The honor is all mine, William…So tell me, how is life as a spy?"

"Pure hell, Mr. President," answered Lytham, bringing a chuckle from all. "But I have no regrets. I realize espionage is crucial if we are to have any chance at offsetting our lower number of soldiers and weapons. So, I am glad to be serving our beloved South in this capacity. I believe I have a talent for spying, Mr. President. I thrive on the thrill and the excitement of it all. But, as a whole, the job is very dangerous. In fact, I narrowly escaped death."

"My word, William. I know, spying is very dangerous; yet at the same time, it is most necessary. Did you have to assume various identities?"

"Well, while in Washington, Mr. President, I assumed two identities: a David Stenner and a Brett Brinson. As David Stenner, I was a wealthy Bostonian willing to provide the Union military with financial help." Davis chuckled. "Then, when it became unsafe for me to continue that alias, I assumed the identity of Brett Brinson—a hobo from New York looking for work." Davis smiled.

"You are very creative, William. I'll definitely give you that. Did the disguises bring you success in ascertaining Union strategy?"

"Indeed, Mr. President! As David Stenner, I discerned the strength and movements the Union army employed at Bull Run, while as Brett Brinson I discovered the fragile hold the Yankees have on their capital."

"Fragile hold?"

"Yes, Mr. President. Washington is poorly defended."

"Well, then, we must attack!" Davis looked to Beauregard and Johnston for agreement.

"Mr. President, I would love to attack. But, unfortunately, William's information is months old," Johnston said.

"Months old?"

"Yes, Mr. President. I found out about Washington's vulnerability in August through a conversation between General McClellan and Lieutenant Duckworth. As soon as I found this out, I notified Rose Greenhowe, who informed me that she would immediately alert General Beauregard."

"Oh. I see," Davis sadly said. "Unfortunately, our beloved Rose was captured by the enemy around that time, William. Had we only known of this in August, we would have surely overrun the Union capital by now and in so doing would have put a stranglehold upon the Union."

"Mr. President, we can still do that," Lytham appealed. "Washington is still vulnerable! These past months, I have been scouring the streets to see if the fortifications and manpower necessary for its defense have been installed. They haven't, Mr. President. Although the Union's defense is stronger than it was in August, with a concerted effort on our part, Washington can still be overrun." Lytham recalled the letter but decided to leave it to Beauregard to bring it up. "Even if they have everyone working day and night on its fortification from the time I left, it will still take them more than a month, at the very earliest, before their capital can be considered secure."

"Pierre?"

Beauregard believed Lytham, thus he decided not to bother informing the president of the letter. "Mr. President, I agree with William. I do believe we should attack the Union capital. Such an opportunity may never come to us again. With Washington being as defenseless as it is, I believe it imperative that we take advantage of this and attack. If we are successful, of which I have no doubt that we will be, our recognized independence from the North may be only days away."

"Joe?"

"I don't know, Mr. President. The troops we have on our side of the Potomac River, stationed at my fort, are not sufficient for such an enterprise."

Davis contemplated.

"Mr. President, I agree General Johnston's numbers at the border are not enough for the overrunning of Washington. I do believe, however, that if we could quickly summon troops situated at our other locations, we would then be in a position to overtake the Union capital," Lytham pleaded.

"Generals? What do you think? Can we afford to bring troops from our various other posts for an attack on Washington?"

Johnston looked to Beauregard.

"Mr. President, I believe we can safely bring more than enough troops necessary for an attack on Washington," Beauregard answered. "It would take, however, about two weeks for them to be brought here and to be ready to attack."

"William, do you think even with the passage of two weeks we would have enough time for a successful attack?"

"Absolutely, Mr. President. Absolutely!"

"William, would you excuse us for just a moment?"

"Of course, Mr. President." Lytham saluted and, with a return salute from Davis, exited.

"Men, I don't know. I trust William's assessment, but at the same time his original source is now months old. I realize he has since been surveying Washington to make sure that it is still vulnerable, but the Union could be fortifying their capital in places where William has not seen…Joe?"

"I agree, Mr. President. I love William as if he were my own son, but, as you say, his information is now months old, and in this war it may as well be years old."

"Pierre?"

"I trust William, Mr. President. I believe he has been diligently making sure Washington is still vulnerable and would only give his consent to attack if he felt more than certain we would win. William has proven his reliability many times over already. I believe we should attack!"

"But, Pierre, we can't risk losing such a battle," Johnston responded. "If we enter upon this enterprise and have miscalculated the Union's weakness, they will be able to march right into our capital uncontested. Their victory would then be assured."

Davis was frightened at Johnston's warning.

"But, Joe," Beauregard countered, "William has unequivocally stated that Washington is still vulner…"

"Pierre, Joe is right. We can't risk being wrong on this one. We have come so far and have fought so hard, and to jeopardize our very cause upon young William's information—no matter how credible he has been in the past—is far too risky. I'm sorry, Pierre, but in this matter I must concur with General Johnston. Inform William of our decision and return. I would like the three of us to go over some military strategy I have been devising for the Western front."

"Yes, Mr. President." Beauregard, with a salute, and then a return salute from Davis, left.

Davis was confident in his decision. "So, Joe, how is the situation at the border?"

"Fine, Mr. President. We are strongly secure!"

"Good. When are your boys expecting you back?"

"Not for a few days, Mr. President."

"Good, then stay in Richmond for these next few days and enjoy yourself. I am sure you will most enjoy our New Year's Eve dance tomorrow night."

Johnston was highly pleased. "Thank you, Mr. President. I have no doubt I will!"

Leaving the president's office, Beauregard informed William of Davis' decision. Lytham was downcast.

"Don't worry, William. We'll attack Washington one day," Beauregard said in a hopeful vein.

"Yes, General. But this is such an opportune time for us to attack. Who knows if we will ever be in such an advantageous position again?"

"I agree, William, but the president is worried that if our calculations are wrong, Richmond would be dangerously exposed."

"True. But I am certain that we would not fail."

"So am I. I told him as much. But he is, after all, our president and so we must trust his decision."

"True. General, what would you like me to do now?"

"Well, if Washington is as bad as you say, with you being a wanted man, it is best that you stay here for the time being while I deliberate upon where I should next send you."

"Yes, General."

"William, I have to go back and converse some more with the president and General Johnston. I am not sure how long it will take. In the meantime, go to the Spottswood Hotel and inform them that you have been sent by me to request a room for an indeterminate duration. They will give you keys to a room and you can reside there while in Richmond."

Lytham was thrilled, knowing the Spottswood Hotel to be luxurious—something he had missed for far too long. "Thank you, General. I am humbly grateful."

"My pleasure, William. Anyway, get a good night's sleep tonight, for tomorrow is the New Year's Eve dance. You do know about the dance tomorrow night, don't you?"

"Yes, General."

"Good. I'm sure there'll be plenty of pretty young ladies there, William," Beauregard continued, smiling.

"I am definitely looking forward to that, General," Lytham said.

7

Arriving in New York, McDowell headed to the New York division and was cordially welcomed by Lieutenant Darren McKenny—who had been telegraphed by McClellan of McDowell's pending arrival.

"Good morning, General McDowell. I am Lieutenant Darren McKenny. We have been eagerly awaiting your arrival."

"Good morning, Lieutenant McKenny."

"How was your trip?"

"Tiring."

"Yes, but you made good time. I wasn't expecting you for at least another day."

"Well, due to the gravity of the situation, I came here as fast as I could."

"Yes, I was telegraphed that a rebel spy ascertained our military plans at Bull Run and that is why you have come—to meet code decipherer Colonel Brian Togging of my division to see if he can decode a message the traitor left."

"Yes, Lieutenant. General McClellan has set me on this assignment, and the president is eagerly awaiting the results of Togging's work."

"Well, let's not waste any time then. I'll bring you to him. He is anxious to meet you."

"Thank you, Lieutenant."

Darren entered his division quarters. "Good morning, men."

"Good morning, Lieutenant McKenny," the soldiers greeted, saluting.

"Colonel Togging."

"Yes, Lieutenant McKenny," he answered as he approached.

"Brian, I would like you to meet General McDowell."

"Good morning, General. It is a pleasure to meet you, sir."

"It is a pleasure to meet you too, Colonel. They say, Brian, you are an expert in code deciphering and in discerning the identity of persons who use such means to send information."

"All my life, General, I have enjoyed the challenge of decoding messages and placing a face and then a name behind the writer. I must admit, I have had more than my share of success. I believe this is a talent of mine."

"Colonel Togging is by far the best in his field, General. Whenever we come across a coded message, we send Brian upon it, and nine times out of ten he'll either know who wrote it or give us a good indication of the type of person we're looking for."

"Splendid! Well, the government desperately needs your services here, Brian."

"I'll leave you two with your work. If you need anything, General, please don't hesitate to ask."

"Thank you," McDowell said as McKenny exited.

"Brian, for the past five months we have been looking for a man under the alias of David Stenner. We believe him to be a rebel spy. I met the man and have brought a sketch of him here. The traitor has also assumed the name of Brett Brinson; I have his handwriting both from a letter he gave to a Mrs. Smith and from a coded message he wrote to his rebel friends." McDowell presented Togging with the picture and the handwriting samples.

Togging studied them, in particular the secret communiqué. "Well, it's definitely a coded message, General, though a weak one."

After a span of thirty minutes, Brian successfully decoded the entire message—save the signature.

"That's what I deem the content to be, General."

McDowell read it. "Great work, Brian. The bastard, informing his fellow rebels of the time we still need to fortify our capital and thus urging them to attack us now! Dammit! How about the signature? Who does it belong to?"

Togging studied the signature again. "Well…well, I believe *S* more than likely stands for South. *O*…um…let me see. *U*…well…*U* may very well stand for Union?!" Togging was impressed with his own resourcefulness.

So was McDowell. "Great work. Keep going!"

"Well, we may have South, *O*, Union, *L*. Hum…over? That's it! *O* must stand for over!" proclaimed the colonel, excited at his discovery. "Yes! South over Union *L*!"

"Excellent, Brian. Excellent! One more." *One bloody more!*

"*L*…hmm…*L*. Let me think…South over Union *L*. South over Union Lawn? No. South over Union Larry? No, probably not. South over Union, hum. South over Union Lamb?"

"Lamb? Is it Lamb?" McDowell asked with anticipatory hopefulness.

"Maybe not."

McDowell was downcast.

"*L*…hmm…that *L*. General, it must signify the initial of his name. It must start with an *L*."

"His first name or his last name?"

"Probably his last name."

"What? What do you think his last name is, Brian?"

Togging thought intensely. "Lonning, Lethley, Landry. I don't know, General. It could be anything. I'll have to work on it some more."

Though disappointed, McDowell realized that to decipher a name with just one initial was no small feat. "That's fine, Brian. You take your time. Concentrate. You've done well so far. Just one more hurdle, Brian. Just one more hurdle!"

"Yes, General."

"I'll come by first thing tomorrow morning to see how you're doing."

"All right, General. I'll see you tomorrow morning. Hopefully then the rebel's name will be a mystery no longer."

"Right you are, my son." *Right you are.* McDowell thought as he left.

The following morning, the general returned to the New York division.

"So, General, how are the two of you coming along with the coded message?"

"Well, yesterday the colonel deciphered the entire message, along with three of the four letters in the rebel's signature. He seems to believe that the final letter in the signature is the initial of the spy's last name."

McKenny was impressed, but he was not really interested. "That's great, General. Well, let's go see how he's progressing, shall we?"

"Yes, Lieutenant—thank you." McDowell was aware that before the war, McKenny had lived in the South and had spent time at Mobile Academy. "Say, Lieutenant?"

"Yes, sir?"

"How was it like, you know, in the South and all—growing up and attending Mobile Academy?"

"Those were interesting years, General. I met many people and, in fact, I was deceived into believing the South was better than the North in all things. Boy, was I wrong. I'll tell you one thing, Irvin," McKenny continued, losing focus as he recalled the Jedd and Shen conversation, "Southerners will never accept Northerners—no matter how much the Northerner tries."

"Well, who would want to be a backward Southerner anyway?" McDowell chuckled, without the return emotion from McKenny.

"It is my mission in life to destroy the South, completely!" McKenny said, totally losing focus as he recalled William. "From the top," McKenny continued as he thought of William, "to the bottom," as he thought of Jedd and Shen. "I will not rest until my goal is achieved—whether we win this war or not!"

McDowell looked at McKenny with confusion.

"I mean, we will win this war and thoroughly destroy the South in the process!"

McDowell gave a half smile.

"Good morning, Brian! How are you today?" McDowell greeted as the men entered Togging's quarters.

"I could be better, General."

"What's up? Did you decipher the last letter in the rebel's signature?"

"General, there is nothing I want more than to accomplish that very task. I have been up all night trying to achieve such but without success. The final initial, *L,* could mean any last name starting with *L*: Lorry…Loing…Lottoning…?"

Leaving the room as the two resumed their business, Darren halted upon hearing the twelfth letter of the alphabet.

"What did you say, Brian? The last letter is *L*?"

"Yes, Lieutenant. We believe the last letter, *L,* is the person's…"

"Let me see the message and the sketch."

"Oh, don't worry, Lieutenant. This is something that is occurring in faraway Washington. We don't believe he is in New York," McDowell intervened.

Darren looked intently at the signature and drawing. "The picture! The eyes! Those sparkling eyes! It's him! Oh my God! It's him!"

"What? What are you saying, Lieutenant?" McDowell inquired, with a troubled look.

"Lieutenant?" added Togging, concerned.

"It's William Lytham. He's the Soul of the South!" McKenny exclaimed, examining the S.O.U.L. signature.

"William? *The* William Lytham? Commander of our troops at Mobile Academy?"

"Yes, General! When Brian stated the last initial *L*, William's last name immediately entered my mind. Then, after looking at the picture, I knew it was William. Disguises are convincing, but one can never disguise the eyes. They say the eyes are the window to the soul. And this man is truly the Soul of the South. I know those sparkling eyes; they belong to William. And the handwriting: that's also Lytham's."

"This is great news!" McDowell said.

"Take me to the president, General. At once!"

"But, Darren, you are a lieutenant of a division here in New York."

"Irvin, William can do more damage to our cause than the elimination of ten times the size of my division. I know how to capture the man. I was his best friend for the majority of his life. If anyone knows how to catch him, it's me. Moreover, if we don't catch him, I fear our entire goal to suppress the rebel states will be lost. William can almost single-handedly achieve independence for the South, and the South knows this. Why else would they not have insisted that he be an officer in their army, especially with his glorious military career at Mobile Academy? This is because they believe in him and in his passion. And I, if anyone, can see why. It is because of William that I became one of the staunchest of all Southerners at Mobile. He knows things no one else knows. The information he ascertains is reliable, and the way in which he boldly goes about getting it is incredible!"

Recalling his meeting with Lytham as David Stenner, McDowell nodded in approval.

"I must immediately accompany you to Washington, General. We have no time to waste. An attack upon our capital may come at any minute."

McDowell was now totally convinced that McKenny must indeed accompany him to Washington. "Yes. Yes, Darren. You must indeed come. We have but little time left!"

Quickly, Darren summoned his division and stated that his presence in Washington was immediately required and that in his absence Officer George Drinning would be in charge. McKenny then packed his bags and with McDowell—who already had his belongings on him—boarded the next train to Washington.

8

After a refreshing night's sleep in the Spottswood Hotel, William awoke rejuvenated. *Luxury sure does have its place in the world,* he thought. Washing up, William toured the main streets of the Confederate capital—not only to see its beauty, but also in the hopes of finding a nice suit to wear for the evening's New Year's Eve dance. Although taking in the splendor of Richmond, William found it hard to concentrate on his task—due to the many beautiful women. William truly admired pretty ladies and was glad that he could now just be himself around them, without any aliases. However, with the many ladies stopping him, smiling, asking for his autograph, telling him their name and what they would be wearing for the dance, William saw much of his day pass quickly by. It was already five in the afternoon and he was still without a suit. Finally, just after 5:15 p.m., William's fortunes changed when he entered Chrisham's Clothing Store. The person who greeted him was Charles Chrisham, one of his former professors at Mobile Academy.

"William, good afternoon!"

"Professor Chrisham!"

"Yes," he happily replied as he shook Lytham's hand. "How are you?"

"Fine, Professor," Lytham answered with merry surprise. "How are you?"

"Most fine, thank you!"

"When did you come to Richmond? I never thought you would have left Mobile Academy, where you loved teaching."

"Yes, William. I do love teaching. It is what I have done my entire life. There is nothing I take more pleasure in than in helping students learn. At the start of the war, President Davis, who was also once a student of mine, asked me if I would come to Richmond and teach the new recruits here, as well as provide them with the moral solace necessary in this time of crisis. Without hesitation, I said yes—grateful that I could assist our cause. With today being New Year's Eve, and thus no school, I decided to come to my grandson's clothing shop and help him out. I like to think I know something about the clothing business, for clothing has been in the Chrisham family here in Richmond for generations. I must admit, I was considered a rebel—fittingly so, wouldn't you say—for being the only Chrisham to leave the family business and enter the teaching profession. I must say, though, I have no regrets, and my family, although hesitant at first, have fully supported me ever since."

"That is fantastic, Professor. Well, it looks like I have come to the right place. If your grandson is as good a clothier as you are a teacher, then I know my suit for tonight will be splendid!"

"Well, thank you, William," Chrisham humbly replied. "I am sure you have come to the right place indeed." Charles saw his grandson Robert Chrisham approach. "Robert, I would like you to meet one of my former students, William Lytham of Mobile, Alabama."

"Mr. Lytham, it is a pleasure to meet you, sir," he greeted with a slight bow, shaking his hand.

"Please, call me William. It is also a pleasure to meet the grandson of the admirable Professor Chrisham. Robert, I am attending the New Year's Eve dance tonight, but I am without a suit. I was wondering…"

"Say no more, William, you have come to the right place. Our selection of suits is paralleled by none—not even by the clothiers of Paris or Rome."

"Splendid. Well, what do you think would best agree with me?"

Robert looked at William's features. "Well, I think black wool trousers, a white cotton shirt, a black wool vest, a black wool tailcoat with a black silk bow tie and matching silk handkerchief would look just fine. What do you think?"

"I think that would be magnificent!"

Robert went on to fit William into the sharp-looking suit, equipped with dashing black leather shoes. To put it mildly, he looked extraordinary.

Chapter Eight

"How do you like it, William?"

"I love it, Robert. I'll take it," Lytham answered as he proceeded to pay for the suit. "Well, it sure has been good to see you again, Professor Chrisham."

"It has been good to see you again also, William. Have a wonderful night tonight!"

"I will. Thank you ever so much, Robert, for your help. The suit is fabulous!"

"My pleasure, William. Come by anytime."

At that, Lytham left the shop smiling and proceeded to the hotel for a quick supper, bath, and shave before the dance.

At seven in the evening, Officer Childs knocked on Lytham's door.

"Mr. Lytham? William?"

Lytham emerged from the bathroom as he just finished his shave. "Yes?"

"Mr. Lytham, I am Officer John Childs. General Beauregard said that you would be expecting me."

Lytham opened the door. "Why, yes. Please, come in."

"Thank you." Childs entered and shook Lytham's hand. "It's a pleasure to meet you, Mr. Lytham."

"Please, call me William. It is a pleasure to meet you too, Officer Childs."

"John is also fine for me."

Lytham smiled.

"Sharp suit, William!"

"Yours too, John!"

Childs' attire was similar except that his bow tie was white.

"So, John, are you ready for the dance tonight?"

"I certainly am, William. How about you?"

"I sure am," Lytham said as the two left to meet up with Beauregard. "It has definitely been a while since I've had a relaxing night out, John. In fact, it has been over eight years since I've even been to a dance; and that was my senior high school graduation dance."

"Was the woman you brought lovely, William?"

"She sure was. Her name was Beth Bronson. We had known each other since we were children. In fact, my parents thought we were destined for each other."

"What happened?"

59

"Well, I joined the army and in becoming wrapped up in it, I neglected writing to her. I guess I felt it wasn't meant to be between us. She would never write. I believed she was waiting for me to write first. Finally, when I did write to her, on my twenty-fifth birthday, it was too late. Her return letter informed me that she had been married for over two years and that she had waited for me to write up until then; when I hadn't written, she believed I wasn't interested in her. As a result, she allowed herself to be courted by another and was married shortly thereafter. My loss, I guess."

"No, William. That was just meant to be, that's all. You weren't meant for each other. Your time will come. I know it will." Childs chuckled. "In fact, I'll bet if you ask any of the women tonight to marry you, they would say yes right on the spot."

Lytham chuckled in return. "Well, I want a woman who will move me, John. I want a woman for whom I would trade in all the money in the world. In fact, I have felt that way about only one woman in my life, and that was for a widow whom I knew it wouldn't be proper to court: Rose Greenhowe."

"Ah, yes! Rose is sure a fox, even at her age. And her passion for the South is incredible!"

"You're right, John. Rose is truly one-of-a-kind. If I could find someone even close to her, I would be a happy man."

"Well, you never know, William, tonight you may meet such a woman."

"You never know, John. You never know. So, what about you? Are you a bachelor, married...?"

"I am proud to say that I am a happily married father, William. My wife Emma and my baby girl Nicole are the loves of my life. And yet I haven't been home to Jackson, Mississippi, to see them in over ten months. I sure miss them."

"It must be tough having a wife and a child and yet not being with them. That is the only reason why I am glad that I am not committed. It would break my heart not to be with my loved ones, especially if the unthinkable occurred."

"You are right, William. But knowing that I am loved gives me all the more determination to make sure that I make it back home alive."

"That's the right attitude to have, John. You just keep thinking that and not only will we win this war, but you will also return home safely to your family."

9

Arriving in Washington, McDowell and McKenny made haste to the White House. Lincoln was with General McClellen.

"Mr. President, I would like you to meet Lieutenant Darren McKenny of the New York division," said McDowell.

Lincoln was somewhat taken aback, expecting Brian Togging. "Pleased to meet you, Lieutenant."

"Mr. President, it is truly an honor," McKenny replied.

"Mr. President, as soon as I arrived in New York, I met up with Colonel Brian Togging, and he was able to decipher the contents of the rebel message, save the last letter in the signature of S.O.U.L." McDowell presented the deciphered letter to Lincoln.

"Just as we thought, George: a communiqué informing the rebels of Washington's vulnerability and thus urging them to immediately attack!" Lincoln then handed the letter to McClellan.

"The bastard!" McClellan uttered, reading the same.

"What about the last letter in the signature of S.O.U.L., Irvin?"

"Mr. President, the colonel believed that the last letter was an abbreviation of the rebel's last name. When I met Brian the following morning with Lieutenant McKenny, he was still unsuccessful in deciphering the name. Hearing of our trouble, Darren asked to examine the spy's letter and sketch. After only briefly looking at those two items, Lieutenant McKenny identified the traitor's true identity."

"Is this true, Darren?" questioned an astonished Lincoln. "You know who the Soul of the South is?"

"Yes, Mr. President. It is none other than William Lytham!"

"Lytham, William Lytham?" responded Lincoln in shock. "My God, I can't believe it! When Alabama seceded, I sent a dispatch to William instructing him to report to Washington to partake in operations to maintain the Union. When he did not report, I presumed that he was either killed or had fled to another country—not being able to stomach the thought of our civil conflict. I never believed that William defected to the Southern cause. He and his family were staunch, loyal citizens. In fact, I put my hope, and indeed the hope of the nation, in his assuming an officer's role in the Union army. His intelligence, natural persuasion, and kindness are all attributes I believed would have been employed by us to sway the South into accepting my presidency." Lincoln pondered and was now worried. "I am starting to realize the gravity of the situation. If William is as focused on Southern independence as he previously was to U.S. patriotism, we have a major problem on our hands. I know William will not stop until the South achieves its goal. In fact, for him to cast away all that he and his family have achieved as United States citizens for generations illustrates, beyond any doubt, that he is determined to see Southern secession through to the bitter end."

"That is precisely why I have come, Mr. President. I know William. I have known him since we were children. I know his passion, his drive, his ability to get what he wants when he sets his mind to it. When my family moved from New York to Mobile some twenty years ago, I was immediately attracted by William's persona. His frankness, kindness, and influence are unmatched. In fact, it was because of William that I became a loyal Southerner. I know the man's heart, Mr. President. I know his soul. His soul is with the South. He honestly believes that when the South becomes independent, he will set about ending slavery; and, knowing the man, I know he will succeed. He captivates his people, Mr. President. They put their entire hope and trust in him and not without reason. The kindness and love he has for the Southern people cannot be expressed in words. He truly is the Soul of the South, Mr. President. That is why I have come to Washington: to serve the Union in his apprehension. As I've said, I know the man better than anyone. I know how he thinks and how he goes about accomplishing his tasks. If you set me upon him, Mr. President, I have no doubt that it will be the best decision the Union will ever make. For if we are unsuccessful in his apprehension, I truly believe that the preservation of the Union might be jeopardized."

Chapter Nine

"You realize that if I set you upon this assignment, Darren, there is no guarantee that you will see it through alive. William has already killed one man that we know of. I wouldn't doubt that you might share the same fate if it meant, to William, the defense of the South."

"I realize this, Mr. President. But if I die in the attempt to preserve our country, then I will die a happy man—not that I think that I will die in this assignment, however. But I realize the risks involved, and I am willing to take those risks."

"George?"

"I believe Darren should be given the assignment, Mr. President. Darren knows the man. If anyone can catch William, I believe it's him. Are you sure you realize the risks involved, lad?"

"I do, General. I do."

"All right then," continued Lincoln, "the assignment is yours. We believe William to be in Richmond—no doubt conferring with Davis and his rebel generals. I would like you to bring him back alive, Darren. But if such is not possible…" Lincoln pondered, somewhat reluctantly, "then do what you must. William must be stopped! He has brought immeasurable harm to the Union already."

"Thank you, Mr. President. I won't let you down."

"I'll arrange for you a meeting with disguise specialist Glen Hammer. Although I asked our premier disguise specialist Mittle Tobbs from South Carolina to come to Washington to set up shop for us here, he gave me a resounding no. As a consequence, Glen is now our best disguise specialist. So, I'll send you to him. General McDowell will inform you of the time and day of the meeting. In the meantime, I would like you to stay at the Willard Hotel. General McDowell will accompany you there to book your room." Lincoln looked to McDowell as McDowell fervently nodded.

"Thank you, Mr. President," McKenny answered happily, aware of the legendary luxury of the place.

With that, McKenny and McDowell saluted the president and, with his return salute, the two proceeded to the Willard Hotel.

The president turned to his general. "I never would have believed it, George—even if I had seen it with my own eyes. I never would have thought that William would leave the Union. But since he has, I realize the extreme importance of stopping him. I am sure Davis is overjoyed that William is in their service. If there is anyone who can achieve independence for the South, it is William Lytham. We must stop him,

George! We must do so before it's too late. Look what the man has already done to us in just this short time."

"Indeed, Mr. President. He must be stopped. I never met the man, but I've heard of his legend: of his ability to garner victory against formidable odds. I think sending Darren upon him will bring forth abundant fruit. If anyone can catch him, I believe it's McKenny."

"Let's just hope he's successful, George. We can't afford to have William at large. Our goal of preventing Southern secession depends on it."

"Agreed, Mr. President."

Later in the week, McDowell went to see McKenny at the Willard Hotel.

"So, has the president arranged for me a meeting with Glen Hammer?" asked McKenny.

"Yes, Darren. You are scheduled to meet him this afternoon at two o'clock. At that time, he will provide you with all the particulars for your mission."

"Perfect, General."

"Darren, I want you to be careful. William is no fool. He is sly, cunning, and smart. But I'm sure you already know this."

McKenny nodded.

"Okay then, so get that son of a bitch if it's the last thing you do! There's no one who wants that Lytham more than I."

Perhaps I, General, Darren thought. "I will, General. I'll get that Lytham!"

At the scheduled time, McKenny met Glen Hammer at the latter's shop.

"I've heard many good things about you, Glen. Your talent in disguises is well known."

"Well, thank you. We must all fight rebeldom in one way or another. And I'm glad to be fighting the rebels in the service of deception."

"Well, I'm sure it's because you're the best."

"Damn right I'm the best! I'm better than anyone, especially anyone from the South," Hammer stated, as he thought of Mittle Tobbs. "Anyway, the president has fixed everything for you. The name you are to assume is Henry Rolding. Here are your identification papers." Hammer handed them to him. "Your instructions are as follows. You are to cross the Potomac this evening under the cover of darkness. Upon crossing, inform the rebels that you are a Southerner and had been detained in Washington on the charge of being a rebel spy. Yet you, along with two others, escaped one of our holding stations prior to being sent to Capitol Prison. The two, however, were shot and killed in the subsequent pursuit. But you managed to cross the Potomac River and now want to enlist in the Confederate army to exact revenge on the Yankees. Here are a pair of handcuffs. Put these on after you cross the river. It will help in the believability of your story. Have the rebels take them off. I am to shave your head, and then you are to put on these clothes." Hammer showed McKenny a ripped shirt, some torn-up pants, and a pair of well-used boots.

Glen proceeded to shave Darren's head and, upon finishing, had him dress in his new attire.

"How does it fit?"

"It fits well, Glen. Thank you."

"My pleasure. You look like a totally different person."

"Indeed, I do!"

"Good luck, Darren. Get those Southern bastards!"

"I will!"

10

The New Year's Eve dance was held at the Richmond Roar, a hall located on the first floor of the Spottswood Hotel. As Beauregard, Childs, and Lytham entered the Roar, they were welcomed by President Davis. After exchanging pleasantries, the president went on to welcome other guests while Beauregard asked Childs and Lytham what they thought of the place.

"Very impressive, General," Childs answered.

"The place is fabulous, General," Lytham echoed.

"Well, do enjoy yourself, lads. I'm off to say hello to General Johnston."

"Thank you, General."

"Pretty amazing, don't you think, William?"

"I'm highly impressed, John. The place is remarkable. Look at those expensive chandeliers and the marble flooring. This hall must have cost a fortune to furnish!"

"Look at the pretty women, too, William. Pretty gorgeous, wouldn't you say?"

"I would indeed," Lytham answered as three ladies approached.

"Hi, William," the ladies greeted with happy giggles.

"William, would you like to dance?" asked one.

"Maybe later, sure…"

"Let's go for a stroll, William," entreated another.

"Ah, ahhhh…"

"Come, William, I want to introduce you to my family," beseeched a third, grabbing his hand.

Childs saw Lytham's reluctance. "Please, ladies. William will be happy to spend time with you all. But I have been ordered to show him around the premises first," Childs lied.

"Well, we'll see you later then, William," the women exclaimed, smiling and winking at him as they left.

"My gosh, I can't believe it. Have I died and gone to heaven?"

"Come, William, let's sit at our table; supper is about to be served." Childs smiled.

As Lytham and Childs, along with the rest, finished eating their supper, music began.

"Say, John, who's that lady over there?" Lytham asked, noticing a woman at a table not far off.

"Oh, that's Melanie Wenning. Her parents split up some nine months ago. Her father lives in the North and is a Union officer, while her mother lives here and runs a shoe shop. They say the war wrecked their marriage. Her father is a Federalist, while her mother is a staunch Southerner. Such a polarizing of loyalties is common here in Virginia. This is not Mississippi or Alabama, you know."

"True. Do you know her?"

"Not really. I met her the other day at her mother's shop while I was getting a pair of shoes for tonight's dance. She helps her mother there and was the one that attended to me. We started some small talk and that is how I found out about her parents' situation."

Lytham was amazed at her beauty. "Do you think you could introduce me to her?"

"I'm sure you don't need any introduction, William. But I will if you want me to."

"It would probably be best."

Childs and Lytham walked to her table. "Hi, Melanie."

"Hi, John. How are the shoes?"

"Perfect. They fit and look great!"

Melanie nodded with a smile.

"Melanie, I would like you to meet a friend of mine, William Lytham."

"Hi, Melanie," William greeted.

"Hi, William," Melanie replied, shaking his hand. "It's a pleasure to meet you!"

"Well, I have to go and say hello to an old acquaintance," Childs said, aware that his introduction was complete. "It's good to see you again, Melanie."

"Good seeing you again, too, John," Melanie echoed as Childs left.

"Would you like to dance, Melanie?"

"Sure, William."

"It certainly is a lovely ball," William commented as they danced hand in hand.

"It sure is."

"John told me that you and your mother run a shoe shop?"

"Why, yes. It's quite successful, actually. We've been in the business my entire life. You know, you're quite the legend around here, William Lytham."

Lytham blushed. "Well, it's nice to be home."

"Oh, are you from Richmond?" Melanie asked, knowing the answer.

"Actually, I meant home here in the South. I'm originally from Mobile, Alabama. Have you heard of it?"

"Why of course I have."

"It's quite a lovely place."

Melanie smiled. "Have you recently come from some place other than the South then, William?"

"Oh, ah, yes. I've just returned from a vacation."

"Yeah, sure. You don't have to worry about me, Mr. Lytham. I am a Southerner. I'm sure John has told you about my father being a Union officer."

"Well, I think someone may have mentioned it."

"Well, I am a Southerner, through and through. Just like my mother. In fact, the Yankees ruined my parents' marriage. My father has Southern sympathies but felt that, as a Federalist, he had to join the Union army. My mother was shocked to the core and told him that if he left to fight in the Yankee army, she didn't want to see him ever again. My father desperately tried to explain the reasons for his decision, but my mother would have none of it. Thus, I am without a united family. It is terrible, William."

"It must be hard to have a mother and a father, both of whom you love so much, to be on opposing sides in our conflict. I cannot even imagine what it must be like."

"Well, it has made me a stronger person."

Lytham was impressed. "Would you like to go for a walk, Melanie?"

Melanie nodded with a smile. "The night is beautiful, don't you find, William?" Melanie asked, admiring the breathtaking stars and the soft warm breeze.

"Yes, but not as beautiful as you, Melanie."

"Oh, William," Melanie said, blushing.

The two strolled outside for about an hour. They then returned to the ball and danced together for the remainder of the night, sipping champagne along with the rest in welcoming in the New Year. As the gala came to a close, William offered to escort Melanie home, which she happily accepted.

Arriving at the Wenning abode, William bid Melanie good night—kissing her softly on the cheek in front of the porch—and was overjoyed that she wanted to see him again the next day. Returning home to the hotel, William wondered if he was in love.

He could hardly wait for the next morning. Arriving at her door, William was greeted by Melanie's loving embrace.

"William, how are you? I knew you'd come."

"I wouldn't have missed it for the world, Melanie," William said, hugging and kissing her affectionately on the cheek. "So, what would you like to do today?"

"Anything you want. As long as we're together!"

"Well, I thought we could first tour Richmond to see the town and its monuments, then have lunch with some fine French wine in the open fresh air, and after that…who knows?" William smiled.

"Sounds perfect, William. First, though, I would like you to meet my mother. Since I told her about you last night, she has been anxious to meet you."

"Of course, I would love to meet her!" William and Melanie went inside.

"William. William Lytham. It is an honor to meet you!"

"Good morning, Mrs. Wenning. It is an honor to meet you too! Your fidelity to the Southern cause is well known."

"Well, I lost a marriage because of it," Mrs. Wenning said. "But I have no regrets. I love my husband and I believe, in the end, he will beg me to accept him back. But whatever happens, my heart and soul will always be with the South."

"Mine, too, Mrs. Wenning," Lytham replied, smiling.

"Mother, William and I are going to tour the city."

"Sounds fabulous. How about supper tonight at our house, William?"

William looked to Melanie, who fervently agreed to it. "Sure. I'd love to, Mrs. Wenning."

"We'll be home at six, Mother. Is that all right?"

"Yes. Six it is. Supper will be ready then."

"Thank you, Mrs. Wenning. That is certainly nice of you."

"Think nothing of it, William. I am honored to have you dine at our table."

Lytham blushed with a humble smile.

With that, William and Melanie, hand in hand, took in the beautiful sights of Richmond.

"Richmond is sure grand and beautiful, isn't it, William?"

"It certainly is, Melanie."

"How about Mobile? Is it nice?"

"Well, it isn't as large as Richmond, but it is still pretty. In fact, it has a very serene, peaceful atmosphere. The people there are so friendly. It is more of a coastal setting."

Melanie smiled. "What would you like to do when this war is over, William?"

"Well, I haven't really given it much thought. I probably would like to be an officer in the Confederate army or something."

"What about owning a plantation, growing cotton? They say England loves our cotton. We…I mean, you, could make a fortune." Melanie smiled.

Lytham gave a return smile. "Well, as for a plantation, if I had one, it would be with paid labor."

"What about slaves, William? They're cheap and do a good job."

"When this war is over, Melanie, I am going to make sure slavery is abolished. It is truly wrong. But the North is to blame for this, not us. We have wanted to end slavery for many years, but because the powerful Northern economy dictates that it is necessary for us to produce goods such as cotton, we have been unable to end it. Once we get a country of our own, none of us will be slaves to the North; we can then set about ending slavery here in our own society."

"You're right, William. We've truly been slaves to the North—both white and black. I hope we win!"

"Me too, love. Me too!"

Just then, William realized that he had called Melanie "love." *Perhaps she is my destiny? Perhaps?*

The two continued to enjoy Richmond's fine scenery and fresh air. At about one in the afternoon, the couple entered a corner store where he purchased a bottle of choice French wine and exquisite blue cheese and bread. The two then found a beautiful park where they had a delectable lunch, sitting on a blanket and enjoying the beauty of the day.

"Where do you see yourself living when this war is over, William?"

"Well, if I'm an officer in the army, I will probably be living here in Richmond. How about you, Melanie?"

"In Georgia or Florida, William. They say it is beautiful down there—with the blue ocean, the warm sun, and the lovely soft sand."

"Yes, that would be a nice place to live, wouldn't it?"

"Indeed!"

Finishing their lunch, the two doted upon each other, wherein they kissed on the lips, which progressed to more passionate kissing. With the passage of a half hour, the two set upon visiting the rest of Richmond.

Having toured as much as their legs could stand, they realized 5:30 p.m. had arrived. William was truly looking forward to some good home-style Southern cooking, which he had been in the absence of for far too long. Upon arriving, Mrs. Wenning welcomed the two, and after having them seated, she served the food.

"I hope you two like it. It's Hoppin' John."

"I love it, Mrs. Wenning!" Lytham answered as all were eating the stew.

"This is great, Mother."

"Thank you," Mrs. Wenning humbly acknowledged. "So, William, how long will you be staying in Richmond?"

"Probably until the end of the week, Mrs. Wenning."

"Where will you go then?"

"I'm not sure. It's up to General Beauregard. I hope it's still here in our capital," Lytham answered but only half hoping so; the other half knowing the necessity for him to continue his mission wherever he was needed.

"I hope so, too, William!" Melanie exclaimed.

Every time Melanie called William by his name, his heart melted. He loved hearing her call his name. William was slowly falling in love with her. The man was starting to believe more and more that she was the one for him.

After enjoying supper, William and Melanie decided to catch the Shakespearean play *A Midsummer Night's Dream* that was currently running at the Marshall Theater. Thus, after thanking Mrs. Wenning for dinner, the couple went out into the starlit Richmond night, walking hand in hand to the theater.

Watching the play, William recalled his lifelong dream of being born in Elizabethan England, performing one of Shakespeare's characters on stage.

"I think I could do that, Melanie."

"Acting? You think you could be an actor, William?"

"I think so."

"Well, what kind of acting experience do you have?"

William chuckled inside, not willing to reveal his success as a spy. "Well, not much I guess. But I still think I could do it."

Melanie chuckled at her belief in William's naivety. "I'm sure you can, honey. I'm sure you can."

With the conclusion of the play, the two made their way back to the Wenning abode.

"I've had a wonderful day, William. This has been, by far, the best day of my life."

"This has been, by far, the best day of my life, too, Melanie."

Now at the Wenning residence, the two kissed on the porch. "Can we do it again tomorrow, William?"

"We will, love. We will!"

11

Having crossed the Potomac River, Darren was now in Confederate territory. *It has been quite a while since I have been in the South*, he thought. *Now is my time to show these Southern bastards, and William in particular, the power of a determined McKenny.*

Realizing that he had been spotted by a Confederate soldier who was now approaching him, McKenny, with handcuffs on, walked like a man who had just survived a Napoleonic battle on the losing side.

"Help! Help!" McKenny cried, in his Southern accent.

"Who goes there?" the advancing trooper, Steve Jesson, questioned.

"It's me, Henry Rolding from Maryland. I have just managed to escape from the tyranny of the North. Help! Get me out of these abhorrent chains!"

"Don't worry, Henry, I'll get you out of those detested Yankee shackles in no time." Jesson proceeded to open the handcuff lock with his pick.

"Thank you," McKenny said, rubbing his wrists.

"The name's Jesson, Steve Jesson." Steve extended his hand. "Welcome to your true home!"

McKenny shook hands with him. "Thank you, Steve. It's truly a pleasure to be in friendly confines." Darren proceeded to glance at the nearby fort. "Who's in charge of that fort?"

"Why, none other than our own General Johnston. But he's not there right now. He's gone to Richmond with William Lytham to discuss military plans with the president."

McKenny was most pleased to have ascertained William's whereabouts. "Well, I want to immediately enlist in the Confederate army, Steve, and give back to those Yankees all the hell that they have given me. Ever since the outset of our struggle, I made it no secret that I was firmly in favor of Maryland's secession from the Union. As a result, the Yankees became suspicious of me—believing me to be a spy for the Confederacy—and arrested me without just cause. They then put me in a holding station where I was to be sent to Old Capitol Prison when I, along with two other Confederate sympathizers, made a daring escape. Although I survived, the Yankees managed to shoot and kill the other two."

"Those bastards!"

"Indeed they are! Is there anyone at that fort who can enlist me in the army, Steve?"

Jesson was fully convinced of the man's Southern allegiance. "Why, yes. You need not worry, Henry. Officer Torring is in charge in General Johnston's stead. I have no doubt that he will immediately enlist you, especially after all that you have gone through at the merciless hand of the enemy."

With that, Jesson led McKenny to the fort, just as John Jedd emerged.

"Look, Henry, it's my lookout partner, John Jedd. Tell him of your ordeal. He detests Northerners more than anyone I know. He'll warmly receive you!"

Jedd. No. It can't be! What are the odds? Yet it must be. I can't afford to take any chances. McKenny remembered his former friend, John Jedd, who had questioned his Southern allegiance at Mobile Academy. *For sure he will recognize me and I will be charged with high treason and be sent to Castle Thunder to be hanged. I can't run the risk of him recognizing me, even with my disguise and alias.*

"John! John! I have a patriotic Southerner who has just escaped the tyranny of the North. Come see."

As Jedd approached, Darren took a quick look to see if it was indeed the man he had known at Mobile Academy. It was. McKenny immediately turned his back and decided that when Jedd was within striking range, he would administer the fatal blow. Darren reached from under his shirt for the knife he had placed there, just in case of such an emergency. Timing was of the essence. Two swift silent killings were all McKenny wanted.

"John, this is Henry Rolding, a Southerner from Maryland who wants to enlist in our army."

Immediately, McKenny turned on Jesson and propelled the knife straight into his heart, killing him instantly and without any noise. Darren then leaped on Jedd who, in a state of complete shock, failed to react, making it easy to administer a knife slice into his neck, severing the vital arteries. John lay grabbing his neck, sprawled on the ground, clinging to his final seconds. Savoring the kills of his enemies, and especially his revenge upon Jedd, McKenny could not help but reveal his elation.

With John lying half dead on the ground, Darren approached him; Jedd recognized McKenny.

"That's right, you no good Southern bastard! So you know before you die, it was I, Darren McKenny, who killed you. I overheard you and Shen question my Southern allegiance at Mobile Academy. There was nothing I wanted to do more than to serve the South. But after that conversation, I realized that I would never be accepted as a Southerner. That I, in essence, am from the North and am a Northerner through and through."

Jedd gasped for breath.

"Die like the pig you are, John; you traitorous Southerner!"

Jedd died.

With that, McKenny wiped his blade, saying, "For the North!"

With the two dead, Darren quickly removed Steve's uniform and identification, buried the bodies, and then covered as much of their blood as he could with the river's sand. McKenny proceeded to assume the clothes and identification of Jesson, who was about his size and stature, and headed to Richmond—completely apparelled as a Confederate soldier.

Halfway into his trek, McKenny was halted by soldiers Doug Stanner and George Turner—men who were stationed at the checkpoint between Richmond and Johnston's fort at the border.

"Who goes there?" Stanner demanded.

"Me, men. Steve Jesson of General Johnston's unit."

McKenny was hoping that the troopers did not know Jesson, due to his young age. They didn't.

"What business have you heading toward the capital?" Turner inquired suspiciously.

"Men, my general is in Richmond, as I'm sure you well know. I have been dispatched by Officer Torring to inform him of an impending Yankee attack on the border. Now you either let me inform the general of this now so that we can devise a strategy to defend ourselves, or keep me here and let everything we've worked for be totally lost—with you two being solely responsible!"

The soldiers looked at each other, not wanting the least bit of blame cast upon their heads. "Godspeed, Jesson!" they responded.

With that, McKenny continued on to Richmond. Reaching the city's outskirts, it was nine in the evening and Darren was completely exhausted. He set up camp for the night, deciding to find William on the following day.

* * *

At the New Year's Eve dance, Johnston had the time of his life. The general truly cherished saying hello to old friends and conversing with the president as if he were just "one of the guys." In fact, the whole extravaganza was free from the worries of the present. Johnston was very pleased with his "vacation," as he called it, and felt it was just what he needed to reinvigorate his spirits. Johnston continued in this merry mood for the remainder of his stay in Richmond. When he finally departed the Confederate capital with his entourage on the following morning, his carefree disposition was given a sharp jolt back to the reality of the times when Stanner and Turner met him at the checkpoint.

"Good day, General. Sorry about our holding of Jesson. But we had to make sure that he was truly a Confederate soldier and not a Yankee spy," Stanner said, believing that Jesson had told Johnston about his temporary detainment by them.

"Jesson? What are you talking about?" Johnston inquired, concerned.

"Steve Jesson, General. He told us that he was going to Richmond to inform you of Officer Torring's dispatch of an impending Yankee attack on the border," Turner continued.

"I've received no such news!" Direly concerned of events at the border, Johnston immediately addressed his troops. "Men, follow me! Make haste to the border!"

Arriving at the border, Johnston called out to Torring.

"Torring! Torring! What news have you? Have the Yankee forces attacked? Where are their movements?"

Torring rushed outside his office quarters to meet Johnston. "What movements, General? Where are the Yankee forces? I've had my men on continual patrol and they've reported no such thing."

Chapter Eleven

"Jesson! I was informed that you sent Steve Jesson to deliver me news of an impending Yankee attack."

"Jesson? He and Jedd have been missing for the past two days. They must have gone to inform you of such then. But they should have informed me of this first. I've received no such news of any impending Yankee attack, General. In fact, the soldiers whom I've placed in their stead while we've been looking for them report no such Yankee build-up."

"This is so unlike Jesson and Jedd to leave their post without notification."

"Truly, General, especially when there is no enemy build-up to speak of."

"We may have a Union spy disguised as Jesson heading toward the capital, no doubt attempting to ascertain Confederate strategy."

"But what of Jedd and Jesson, General? How can their disappearance be explained?" Torring asked, fearing the worst.

"Perhaps the spy killed them," Johnston sadly said.

"But we have looked everywhere and have been unable to find them."

"The man probably buried the bodies." Johnston now addressed his soldiers. "Men, search the entire area where Jesson and Jedd were last stationed and unearth the soil."

"Yes, General," they replied.

After searching for the better part of two hours, three soldiers came upon the bodies of the men.

"Oh my God!" stated one.

"Killed in cold blood!" cried another.

"General. General Johnston," called the third.

Johnston immediately arrived. "What? What is it?"

"It's Jedd and Jesson, General!" the third declared.

"Oh my God. Poor souls!" Johnston exclaimed as he saw the dead bodies. "God bless you, lads. Your deaths will not be in vain! Get me my horse," Johnston continued to one of his soldiers. "There is a spy in Richmond." Johnston now addressed ten of his troopers. "Men, you will accompany me to Richmond. Ken, you are once again in charge until my return."

"Yes, General," Torring replied as the assigned soldier brought Johnston his horse.

"We will requite your deaths, boys. We will get that scoundrel and bring him to justice. Let's go, men, away!"

12

William arose from his sleep the following morning in a wonderful mood. He had had a perfect time with Melanie the previous day and was looking forward to yet another one when he heard a knock on the door. "William. William! It's me, John Childs."

"What, John? What is it?" Lytham questioned as he let Childs in.

"General Beauregard sent me to inform you that your stay in Richmond is to be over. He wants to speak with you on the matter immediately."

"Well, let me just wash up and we'll go."

"Of course. So, how was your time at the dance with Melanie, William?"

"Actually, it went very well. In fact, I spent all of yesterday with her. I think I'm in love, John."

"Well, if you are, I can see why. Melanie is sure a beautiful woman."

"That she is, John. We seem to have connected right from the start."

"Splendid!"

After quickly rinsing himself, William, with John, made for Beauregard's headquarters.

"General, William's here."

"William, please come in. Thank you, John."

"William, as you are aware, I have been deliberating upon where you could next be of best service for our cause. Can you speak French?"

"Well, I studied the language as a child and I got to practice some of the same in my discourse with a French chef while in Washington. Enough to get by, I guess," Lytham answered, wondering why.

"Good. William, as I'm sure you know, you are a wanted man in Washington, with even a price tag on your head. Your David Stenner picture and your handwriting are displayed everywhere. To send you back to Washington would be risky, if not stupid."

Hearing the news, William was frustrated and downcast.

"Not to worry, though, William. In fact, after conferring with the president, we believe you can be of vital service in another way."

"Yes, General?"

"By going overseas."

"Overseas?"

"Yes, William. We would like you to go to England and France to seek our international recognition. As it stands right now, although on land we are holding our own, at sea the Yankees are gradually blockading all of our ports. As a result, they are preventing us not only from exporting our cotton, but also from importing vital munitions. Thus, if we can solidify Britain or France's support, then our ability to defeat the Yankees at sea and win this war will be that much greater. For even during the American Revolution, if France had not provided us with a much needed navy as well as soldiers, we might well have lost that war. So, we would like to send you, William. You are educated and a true gentleman. We have no doubt that you will make quite an impression on the dignitaries of those two nations."

"Yes, General. I will be honored to serve the South in this capacity," Lytham answered as he realized the importance of this role.

"Great. You will leave first thing tomorrow morning."

"That's most fine, General."

"It seems as if you and Melanie Wenning hit it off quite well at the New Year's Eve dance."

"Yes, we seem to make a good match, General," Lytham replied, a bit taken aback at the change in subject.

"You know her father is a Union officer. Be careful. That's all."

"I know, General. It's all right. She and her mother are true Southerners. There is no need to worry. I have acquired a knack for detecting things like this, you know."

"I know, William. All right, come meet me in my office tomorrow morning, say about eight, and we'll go over the particulars of your mission."

"Yes, General."

Leaving Beauregard's headquarters, William made straight for Melanie's. It was one in the afternoon and Melanie would no doubt wonder why he was late. *I'll just tell her the truth*, he thought. William had become so accustomed to lying as a spy that telling the truth had become a somewhat foreign concept. *At least with Melanie,* William solaced himself, *the shift from lying to speaking the truth is safe and enjoyable.*

Seeing William approach her home, Melanie ran out the door and into his arms.

"What took you so long, William?"

"I had a meeting with General Beauregard, love."

"What? What is it? What did the general have to say?"

"Well…my stay in Richmond is over as of tomorrow."

"Where? Where will you be going?"

"To England and France," Lytham answered as he realized there was no need to be covert.

"To England and France? Why? What for?"

"To seek our international recognition."

"Say you can't make it, William. Say that you are ill. I don't want you to leave!"

"I must, Melanie. International recognition is crucial for us. If we can be recognized as a sovereign nation by two of the most powerful countries in the world, then our ability to win this war will be that much greater. Thus, my job is extremely important. I have to go."

"Say it won't be dangerous then, William. Say that you'll be all right. I'd die if something happened to you!"

Lytham was overcome with emotion, and part of it showed. "I'll be fine, Melanie. Don't worry; it won't be dangerous. I'll be all right."

William had never concerned himself with his own mortality. To him, death was nothing to worry about. *We all die anyway, so why bother fretting about it.* Moreover, he believed his death would not result in much grief. Sure, his parents and siblings would be sad. But at least there would be no one who depended on him, such as a wife and children. Now with Melanie depending on him, William started to comprehend the enormous feat soldiers with wives and children were taking in this war. With so many people counting on their safe return, and the tragedy and sorrow if the unthinkable occurred, William realized that the soldier was the true hero in this war. With these thoughts going through his mind, he was determined more than ever to see secession through and alive—to survive for his Melanie.

"I will be praying for you every night, my love."

Lytham was truly touched. "Thank you, Melanie. I love you tremendously," he exclaimed as they kissed each other most affectionately.

The two toured the rest of the city for the remainder of the day. After another enjoyable outing, the couple arrived back at the Wenning abode, where they kissed on the house porch. William reassured Melanie, once again, that everything was going to be all right.

* * *

After spending a most uncomfortable night and morning in the Virginia woods, Darren, at about one in the afternoon, proceeded to the Confederate capital. After walking for about thirty minutes, he spotted a tavern, which he entered. McKenny hoped to ascertain, from either the bartender or a patron, the location of where Lytham was staying.

"What will you have, friend?" the bartender entreated.

"A cold beer, partner," McKenny answered.

"Coming right up."

As the bartender was getting Darren's drink, he could not help but notice the dirtiness of the man's uniform and presumed that he was a Confederate soldier who had just come from the front line. "What brings you all the way to Richmond, lad?"

McKenny sensed the bartender's presumption and was thus relieved that his disguise was believable. "Well, I've just come from General Johnston's unit at the border to inform him of suspicious Yankee movements."

"We are safe, aren't we?"

"For the time being, yes. But that's why I've come—to make the general aware of the gravity of the situation."

"What? What's transpiring?"

"Well, the information is confidential. However, the Yankee movements aren't anything we can't handle. Not yet, anyway."

"Good. Well I'm sure his time at the Spottswood Hotel will be cut short due to your information. They say that he, his soldiers, and William Lytham are having the time of their lives there; you know, with the New Year's Eve dance the other night and all."

"I know." McKenny smiled, acting as if he knew.

"Well, I'm not sure how long you'll be here, friend, but while you're here, do enjoy the beauty of our city!"

"Thank you. I will."

Ten minutes later, Darren finished his beer and proceeded to pay the bartender.

"Don't worry, son. This one's on the house. Tell General Johnston that we are all doing what we can to help the South win."

"Thanks, partner. I will."

McKenny left the tavern and, happy with a free beer at the Confederate's expense, headed for the Spottswood Hotel with murder on his mind.

Entering the hotel, Darren asked a maintenance person for the floor and the room of William Lytham's lodging. Being informed, McKenny headed to the second floor to his enemy's room, number 225. Adrenalin rushed through his veins as he advanced toward William's lodging. Since Lytham was not a general, he did not have the same type of security—a soldier continually on watch outside the hotel room entrance—as Beauregard and Johnston did. In fact, William's only security was a pathetic lock on his door. As McKenny approached Lytham's room, he was ecstatic to find that there was not even a soldier in sight.

Outside William's room, Darren could not believe where he was. Since leaving Mobile, he desperately wanted to settle his score with Lytham. His own failed mutiny and subsequent banishment by William from the Academy burned Darren inside. *I will exact my revenge upon my archenemy one day*, McKenny had always said to himself. At first, Darren believed that his revenge would manifest itself on the battlefield. When McKenny left Mobile, Lytham was an officer, and Darren presumed that William would eventually assume this rank for the South once the conflict ensued. Thus, with him being promoted to lieutenant upon his arrival in New York, McKenny believed that an eventual showdown with Lytham on the battlefield was destined. Yet when there was no word of William's whereabouts, Darren deemed that, in the end, although Lytham was committed to the South, he would never turn against the Union and bring disgrace upon his family. Rather than fight his own people, Darren believed that William had fled to Mexico and was waiting until the conflict was over. McKenny was thus disappointed and felt that his revenge would have to bide until the conclusion of the war—perhaps in the form of assassination. His hatred for William was that intense. Having found out that Lytham was, in fact, a Southern spy and with him now being a Northern one, the opportunity for revenge on the battlefield, albeit perhaps in another form, occupied and excited McKenny's mind.

Murder and primal instinct now consumed Darren's being. *Oh, how Lincoln, McDowell, and my family will all be so proud of me*, he thought. *My elimination of William Lytham, the Soul of the South.* He would be as cool as ice. His first strategy would be to knock, whereby he hoped William would nonchalantly answer so that he could plunge his knife straight into Lytham's neck to make him suffer an agonizing death, just like Jedd. If there was no answer, Darren would pick the lock and hide inside William's room and wait until he returned: strategy number two. If William returned during daylight, Darren would plunge the knife right into his neck. If William returned at night, Darren would attempt to kill him with a knife blow to the stomach and then up to the heart; for, much to his dismay, McKenny could ill-afford the chance of missing Lytham's neck due to darkness. After killing his archenemy, Darren would make a quick escape out the back window and into the dense Virginia woods.

Sweat poured down McKenny's face. After three knocks without an answer, Darren employed strategy number two. Looking down the hallway and not seeing anyone, Darren easily picked the lock, entered William's premises, and stood to the side of the door. As soon as Lytham entered, McKenny would be in a perfect position to lunge at him with his knife. It was now nightfall, and there was still no sign of William. Darren continued to wait anxiously.

* * *

Walking home from Melanie's, William was entranced in love. *Oh, I have to survive this war to make it back home so that I can be with my Melanie. We can then be married, have a wonderful family, and live on the coast in Georgia or Florida.* His thoughts were that majestic. Heading home, William also focused himself on his new role for the Confederacy. *So, the general wants me as a diplomat in England and France. This could be enjoyable!* Never before had William traveled outside America, and now his beloved South wanted him to travel to the two great European countries. Incredible! William had always wanted to visit Europe. In particular, he wanted to visit England—the place of his roots. William decided that once he was there, he would make time to travel to Lytham, England, to see where his ancestors had lived prior to their emigration to America. William hoped to even see and visit a distant relative, for not all the Lythams had left

England. Although some moved to America and others settled in France, some did remain. *I sure look forward to going to England*, he thought.

And France too. William loved the French. After all, France's assistance in America's independence through its provision of both a navy and soldiers was something not to be forgotten. Moreover, the French Louisianans who had supported the rest of the South in her struggle for independence were also something to be cherished. And then there were the French women. *Ah, yes, the French women!* William considered the French woman only second to the Southern belle as the most beautiful of all women in the world. Even the name Southern "belle" came from the French language. *Yes,* thought William, *I do want to go to France.* But then William thought of Melanie. *Melanie, my love Melanie! What happens if I meet a beautiful French woman? No*, thought William, *Melanie is my love. She is my destiny. I will just have to restrain myself, that's all.*

Darren could hear footsteps coming from one end of the hallway toward William's room. *Well,* thought Darren, *could it really be William?* Adrenalin rushed through his veins as he clutched his knife with his heart racing.

Seeing the door open, Darren tried to maintain his composure. He wanted to wait until the precise moment when William would turn his body toward him when he closed the door and thus be completely vulnerable to attack.

As Lytham opened the door, the quietness of the night astounded him. *It is as if you can hear a pin drop*, he thought. The heavens must have allowed such a setting, for, as William was about to enter his room, he was startled by a faint scrape behind the door.

Consumed with pure adrenalin in anticipation of the fatal blow to his mortal enemy, Darren was unable to prevent his right hand—which carried the knife—from shaking. As a result, the knife, ever so slightly, scraped part of the door. Had it not been for the extreme quietness of the night, the sound would have gone unnoticed. Yet Darren realized that William must have heard it. McKenny had no time to lose. He emerged from behind the door and lunged with the knife toward William's heart. Lytham, however, alerted by the faint scrape, blocked the knife's entrance into his heart with his left arm, though that arm began bleeding profusely from a grazing blow. A successful warrior since childhood, Lytham punched the man's ribcage with his right hand. The forceful blow broke McKenny's right ribs and, in the process, completely knocked the wind out of him. With the man now bent down, William kicked Darren in that same area with all his might. Darren, however, quickly turned during the strike, receiving only part of the right leg blow. In the process, he sent his knife forcefully into William's right leg. Blood began gushing from that leg as well.

William lunged forward, grabbed Darren's right arm and broke it against the door—sending the knife flying across the room. With his knife out of his possession and his arm and ribs broken, McKenny realized he would not be able to finish the job. Moreover, Darren realized that if he didn't leave soon, he might even be defeated. Flashbacks of his thorough defeat at Lytham's hands as a child entered his mind. Accordingly, Darren darted for the door and fled down the hallway. Seeing the man leave, William collapsed on the ground and lay semiconscious. He managed to make a haphazard call for help, loud enough for a soldier patrolling the floors and now on the second floor to hear him.

"Oh my God! William! Are you all right?" the trooper cried, entering the room.

"Get him."

The soldier looked around the premises and spotted a trail of William's blood stretching down the hallway. At once, the soldier followed it, while frantically calling for someone to help William Lytham in room 225.

By this time, Darren had escaped out the back door and was now approaching the outskirts of Richmond, where woods were visible.

Two soldiers, one with a stretcher, arrived to attend to William. "It's all right, William," stated one.

"You're going to be fine," implored the other. "A doctor is on the way."

Lytham believed he was about to die. "Tell Melanie that I love her. Tell my family that I love them too." The doctor arrived and immediately administered to him. "Tell them all that my death was not in vain, that I died for the glory of the South," William exclaimed, losing consciousness.

"How is he, Doc? Is he going to live?" cried the first soldier.

The doctor dressed the gaping wounds. "I hope so. He's lost lots of blood. Had we arrived only minutes later, we would have certainly lost him. We still might. He must be taken to the hospital at once!"

Troopers immediately carried Lytham on the stretcher to the hospital. "You're going to be all right, William," beseeched the second soldier. "And we'll get that son of a bitch who did this, William!" continued the first.

13

Arriving at the checkpoint, Johnston immediately sought a description of the man who had portrayed himself as Steve Jesson.

"Good day, General," welcomed Stanner and Turner.

"Good day. Boys, what did this Jesson, whom you saw two days ago, look like?"

"General, he looked to be in his late twenties, five foot ten, maybe one hundred eighty-five pounds, rather stocky with a shaved head and brown eyes," Stanner answered.

"Anything else?"

"Well, he spoke with a deep Southern accent, General," Turner added.

"Hhmmm. Well, at least we now know what he looks like. Men, the man whom you have just described is not Jesson. Rather, he is a Yankee spy who killed Jesson and another one of my men. He is no doubt now in Richmond, doing goodness knows what else."

Stanner and Turner were shocked and mortified. "We're so sorry, General. We didn't…" they cried.

"Don't worry. It's over now. I want both of you to accompany me to the capital to tell the president exactly what you have just told me. He will want to know firsthand what this man looks like."

"But what of our posts?" Stanner inquired.

"Two of my men will stay here and maintain patrol in your absence." Johnston chose the two men and said to the rest, including Stanner and Turner, "All right, men, off to Richmond!"

After a cumbersome journey, stretching into the early morning of the next day, Johnston and his entourage finally reached the Confederate capital. It was now two in the morning. Johnston thought it best to first inform Beauregard of the news and then decide, with Pierre, if it would be prudent to inform the president at that hour.

Entering the Spottswood Hotel to inform Beauregard, Johnston was alarmed at the panic and mayhem gripping the hotel. The general, unsure of what was transpiring but firmly believing that it had something to do with the Union spy, immediately asked one of the hotel guards, "What is going on here?"

"General, there has been an assassination attempt on William Lytham."

Johnston was horrified. "William? No! Is he still alive?"

"Barely, General. He is currently being treated at Winder Hospital. He has deep wounds to his leg and arm. The doctor says that his blood loss was extreme. Had we reached him only minutes later, he would have most certainly died."

Johnston was completely shocked but consoled that William was alive. "Are the president and General Beauregard aware of this?"

"Yes, General. They have dispatched soldiers to apprehend the person responsible for this heinous crime. They themselves are at the hospital."

"Do we know where that bloody scoundrel fled?"

"Apparently he left a trail of either his blood or William's blood leading straight into the woods outside Richmond. Although we are presently searching the forest, our chances of spotting him are severely limited due to the darkness of the night. We'll have much-better luck searching for him come daybreak. We fear, however, that he'll be long gone by then."

Johnston addressed six of his soldiers. "Men, join the rest of your brethren and search the forest. Identify who you are and help them find this most foul villain!"

"Yes, General," replied the troopers as they quickly exited.

"Does anyone know who this person is?" Johnston continued to the guard.

"Not as of yet, General."

"What about suspicious persons? Such as a man in a Confederate uniform claiming to be Steve Jesson?"

"No, it doesn't ring a bell, General."

Johnston, not wanting to waste any more time, addressed the rest of his troops. "Men, to Winder Hospital!"

With that, Johnston and his entourage raced to the hospital and, upon entering, saw Davis and Beauregard in sorrow.

"Mr. President."

Davis was surprised at Johnston's presence. "Joe!"

Beauregard was just as amazed. "General!"

"Mr. President, the person who did this heinous crime to William Lytham is a Yankee spy who has also killed two of my most loyal soldiers. He has assumed the name of one of them—Steve Jesson. As soon as I became aware of this, I immediately made straight to Richmond to inform you. It seems as if I am only minutes late, however," Johnston sadly stated.

"Yes. What of his name, Joe? Do you know his real name?"

"No, Mr. President, but I have brought two men here who have seen him and can describe him."

Davis eagerly awaited the description.

Johnston nodded for Turner and Stanner to speak.

"Yes, Mr. President, we saw a man claiming to be Steve Jesson some two days ago who had a very convincing deep Southern accent. He stated that the border was about to be attacked and that he was sent to Richmond to inform General Johnston of the gravity of the situation," Turner said.

"Mr. President, he looked to be in his late twenties, five foot ten, one hundred eighty to one hundred ninety pounds, rather stocky with a shaved head and brown eyes," Stanner continued.

"Men, send out word of this description to the others," Davis addressed his soldiers.

"Yes, Mr. President," the troops replied as they left.

"How's William, Mr. President?"

"Not good, Joe. But we're lucky he's still alive. I can't believe it: someone going after William. But then again, maybe I can. Pierre informed me that the Yankees now know that it is William who has been assuming these aliases. Perhaps they found out that he was currently in Richmond and wanted to eliminate him before he had the opportunity to inflict more damage on them. Yet it is still despicable. To come into our territory and do this terrible crime is far beyond the pale! We're lucky they didn't succeed. From now on, Pierre, I want William to have twenty-four-hour security wherever he goes. He is our potent weapon, a weapon the North cannot counter. Why else would they have set upon his elimination? We can't allow them to succeed. We can't and we won't!"

"Yes, Mr. President," Beauregard said. "He will be guarded by two of my most trusted men."

"Good. I still want William to go to Europe, Pierre. As soon as he is well, I want him sent. We need him there to gain our recognition. As we have discussed, and as you've articulated to him, he is perfect for the job."

* * *

The Confederate soldiers continued to search the Richmond area for the fugitive throughout the night. Darren, however, was now safe in the dense, vast, and dark Virginia woods. Knowing that he was out of immediate danger, McKenny, barely with breath, collapsed on the ground. The pain in his arm and in his ribs was excruciating to the core, and Darren vented his anger. "Dammit, I messed it up! No doubt William's still alive, and I am now being hunted down like a dog. Dammit! Ahhhhh, my arm, my ribs!" The pain would not subside. McKenny attempted with partial success to prevent himself from continually thinking of the pain. *What am I to do now? Concentrate. In the morning, I will be exposed by the sun and a massive manhunt will be in full force. Moreover, I'm sure Johnston and his soldiers have discovered the dead bodies and are on their way here with a full description of me. What am I to do?* After deliberating, Darren deemed it best to head back across the Potomac and into Washington to recuperate until he was healthy enough to resume his assignment. *But the river is a long journey. Yet I must go! There is no way I'll survive here in my condition.* Accordingly, Darren traveled to a nearby farm and after stealing one of the horses, made haste for the border.

* * *

The search for the "villain" continued in earnest at daybreak. While his soldiers were still relentlessly searching, Beauregard went to visit William in the hospital. He proceeded into William's room and, upon entering, saw Lytham's left arm and right leg tightly wrapped up in bandages with Melanie by his side.

"How are you, son?"

"I could be better, General," Lytham answered weakly. "I never thought I could have been so careless as to let my guard down like this."

"It's not your fault, William," Melanie said. "You had no idea that there was a man behind the door waiting to kill you. Who would?"

"Melanie's right, William. The fact that you survived is a miracle in and of itself. You're lucky to be alive!"

Lytham gave an acknowledged smile.

Beauregard glanced toward Melanie and then looked at William; Lytham understood the message.

"Love, would you excuse us for just a minute?"

Melanie also realized that the general wished to converse with William in private. "Sure, hon. I'll just be outside the room," Melanie answered with a quick kiss.

"Thanks, love." Melanie left. "I can still make the voyage by this afternoon, General," Lytham said in a hopeful voice, yet realizing such was not realistic.

Beauregard gave a kind smile. "Don't worry, William. You're not going anywhere for the next while. This morning I made all the new arrangements. You will still be going overseas, however. In fact, there is no one the president and I would rather have overseas seeking our recognition than you, William Lytham."

"Thank you, General," Lytham humbly replied.

"And you need not worry about another incident like this again. When you leave, you will have around-the-clock security wherever you go. "

"Thanks, General."

Beauregard became pensive. "I'm so sorry, William. Your quarters should have been under guard just like the generals' quarters. I just thought…"

"No. Don't worry, General. Had that even been suggested to me, I would have been most reluctant. I am not a general. Like you, I never would have suspected anyone coming after me. Has the man been apprehended?"

"Not yet. But we'll get him. Did you manage to get a good look at him, William?"

"No, General. It was so dark; I couldn't make out his description. All I know is that he's as strong as a bull."

"How about the confrontation, William? Anything there that we can go on?"

"I may have broken some of his ribs on his right side. I think I also broke his right arm. He came at me with a knife, but I believe I knocked it out of his hand during the confrontation."

"Yes, William. We retrieved the weapon."

Lytham gave an acknowledged smile.

"Don't you worry, William. We will find that villain and bring him to justice."

* * *

Having successfully passed the new mid checkpoint soldiers under the cover of darkness, and later swimming across the Potomac River, Darren was back in the Union. Yet, after crossing the river, quick-tempered Federal soldier Bruce Buttermilk spotted him.

"Freeze or I'll shoot you down, you rebel dog!" Darren was still wearing the Confederate uniform.

"Wait. I'm a Federalist too!"

"Bull! Put your hands up in the air and don't make a move, or you will be my next trophy of rebel dead men!" Bruce boasted of killing twenty Confederate soldiers at the battle of Bull Run.

"Fine." McKenny raised his left arm, but his right arm was only slightly raised—due to its brokenness and his broken right ribs.

"I said both of them!"

"Please, my right arm is badly broken by the hands of a rebel. I have not slept even an hour's sleep this past night because of the enemy's pursuit upon me. Please, take me to General McDowell, General McClellan, or even the president. I am Lieutenant Darren McKenny, and they will all vouch for my legitimacy."

Buttermilk was now somewhat less suspicious. "Fine. Follow me."

Bruce marched Darren straight to McDowell's headquarters. He thought that since McDowell was the most junior of the three, it was at least better to waste his time rather than McClellan's or even the president's if the man was in fact a fraud.

"General, I have a man here who claims to be a Union lieutenant whom you know. However, I believe that he is a rebel spy who has crossed the Potomac to find out the strength of our fortifications. But just in case his alibi is authentic, I brought him to you."

"What's his name?"

Chapter Thirteen

"He says his name's Darren McKenny, General."

"McKenny? Send him in!"

"Come," Bruce called to Darren.

"General McDowell, I need a doctor," McKenny cried, half-delirious, as he collapsed on the ground.

"Get my friend a doctor, now!" McDowell commanded Buttermilk.

Bruce accordingly realized his mistake. "Yes, General!" Buttermilk replied, exiting.

"Don't worry, Darren. You're going to be fine," McDowell said.

McKenny was now unconscious.

The doctor entered with Buttermilk, who held a stretcher while the doctor immediately attended to McKenny.

"He has severely broken right ribs and a badly broken right arm, General. My gosh, it's a miracle that he's still alive!" the doctor asserted, noting that his injuries occurred some time ago.

"Is he going to be all right, Doc?"

"I believe so, General. But we should take him immediately to the Patent Office Hospital for treatment."

"Bruce, help me with him."

"Yes, General." The two proceeded to carry McKenny on a stretcher to the hospital.

"Don't worry, Darren," McDowell pleaded. "Please, be strong!"

Spending the remainder of the day in the hospital, Darren, although he was still in much pain, felt much better. His arm and ribs were painfully sore, but the medicine he was given to ease the pain worked, which lifted his spirits. Although his body felt better, his mind was filled with worries. He realized that his mission was a failure. *Damn! What am I going to tell McDowell?* Darren felt humiliated.

McDowell entered McKenny's room the following day. "Good morning, Darren. How are you feeling?"

"Much better, General. Thank you."

"You gave us quite a scare yesterday."

McKenny gave an acknowledged smile.

McDowell gave a return smile and was now unable to hold back. "So, Darren, how'd it go?"

"Not as well as I hoped, General," McKenny answered, downcast.

"What? What happened?"

"Well, I successfully entered rebeldom with my disguise—so much so that the first rebel lookout man I met believed my story immediately. When his partner emerged, a man whom I had known at Mobile Academy, I had no other course of action but to kill them both."

McKenny believed that McDowell would be happy to hear of him killing rebels. He was right. "Great work, Darren!"

"Anyway, I then assumed the first rebel's name and uniform—believing that since he was young, few would know of his person. So if I claimed I was him, my chances were good that I would not be suspected. It worked."

"Smart thinking, Darren. Go on."

"Well, my disguise enabled me to enter the Spottswood Hotel, the place where William was staying. Upon entering, I headed straight to his room. My hope was that when I knocked on the door, William would answer, whereupon I would kill him with my knife. Since he wasn't in at the time, I picked the lock and waited until he emerged."

"Good. Go on."

"When William finally entered at about one thirty in the morning, I attacked him. However, he managed to fend me off," McKenny continued, though unwilling to admit his slip up. "But not before I administered two slicing strikes—one into his arm and the other into his leg."

McDowell was pleased that William was wounded, but upset that he wasn't killed.

"When he managed to separate the knife from my hand, I was unable to retrieve it, due to the darkness. Since I knew that with my broken ribs and arm there was no way I would be able to finish the job, I thought it best to return to Washington to recuperate before setting upon him again."

"That's all right, Darren. At least you inflicted weighty damage upon him. I have no doubt that next time you'll finish the job."

"I will, General. I will!"

"Good. Anyway, rest here for the next while and once you recover, we'll determine what you are to do next."

14

After weeks of recuperation with Melanie by his side, the pain and cuts on William's arm and leg had largely healed and he had regained the blood he had lost. However, the psychological trauma of the episode was far from conquered. William could not believe how close he had come to death. He started to realize the true frailty of human life. He even started to have second thoughts about his mission—though such thoughts were quickly dispelled. William was a soldier, a soldier for the South. He now fully appreciated what he and his fellow countrymen were prepared to sacrifice for independence. For William, death was no longer an abstract thought. Having been at death's door, he realized that dying was a reality, yet a reality he was prepared to take for his beloved South.

On February 20, 1862, Lytham's final full day at the hospital, Beauregard paid an early visit.

"Good morning, William. How are you today?"

"Fine, General. I feel great."

"The doctor says that your recovery is progressing faster than had been expected and that he plans to release you tomorrow."

"The doctor told me the same thing prior to your arrival, General. I'm ecstatic."

"So, William, are you still up to going overseas?"

"Absolutely, General. Absolutely!"

"How about tomorrow afternoon then? I know that it will be only hours after you are released, but we have a ship leaving and the sooner you get overseas, the better."

So, I am going to Europe tomorrow. I can't wait. France and England: amazing! The voyage, however, will take at least a few weeks. But that's all right. I've waited my entire life; another few weeks won't be the end of the world. These thoughts occupied William's mind until Melanie arrived at her normal time of eight in the morning.

"Good morning, William!"

"Good morning, Melanie; how are you today?" he asked with Melanie kissing him.

"Fine," Melanie answered, still kissing him. "I could do this all day."

"Me too…Melanie, General Beauregard came to see me this morning." Melanie stopped her kissing. "What did he want?"

"Well, the doctor is releasing me tomorrow, and the general would like me to start on my new assignment then."

"But I thought he was going to wait a few days after your release before sending you to Europe."

"I thought so too," Lytham answered, yet not really believing it. "But the ship is leaving tomorrow."

"Oh, William, I don't want you to go. I fear for your safety."

"Melanie, I have to go. Don't worry, I'll be all right. General Beauregard is providing me with twenty-four-hour security."

"I love you, William. With all my heart! Please, please be careful!"

"I love you too, Melanie. Don't worry, love, everything is going to be fine," he reassured her as the two embraced.

The following morning, upon his release, William was greeted by Melanie and Mrs. Wenning at Winder Hospital's front entrance.

Melanie embraced him. "Please be careful, William. Gain our recognition, but come back safely."

"I will, Melanie. I promise," Lytham replied as the two hugged each other.

"Good luck, William. Do our country proud!"

"Thank you, Mrs. Wenning. I will!"

As William headed to Beauregard's office quarters, the young man was overcome with emotion. He was starting to believe that Melanie was the one for him, and thus his good-bye to her hurt him to the core. Yet, William realized that he had to travel overseas. *Yes, I have to go to Europe. I have to gain recognition for the South. I will give it my all. I must succeed. I will not take no for an answer!*

After greeting General Beauregard, the two got down to business.

"All right, William, first Britain. As of now, although Queen Victoria has officially announced Britain's neutrality, she has acknowledged us with the status of a belligerent power. In laymen's terms, it means that while we are not yet recognized as a sovereign nation, we are still considered a legitimate principality conducting war. As a result, we can purchase munitions from neutral countries as well as capture Yankee ships at sea. Your task is to have Britain take the next two steps: to formally recognize us as a sovereign nation and to gain military support from them. My sources in England tell me that the British prime minister, Lord Palmerston, and Her Majesty, Queen Victoria, are very sympathetic to us. In addition, the aristocracy and the *Times* of London are largely on our side. I'm sure this is because we are close to Great Britain both in trade and in our entire chivalric way of life. Furthermore, despite Britain's official neutrality, British shipbuilders are secretly constructing blockade runners to break through the Union blockade to deliver their products to us, as well as to transport our cotton back to their island. Finally, the majority of liberal men also support us. In short, they consider our aspiration to escape the North's tyranny meritorious."

"Great."

"Now for the not-so-good news. A large portion of the population favors the Union. Many British businesses, especially the shipping industry, have strong trade relations with the Yankees. Moreover, the influential British humanitarian associations, in particular the antislavery leagues, are having difficulty in sympathizing with us. Since the bulk of these associations are made up from the lower class, it would be safe to say that the lower class is generally on the Federalists' side. Finally, there is the middle class, the majority of the population, in the middle of all this. If they can be swayed, then I believe that the British politicians will openly come out in our favor."

"Understood, General."

"Now for France. The situation there is less complicated but perhaps more difficult. My sources tell me that Emperor Napoleon III has expressed sympathy for our cause, perhaps even more so than Lord Palmerston and Queen Victoria. In addition, while France's antislavery coalition is finding it hard to sympathize with us, there is a sizeable segment of the population that does support us. Moreover, there is currently in session an assembly of ministers formed by the French cabinet and initiated by Napoleon who are deliberating upon our recognition. As a result, we believe that the emperor wants to take some measure that will officially recognize us."

"Wonderful."

"Yet, at the same time, Napoleon is hesitant. Though he secretly supports us, he is fearful of acting alone. He fears war with the United States and presently would only consider recognizing us if Britain does so first. That is why we are sending you to England first, William. If you can get Britain to recognize us, then your assignment in France will be that much easier. If, however, England is dragging her feet, we may still send you to France, where you must do your utmost to allay Napoleon's fears of acting alone."

"Yes, General."

"Good. You will board one of our merchant ships under the British flag in order to ensure safe passage through the Union blockade. When you arrive in London, you will meet our ambassador Mr. James Mason at Trafalgar Square. I sent him word that you would be arriving in about three weeks."

Lytham nodded in approval.

"For your security, you will be accompanied by two of my most trusted soldiers, George Sawton and Charles Champson. They will make sure that you are protected at all times. Both are presently outside my office."

"Thank you, General."

"When you arrive at Trafalgar Square, Mr. Mason will be wearing a black suit, a black hat, and will be reading the *Times*. When you see such a person, you are to say, 'Good day, gent. Lovely day in the heart of London, wouldn't you say there, chap?' If you are speaking to Mr. Mason, he will respond with, 'Yes, the heart of London is by far the most beautiful place in all of Britain.' If he does not respond with that sentence, then you have not yet found him."

"Yes."

"Is it locked in your memory, William?"

"Yes, General. I say, 'Good day, gent. Lovely day in the heart of London, wouldn't you say there, chap?' And he responds with, 'Yes, the heart of London is by far the most beautiful place in all of Britain.'"

"Good. Any questions?"

"No, I don't believe so, General. I am ready to gain our recognition!"

* * *

Chapter Fourteen

Having been released from Patent Office Hospital after weeks of recuperation, McKenny made straight to McDowell's headquarters.

"Good morning, General. I hope I didn't get you at a bad time."

"No, not at all, Darren. Please, come in."

"Thank you," McKenny replied as he entered. "General, I am ready to apprehend William Lytham again."

"All right, Darren. I will bring it to the attention of the president."

"Thank you, General."

"In the meantime, I would like you to stay at the Willard Hotel. I knew you were being released this morning, so I booked a room for you there—room 132. Here is your key. I'll come by later today to inform you of the president's decision."

"Yes, General. Thank you."

Later that day, McDowell met with Lincoln.

"Good afternoon, Mr. President."

"Good afternoon, Irvin. Please, come in."

"Thank you, Mr. President," McDowell replied, entering. "Mr. President, Darren McKenny was released from the hospital this morning and came to see me, stating that he is ready to serve the Union once again in William Lytham's apprehension."

"Yes. Well, William is off to England, Irvin."

"England, Mr. President?"

"Yes. One of our spies in Richmond informed me that he left to seek rebel recognition."

"Would you like to send Darren to England to apprehend him, Mr. President?"

"For the time being, Irvin, it would be better to hold off. Ambassador Seward assured me that the British government will not recognize the South while we are at war, under any circumstance."

"Does Ambassador Seward know William is now a member of the rebel delegation?"

"Yes. I dispatched this information to him and he adamantly assured me that not even William's persona could turn British neutrality into Southern support. It is therefore best, for the present anyway, to have Darren resume his post as a lieutenant in the New York division."

"Yes, Mr. President. I will inform Darren at once."

McDowell immediately headed for the Willard Hotel.

"Darren, the rebel government has sent William to England to seek international recognition for the South. Ambassador Seward has assured the president that Britain will not recognize the South, regardless of William's presence. As a result, Lincoln believes William will pose no threat to us there and thus his apprehension is not necessary at this time. He has therefore decided that you are to return to New York to resume your lieutenant post."

McKenny was upset with the president's decision but was willing to accept it. "Yes, General. I am happy to oblige. When am I to depart?"

"At once, Darren."

"Thank you, General."

15

Voyaging across the Atlantic Ocean, William frequently conversed with his protectors Champson and Sawton, and, in doing so, became fascinated with their backgrounds. George Sawton was forty and had served valiantly as a soldier in the Mexican-American War. In fact, he soon gained the distinction as America's fiercest Mexican fighter. Perhaps Sawton's fervor to defeat the Mexicans resulted from him losing his father at the Alamo. His father's merciless death at the uneven battle had filled George with wrath. Accordingly, when the situation presented itself to exact revenge during the Mexican-American War, Sawton enthusiastically joined the Federal army and played a vital role in America's subsequent victory.

With the onset of the Civil War, Sawton viewed the Union as he had previously viewed Mexico. Since the Union was responsible for the death of his only brother, Matthew Sawton, at Bull Run, George felt the Union had to pay, as the Mexicans had years earlier. Prior to Bull Run, Sawton debated whether he should join the Confederacy or remain in the Union. Being from Texas, George empathized with the large segment of the population, headed by Sam Houston, who desired to keep the Lone Star State in the Union. However, after his brother joined the Confederacy and was killed at Bull Run, George was consumed with rage toward the United States and earnestly sought to avenge his brother's death. General Beauregard happily enlisted him in the service of the South, even making Sawton one of his consorts. In the Confederates' huge victory at Ball's Bluff in October 1861, Sawton killed seventy-five Union soldiers. He was subsequently nicknamed "slinger" for his ability to fire quickly and with deadly precision.

Charles Champson, just twenty, was born and raised in North Carolina. At the time of secession, there was a fervid Union movement in North Carolina's legislature. Champson's father belonged to that movement and was committed to keeping the Union together. However, when Lincoln mobilized the military for the suppression of the Confederate states, Champson's father burned with anger. He resented Lincoln's action because he believed that the best way to keep the Union preserved was to persuade the South, through peaceful means as he was doing, on the merits of remaining in the Union. Champson's father now felt he had little choice but to defend his homeland. Charles loved his father dearly and embraced his decision. After enlisting Charles in the army and seeing his commitment to the cause, Beauregard made him another of his consorts. When the general decided to have another protector for William and accordingly asked Charles, the same enthusiastically agreed—stating he would be honored to do this for his beloved South.

Notwithstanding their frequent friendly conversations, the voyage across the Atlantic was a perilous crossing. Though the ship managed to pass the Union blockade, the weather was so atrocious that William many times thought they weren't going to survive. "Know that I love you, God. Know that there is no love I have greater than for you." William said these prayers many a time on the journey, believing death was imminent. Yet time and again, just when it looked like the ship was going to capsize, the water became still and the sun pierced through the overcast sky. William believed this was divine intervention and that these happenings were for a reason.

On the last episode of treacherous weather, the captain sailed for Dublin, deciding to remain there until the climate improved. Accordingly, William believed that it was meant for him to be in Ireland. Perhaps his Irish grandmother in heaven asked God to let him see the lovely green isle at least once in his life. Thinking of this, he noticed a beautiful dove hovering over a rainbow in the now bright blue sky. *Yes,* thought William, *this is meant to be!*

Arriving in Ireland, William was greeted by the friendliest of people. In fact, the Irish were the warmest people he had ever met. William even had thoughts of living in Ireland for the rest of his life. And who could blame him? There was something about the Irish that could always bring a

Chapter Fifteen

smile to one's face. The Celtic people seemed to look on life differently than the rest. They seemed to look on the world as something to enjoy, not to fret about, perhaps because of our short time on Earth. And did they know how to celebrate. True, they had problems of their own; yet they had that ability to overcome any obstacle with a sincere, exerted effort. Perhaps it was the island itself—full of rich history and a beautiful landscape—that gave them this ability.

In Dublin, William and the crew were greeted by city magistrate Brian Higgins.

"Good evening, gentlemen. It's a bad one out there tonight, isn't it?"

"Sure is," the ship's captain answered. "Would it be all right if we docked at your port until the weather subsides?"

"Absolutely. Have your men check in at the Gresham Hotel over across the street. I will arrange everything. Welcome to Ireland!"

There it is, thought William, *that Irish friendliness.*

After unpacking their belongings in their hotel rooms, the captain called the men together and stated that foul weather was expected to continue for another two weeks and that it was a miracle that they had made it this far. The captain went on: "The magistrate has graciously granted us these rooms for the next two weeks, and during this duration, we are welcome to tour the city." Cheers of "Hurray! Hurray!" came from the crew. Like William, this was the first time they had ever set foot on Irish soil, and once there, they all had the time of their lives. Free from the worry of the war across the Atlantic, William and the men reveled the whole time. *Oh, this is the life,* thought William. During this time, William also visited his grandmother's birthplace on the west side of Dublin. After telling Champson and Sawton of his wish to visit the place where his grandmother was born and raised, the two men were more than happy to accompany him. While there, William met his grandmother's great nephew—Sean O'Reilly—by a fluke at a local tavern. Sean, the pub's bartender, was shocked when William stated that his grandmother Lucy O'Rourke was born and had lived in west Dublin prior to her family's leaving for Mobile, Alabama, in the early 1800s. Sean told William that his grandfather Kevin O'Rourke had a first cousin named Lucy O'Rourke who left for America around that time. They soon realized that they were distant cousins and Sean invited William, along with his protectors, to the O'Reilly manor for dinner.

At the O'Reilly residence, William met his great-uncle Kevin O'Rourke, now ninety years of age. Sean informed his grandfather that William was the grandson of his first cousin Lucy O'Rourke and that he had come from overseas to seek European recognition for the Confederacy.

"It is an honor to meet you, William."

"The honor is all mine, Mr. O'Rourke. I never believed I would meet distant relatives here in Ireland. This must be the will of my grandmother in heaven. I knew that when we stopped in Ireland it was for a reason."

"Your grandmother and I were the best first cousins that ever existed, William. We played games, watched the ocean, and dreamed of the future together. When her family left Ireland, it was the saddest day of my life. Seeing my best friend leave made me melancholy beyond belief. She always said she would return to visit me someday. I promised myself that I would not die until she came," O'Rourke said as tears formed in his eyes.

"Well, that day has now come, Uncle," Lytham replied, overcome with emotion. "Through me, my grandmother has returned," Lytham said as he embraced Kevin.

"Now I can die in peace, William. Lucy has finally come home!" Mr. O'Rourke voiced as tears flowed.

Sean interjected, emotionally shaken. "How long will you be staying in Ireland, William?"

Lytham was trying to maintain his composure but was only partially succeeding. "We're not sure, Sean. We are to leave as soon as the weather subsides."

"Well, you and your men are welcome to stay the night," Sean offered.

"We would more than love to, Sean, but we must report back before our curfew of two in the morning. We are staying at the Gresham Hotel."

"Well, you boys are definitely staying for supper then," entreated Sean's mother, Mrs. O'Reilly. "We are having steak and potatoes."

"We wouldn't miss it for the world, Mrs. O'Reilly," Lytham answered. "Thank you!"

"Come, William, I want to show you some poetry your grandmother and I wrote together." Mr. O'Rourke now led William to the family den.

Later they proceeded to have the best meal any of them had had in a long time. For Kevin, it was his best meal ever. He saw Lucy in William's eyes, and the bliss in his soul could not be expressed in words.

Chapter Fifteen

William's departure from the O'Reilly manor was emotional. The family entreated William to visit anytime and William reciprocated the favor if they ever visited Mobile. However, they all knew that this would probably be the only time they would ever see each other.

After William and his friends departed, the O'Reilly household marveled at the miracle visited to them that night.

"You're very special, William," Sawton said as the three returned to the hotel. "I cannot believe what my eyes have observed this day."

"Goodness, William," Champson continued, "what were the chances of you meeting your grandmother's long-lost first cousin?"

"A billion to one? But I guess with God all things are possible."

"That's for certain, William. That's for certain!" they affirmed.

"What time is it anyway?"

"One thirty in the morning, William," Champson answered.

"Will we make it back to the hotel in time?"

"Barely, William," Sawton followed. "Under any other circumstance, I would have picked you up and carried you to the inn to make sure we were on time."

Lytham smiled.

By the end of the second week, the weather had subsided, so the captain called the men together and told them to pack their belongings and board ship for their sail to England. After thanking Gresham Hotel's owner as well as magistrate Higgings for their generosity and hospitality, William and the crew left the lovely green isle. The sail to England was ideal, with a tranquil sky, sea, and wind. Onboard, William focused on the job at hand. *All right, I am to meet Mr. James Mason at Trafalgar Square. He will be wearing a black suit, a black hat, and reading the* Times. *When I arrive in London, I will immediately check into a hotel and then go to the Square. The sooner I meet Mason, the better!*

On April 18, 1862, the ship approached England. William eagerly looked forward to visiting the place of his ancestry. Sawton and Champson were also anxious to visit the Anglo-Saxon island. Like William, they were of English descent, and they were also first-time visitors. As they advanced closer, they entered a thick fog—preventing them from seeing even two feet ahead. However, once the fog cleared, their eyes saw a splendid sight.

"There it is, men. The land of England!" Lytham happily proclaimed.

"Magnificent!" Sawton asserted.

"Look at it. It's beautiful. Absolutely beautiful!" Champson confirmed as William and George nodded in agreement.

"After we check our belongings in at a hotel, I have to meet Mr. James Mason at Trafalgar Square."

"That's fine, William," Sawton responded. "We'll follow at a distance."

The ship took the crew up the Thames River to London. William savored the moment when he stepped onto English soil. For William, the English were special. His roots and family history up until the middle 1600s were English. Regardless of the difficulties his family had experienced at the hands of English kings and queens in the past, William's blood was Anglo-Saxon and, as such, he would always have a special love for the "island race."

The Lytham name was still held in high regard in Britain. There was a town named after William's ancestors, Lytham, England, and the Lythams did more for the glory of England than did any other family. It was a Thomas Lytham who fought alongside Alfred the Great when the very existence of the Anglo-Saxon race was put in jeopardy by the Vikings. In fact, the Viking annals mention a "Thomass Lythamm" as the most formidable Anglo-Saxon they ever came upon. It was a John Lytham who accompanied Henry V on his battles in France and gained notable wealth and rank because of his valiant service.

Although the Lythams suffered hardship because of their Catholicism during the Reformation, they were still viewed highly in Britain. When Thomas More and his friend Geoffrey Lytham refused to acknowledge King Henry VIII as supreme head of the English Church on Earth, Henry sighed, saying, "I will forever live in sadness because of my two favorites' refusal to obey my command." If Thomas had not implored Geoffrey to flee for the continent to escape what was about to befall disobeyers of the king's will, he would have suffered the same fate as More. Henry was so tormented by his decision to disassociate himself from More and Lytham that he silently asked for their forgiveness on his deathbed. Many say that his leg, in the end, caused him the greatest grief. In reality, his greatest sorrow in life came from his treatment of More and Lytham. Thus, even at the height of religious change in England, the Lytham name was still highly regarded.

When Queen Elizabeth ascended the throne in the mid-1500s, she desired to have Lythams in her Privy Council. Yet, because of their

Catholicism, she, in the end, refused to accept them. The queen, however, continued to entreat them to change their faith. After their continual refusal to do so, she thought persecution and removal of their once-held titles would make them conform. But it didn't. It was at this time that some of the Lytham lineage fled Mother England and settled in France. Others, however, chose to remain, enduring persecution and even death because of their faith. At the end of her life, Elizabeth regretted how she had treated the Lythams and asked for forgiveness from her confessor: "My intentions were always good, yet I now realize that I went about it severely bad."

After the reign of Queen Elizabeth, English kings and queens continued to have Lythams in their service, always looking the other way while knowing of their Catholic faith. When Oliver Cromwell became protector in the mid-1600s, the Lythams worried that such a staunch Puritan would destroy both their Catholicism and their royal name. When it became evident that King Charles was going to lose the English Civil War, William's lineage fled to the New World and settled in the South. They didn't tell their remaining relatives where they were going in case Cromwell forced it out of them and, accordingly, hunted William's family down. The Lythams who remained in England, however, much to their thankful surprise, were treated with a respect, albeit a silent one, by Cromwell and his ironclads. Cromwell gave specific orders that the Lythams' Catholicism and royalty were not to be touched. Thus, in the end, even Republican Cromwell desired the preservation of the Lytham family. In fact, he even secretly employed a Lytham under the surname Butler as one of his confidants. The Lytham family was that valued. Their absolute kindness, lack of bitterness, and true loyalty were qualities not to be overlooked. Such was the legacy of the Lytham name in England.

After checking in at a hotel, William and his protectors unpacked their belongings and went to meet Mr. James Mason at Trafalgar Square. As promised, Sawton and Champson followed at a distance.

Approaching the Square, William noticed a man with a black hat and a black suit who was reading the *Times*. *That must be him. I'll go over and find out.* Standing next to the man, Lytham stated the secret code: "Good day, gent. Lovely day in the heart of London, wouldn't you say there, chap?"

"Yes, the heart of London is by far the most beautiful place in all of Britain."

"William Lytham." Lytham extended his hand.

"Nice to meet you, William; James Mason." The two shook hands. "How was your trip?"

"Rather hectic. The weather was atrocious; so much so that we docked in Dublin for two weeks. Then the weather subsided, and it was clear sailing."

"Yes, I thought you might have run into foul weather."

Lytham gave an acknowledged smile.

"So, are you ready to start your diplomatic career, William?"

"I certainly am."

"Good. It would be nice if you started with the stakes not being so high, but they are."

"Well, I am going to give it my all, Mr. Mason."

"Please, James is fine."

Lytham nodded.

"Meet me at nine tomorrow morning at Royalton's pub in downtown London, and we'll go over the details of your diplomatic mission."

"All right, James. Thank you."

Mason, with a smile, left.

James Mason was in his early sixties and was a true diplomat. Born and raised in Virginia, he previously was a lawyer who had also been a member of the Senate Foreign Relations Committee. Although initially hesitant at the South's secession from the Union, once his state legislature voted to leave, James became fully resolved to join the Confederacy and defend his beloved homeland. Due to James' foreign-relations experience, President Davis deemed it best for him to continue his career but as a diplomat for the Confederacy in England. His job was to convince the British government to support an independent Confederate nation.

Before even setting foot on European soil, Mason and colleague John Slidell—who was Mason's counterpart in France—almost accomplished their missions. Traveling to Europe on the British steamer *The Trent* in the fall of 1861, Mason and Slidell were arrested by Union Captain Charles Wilkes from the Federal ship *San Jacinto*. The two were subsequently sent to Boston onboard the *San Jacinto* and were imprisoned upon their arrival.

The British were furious when they heard of the "Trent Affair." In fact, they demanded that the Union either release Mason and Slidell or face war. Learning of the British ultimatum, President Lincoln realized it was better to release the diplomats rather than risk war with both the Confederacy and Great Britain. Accordingly, at the start of 1862, Lincoln had Mason and Slidell released.

In England, James successfully convinced Queen Victoria to continue Britain's position of recognizing the South as a belligerent power; for there were many times when she was about to change her mind and openly declare for the Union. Yet, Mason's diplomacy prevented her. Furthermore, when the queen leaned toward having British businesses cease their production of blockade runners, James' diplomacy once again prevented her.

James knew of William, but he looked upon him as more of a kid who, with no diplomatic experience, was assigned to perhaps the most crucial of all positions in the conflict. Moreover, Mason believed that he alone could gain recognition from the British. Accordingly, when informed that William was going to join him, the ambassador viewed this as a slight on his ability. As a result, his first meeting with William was conducted with the cynicism of a seasoned veteran having to work with a young rookie.

After departing from his meeting with James, William walked home pondering his audience with the Confederate ambassador. Lytham had learned of Mason's renown from Beauregard. Accordingly, although he sensed James' cynicism, he realized this was to be expected. After all, Mason had played the international diplomatic game for many years, and now, having to work with someone without any international diplomatic experience with the stakes being extremely high, it was more than understandable that James would be cynical. William thus decided that he would make it known to James, through his demeanor, that he was the student and Mason the professor.

Later that day, Lytham toured London. *So much beauty and history is here*, he thought. In fact, there was so much to see and do that William did not even know where to begin. And then there were his ancestors. He definitely wanted to visit Lytham, England, and perhaps even meet some distant relative. *Relax, lad, you are going to be here for a while. Take your time. You will accomplish everything you want, but all in time.* These were the words William used to sooth himself. They worked. Accordingly, Lytham's first day in England was leisurely spent touring London's many enchantments.

Walking down the various streets, William marveled at the many shops. It was like nothing he had ever seen. Mobile was small, Richmond was bigger, but both paled in comparison with the metropolitan of London. His protectors, now at his side, were also highly impressed.

"Well, what do you think, men?"

"Breathtaking, William," Champson replied. "I've never seen anything like it. I cannot believe the size of this city!"

"Me neither," Sawton said. "London is grand beyond belief!"

"Well, while we are here, we may as well enjoy ourselves."

They continued to walk the streets for the remainder of the afternoon, relishing London's captivating monuments, buildings, and stores. At six in the evening, the trio traversed to a popular tavern—where they had supper, conversed with the Londoners, and enjoyed the nightlife of music and merriment. At ten in the evening, the three called it a night. Although they wanted to stay longer, they realized there was a war overseas and that it was best if William was fresh for his meeting with Mason on the following day. They all knew the importance of gaining British recognition and did not want to jeopardize their chances by their carelessness.

The hotel where they stayed was of humble origins. Each room was small and contained only enough space for a bed and tiny closet. Yet a bed was all William really wanted anyway. He was in England to gain Southern recognition, not to live in luxury.

William's security at the hotel, however, was very impressive. Sawton would first enter William's premises, search the entire room, and when he deemed it safe, Lytham, with Champson, would enter. Then Sawton would guard Lytham's entrance, while Champson slept. Halfway into the night, the two would switch places. After the calamity at the Spottswood Hotel, the Confederacy was going to great pains to make sure that a similar episode did not happen to William again. Lytham was truly grateful for the meticulous effort given to him concerning his safety.

At eight fifteen the following morning, William went to meet Mason at Royalton's, with Sawton and Champson following at a distance. James was already seated when William arrived.

"What are you having?" asked Lytham.

"English tea—the best in the world, you know."

"I know." Lytham smiled. "I'll have the same."

"Waiter, this man would like a cup of tea, please."

"Yes, sir, coming right up."

"So, how do you like London, William?"

"I love it, James. It is most beautiful, as well as spacious."

"And important too. This is the city that can give us something vital to our war effort."

"Indeed."

"William, some six weeks ago I arranged an audience with the queen for tomorrow; so you've come just in time."

Lytham smiled, yet butterflies filled his stomach.

"I did not tell you yesterday because I was afraid you would get nervous. Thus, telling you now doesn't give you as much time to worry about it."

Lytham realized such was a wise move due to his extreme nervousness. "True, James."

"Actually, the queen smiled when I informed her that you would be accompanying me. In fact, she is looking forward to meeting you. I believe she has a Lytham in her services and is highly impressed with his dutifulness. When we meet the queen tomorrow, William, you must remember that she is royalty, and the English are very particular about how royalty are treated. They deem the queen above us mere mortals. To them, the queen is more on a par with God. When you meet her, you are to bow and present yourself in total humility."

Lytham nodded in understanding.

"While we are there, we are going to present our case. Our aim is to have her see that we are just striving to have a country to call our own and, in so doing, we are defending our homeland from Northern aggression. Yet, in order to solidify our aspirations, we need British support. Great Britain's formal recognition will send a clear message to the North that we are indeed our own country and that their aggression must stop."

"What about military aid?"

"One mountain at a time, William. First, let's gain our recognition and then we can go about gaining military aid."

Lytham nodded in agreement.

"I have already had two meetings with Her Majesty—both ending in partial success. The first meeting secured our status as a belligerent power. The second meeting solidified Britain's commitment to continue in their production of blockade runners. The queen reiterated that if she was asked publicly if she sanctioned this activity, she would categorically deny it. I was hoping that either meeting would have gained us British recognition, but such a hope so early on was probably unrealistic. What I did achieve, at least, was better than nothing."

"Much better, James."

"In this third meeting, I am hopeful that we will gain our recognition or at least see Her Majesty convincingly heading in that direction."

"Yes."

"The problem here is Seward—Lincoln's ambassador in London. He is a strong diplomat, and the English like him. While the queen, the prime minister, and the majority of the aristocrats are inwardly cheering for us, they are hesitant to outwardly acclaim us because of Seward's popularity. The queen is meeting with him later in the week. No doubt she will hear from both sides before making a decision."

"True."

"So, any questions?"

"No, James. Everything is clear."

Mason was pleased. "Good. I will come and pick you up tomorrow morning at nine. We are meeting the queen at ten. Dress formally but not extravagantly. A nice conservative blue suit will do."

"All right."

"Let me do the talking, William. But if the situation calls for you to speak—I hear you are quick on your feet—so follow your heart as it tells you what to say."

"Yes, James. I will."

After finishing their tea, James paid the bill and the two left the tavern, each going their separate ways. Mason left the meeting very pleased with his young associate. *Maybe William is going to be a good diplomat after all*, he thought. *We shall soon find out. I hope he does well tomorrow.*

William toured more of London for the remainder of the day. While touring, he purchased a nice conservative navy blue suit. *I hope the queen will be pleased.* Walking home, William thought upon his meeting with Victoria. *My goodness, I am going to meet the queen of England tomorrow. It has been a while since my lineage has conversed with royalty. Hopefully, my genes will portray me as I should be portrayed.*

16

The next day, April 20, 1862, James, as scheduled, went to pick up William. After the two left the hotel, they boarded a carriage to Buckingham Palace.

"How do you feel?" Mason asked during the carriage ride.

"Extremely nervous, James. I hope I don't make a mistake."

"Don't worry, William. You'll be fine," Mason encouraged.

The carriage pulled up to Buckingham Palace, where one of Victoria's servants opened the carriage door and escorted them in. William and James were then informed to tarry in the waiting room. After fifteen minutes, another of the queen's servants addressed them.

"The queen will now see you, Mr. Mason and Mr Lytham,"

"Thank you," Mason said as the two were escorted to Queen Victoria's conference room.

"Good morning, gentlemen."

"Good morning, Your Majesty," Mason greeted, bowing, with Lytham imitating James' bow. "Your Majesty, I would like you to meet William Lytham of Mobile, Alabama."

Lytham bowed again. "Good morning, Your Majesty."

"Good morning, William Lytham. Lytham," Victoria happily pondered. "That is a very special name in England. The Lythams in England trace their roots back to the time of King Alfred the Great. Your family must be originally from England, William."

"Yes, Your Majesty. We left during the protectorate of Cromwell."

"Yes. That was a turbulent time indeed."

Lytham acknowledged such with a humble smile.

Victoria was enamored of his appearance and legendary name. "Actually, William, I have a Lytham, an Alfred Lytham, in my service. In fact, he is my personal emissary."

Lytham continued his humble smile.

"So, William, how is the situation in the South?"

Expecting Mason to be asked, William looked to James who, in turn, nodded to William. "Well, it could be better, Your Majesty. Although we are holding our own on land, our ports are gradually being closed by the Union naval blockade. As a result, we are limited in our ability to export goods such as cotton in exchange for much-needed supplies."

"Yes, this conflict has truly hurt our importers of Southern cotton. Well, we are allowing you to build blockade runners here to help the Confederacy free its ports from the blockade."

"Yes, Your Majesty, but we need more. We are desperate for your recognition. If Great Britain could recognize our sovereignty, our potential to win this war would be greatly increased. The South, Your Majesty, is more like England than any other part of the world outside the British Empire. In fact, unlike the North, where peoples from countries such as Germany and Holland have settled, in the South, much of our ancestry has come directly from your island. Our ties are much closer to you than they are to the North. We look upon you as our Mother Country. We desperately need your support!"

"Spoken like a true Lytham. William, I have no doubt the Southern people know that I, the prime minister, and the bulk of the aristocrats are on your side. I will be blunt with you. The problem here is twofold. For starters, there is a large portion of the population who look unfavorably upon your cause; they look upon your cause, as effectively articulated by Lincoln's ambassador Seward, as a slave-loving cause."

"Your Majesty, this may be the perception, but it is not the reality. We have wanted to end slavery for many years. Yet, the North has prevented us from ending it, as they demand that we must grow crops such as cotton and sugar to be economically sound. Had the North even suggested that they would help us diversify our economy, slavery would have been eliminated immediately. The Southern people are not slave lovers, Your Majesty. We are a people who have been boxed into a corner and this is the only way in which we can break free. Once we are free, having a country to call our own, then none of our society will be slaves to anyone—neither to the North thus nor to each other. All of us will be free, both in reality and in legality."

Mason was astounded at William's oratory and now realized why Davis sent him.

"Well spoken, young man. Well spoken, indeed! Yes, William, I am truly starting to see the South's position in all this. But, secondly, there is the problem of the United States. If we formally recognize the Confederacy and provide the South with military aid, we then risk war with the Union. Although we were fortunate enough to prevent the Union from taking over Canada in 1812, how are we to know that we will again be successful? I want desperately not to lose my British North America."

"Your Majesty, when Great Britain fought the Union in 1812, it was not only against the North but it was also against the South. The entire United States of America fought Britain in that war, and still Britain succeeded in preventing Canada from being annexed to the Union. Now, Your Majesty, if war between Britain and the Union transpires, you will no longer be alone. Britain will have part of the former United States of America fighting by her side. As a result, not only will the Union be contending with Great Britain to its North, but it will also be contending with us to its South. There is no way that they will want this, and if they do engage in such, they will most surely lose. They are having more than enough trouble with us; there is no possibility they'll be victorious over both our nations."

"True, William. Very true. Well, as I'm sure you both know, I am scheduled to meet Ambassador Seward later this week."

"Yes, Your Majesty," Mason replied as Lytham nodded.

"I will hear what he has to say. It is only prudent that I listen to both sides before reaching a decision."

Mason and Lytham nodded.

"Both of you are scheduled to meet the prime minister on May twenty-fifth, are you not?"

"Yes, Your Majesty," Mason answered.

"Good. For the interim, I'll determine when the four of us can convene to further discuss the South's aspirations. In the meantime, do enjoy your stay on our island, William. Perhaps you could even visit Lytham, England—the home of your ancestors."

"I plan on doing that very thing, Your Majesty," Lytham happily said. "Thank you."

"Thank you for coming, William. I see President Davis has made a most sound decision in sending you here!"

With that, Mason and Lytham bowed to the queen, left Buckingham Palace, and boarded a carriage awaiting them. In the carriage, James informed the chauffeur to take them to Royalton's where they could dine for lunch.

At the pub, Mason praised Lytham on his performance. "Great work, William. The queen is highly impressed with you."

"Do you think so? You don't think I spoke too strongly?"

"At first I did, but she seemed to like it. I am very impressed, William!"

Lytham smiled in gratitude.

"But let's not get our hopes up too high. I've played the international game for many years, and I know how swiftly currents can become still waters without even a moment's notice. We still have to meet the prime minister next month; a date that I earlier arranged for us. And remember, the queen can't recognize the Confederacy without him."

"True."

"But we are definitely off to a good start! I must say, I was extremely nervous when the queen asked you to answer her questions. But when she did, I remembered what Beauregard had said: 'Just let him answer with his heart; he'll do fine, no matter what the topic.' Even yesterday, when I told you to follow your heart if the situation arose for you to speak, I did so most hesitantly. But now my doubts have been thoroughly dispelled. You truly have a way with people, William."

Lytham smiled.

The two proceeded to have generous platefuls of fish and chips, arranging the date of May 24 at ten in the morning at Royalton's to prepare themselves for their meeting with Lord Palmerston.

The following day, William embarked on his visit to Lytham, England. He eagerly looked forward to visiting the place of his ancestors. He even hoped he might meet a distant relative. Conversing with Champson and Sawton about his plans, the two agreed to accompany him.

Upon their arrival, they could not help but marvel at the beauty of the place. It was very picturesque, with thick green trees blowing ever so carefree upon the lush landscape. Cows grazing and farmers attending to their crops made William think of what it must have been like hundreds of years ago. *Perhaps my ancestors, prior to their royal ascension, were farmers,* he thought.

In downtown Lytham, William entered the magistrate's office. He believed that if anyone knew of his ancestors, it would be the town's magistrate.

"Good morning, sir," William greeted.

"Well, good morning, gentlemen. Welcome to Lytham, England. My name is Peter Lytham, and I am the city's magistrate."

"Pleased to meet you, Peter. My name is William Lytham from Mobile, Alabama. My ancestors lived here before immigrating overseas, and I have come to see if you knew where in Lytham they resided."

"When did your lineage leave Lytham?" Peter asked, taken aback.

"During the protectorate of Cromwell."

"My gosh, we are distant relatives! I am from the family who remained. We have kept in contact with our relatives who migrated to France during the reign of Queen Elizabeth, but we have been unsuccessful in finding out where in the New World your lineage settled."

"Yes, my father told me that when we fled, we purposely did not inform anyone as to our new location in case Cromwell and his ironclads managed to find out and hunt us down."

"Yes, that was a turbulent era indeed, William. We who chose to stay believed persecution was imminent. However, by the grace of God, Cromwell showed us mercy—allowing us to maintain our name and faith."

"How has it been, Peter, enduring all these years?"

"At times, extremely difficult, William. The Lythams are of royal ancestry since the time of King Alfred the Great. We enjoyed this privileged position up until the reigns of King Henry VIII and Queen Elizabeth. Yet, during those eras, we suffered hardship, bigotry, and even death because of our refusal to relinquish our faith. However, the royals knew that we were faithful and loyal. Accordingly, after years of persecution, we were eventually admitted back into the royal fold. In fact, my brother Alfred is the queen's personal emissary."

"Yes, she told me."

"Who? The queen?"

"Yes. I had a meeting with Her Majesty yesterday."

"Incredible! A Lytham returns to his original home and is immediately given an audience with the queen of England!"

"Actually, I don't believe it was that easy, Peter. I am on a diplomatic mission for my government."

"Oh yes, the United States is always sending us delegations."

"Actually, I am a representative of the Confederate states."

"Oh! Yes. How could I have forgotten? Please forgive me, William. So, the Lythams are Southerners. Well, it only makes sense they would be. The South has always been closer to England than the North. Their entire chivalric way of life is characteristic of the Englishman."

"In fact, much of our ancestry has come directly from your island, Peter; while, in the North, they have more of a German and Dutch mix. So, it is not surprising that we are similar to England. Our blood is the same."

"That it is, William. In fact, your blood is royal blood!"

"Well, living in America, we don't really look on royalty in the same way as England does."

"Oh yes." Peter sighed. "You broke free from us, didn't you? It still pains our hearts. Yet, King George III was corrupt and I don't blame America for leaving. Anyway, I must show you the family archives. Come! If you ever visit France, William, do visit Marne la Vallée, east of Paris. That is where the Lythams who fled England during Queen Elizabeth's reign settled."

"Thank you, Peter, I will."

Peter led William across the street to the Lytham Registry, where the town's archives were kept. Later in the day, he invited William and his protectors to the Lytham manor to meet more of the family. After a delicious supper, Peter entreated them to reside at the manor during their stay. Peter informed William that Alfred would be returning home on the weekend and that it would be to his advantage to converse with him. William gratefully accepted Peter's invitation and eagerly awaited Alfred's arrival.

That same week, Union Ambassador Seward was feeling confident as he entered Buckingham Palace for his one o'clock afternoon meeting with the British monarch. After having been previously assured by Her Majesty that Britain would not recognize the South as long as the war continued, Seward felt that his mission was complete.

"Good afternoon, Your Majesty."

"Good afternoon."

Seward was puzzled at the indifferent greeting. "Your Majesty, the president brings good news; namely, that the smashing of the rebels is continuing very well. We are in the process of closing all their ports. Though they are demonstrating stubborn resistance on land, their rebellion will very soon be crushed. Then, as one united country, we can strengthen our already strong relationship with Great Britain."

"Oh, that is interesting."

"Your Majesty?"

"Well, I met William Lytham earlier this week and he seems to think the South will eventually win your war."

Seward's heart raced. "Your Majesty, I assure you, there is no way the rebels will succeed."

"Yes, on their own accord, perhaps they won't."

Seward was crushed at the implied message. "Your Majesty, you are not really considering…"

"I am not considering anything, Seward. All I am saying is that William Lytham is tremendous in articulating the Southern point of view, as you are doing for the Union. It would be incorrect for all my empathy to go to the North in your conflict. Do you not agree?"

"Your Majesty, you have already granted them the status of a belligerent power. Please, don't go any further…or else our strong ties would be jeopardized." Seward chanced the veiled threat.

"Well, if they are jeopardized, it won't be at our doing," Victoria fought back.

Seward realized his veiled threat miserably failed. "I know it won't, Your Majesty. The president ardently desires to continue our strong relationship. Please, just reassure us that Great Britain will continue to stand by our side."

"I am not saying anything anymore, Seward. I just want you to know that I am keeping closely apprised of events overseas and that William Lytham is a fine diplomat for the South."

Seward was shocked at the transpiring events; in fact, he was nearly speechless. "Points taken, Your Majesty."

"That is all. You may go."

"May we meet again? Perhaps some time next month, as usual?" On previous occasions, the queen would always arrange a time and day for them to meet in the succeeding month.

"One of my servants shall inform you when I will next give you audience. That is all."

"Yes, Your Majesty," Seward responded lowly.

Seward left Buckingham Palace for dispatcher Gary Collins' residence in complete dismay and anger.

"Collins!" Seward shouted, banging on the hotel room door.

"What? What is it, Seward?" Collins asked, opening the door.

"Gary, we have a major problem on our hands!"

"What problem?"

"William Lytham! He's our problem!"

Collins gave a bewildered look.

"William met the queen earlier this week, and in that one meeting has set British foreign policy on course to recognize the rebel government."

"But you told the president that no one, not even William, could jeopardize Britain's neutral position."

"Well, I was wrong! Good old Queen Vic made it abundantly clear to me today that Britain's friendly relationship with the United States has made a complete one eighty."

"Well, who's to say William's to blame?"

"Who else could it be? She blatantly told me she is highly impressed with him. What else are we to think?"

"My gosh. We're in trouble!"

"Trouble? We're in deep. Dammit! Since my arrival, I've been working incessantly to sway the queen, the prime minister, the aristocrats, and the *Times*. Although I have been unable to sway the newspaper, I have made inroads with the aristocrats, and, to a lesser degree, with Victoria and Palmerston. Now William Lytham, who arrived here only days ago, has significantly moved the queen to the South's side and will no doubt soon do the same to the aristocrats and to the prime minister."

"What do you want me to do?"

"I want you to board the next ship to Washington and inform the president of the situation. Ask him what he wants done. Tell him if something is not done and soon, he can expect British arms assisting the rebels as early as this spring."

"Oh my God. My God! I will Seward. I will!"

17

During his week in Lytham, William had the time of his life. *Yes,* he thought, *this is where my roots are. Everyone should visit the place of their roots at least once in their lives.* William believed that in order to know oneself, one needed to know one's heritage. Thus he was glad all the more to have visited Ireland and now England. In his times of leisure, William would leaf through the family archives in the hopes of finding Roman blood in him. *Yes,* he thought, *to have blood from the only race in history that simultaneously ruled Europe, Africa, and Asia would truly be an honor.* William hoped the first Lytham was a Roman legionnaire who settled in England during the Roman habitation of the island. After much searching, William discovered an Augustus Lythamvus who settled in Lytham, England, around AD 300. *There it is,* he rejoiced. *I do have Roman blood in me!*

It was now the weekend and William eagerly awaited the arrival of Alfred Lytham. At five in the afternoon on Saturday, he arrived.

"Alfred, I would like to introduce you to William Lytham from Mobile, Alabama, a member of the Lytham lineage that immigrated to the New World during the protectorate of Cromwell."

"It is a pleasure to meet you, William. I've heard many goods things about you from Her Majesty. Your meeting with her went very well. The passion with which you presented your case impressed the queen immensely!"

"Really, Alfred?"

"Most certainly. In fact, she is highly pleased you are serving the South as a diplomat. She likes Mason, and the same is very persuasive, but you bring a fresh vitality to the cause. You speak with conviction. When you talk, people hang on your every word. This is because they know that when you speak it comes from your heart, your soul. Word has spread that you are the Soul of the South. Hearing the queen's accolades given to you this week, I can see why. If anyone has a chance at bringing Great Britain over to the South's side, it is definitely you, William."

"Well, I desperately want to accomplish that very task, Alfred."

"Well, you just keep up the good work, son, and I have no doubt that Southern recognition will be forthcoming."

"I will, Alfred, thank you." William now recalled Seward's scheduled meeting with Victoria that same week. "What about Ambassador Seward, Alfred? How was his meeting with Her Majesty?"

"Terrible for him, I must say. I am sure he was shocked to learn of your successful audience with her."

Lytham humbly smiled. "Thank you, Alfred, for all your help. Your information is most appreciated!"

"Anything to help out a fellow relative, no matter how distant that relative may be," Alfred responded with a kind smile. "I will continue to keep you apprised of the situation at court. Any information relating to America, I will immediately inform you."

"Thanks so much, Alfred. Truly blood is thicker than water, and no matter how far we have been separated and the years therein, Lythams truly look after their own."

Alfred smiled in acknowledgment. "Let's have a toast!" Alfred poured a glass of champagne for the assembly, and then raised his glass. "For the South!"

"For the South!" William echoed, raising his glass as the rest joined in.

* * *

Arriving in Washington from the voyage across the Atlantic, Collins rushed to the White House.

"Mr. President, I bring dire news from England."

"What dire news?"

"William Lytham, Mr. President! Seward had an audience with the queen just prior to my departure, and from that meeting Seward gets the distinct impression that because of William's influence, Britain is on course to recognize rebeldom with arms to follow as soon as this spring."

"What? What are you saying? I cannot believe my ears! Seward assured me that as long as we were still fighting, there was no way Britain would support the South. And you mean to tell me that he now believes that England is changing her position over the person of one man? I know William is persuasive, but Seward assured me that not even William could change the British position."

"Well he is, Mr. President, and unless we act fast, Britain will soon be an active participant on the South's side."

Lincoln called out to his secretary. "Stoddard! Stoddard! Get me the British ambassador here at once."

Stoddard shortly returned with British ambassador Lord Lyons.

"Lyons, what news is this of Britain contemplating a change in her position regarding our conflict?"

"Britain is doing nothing of the sort, Mr. President."

"Well, I have just been informed that Seward met Her Majesty some weeks ago and got the distinct impression that Britain is considering supporting the South."

Lyons was aware of Britain's changing position but was unwilling to divulge it. "Mr. President, we have continually stated that our official position is not to interfere in your domestic matter."

"Don't give me that official bull, Lyons. I want to know the reality," snapped Lincoln.

Lyons realized that he must budge. "Well, the queen is impressed with the South's new diplomat, William Lytham, Mr. President."

"I knew it! The queen is going to change British policy over a royal ancestor of hers," Lincoln replied, aware of William's lineage.

"Britain is doing nothing of the sort, Mr. President. The queen likes William and the way in which he articulates the Southern position. Although she believes the South is not entirely without sympathy in your conflict, that is all, Mr. President. Nothing more."

Lincoln paused, not wanting to aggravate the situation further. "Fine. Thank you, Lyons."

"You're most welcome, Mr. President. Good day." He nodded, exiting.

"What do you think, Gary?"

"I don't know, Mr. President. It seems as if he's hiding something."

"I get the same impression."

"What would you like done, Mr. President?"

"Well, for starters, I want you to immediately return to London and inform Seward that he is to continue to get British opinion on our side. The queen is unable to act on this matter unilaterally. She needs the consent of the prime minister, and I'm sure both would desire the consent of the British populace."

"What of William, Mr. President?"

"Detain him. What I have always feared, notwithstanding Seward's assurances, is coming true; namely, that the longer William is overseas, the greater is his potential for gaining international recognition for the rebel cause. He must be stopped! It is definitely time to act. Inform Seward to have his protectors apprehend William, then bring him straight to Washington where he will be brought to justice."

"Yes, Mr. President. I will."

"Continue to have Seward keep me apprised of all events overseas."

"Yes, Mr. President!"

* * *

After a magnificent time in Lytham, England, William said good-bye to his relatives. William was pleased that he and his family were given an open invitation to visit Lytham, and William was more than happy to exchange this pleasantry.

"Good luck to the South, William!" The Lythams saluted.

"Thank you!" William gratefully replied.

With that, William returned to London with Champson and Sawton. On May 24, he met James at Royalton's.

"So, are you ready for our meeting with Lord Palmerston tomorrow?" asked James.

"I am eagerly looking forward to it."

"Me too. If we can have as much success with him as we had with the queen last month, then our chances for recognition will be that much stronger. For, as I stated before, both must agree if recognition from Britain is to come."

"Indeed, James."

"So we have to be at our best, William."

"Well, I know that I am going to give it my all. Truly, there is nothing I want more on earth than for us to have a country to call our own."

"Agreed. I'll pick you up at ten tomorrow morning; our audience with the prime minister is at eleven. Once again, William, dress conservatively."

"I will, James. See you at ten."

* * *

Back on English soil that same day, Collins immediately headed to Seward's residence. "Seward? It's me, Collins."

"Coming," Seward replied as he opened the door. "What news from the president?"

"Your protectors Terx and Yieps are to apprehend William and then send him straight to Washington to face justice."

"Fine. Go inform them of this, but tell them to be careful. I'm sure William has protection. Rebel Davis would definitely not leave the South's pride and joy without any. And the protection he has is probably the best."

"Agreed. I will, Seward."

"I am not sure if you are aware of this, Collins, but William and Mason have an audience with the prime minister tomorrow."

"Do you believe Palmerston will grant them official recognition at that time?"

"I don't know. The aristocrats I have on our side say Britain has no intention of recognizing the South. But they might just be telling me what I want to hear."

"Have you managed to get an audience with the queen since your last meeting with her?"

"Not yet, but I've been continuously working on it. I hope to get one soon—before it's too late."

"What about William and his meeting tomorrow? Should we send our men upon him tonight?"

"I don't know."

"I think we should! The sooner we get William, the better. No doubt if the prime minister recognizes the South, he will want to tell it to William personally. The English love him that much here."

"True. All right, send Terx and Yieps upon him tonight."

Collins immediately proceeded down the hotel hall to Terx and Yieps' room.

Collins knocked on their room door. "Guys, it's me!"

Terx opened the door. "What's up, Collins?"

"Important news!"

"What news?" Yieps asked.

"Men, the president wants you to apprehend William Lytham; and you are to apprehend him tonight before he has a chance to meet with the British prime minister tomorrow morning."

Terx was enthusiastic. "It would be our pleasure!"

Terx Gordon was twenty-five years of age, born and raised in Massachusetts. He was not an educated man. In fact, he was by all accounts a no-good rotten bum. If it weren't for the Civil War and serving first as a soldier in the Federal army and then as a protector to Seward overseas, Terx would still be involved in burglary, as he had been doing all his life in Boston.

Terx heard of the fame of William Lytham through bar conversations with fellow soldiers prior to his assigned protectorship of Seward in England, and he viewed the same jealously. William's good looks, kind personality, and powers of persuasion were attributes Terx lacked. He eagerly wanted to kill the Soul of the South and therein give himself immortal fame. Yet because of Lincoln's initial instructions for William to be left alone while in England, Terx was prevented from fulfilling his dream. Now that he had his chance to apprehend William, Terx felt that detaining him was at least the next best thing. Moreover, while in detention, Terx looked forward to giving William many blows to the face and stomach, such that when Lytham arrived in America, no one would be able to recognize him.

Collins was well aware of Terx's disposition. "Remember, Terx, William is not to be eliminated—only apprehended."

"Oh, don't worry, I'll apprehend him," Terx responded with a sinister smile.

"In addition, be extra careful. William, no doubt, has protection."

"I didn't see any. I'm sure he doesn't," answered Yieps.

Yieps York was another thug employed by the North to serve as a protector to Seward. Legend has it that when he was born, his mother screamed in horror, and the doctor mistook the scream as the name she wanted to give her child. Hence his name: Yieps. Most people viewed the legend as pure nonsense, but looking at the man, one could not help but think that the legend was not without foundation.

Yieps was thirty-seven years of age and had enjoyed the rugged frontier life of Iowa. He soon gained the distinction as America's most eminent Indian fighter. To Yieps, the only good Indian was a dead Indian. When the American government started to disapprove of Yieps' immense slaughter of the natives—many times conducting such without any provocation—Yieps retorted, "Somebody's got to do it, and it may as well be me." With the Civil War, Yieps saw his opportunity to kill more of the "enemy." Yet, because of his partially maimed left arm, inflicted by an Indian arrow, the Union deemed him unfit for service. Yet, as a consequence of his dire appeals to Washington to serve the Union in any capacity, the president finally agreed to have Yieps be a protector to Seward. Lincoln felt that Yieps' formidable presence would be enough to prevent anyone from approaching Seward with sinister ideas.

"Well, I'm sure he does, so do be extra careful! Remember, Yieps, no violence."

Yieps slyly smiled. "Of course not."

Collins, who really didn't care if William died at their hands, did not bother to press the matter any further.

"Fine. William is staying in room 221 at the Hashburn Hotel. So, go get him, boys!"

"Right you are, Collins!" they enthusiastically replied.

Outside William's lodging, Champson was on ever alert duty, making sure the Soul of the South was completely safe. In his hotel room, Sawton was only partially sleeping; the seasoned warrior could not fully sleep knowing that at any moment William Lytham, the South's pride and joy, could be apprehended—or even worse. Both protectors were true professionals. When duty called, the two always answered faithfully.

While guarding William's entrance, Champson was eagerly looking forward to the following day—the day when he believed his beloved South would finally be on its way to getting the recognition it so desperately needed. Champson firmly believed in the power of William to get for the South what it earnestly desired from Britain. William had a way of getting things done. One never knew how he would go about doing it; in fact, many times people believed that William didn't even know how. But time and again he always achieved what he set out to accomplish. Champson believed that even the Union knew this—thus the attempt on his life in Confederate territory. Moreover, Champson believed that an attempt on William's life would even be undertaken in England. Thus, like Sawton, Champson took his job most seriously, never slouching for one moment.

Walking slowly up the stairs, Terx and Yieps peaked down the corridor to see if there was anyone guarding Lytham's premises.

"Yieps, there is someone guarding. What should we do?"

"Pretend he's an Indian and shoot him down!"

"Don't be stupid. If we do that, we'll make noise and William will then be alerted. This is not the Wild West, you know. We're in England!"

"All right then. What are we to do?"

"How about you pretend to be a drunk, stating that you have lost your way. When the guard advances upon you, I will grab him, cover his mouth, and knife him. You help me with this once we get him. All right?"

"All right." Yieps began acting like a drunkard. "Help. Help!"

The call for help immediately awoke Sawton—who, even in partial sleep, was always on the alert.

"What? What business have you here?" Charles questioned with gun drawn as he approached Yieps.

"Please, I need help. I feel sick! I've lost my way!"

Always wary of a trap, Sawton immediately opened his door, yelling, "Champson, get back!" The shout instantly awoke William.

Yieps, in panic, instinctively reached for his gun.

Champson, seeing this, immediately fired with deadly precision. Yieps, mortally wounded, died.

Terx lunged for Champson, slicing his neck in the process. Sawton, with gun drawn, immediately fired upon Terx—striking him in the heart; Terx died.

"Champson!" Sawton frantically called. Yet Charles was already dead.

Lytham opened his door. "What? What's going on?" Then he saw the dead body of Champson. "Oh my God!"

Sawton was at Charles' side. "God bless you, son."

Lytham echoed Sawton's sentiment with a deep sigh, totally in shock. "Who are these guys?" Lytham asked as he looked at the two dead conspirators.

"They're Seward's men."

"What are they doing here?" Lytham continued, yet knowing the probable answer.

"To kill you, no doubt, William. You get some rest. You have an important meeting with the prime minister tomorrow. I will clean up and guard your door."

"Don't worry, George. I won't rest unless I help."

Sawton, realizing it was only proper for William to help, did not press the matter any further. Both now overcome with unrelenting grief hugged each other—unable to hold back the tears. To Lytham and Sawton, Champson was someone special. The young man's eagerness to serve the South even unto death was a man right after their own hearts. He was a young kid, giving his all for the glory of the South; and, in the end, he did give his all for his beloved homeland. Such a sacrifice could only be respected and admired.

After saying a prayer over their beloved friend, Sawton and Lytham alerted one of the keepers of the hotel. Realizing there was nothing more to be done, William entered his room and tried to get some sleep. Sawton, for the remainder of the night, guarded Lytham's room with an alertness that could only be described as phenomenal.

18

The next morning, May 25, 1862, William awoke surprised that he even managed to get some sleep. He wished it were under better circumstances, however. Understandably, he had had a tough time getting to sleep the night before; yet he was determined not to allow the previous night's episode to affect his audience with Palmerston.

At ten in the morning, Mason, as scheduled, called on William.

"William, what's wrong? You look as if someone died."

"One of my protectors, Charles Champson, was murdered here last night by Federalists as he was guarding my room."

"Oh, William. The Union is determined to get you. Yet, I never thought they would have gone to such lengths. Those bastards!"

"Well, we must not let Champson's death be in vain, James. We must get recognized."

"Absolutely. What of Sawton?" Mason continued, knowing of both William's protectors.

"He's all right—physically at least."

"What of the killers? Did they escape?"

"No. Champson managed to kill one of them, while Sawton killed the other."

"Do you know their identities?"

"All I know is that they're Seward's men."

"Seward's men? Well, we'll deal with him, but later. Right now we have to focus ourselves on the job at hand. We must perform well in front of the prime minister today, William."

They left the hotel and boarded a carriage to 10 Downing Street. Arriving, they were greeted by one of Palmerston's servants who, in turn, led them to Palmerston.

"Good morning, gentlemen."

"Good morning, Mr. Prime Minister," Mason and then Lytham replied.

"Mr. Prime Minister, I would like you to meet William Lytham from Mobile, Alabama."

"It is a pleasure to meet you, Mr. Prime Minister."

"The pleasure is all mine, William. Welcome to England!" Palmerston shook his hand. "Her Majesty is highly pleased that you are serving the South as a diplomat here on our island, William."

"Thank you, Mr. Prime Minister."

Palmerston smiled. "So, gentlemen, how is the situation overseas?"

William looked to James who was, after all, the main Southern diplomat on the island. "Not bad, Mr. Prime Minister," Mason began, "but it could be better. The situation is much the same as when we last conversed with Her Majesty. Although we are holding our own on land, at sea the Union is still in the process of closing all of our ports. If Great Britain were to recognize us as a sovereign nation, our defeat of the Union on land as well as at sea would no doubt be forthcoming. Moreover, defeating the Union at sea would enable us to send precious commodities such as cotton to Britain without fear of Union interference."

"Yes, those involved in the cotton industry have been stating that very thing. I must admit, gentlemen, that right from the outset of your conflict, I have not been impressed with the Union's tactics. After declaring our official neutrality and giving the South the status of a belligerent power, the Union has not only gone about aggravating you but also us. Initially, they accomplished this by seizing our ship *The Trent* and imprisoning you, Mr. Mason, and your counterpart in France Mr. Slidell. This was a complete violation of international law. I was angry to the core—as was the queen and the entire British populace. In fact, I told Mr. Lincoln in no uncertain terms that he either release you, Mr. Mason, and your colleague Mr. Slidell or face war with Great Britain—with our nation fighting alongside the South. At the time I, Her Majesty, and the entire British populace were more than prepared to recognize the Confederacy. And if Lincoln had not released you and Mr. Slidell, then British recognition and arms would have indeed been forthcoming to the South. Now the Union is closing your ports. Thus, our desire for your cotton has been curtailed. In sum, the

Union's tactics in this whole conflict are not only aggravating you, but they are also aggravating us."

"Yes, Mr. Prime Minister," Lytham said. "That is why if you were to recognize us as a sovereign nation, then we both would be free from Northern tyranny."

"True. Very true, William."

"Moreover, Mr. Prime Minister," Mason continued, "the Union is continuing their underhanded tactics. Last night two of Seward's men murdered one of William's protectors just outside William's room—presumably attempting to seize William, if not worse. Fortunately, they were eliminated by William's protectors before they had that chance."

"Is this true, William?"

"Absolutely, Mr. Prime Minister."

"This is yet another flagrant violation of international law. I am shocked and dismayed! I will immediately bring this to the attention of the queen. She will no doubt discuss it with Seward when she next meets with him. Do you know for certain, however, that the two acted not on their own accord?"

"I am sure that is what Seward will claim, Mr. Prime Minister," answered Lytham. "But I don't believe it for a second. I don't believe those two would have acted without being given specific orders to do so."

"Well, we'll definitely get to the bottom of this. In the meantime, William, I would like you to stay at the Brown's Hotel—where you will be given the securest of protection by Scotland Yard."

"Thank you, Mr. Prime Minister."

"You're most welcome. Well, gentlemen, I will deliberate further on Southern recognition. Such an action on our part should be well thought through. We must take into consideration all things: British opinion, the situation of the war, as well as our ability to win such if recognizing the South results in Great Britain being at war with the United States."

"Yes, Mr. Prime Minister," Mason, then Lytham, acknowledged.

"Her Majesty would like all of us to meet at eleven in the morning on July fifteenth at Buckingham Palace to discuss, in greater detail, the aspirations of the South. Would that be acceptable?"

"Yes, Mr. Prime Minister; thank you," Mason answered as Lytham nodded.

"Good. I will inform the queen of such then, gentlemen. In the meantime, if you could do your utmost to gain British opinion in favor of Southern recognition, it would make our decision to declare for the Confederacy that much easier."

During their carriage ride home, the two were much pleased with the meeting.

"Good work, William. I hope we are now well on our way."

"Indeed. Good work to you too, James. You did a fantastic job!"

"Regarding the incident the other night, William, I will send dispatcher Andrew Millson overseas to inform President Davis and see what he wants done. In the meantime, we must do our utmost to get British opinion on our side. As we've heard from Palmerston, such would make their decision in declaring for us that much easier."

Mason proceeded to arrange the date of July 14 at eleven in the morning at Royalton's where the two would meet prior to their audience with the queen and the prime minister. Dropping Mason off at his hotel, the carriage proceeded— with Sawton following at a distance in another carriage—to the Brown's Hotel. Inside the hotel, Lytham informed Sawton of the additional protection. Hearing the news, Sawton was much relieved; he realized that, on his own accord, it would be extremely difficult, if not impossible, to secure William's safety.

* * *

Learning of the fiasco, Collins made straight to Seward's residence.

"Seward, it's me, Collins!"

"What news, Collins?" Seward eagerly asked as he opened his hotel room door.

"Terrible news! William's guards killed Terx and Yieps before they had the opportunity to get to William. Yet, if it is any consolation, one of William's guards was killed in the struggle."

"Dammit, that is no consolation, Collins. Those fools! We'll just have to claim that they acted on their own accord."

"I agree. Should we inform Lincoln?"

"Of course. Go overseas and inform him. Tell him that we're going to deny any involvement, and ask him what he would like done next."

Later that week, the queen scheduled a meeting with Seward at Buckingham Palace.

"Ambassador Seward, the reason I called you here today is that two of your men were found dead in front of William's hotel room—presumably going after him."

"Yes, Your Majesty, I read the same thing in the *Times* just the other day. I am shocked to the core!"

"Well, who's in charge of them, anyway?"

"They answer to my dispatcher, Gary Collins, Your Majesty."

"Have you spoken to Collins about the incident?"

"Unfortunately not, Your Majesty. The day after the incident I sought an immediate audience with him—only to find out that he had already boarded a ship for overseas."

"Well, I suggest you send another dispatcher overseas and inform your president of what transpired here. Such an action on the part of the Union is absolutely illegal—as I'm sure you well know. Britain will not stand for another fiasco like *The Trent* affair. Is that clear?"

"Abundantly clear, Your Majesty. I will immediately inform President Lincoln of the incident and I am sure Collins will be questioned accordingly."

"Good. That is all."

Seward wanted to speak more about the situation overseas but he realized such would not be prudent at that moment. Accordingly, "Yes, Your Majesty," was his response and he made a humble exit.

* * *

Arriving in Washington, Collins immediately headed to the White House and informed President Lincoln of the mishap in London. Needless to say, the president was not pleased.

"Dammit! But how? How did they fail?"

"Apparently, William's room was strongly protected, Mr. President, and in the attempt to seize him, Seward's men met their fate."

"What of Britain? What is their reaction?"

"I'm not sure, Mr. President. When I left for Washington, Seward was still seeking an audience with the queen. He told me to inform you, however, that we will deny any involvement regarding William's attempted abduction."

Lincoln was somewhat relieved. "Good."

"In addition, Seward wants to know what you would like done next."

"Well, it's best if we just let things cool down for the time being. To attempt another abduction upon William on the heels of this one will look suspicious."

"True, Mr. President."

"On the next ship leaving for London, then, I want you to board the same and inform Seward of my deliberation upon your arrival. In addition, two of my men, Hugh Ritt and Manfred Treven, will accompany you to replace Terx and Yieps as protectors to Seward. This might be all the more necessary if the rebels believe that we were indeed involved and thus set upon Seward in retaliation. Once again then, Collins, when in London, inform Seward that everything must be allowed to cool down before we set upon William again."

"Yes, Mr. President. I will."

"How is Seward doing, anyway, on swaying British public opinion to our side?"

"Not badly, Mr. President. Apparently, Seward is having much success in getting the aristocrats, previously sympathetic to rebeldom, on our side."

"Good. Hopefully our failed abduction will not sway the momentum to the rebel's favor."

* * *

Receiving the news of the incident from Andrew Millson, President Davis immediately suspected the Union was behind it.

"Damn that Union! They are doing it again. First they attack William in Richmond and now overseas. What a complete violation of international law. I am continually shocked at the underhanded means that Lincoln employs in his attempt to suppress us."

Millson nodded.

"I guess we are left with little else but to fight fire with fire. A message must be sent to Lincoln that William is to be left alone, and, if he isn't, then we are prepared to employ the same tactics. Where is Union dispatcher Collins now?"

"I believe he is presently in Washington explaining these recent events to Lincoln, Mr. President."

"Then I want you, along with two soldiers that I will assign to you, to make straight to Washington; and when you deem it an opportune time to set upon Collins, then…do what needs to be done. The Union will soon realize our resolve not to be intimidated."

Millson understood the message. "Yes, Mr. President."

19

In England, William was also doing his utmost to persuade the populace to the South's side. And his hard work was paying off. Gradually the majority of the aristocrats, after listening to the true passion and conviction in the young man's voice, were coming over. In addition, meeting people on the street and in the local pubs, William was making a great impression upon the middle and lower classes of British society. Slowly but surely, the mass of British opinion was being swayed to the Confederate side.

As a result, when Palmerston met Victoria for their scheduled meeting on the twentieth of June, many believed the meeting would result in Confederate recognition. The newspapers were buzzing, the *Times* in particular: "The prime minister is to meet Her Majesty today. The topic, no doubt, is Confederate recognition. Many believe Her Majesty and the prime minister will come out in favor of the Confederacy today." The anticipation for their scheduled meeting was thus electric. As a result, Palmerston's visit to Buckingham Palace was met with throngs of people.

"Recognize the South, Mr. Prime Minister!" chanted some.

"No. Stand by the Union!" exhorted others.

The division amongst the populace was sixty-five to thirty-five—with the majority favoring Confederate recognition. While being escorted to the queen's conference room, Palmerston himself was nervous. He realized that at the conclusion of their meeting, Britain might very well be on course for war against the United States.

"Good morning, Mr. Prime Minister."

"Good morning, Your Majesty."

"How is it outside?"

"The weather, Your Majesty?"

Victoria was somewhat taken aback; then she realized the question could also be interrupted as the feeling amongst the populace. "Yes."

"Actually it looks to be a beautiful day. Mild weather, clear blue sky, and a bright shining sun."

"Lovely. How about the feeling amongst the populace?"

"Well, it looks as if the majority now thinks that we should recognize the South, Your Majesty."

"And what do you think?"

"I am not sure what to think, Your Majesty. My sympathy is with the South, but I am not sure if declaring for them would be our best course of action."

"My sympathy is also with the South. Yet I, like you, realize the full implications that this sympathy, if put into action, would take. How are they doing on land?" she asked, already aware of the situation at sea.

"They are still holding their own, Your Majesty."

"What of France? What are they saying in all this?"

"At present, Your Majesty, all they are saying is that they will only consider recognizing the South if we do so first."

"Are our soldiers stationed in Canada presently positioned?"

"Yes, Your Majesty. We are ready."

"What do you advise?"

"Well, to be honest, I would feel much more comfortable if France guaranteed her support for the South with us."

"How could we secure such a guarantee?"

"Perhaps we could inform William that if he were to gain France's guarantee to recognize the South if we did so first, we would have no hesitation in declaring for them."

"Yes, it is indeed better if we act not alone on this. There is no possibility the United States would want a war with us, France, and the South simultaneously. They would have no other recourse but to let the South determine her own destiny. Accordingly, with an independent South, the balance of power would be even more firmly in our favor. There will no longer be a huge United States conducting its affairs unchecked by any other comparable power overseas. I fear, however, that if we act alone and have miscalculated the strength, or lack thereof, of the

South in this, then our British Empire in North America might very well be lost."

"My thinking precisely, Your Majesty."

"Good. We will both inform William and Mason of our deliberation when we meet them next month."

With that, Lord Palmerston left Buckingham Palace and returned to number 10. When asked by reporters if Britain was about to recognize the South, Palmerston stated that the position of the British government had not changed but that he and the queen would meet with William Lytham and Ambassador Mason next month to discuss the matter more fully.

* * *

Having boarded in Washington the same ship Collins and his associates were taking to London, Millson, with soldiers Ian Letton and Les Retson, waited for the opportune time to strike.

The sail to England was a stormy affair. In fact, it was so bad that Collins' associates got seasick. They had never been at sea before and were thus not accustomed to its characteristics. Collins just smiled, entreating them to rest and recover in their cabins. Although they insisted that they should stay at his side to ensure his safety, Collins assured them that it was Seward who needed the protection, not him. Accordingly, they went to their cabins to receive some much needed rest and recovery. On deck, Collins marveled at the power of the sea. *So vast and ominous a presence,* he thought, *that no one should dare treat her with disrespect.* Seeing Collins by himself, Millson commanded Letton and Retson to set upon him.

The two approached Collins nonchalantly.

"Sure is a terrible storm out there," Letton began.

"It certainly is," Collins concurred, staring at and entranced by the power of nature. "The wind, rain, and sea are a powerful combination."

Retson nodded in agreement.

"Well, we best get inside, men, before we ourselves become part of it," chuckled Collins, trying to elicit humor.

Letton was not amused. "Actually, we think it would be better if you went for a swim."

Immediately, Letton and Retson seized Collins and threw him overboard. Collins gave out a frantic call for help, but because of the violent storm, not even Letton and Retson could hear his cry. Subsequently, the waves covered Collins—drowning him in a powerful rage.

"Well, so much for that one," Letton declared.

"That's for sure," Retson agreed. "Hopefully the Union will now leave William alone."

The two then returned to Millson and asked him if they should give Collins' associates the same fate.

"No, the president commanded only Collins be taken care of. Anyway, someone has to arrive in London to inform Seward of the fate of his dispatcher. This should send chills down the Yankee spine."

Accordingly, Ritt and Treven were allowed to live. After feeling much better from their seasickness the following day, the two emerged from their cabins to rendezvous with Collins. Yet, after repeated knocks upon his cabin door with no answer, the two decided to enter by picking the door lock. Entering, Collins was nowhere to be found. In the end, they believed rebel sabotage was at work in Collins' disappearance. As a result, when they landed in England, they immediately notified Seward of Collins' disappearance on ship. Shocked and horrified at what presumably happened to his dispatcher, Seward instructed Ritt to return to Washington to inform Lincoln. Treven then went on to inform Seward of Lincoln's instructions regarding William, having been previously told of such by Collins.

Hearing this, Seward was relieved. The situation in England was becoming extremely tense. Many held the Union responsible for William's attempted abduction and, as a result, were switching to the Confederate side. In addition, for entirely personal reasons, Seward was also relieved that William was to be left alone. He feared that if the Union persisted in its attempt to apprehend William, especially on the heels of their failed attempt, the Union ambassador's own life would be at risk. Seward had no better illustration for this concern than in the disappearance of Collins.

Millson, Letton, and Retson met up with Mason upon their arrival on English soil and told him of Collins' fate. Mason was relieved. But to be on the safe side, he sent Letton and Retson to the Brown's Hotel to assist Sawton and Scotland Yard in William's protection. After being checked by Scotland Yard and confirmed by Sawton, Letton and Retson now joined in the protectorship of Lytham. The next day, July 14, Mason and William met at Royalton's.

"Well, this could be it, William. After tomorrow we may be recognized as a sovereign nation by powerful Britain. This will undoubtedly give new vigor and hope to our cause!"

"Indeed, James. I must admit, I am pretty nervous."

"Don't worry, William. I, too, am nervous, and I am more than twice your age," Mason consoled as Lytham humbly smiled. "The key is to turn your nervousness into determination. With that, there is no mountain you can't climb."

The following day, July 15, London was buzzing. "Will the Confederacy be Recognized Today?" headlined the *Times*. The anticipation was high. William had succeeded in swaying a great majority of the aristocrats and the British populace to the Confederate side. With his sincere, convincing persuasion, as well as his illegal attempted abduction, the British were coming over.

At ten in the morning, Mason knocked on Lytham's hotel room door, and the two left the Brown's Hotel and boarded a carriage awaiting them—"compliments of Her Majesty," said the chauffeur.

Getting ready, the queen was still upset that Britain would not recognize the Confederacy unilaterally. She desperately wanted to. Yet, in the end, she concurred with Palmerston's reservations. *Yes*, she convinced herself, *it is better if France comes along. I am sure William can get the French on their side. Oh, I hope you do, William. There is nothing I want more than to declare for the South and to tell you the news personally.*

The carriage approached Buckingham Palace with Alfred Lytham awaiting the two. With the queen's arrival to the royal den some five minutes later, she and the prime minister proceeded to the conference room and welcomed William and James. After exchanging pleasantries and smiles, Palmerston broached the heart of the meeting. "So, gentlemen, what is the situation overseas?"

"We are still strongly holding our own on land, Mr. Prime Minister," Mason began. "But the Union blockade is still effective."

"Yes, Mr. Prime Minister," William followed. "We desperately need Great Britain's support in this matter."

Palmerston and Victoria looked at each other deeply; a long pause ensued.

"I will be frank with you, gentlemen. The queen and I desperately want to declare for the South. Yet, at this stage, we are hesitant. We realize you are holding you own on land, but at the same time, the Union has a great edge in military resources. As a result, even if Britain recognizes the Confederacy, victory by both our nations would still be cumbersome, if not impossible. Yet, if France could join us, Britain would have no hesitation in declaring for the South. My sources inform me that Napoleon has sympathy for the South but would only go about recognizing her if we did so first. We are now willing to do so."

"So, if we gain France's pledge to support us, informing them that Great Britain will do so first, you will then declare for us?" Mason asked.

"Precisely!" Palmerston answered.

"And that is the only way in which Great Britain will support our cause?"

Victoria was reluctant, yet resolved. "Yes, William. At the present time it is. I know you can do it, William. With your personable character, I have no doubt you will accomplish for the South not only our recognition but France's as well. Your cause then will be assured. I will have one of my servants come by the Brown's Hotel later today to give you all the necessary documents verifying Great Britain's pledge to recognize the South along with France."

"Thank you, Your Majesty. Well, if such is what it will take to make us sovereign, I will seek French recognition."

"Good! Report to me at once, William, when you accomplish your task," Victoria said, having total confidence in him.

"I will, Your Majesty. I will!"

William and James, after exchanging warm good-byes with the queen and the prime minister, left Buckingham Palace and contemplated upon what had just transpired. At last Mason broke the silence.

"Well, William, I must admit, I did have my doubts about Britain recognizing us unilaterally. Hopes of such recognition were probably unrealistic. I realized from the commencement of our diplomatic missions to Britain and France that recognition by both countries, in concert, would help allay the fears of each in declaring for us. Strength in numbers, you know."

"Yes, but I was thinking that maybe…"

"William, I have been in this game a long time. I know all too well how difficult it is for a country to commit to something bearing in mind all the ramifications that such might entail."

"True."

"So you must head to France, William; the sooner the better. I will send dispatcher Millson for France this afternoon to inform our ambassador John Slidell of your pending arrival. When you meet the emperor, William, you must do your utmost to get him on our side."

"Indeed."

"I will inform Millson to have Slidell meet you at the Arc de Triomphe wearing a navy blue suit, a navy blue hat, and reading *Le Temps*. As soon as you arrive at the French capital, head to the Arc de Triomphe and look for such a man there."

"I will."

"In addition, when you see such a man, say to him 'Bonjour, Monsieur. *J'aime Mobile.*' If it is Slidell, he will say, '*Oui, J'aime le Sud.*'"

After dropping Mason off, the carriage continued to William's abode. Arriving at the Brown's Hotel, William spent the remainder of the day assembling his belongings for his voyage to France. *So, I am going to France. The country of the French Republic. Incredible! Truly, an historic nation. I wish the stakes weren't so high, however, so that I could leisurely enjoy myself. But I know there will still be time to take in all that France has to offer.*

20

Having been informed that Southern delegate William Lytham was shortly to arrive in France, Emperor Napoleon III suggested to Scotland Yard that William sail to Normandy, where he would be greeted by French emissary Pierre Charleau—who would then escort him to Paris. Accordingly, later that week, with the weather being perfect and having all of the necessary documents for his mission, William, with Sawton, Letton, and Retson, boarded a ship for the Norman shore and experienced smooth sailing all the way. *Oh, France,* William sighed to himself as they were crossing the English Channel, *the land of love!*

After an hour into the Channel's crossing, William and his protectors could see the magnificent shore.

"Look. There it is, men. Fabulous France! Look how beautiful she is!"

"Truly, William," Sawton and Retson confirmed.

"Indeed, William; France is most beautiful!" Letton added.

Arriving on the shores of Normandy, the three were welcomed by six French soldiers headed by Pierre Charleau.

"Good afternoon, William Lytham. Welcome to France!"

The man's English was impressive. Although one could detect the obvious French accent, William was still highly impressed with his fluency. "If only I could be bilingual like that," thought William aloud, "my mission in France could be that much smoother."

"Don't worry, William," comforted Sawton, "it is the passion in you that is the key, not your mastery of the language."

"William, I am Pierre Charleau, Emperor Napoleon's personal emissary." The two shook hands. "The emperor warmly welcomes you to France. It is an honor to have you on French soil!"

Pierre Charleau was a member of the legendary Charleau family that served the French Royal Court, and the French Republic thereafter, with supreme distinction. In fact, the Charleaus were the counterpart of the Lythams in England; and when the Lythams fled England and settled in Marne la Vallée in the late 1500s, it was the Charleaus who welcomed them.

Lytham knew of the Charleaus from his father. "The honor is all mine, Pierre! Thank you for welcoming me as you did my ancestors some three hundred years ago. It is great to be on French soil!"

Charleau was impressed at William's knowledge of family history. "Yes, William. Your ancestors' descendants are good friends of mine. They are a most patriotic, loyal family."

Lytham was much pleased and smiled.

"Yes, in due time, I will show you the place where they reside."

"Thank you very much, Pierre."

"Well, let's embark on our journey to Paris, shall we?"

"Yes indeed, Pierre. Thank you."

The journey from Normandy was fantastic. William was able to see the vast French interior with its beautiful landscape. Moreover, the French women impressed him all the more. William truly realized he was in the country of love.

Traveling through the French interior, William continued to remind himself of the job at hand. He was in France to gain French recognition. He would not take no for an answer.

At around seven in the evening, the entourage had reached the town of Rouen, and Pierre informed William that they would reside there for the night. Pierre was to meet the town's new mayor, Luc Remmier, and he was to accompany the entourage to Paris.

Checking in at the local hotel, the men became aware of, and were invited to, a party that evening being held for the city's newest mayor in honor of his recent election victory.

At the gala, William was amazed at the friendliness of the French people, especially the women. *Truly, their beautiful countenances makes one want to kiss them right on the spot*, he thought.

"William, I would like you to meet Luc Remmier, Rouen's newest mayor," said Charleau.

"Bonsoir, Monsieur Remmier," greeted Lytham, shaking his hand.

Luc was impressed with William's accent. "Bonsoir, William. Luc is fine. Monsieur Charleau has just been telling me about you. I have no doubt you are serving the South with the same zeal and loyalty your relatives in France have been doing here in their new home for generations."

"Well, I am sure giving it my all, Luc. Merci. It is truly good to be in France!"

"Is this your first time?"

"Indeed."

"Well, I warmly welcome you to France, William, and to Rouen in particular. Be sure to have a good time during your stay!"

"Thank you, Luc. I will."

Luc proceeded to invite the entourage to the large table situated at the front of the dance hall. Being the town's new mayor, Luc and his family were privy to the best seats in the house.

"William, I would like you to meet my family: my wife, Jeanne; my daughter, Nathalie; and my son, Jacques."

"Nice to meet you all," William humbly greeted.

William continued to enjoy the evening thoroughly. The young man, however, could not help but notice that Luc's daughter was continually looking at him and smiling. Nathalie was twenty-two years old and a pure beauty. Her blond hair, five foot four stature, and green eyes were breathtaking. But he realized that he was a professional, on duty, and that he would do nothing to insult his host. Accordingly, William just smiled back but did not press the matter any further. At any rate, he had a girlfriend back home whom he loved tremendously.

"Would you like to dance, William?" Nathalie entreated.

Lytham was taken aback. At the time, he had been conversing with Luc on the beauty of Rouen. "Ah…well…sure, if it's all right with your father."

"Why certainly, William. Go right ahead."

Although reluctant because of Melanie, William realized that he couldn't dare chance offending his host.

"You are sure a good dancer, William," Nathalie exclaimed as the two continued in their waltz.

Lytham was somewhat uncomfortable. "You are too, Nathalie."

"How is the South, William? Is it beautiful?"

Lytham was pleased at the change in subject. "It's actually very beautiful, Nathalie. Very beautiful, indeed. Just like France."

Nathalie smiled. "Well, I would truly like to visit the South someday."

"I'm sure you would like it."

"So, when do you leave for Paris, William?"

"Tomorrow morning, actually. We have important business at hand."

"Yes, my father told me. I hope our ride will be comfortable."

"Our ride?"

"Yes, my family is accompanying Pierre and yourself. The emperor is giving my father a congratulations party on being elected Rouen's newest mayor and has invited the entire family to attend."

Lytham was shocked. "Oh. Well, ah, that's great."

Nathalie smiled radiantly. "Perhaps I can show you around the capital, William?"

"Perhaps," Lytham replied with a hesitant smile.

William had to force himself not to pursue Nathalie. He found her absolutely gorgeous. In fact, she was the most beautiful woman he had seen in Europe. Yet, he realized that he was loved back home and wanted to remain faithful.

On the following morning, the new entourage proceeded to get ready for their journey to Paris. William was completely taken aback when he learned that Nathalie was to ride with him. Since Nathalie had the best command of English and French, she successfully argued that it was better if she were with William on the journey to help prepare him for his meeting with the emperor. William, however, desperately wanted Nathalie not to sit next to him. Not because he didn't want to learn French, but because the French he believed he was going to learn would not be the language. He found her captivating, and he knew that she felt the same about him. As a result, William wanted to keep Nathalie at a distance. He did not want to fall into the temptation. Yet, in the end, he did not want to chance upsetting Luc and Pierre. William realized that Pierre, and perhaps now Luc, had tremendous influence upon the emperor; and the young man needed any advantage he could get for his beloved South. Accordingly, after some initial hesitation, he agreed.

"France is truly beautiful, isn't it William?" Nathalie asked during the ride, smiling radiantly at him while hoping he would notice something else of beauty.

"Yes it is, Nathalie. It sure is. So, do you have a boyfriend?" Lytham asked, trying to distract her away from him. "I am sure a woman as beautiful as you must have one."

The intended effect backfired. "Actually, I was going out with a man for the past five years. He is currently serving the army on France's eastern border. So, you find me beautiful, William?" Nathalie asked, smiling.

William was losing the momentum fast, and didn't know what to say next. "Well, sure."

"I find you beautiful also!"

"Nathalie, actually I have a..."

Yet before William could finish his sentence, she kissed him on the lips. The kiss melted William. Being kissed by a French woman was something he had always dreamed of. *What an amazing woman*, he thought. *What am I to do?* The kiss lasted a good fifteen seconds.

"Well, what did you think, William?"

"Well, I..."

Then she kissed him again. This time the kiss lasted some thirty seconds.

"You sure are a good kisser, Nathalie. I must say."

"I have always wanted to meet someone from the South, William. Some of my relatives who settled in Louisiana say that the Southern man is the gem of the earth. Yet, on top of that, you are the most gorgeous man I have ever met. We French love to love, William!" Nathalie exclaimed, kissing him again.

William could not believe, and yet he did believe, what was taking place. There it was, the Latin race. Of all the races in the world, it was the Latin race that knew how to love best. *It must be the fire in their hearts*, he thought. The Anglo-Saxons were more of a diplomatic sort. They did not possess the fire of love. The Celts looked upon women as goddesses and, accordingly, treated them with more of a spiritual reverence rather than a physical love. Yet the Latins, the Latins. They looked upon women as something to love completely. *Incredible!* William always believed that he possessed at least some of this blood. He knew he possessed Celtic blood by the way he truly cared for his sister. He knew that he was Anglo-

Saxon by his ability to be as cool as ice, not breaking under pressure. Yet there was still another part of William that possessed a fire for women. William knew that the Latins were orchestrators of this fire. Thus when he found out that his original ancestor was a Roman legionnaire, his strong suspicions about having Latin blood in him were happily confirmed.

William always believed that he could resist a woman of Celtic or Anglo-Saxon origin. This was because they possessed that same type of reserve that was also part of his disposition. Yet William knew that if he ever found a Latin woman attractive, and the feeling was reciprocated, the chance of him maintaining his reserve would probably be nil. Instead, his Latinness would come out. Now, here was Nathalie, a true French woman who loved with the Latin fire. *Oh no,* sighed William, *I think I am lost. Yet I will still try.* All efforts of trying, however, were quickly failing. Nathalie found William irresistible, and she knew that he felt the same about her. Nathalie realized that William was hers. She, unlike others, could take him out of his shell, and the man would then be at her mercy. This is what Nathalie wanted. This is what Nathalie was determined to do.

Lytham came up for breath. "Nathalie, aren't you supposed to be teaching me French?"

"I am, lovely William. I am!"

Nathalie then kissed him all the more passionately, and William could resist her no longer. Continuing on their journey to the French capital, the passion and love of Nathalie went on and on and on.

"William," called Charleau from the other carriage as the entourage was now within a mile of Paris.

"Yes, Pierre?"

"William, we are approaching the capital. We will stop at the Hotel Britannique. That is where you and your friends will be staying, along with Luc and his family. I am sure you will like it. The hotel is famous for its luxury and hospitality—in addition to its twenty-four-hour security."

"William! We will be staying at the same hotel!" Nathalie exulted, kissing him ever more fervently.

"Merci, Pierre," William responded, returning her kisses.

At the Hotel Britannique, after informing Nathalie that he had to leave for a bit to meet with a colleague, William quickly unpacked his belongings and made straight haste, with Sawton, Letton, and Retson following at a distance, to the Arc de Triomphe.

Chapter Twenty

Within twenty minutes, William had arrived at the Arc and had spotted a man wearing a navy blue suit, a navy blue hat, and reading *Le Temps*. Approaching, William said the secret code: "Bonjour Monsieur, *J'aime Mobile*."

"*Oui, J'aime le Sud*. John Slidell." Slidell extended his hand.

"William Lytham." The two shook hands.

John Slidell was in his late sixties. Although born in New York, he moved to New Orleans in his middle twenties to practice law; upon laying eyes on the beautiful city and its people, he decided to live there for the rest of his life. When the conflict in America broke, John enthusiastically joined the Confederate side, viewing himself more as a Southerner. Having learned French living in Louisiana, President Davis thought it best for the lawyer to represent the Confederacy as an ambassador to France. Accordingly, Slidell, along with Mason, boarded the infamous *Trent* ship and set sail for overseas. Upon their release from imprisonment in Boston, Slidell made haste to Paris—entreating Napoleon to recognize the Confederacy as an independent nation.

"So, is this your first time in France, William?"

"Yes."

"What do you think so far?"

"Beautiful, John. Truly beautiful. Pierre Charleau, Emperor Napoleon's personal emissary, welcomed me in Normandy, where we made an overnight stop in Rouen before arriving in Paris. The scenery all along the way was breathtaking."

"The women are breathtaking also, aren't they, William?" Slidell smiled.

"They sure are, John. In fact, I have met a lovely woman, Nathalie is her name, who has offered to show me around the city while I'm here."

"You mean to tell me that you've only been in France a short while and you already have a French woman?"

"Actually, Nathalie is just a friend."

"Sure, William, no French woman is just a friend."

Lytham smiled back. "Anyway, how is the situation in France?"

"Not bad, but it could be better. France, like Britain, has granted us the status of a belligerent power. In addition, the emperor has allowed us, albeit unofficially, to produce war ships here on French soil. Dayton, however, the Union ambassador in France, is doing his utmost, and with some success, to sway the French into continuing their neutral stance."

Lytham nodded.

"How is the situation in Britain?"

"Well, Mason and I had an audience with the queen and the prime minister shortly before I left. In the meeting they pledged that if France agrees to recognize the Confederacy, then Britain will too. Our task, then, is to inform the emperor of Britain's new position and hope that he will now agree to recognize the Confederacy with Britain."

"If Britain held this position prior to the fall of New Orleans, William, I am sure France would have agreed to such a joint recognition. Yet, since the fall of New Orleans, the emperor's original optimism for our cause has waned. Napoleon loves the French throughout the world and knows that New Orleans contains many people of French descent. As a result, if he were to support the South, he would want French New Orleans to be part of it."

"Well, we'll just have to convince the emperor that once we are recognized by both his country and Britain, we will not cease fighting until New Orleans is liberated."

"I agree, William. I have scheduled a meeting with the emperor for next month on August the seventeenth. How about we meet at La Republic Cafe in downtown Paris for ten in the morning on the sixteenth."

"Sure, John. That would be great."

"Where are you staying?"

"At the Hotel Britannique."

"Good! The Hotel Britannique is well-known for its security. Here are some papers regarding Napoleon's position." Slidell gave them to him. "Study them in detail. We will discuss them when we meet on the sixteenth."

Returning to the hotel, William saw Nathalie awaiting him outside his room. *My gosh,* he thought. *I cannot believe this woman's passion!*

"Hello, William," she greeted, running up to him and kissing him passionately.

"Hello, my beautiful French woman," Lytham smiled, returning her kisses. "Nathalie, I have some documents to go over for the remainder of the day. Perhaps we can see each other tomorrow?"

"No, William. I want you now!"

At that, she led him into his room and made love to him. William was somewhat bewildered as to what was transpiring. All his life he had purposely abstained from physical intimacy because he wanted to wait until he was married before he made love to a woman. That was the Catholic environment in which he had been brought up. Yet, in the end, the power of Nathalie prevented him. William knew that only the Latin woman possessed such a power over his morals. Thus, when it did happen, he was not so surprised.

"How was I?"

"Like an absolute tiger. You are mine, William," Nathalie said, making love to him again.

William realized this was true. After being a successful spy, an influential diplomat, and a true persuasive individual—whereby everything he did was always under his power and influence—William realized that, with Nathalie, he was at her mercy. No matter how much he tried to deny it, he realized, in the end, it was true. He was Nathalie's and Nathalie knew it.

Lytham was now completely exhausted. "Nathalie, I really have to get to work on these papers. I have a meeting with Napoleon soon and I must be fully prepared."

Nathalie was reluctant yet accepting. "All right, William." Nathalie proceeded to view the papers and saw that some contained French. "But, William, you do need someone to help you sift through the French parts of these documents. I am sure your French is not as good as your French in bed," Nathalie smiled.

Lytham smiled back.

For the remainder of the day, the two looked over the many papers given by Slidell. There were many complexities in them. But, after many hours, they succeeded in getting through much of the work. It was now one in the morning.

"Well, it's getting late, Nathalie. We can finish this later in the morning. You best get some sleep."

"With you, sure William," Nathalie replied, making love to him throughout the night.

21

In the morning, William and Nathalie finished the remainder of the documents, whereupon they toured the city—having a magnificent time.

"Paris is so beautiful, Nathalie."

"Truly it is, William. Paris, I believe, is the most beautiful of all cities."

"I wouldn't doubt it."

"How about New Orleans? They say the city is the Paris of America. Is this true?"

"Actually, I've yet to see New Orleans; but from what I hear, it is."

"Well, that is definitely a city I would like to visit."

"Me too."

The two continued to stroll. They visited the Arc de Triomphe, as well as the many cafes and boutiques that filled the French streets. Later in the day, the two had lunch on the shore of the exquisite river Seine.

Then the two returned to the Hotel Britannique and made love, this time in Nathalie's room. The next day, William and his protectors, at the offering of Pierre, visited Marne la Vallée—the place where William's distant relatives and Pierre's family resided. William asked Nathalie if she wanted to join him, but since she and her family were scheduled to meet Napoleon later that week, she had to decline.

Marne la Vallée was picturesque. It had been settled by the earliest Charleaus since the arrival of the Franks in the sixth century and was filled with beauty and heritage. Pierre took William to the Lytham manor and introduced him to the Lytham family, headed by seventy-year-old Charles Lytham.

"It is truly splendid to finally meet a Lytham from overseas, William. We have kept in contact with our relatives in England, but we were unsure where our relatives who fled overseas situated themselves. So, the American Lythams are Southerners. It looks as if the Lythams in Mobile have the best of both worlds: English speaking in Alabama and yet to its not-too-far West, the French-speaking people of Louisiana. Have you ever been to New Orleans, William?"

"No, not yet Charles, but I hope to one day."

"Good. They say New Orleans is fabulous. It is definitely a place I would like to visit."

"Me too," William said, smiling. "So, tell me Charles, how has it been living in France all these years; living in a country that historically our ancestors have been frequently at war with?"

"Well, we knew it was going to be hard. Yet we believed, in the end, it would have been far worse if we had remained in England. We know for a fact that many Lythams, because of their faith, were sent to the stake by 'good Queen Bess.' After hearing accounts of the persecutions many of our country folk suffered at her hands, I firmly believe the Spanish Inquisition paled in comparison with the 'English Inquisition.' So, we were happy with our decision to flee. Yet, when we arrived in France, we were indeed concerned as to how we would be accepted, if accepted at all. Much to our surprise and relief, however, we were not only accepted by the French but, in particular, by the legendary punishers of the English: the Charleau family. The Charleaus have truly helped us in our transition to the French culture. In fact, many of us have married Charleaus and vice versa. And we are firmly a loyal French race, William; although we dread the thought of having to fight England, if such comes about, we are prepared to do so. After all, it was France that granted us a safe haven in our time of dire need. Accordingly, we owe her our allegiance."

"Agreed. Yes, truly that was a suffering time in England, Charles. In fact, that is why we left for America when Cromwell became protector. My relatives believed Cromwell was going to do even greater harm to the Lythams than did Elizabeth. Since my family was not in the mood for a repeat performance, when they fled England, they made sure they didn't tell anyone where in the New World they would situate themselves—just in case Cromwell's ironclads found out and hunted us down. Much to our surprise, however, Cromwell tolerated and even accepted the Lythams who remained. But we didn't know this at the time of our flight, or we ourselves probably would have stayed. Yet, we have no regrets. My family has loved America ever since setting foot on Southern soil, and we have served our country with great distinction as have yours here in France. It is truly tragic that the situation in America has come to civil war. But again, I am from the South, Charles, and as such, I am giving it my all for my new country the Confederacy just as you have done for your new country France."

"True, William. And such is only to be admired and respected. We Lythams are truly fervent defenders of our homeland—no matter where our homeland may reside."

Lytham smiled in acknowledgment.

"How long will you be staying in Marne la Vallée, William?"

He realized that since Nathalie would be at the Imperial Palace for the next few weeks, there was no immediate rush to return to downtown. "Actually, I'm not sure. Would it be all right if I stay here for the next while, Charles, to spend time with my distant relatives?"

"That would be more than all right, William. Stay as long as you want. There is plenty of room for you and your friends in my manor. We truly have much catching up to do!"

"Indeed, Charles! Thank you."

William and his protectors resided at the Lytham manor for the following three weeks, taking in all that the Lythams and Marne la Vallée had to offer.

After having a magnificent time, William said good-bye to his relatives and, like his kinship in England, they exchanged open invitations.

* * *

On August 16, Lytham met Slidell at La Republic, and they settled down over fresh cups of coffee.

"So, have you had a chance to go over the papers, William?"

"Indeed, John. I believe I'm apprised of the situation in France. To begin with, the fall of New Orleans has hit Napoleon extremely hard. He has always been personally on our side and was even about to unilaterally declare for us, regardless of the actions of Britain, had the Cajun city not fallen."

"Correct."

"In addition, Union Ambassador Dayton is effectively curtailing the French newspapers to the Federal point of view with his pro-Union ads in the French newspapers."

"Indeed. Dayton has truly been a thorn in our side right from the start."

"Finally, a large segment of the Imperial Court is filled with Confederate sympathizers—thanks in large part to the relatives of Confederate soldiers who have made the trek to influence the emperor."

"Correct. Well it seems as if you have done your homework, William. Our goal tomorrow is to inform Napoleon of the commitment you gained from Britain and assure him that by recognizing us as a sovereign nation we will be better equipped to take back New Orleans—that we will not rest until the French state Louisiana is liberated."

"Absolutely, John."

"James tells me that you are quick on your feet."

Lytham gave a humble smile.

"Well, just continue to be, son. No doubt the emperor will direct the majority of the questions to you, since it was you who met with Victoria and Palmerston. I will come by your place at ten in the morning tomorrow. Our audience is for eleven."

"All right, John."

"The emperor, William, is a rather flamboyant sort. So, if you could dress accordingly—perhaps add some colors of the French flag—blue, white, or red—I am sure it will go over well with him."

"All right, John; I will."

The two finished their coffee, with each going his separate way. Outside his hotel room, William was delighted to find Nathalie there waiting for him, having just returned from her family's stay at the Imperial Palace. After exchanging many affectionate kisses, they searched for a nice suit for William to wear.

"Did you have a good time with your relatives, William?"

"Indeed, Nathalie. The Lythams in France are sure nice people!"

Nathalie smiled.

"How about you, Nathalie, how was your family's audience with the emperor?"

"Very good, William. We all had a wonderful time. Emperor Napoleon is truly a great man. He cordially congratulated my father on his recent election victory, and we were his special guests at the Imperial Palace for the entire stay."

"That is great."

"In addition, the emperor asked my father about you and conversed with him about the situation overseas."

"Really? Do you know what was said?"

"Well, for starters, my father spoke fondly of you, which Napoleon received well. The emperor then paused and, with sad contemplation, stated that his heart truly sides with the South but that the Confederate's loss of New Orleans has swayed him from declaring for you."

"How about my demeanor, Nathalie; how should I present myself to the emperor?"

"When you meet Napoleon tomorrow, William, be humble. Ever since the French Revolution, we have viewed our emperors as the Romans used to view theirs—as absolute gods; the world revolves around them and our country and nothing else. In fact, at our revolution, we even produced a calendar that began on the day of our republic. That is how highly we view our race. We view our people as the greatest race on earth.

"Yet, also be forthright. We Latins pride ourselves on our bluntness. While the English always seem to circle around an issue, we Latins get right to the point. It is important for you to remember this and do so accordingly when you meet him."

"Thank you, Nathalie; I will."

The two toured more of the city for the remainder of the day; in doing so, William, with Nathalie's help, picked out an impressive blue suit—the same blue color as in the French flag.

Arriving at the hotel, William told Nathalie that he needed a good night's sleep for tomorrow's important meeting. Although she wanted to be with him, Nathalie understood William's entreaty and therefore did not press the matter further.

At ten in the morning, Slidell called on Lytham.

The two left the hotel and boarded a carriage to the Imperial Palace.

"How do you feel?"

"Nervous. Extremely nervous, John."

"Don't worry, William; just be yourself and you'll do fine."

As the carriage drove up to the Imperial Palace, a French soldier welcomed them, escorting them into the Palace's conference chamber.

"Gentlemen, the emperor will see you shortly. In the meantime, please make yourselves at home," entreated the soldier.

"Merci," Slidell said as Lytham nodded.

After ten minutes, Emperor Napoleon III entered the chamber.

"Bonjour, Monsieurs! *Comme ca va?*"

"*Ca va bien*, Emperor Napoleon," Slidell answered.

"*Oui, ca va bien* Emperor Napoleon—merci," Lytham continued.

"Your Excellency, I would like you to meet William Lytham from Mobile, Alabama."

"It is a pleasure to meet you, William. So, William, tell me, are you enjoying your stay in France?"

"Yes, Your Excellency. France is fabulous!"

"Have you managed to tour the great city of Paris?"

"Oui, Your Excellency! Paris has to be the most beautiful of all the cities in the entire world. It is magnificent. I am truly impressed!"

"I am glad that you like our capital. I want you to feel most at home. France extends her warmest welcome to the Lytham name, just as she welcomed your relatives many years ago. Have you managed to visit them in Marne la Vallée?"

"Indeed, Your Excellency. Pierre Charleau introduced me to them a few weeks ago, and I had the time of my life."

"The Lythams, in France are truly a loyal, friendly, and patriotic people, as I am sure the Lythams in the South are for the Confederacy. You know, William, my sympathy in your conflict has always been with the South. I am aware of the French heritage of Louisiana, and I earnestly wanted that state to remain in Confederate hands. In fact, prior to the fall of New Orleans, I was even about to declare for the Confederacy unilaterally. Yet, when New Orleans fell, I believed that to recognize the South in the absence of French peoples would be something I would have difficulty in doing. Thus, due to the recent Union victories, I feel that it would only be prudent to recognize the Confederacy if Britain did so along with us—with the South's assurance that they would not stop the war until New Orleans is liberated."

"That is precisely why I have come to France, Your Excellency."

Napoleon, unaware of what William had achieved in England, gave a questioning look.

William then articulated the details of his arguments with the queen, while presenting the documents of the British pledge to recognize the Confederacy along with France. "Thus, Your Excellency, if France recognizes the South, they will no longer have to do so unilaterally. France and Britain will now have each other by its side!"

Slidell was impressed at William's articulation and passion.

"Is this true, then? Britain will recognize the South first if we agree to do so immediately thereafter?"

"Indeed, Your Excellency," Lytham answered.

Napoleon read the documents stating that very thing. "And the South will not stop until New Orleans is liberated?"

"Absolutely, Your Excellency," Lytham replied.

"This changes everything. I am scheduled to meet Union Ambassador Dayton next month. It is only prudent that I first converse with him before I decide upon the matter. Let us meet here again, say October twelfth at eleven in the morning. At that time I should have a decision ready."

"That would be fantastic, Your Excellency!" Lytham exclaimed.

"Yes, Your Excellency. Merci. Merci beaucoup!" Slidell echoed.

With that, Napoleon thanked the two for coming. William and John were then escorted by another French soldier to the carriage awaiting them outside the Palace.

"Great work, William! The emperor was well pleased with you and the commitment you gained from Britain."

"Thanks, John. Let's hope that he is pleased enough to grant us our much needed recognition!"

22

Since the fall of New Orleans, Union Ambassador Dayton didn't have a care in the world. With the heart of French Louisiana gone, Dayton believed Napoleon would no longer have any disposition toward supporting the South. And he was right—to some degree. Napoleon more or less articulated this changed demeanor in their subsequent meetings, which the ambassador happily relayed to Washington. Dayton continued in this carefree, confident manner when he met with Napoleon for their September 2 audience.

"Bonjour, Emperor Napoleon. *Ca va bien*?"

"*Ca va bien,* Dayton. *Vous*?"

"*Oui, ca va bien, merci*!"

"So, Dayton, how is the situation overseas?"

"Couldn't be better, Your Excellency. The vast majority of the rebel ports are now blockaded. In addition, more of French Louisiana is back in our hands—with the rest of rebeldom soon to follow. In sum, Your Excellency, the rebel's fate is sealed."

"Indeed it seems such would be the case without assistance."

"Your Excellency?"

"Dayton, I met William Lytham and Ambassador Slidell last month, and I believe it wouldn't be such a bad thing to recognize the South as an independent nation."

"What? Your Excellency. Please! With all due respect, Your Excellency, I cannot believe my ears! The rebels are about to be conquered—thoroughly. Even on land, where they have but only a semblance of an army, they are now being destroyed. Moreover, there is no longer a French presence in the Confederacy. The French state, Louisiana, is firmly in our hands."

"But perhaps with official recognition from both France and Britain, the South may in fact succeed in not only repossessing Louisiana, but also in achieving their quest to have a country to call their own."

"Your Excellency, Britain has assured Ambassador Seward that they will not side with the South."

"And Britain has assured William that they would recognize the South if we agree to do so as well, and he has the documents to prove it."

Dayton was totally bewildered, unaware of what William had attained in England. "Your Excellency, please, we have been France's ally from day one. Had it not been for your country's assistance at our revolution, we probably would not have gained our independence. There is no greater ally we have than France. Please, please don't throw this strong friendship away," pleaded Dayton.

Napoleon was touched. "Dayton. Please. Please understand my position. The South, and Louisiana in particular, has voted to leave the Union—just as your thirteen colonies voted to leave Britain in the 1770s. At that time, we respected the wish of your people. If we were to support the South, we would only be doing the same thing."

"Your Excellency, let's meet again next week to discuss the situation further. By that time, rebeldom may be no more."

"Dayton, we have already discussed the situation at length. We will meet again but, at present, I am not sure when such a meeting will take place. I am to meet William and Slidell in October and inform them of France's position in light of Britain's pledge. I will continue to follow events meticulously overseas until then, but in the end, a people's wish to be sovereign, especially those of French descent, must be supported by the heart of the French: France. Good day, Dayton, that is all."

Dayton left the Imperial Palace in complete shock as to what was transpiring. *I can't believe it! William has single-handedly set Britain and France on course to recognize rebeldom. Damn that Lytham. Lincoln must be informed at once. If William is not stopped, our cause is lost.*

Immediately making haste to Union dispatcher Robert Blanson's hotel room, Dayton, upon arriving, was beside himself.

"Rob. Rob! It's me!" Dayton screamed, banging on the door.

Blanson opened the door. "Dayton, what is going on? We aren't scheduled to meet until next month."

"Next month can't wait. By that time we'll probably be announcing our defeat!"

"What? Our defeat? What are you talking about? We are winning this war. It is only a matter of time, and not much more at that, before we are victorious."

"Not with France and Britain on the rebels' side!"

"What? France and Britain on the rebels' side? Impossible! You had me assure Lincoln that with the fall of New Orleans, France would not even consider recognizing the South, let alone doing such."

"Well, I was wrong. Everything has changed. William Lytham has successfully turned France and Britain to the South's side."

"I can't believe it!"

"At first, I couldn't either, but it's true, Rob. It's completely true. All my work, striving unceasingly to get the French on our side, is now lost. And all at the hands of one man; a man who has been here only a short while. I am in complete shock. No, I'm devastated!"

"Would you like me to head to Washington, Dayton?"

"Yes, Rob. Yes! That is why I came over. You must immediately travel to Washington to inform Lincoln of William's success. Find out what he would like done. Tell him William must be stopped; if he isn't, our cause may be lost!"

Blanson's voyage from Paris to Washington was a long, treacherous journey. It rained the entire way, and there were times when it looked as if the ship was going to capsize. In the end, however, the ship managed to make it to shore—much to Blanson's relief—not only for his own safety, but also for the vital information he was carrying.

Although discussing military strategy with General McDowell—who was in Lincoln's good graces again—the president made time for Blanson, realizing his month-early presence meant something significant.

"Mr. President, Dayton had an audience with Napoleon before I left and was told, in no uncertain terms, that France will likely declare for the South along with Britain."

"What? Why? I don't understand! We are defeating the rebels. The war will soon be over. We have taken back French Louisiana. Why would France and Britain even contemplate, let alone partake in, such action?"

"Apparently, William Lytham convinced France that their recognition would result in British recognition and that, with both, French Louisiana would be retaken with the independence of the Confederacy to follow. In short, Mr. President, if William is not stopped, our cause may be lost!"

"Damn that William. Damn him! How does France know Britain will declare for the South if the former agrees to do so?"

"Apparently, William gained Britain's commitment in England."

"Stoddard! Stoddard!"

Stoddard quickly entered. "Yes, Mr. President?"

"Get me the French and British ambassadors. At once."

Ten minutes later, Lyons the British ambassador, and Mercier the French ambassador, entered the Oval Office.

"Men, what's this about Britain declaring for the South if France agrees to do so?"

"What are you saying, Mr. President?"

"Don't give me that, Lyons! What the hell is going on?"

"Mr. President, I have been instructed by my superiors to state that Britain is a neutral country in your conflict, that is all."

"Mr. President, France has always been, and will continue to always be, a loyal ally to the United States of America," Mercier voiced.

Lincoln realized he was getting nowhere. "All right gentlemen, thank you."

"Mr. President," Lyons nodded, exiting.

"Good day, Mr. President," bid Mercier as he left.

"What do you think, men?"

"I believe they are hiding something, Mr. President," McDowell declared.

"I agree," Blanson echoed.

"All right, Blanson, that is all for now. I will speak with you shortly. In the interim, please wait outside my office."

"Yes, Mr. President." Blanson left.

"What do you think, Irvin?"

"Well, Mr. President, it seems that William must be stopped."

"Yes, but there was an attempt to stop him in England, which ended in disaster."

"How about sending McKenny upon him again? So far he has been the only one to get within striking distance of William. Moreover, Darren knows William's mind perhaps better than anyone. If anyone has a chance at getting him, it's McKenny."

"Go then, Irvin, and send Darren upon him. Take two of your men with you and have them assist him overseas. Inform Darren that I don't want William eliminated, only detained and brought back here to face justice. After all the trouble he has caused, I would finally like to meet the Soul of the South. If he does not return alive, McDowell, then I will hold all individuals involved personally responsible. Do I make myself clear?"

"Absolutely, Mr. President. William is to be brought back alive!"

"Good. Blanson!" Lincoln called out.

Blanson entered. "Yes, Mr. President?"

"Robert, go back to Paris and inform Dayton that very shortly a man by the name of Darren McKenny will visit him who will address the 'William matter.'"

Exiting the White House, McDowell, with soldiers Theo Patlin and Jacob Topson, boarded the next train to New York.

Arriving at the New York division, McDowell greeted a surprised McKenny.

"Good morning, Lieutenant."

"General, good morning! What brings you here?"

"The president, Darren. He wants you to detain William Lytham in Paris, and then return him to Washington where he will face justice."

"The president wants him returned alive?"

"Absolutely, Darren. That is what he adamantly wants. Moreover, it is imperative you get William as soon as possible; for, as of right now, we believe he is in the process of achieving French and British recognition for rebeldom—an achievement that would spell almost certain disaster for our cause."

McKenny was speechless, shocked at the gravity of the situation.

"You will be accompanied by two of my most trusted soldiers, Theodore Patlin and Jacob Topson, who are awaiting you outside your office. They are most loyal, Darren, and should be of vital assistance in your capture of William."

"Thank you, General."

"When you arrive in Paris, you are to meet up with Ambassador Dayton at the Riverie Hotel. He will be expecting you and will be able to provide you with information regarding William's whereabouts."

"Understood!"

23

The day before their scheduled meeting with Napoleon, William and John, as prearranged, met at La Republic.

After exchanging pleasantries and ordering breakfast, the men got down to the business at hand.

"So, William, how has your influence upon the French populace been? As for myself, I managed to make some impact on the newspapers here. After continually articulating our position to them, they are finally starting to speak with more cordiality toward our cause."

"Great, John. I myself have been continuously meeting with leaders of various organizations, especially those originally hostile toward us, as well as ordinary people throughout Paris—illustrating what our cause is all about. And I have had my share of success, such that the public, even those once firmly against us, are now coming over."

"Great work, William. Hopefully our perseverance will yield abundant fruit."

"Indeed, John."

"I'll pick you up at ten in the morning tomorrow."

"I'll be ready."

The two continued to enjoy their breakfast, and William, upon leaving, proceeded to Notre Dame cathedral to attend mass and ask God for help in the South's quest for independence.

Entering the church, William was amazed by its beauty. Its magnificent structure and gothic windows were breathtaking. Being Catholic, William was glad the French had retained their Catholicism. He was also proud they built such beautiful churches, and Notre Dame, Our Lady, was the most beautiful of them all. William always had a fondness for Mary, the Mother of God. He truly believed in her divine intervention whenever he was in need. Praying at Notre Dame, William asked God to be pleased with the decision he and his fellow Southerners made. He prayed that the cause the South was taking up was not a vain cause, not a slave-loving cause, but rather the only alternative as a result of Northern pressure and dictates. William prayed Napoleon tomorrow would agree to Britain's proposal of joint recognition for the Confederacy and would finally give the South her sought after sovereignty. Offering these prayers, William could not help but hear a faint whisper: "Know that we love you and the Southern people and we always will, William." William looked around, yet he could see no one. *Who was this?* Just then a bright beam of light shown radiantly on the alter. Others in the church, along with William, marveled at the light that, after about five seconds, vanished. Contemplating, William concluded that the light and the voice must have been an angel, perhaps Mary, sent to console him. William was grateful for this divine revelation, and, accordingly, left the church with an even greater determination to do his utmost for the glory of his beloved South.

The following morning, October 12, John came by to pick William up. As before, a French soldier escorted William and John into the conference chamber. Yet this time, unlike before, diplomats and servants were scurrying about the premises with papers and folders.

"Perhaps today is indeed the day, William."

"I hope so, John. I sure hope so."

Ten minutes later, Napoleon entered and warmly welcomed his guests.

"Bonjour, Monsieurs Slidell and Lytham. So, gentlemen, how are things overseas?"

"Your Excellency," Slidell began, "we are holding fast. Yet, we still most ardently desire French and British recognition."

"Well, that is exactly what I would like to talk with you both about. William, I conversed with my ambassador in England and he has confirmed your information regarding Britain's pledge to recognize the Confederacy with France. Gentlemen, I have debated at length as to what France should do. I am pleased to announce that the empire of France will indeed honor Britain's pledge of joint recognition for the Confederacy!"

Lytham was visibly moved. "Merci! Thank you so much, Your Excellency. Merci beaucoup. Consider Louisiana back in Confederate hands!"

Napoleon smiled.

"Merci beaucoup, Your Excellency!" Slidell continued. "You will not regret France's wise move in this matter!"

"I know I won't, gentlemen. We are presently preparing all the necessary documents for you, William, to take back to Britain to confirm our part of the pledge."

"Thank you, Your Excellency. I'm ecstatic!"

"As are we, William," Napoleon responded, smiling. "Our paperwork will, however, take another two days. At that time, you will board the *Château*. The ship is only for diplomats. In addition, the *Château* is filled with French soldiers. Both these measures are being taken to ensure your safety."

"Oui," Lytham said. "Merci beaucoup, Your Excellency."

Napoleon smiled, acknowledging their thanks. "In the meantime, gentlemen, please return here this evening to reside at the Imperial Palace as my honored guests. The arrangements have already been made."

Kindly thanking the emperor once again, William and John proceeded to board the carriage awaiting them outside the Palace.

"We did it, William!"

"We did it indeed, John. I can't believe it! President Davis will be overjoyed."

"Absolutely. I'm going to have dispatcher Millson leave for home immediately to inform President Davis of this great news. We best pack our bags and head over to the Palace. Oh yes, the Palace. I am definitely looking forward to living the next two days in thorough luxury, William."

"Me too, John. Me too."

"I will send another one of my dispatchers to England to inform Mason as well."

The carriage traveled to the respective hotels of William and John— first dropping William off and then John. Slidell would be returning to his hotel after two days at the Imperial Palace. William, however, would be immediately off to England and then most likely back to Richmond. Entering the Hotel Britannique, William could not help but be consumed with thoughts of Nathalie. *What am I to do? Do I love her? Do I love her more than Melanie? Does she feel the same way for me as Melanie does?*

For as it stood right now, with all things being equal, William wasn't sure whom he would choose. Both women were very good looking, extremely compassionate, and would make great wives. *Deal with one thing at a time. And the first thing to do is to find out how Nathalie feels about you.* William kept this in mind when he knocked on her hotel room door.

"Nathalie, it's me, William."

Nathalie opened the door, kissing him. "It's great to see you, William. How did your meeting go with the emperor?"

"It went great, *belle femme*. It looks as if Napoleon may recognize the South," Lytham replied, not willing to divulge the emperor's exact pledge. "My colleague and I are to be the honored guests of the emperor at the Imperial Palace for the next two days; whereupon, I am to head to London."

"That is fantastic, William!"

Lytham was unsure of what to say next. "So, how are things with you?"

"Most fine! I received a letter from my boyfriend. He is coming to see me this week."

Lytham realized the reality. "That is great, Nathalie. You've truly been a godsend to me, you know. Your love, your kindness, and your invaluable help in preparing me for my meetings with the emperor will never be forgotten."

"And you, William, you've been a blessing to me. You are the real thing. Your passion for the South, and your willingness to defend it, is something only to be admired—by friend and foe alike. I hope you and the South are victorious!"

"Thank you, Nathalie. You know, if you ever visit Mobile, look me up. I will give you the grand tour. It is not nearly as big as Paris, mind you." Lytham smiled. "But it is beautiful nonetheless. Moreover, if you visit, I will take you to New Orleans, the Paris of America—where we will have the time of our lives!"

Nathalie smiled as tears filled her eyes. "You've truly been lovely, William. I love you. Please, take care!"

"And I love you, Nathalie," Lytham replied, kissing her softly as they embraced.

They realized it was probably the last time they would ever see each other. Yet, they felt the specialness of their relationship and were thus grateful that they had met. After wishing her a most fond farewell,

William left Nathalie's room and, with tears in his eyes, gathered his belongings for his stay at the Imperial Palace.

At the Imperial Palace, William met many relatives of the Confederate soldiers who had entreated Napoleon to recognize the South. Although believing it prudent not to divulge the exact contents of his recent audience with Napoleon, William did tell them that he thought that very soon the emperor would recognize the Confederacy. The relatives were ecstatic and hoped that the plight of their kindred might now be alleviated. William was truly affected by their accounts of the afflictions suffered by their kindred and the general population back home, and one conversation in particular hurt him more than any other.

The woman was from New Orleans and had recently escaped the Union occupation of the city. "Oh, William, it is terrible in New Orleans now that the Yankee army is there. The soldiers are harassing the civilians and especially the women. Yankee General Butler has called the ladies of New Orleans harlots and said that the soldiers are to treat them as such."

"That bastard, Butler!" Lytham vehemently expressed, momentarily forgetting he was in the presence of a lady. "Oh, I'm sorry."

"Don't be sorry, William. We Louisianans all feel the same way. We are helpless. We are at their mercy. I have stated as much to the emperor and he is horrified. Thankfully, he assured me just the other day that the Yankees will soon get their just desserts."

"Don't worry, Annabelle, I believe very soon we are going to give Butler and his Yankees a thorough bon voyage gift."

"Oh, I hope so, William. I don't know how much longer we can endure."

William went on to console Annabelle. Yet her information still troubled him. *The Yankees would stoop that low? War is one thing; but to conduct a war on a civilian population, especially on female civilians, is quite another.*

Later in the day, when Slidell met up with his young diplomat, William informed him of Annabelle's information. Slidell, who made New Orleans home, did not look highly upon the Union's action.

"Those damn Yankees. Well, we'll soon get them, William!"

"Indeed, John. Indeed."

"I can't believe it. I myself am originally from the North, and now I am ashamed to admit it. I would have been shocked if the Union had even contemplated doing such a deed to civilians, especially to women, let alone doing it."

Lytham gave an acknowledged nod.

"Well, we're going to make them pay for their actions, William."

"Absolutely, John. Absolutely!"

24

After a long miserable voyage across the Atlantic, where confronting high seas was the norm rather than the exception, Darren, along with Theo and Jacob, finally landed in Paris. They immediately met up with Dayton at the Riverie Hotel.

McKenny knocked on the ambassador's hotel room door. "Dayton. Dayton! It's me, Darren McKenny. You're supposed to be expecting me."

Dayton opened the door. "Welcome, Darren. Good to meet you. How was the voyage?"

"Actually, it was terrible."

"Yes, they say the Atlantic has been experiencing unseasonably foul weather these past few weeks."

"Anyway, what's the latest on Lytham?"

"Well, I was hoping you would have arrived even one day earlier. William and rebel ambassador Slidell had an audience with Napoleon today and have since been staying at the Imperial Palace as guests of the emperor. Unfortunately, the Palace's security is extremely tight."

"Do you know how long William will be staying at the Palace?"

"No, but in my meeting with Napoleon tomorrow I will seek out that very thing."

"Good."

With that, Dayton headed downstairs to the reception desk and booked a room for the three. Upon receiving the key for their lodging, Darren, along with Theo and Jacob, thanked the Union ambassador and then went straight to their room; whereupon, suffering from complete exhaustion from the ordeal at sea, the men made straight for bed.

The following morning, October 13, Dayton and Napoleon met for their scheduled meeting.

"Bonjour, Emperor Napoleon!"

"Bonjour. Dayton, I have called this meeting to inform you of my decision regarding America."

Dayton was nervously silent.

"Dayton, France ardently loves the United States, as I'm sure the United States ardently loves France. And we wish this relationship to continue."

"We wish so as well, Your Excellency."

"We wish to continue this relationship even with France supporting the South in your conflict."

Dayton was destroyed. "Emperor, please, please..." Dayton pleaded, gasping for words.

"France and Britain would like to honor the wishes of the Confederacy. The South, on her own accord, voted to leave the Union. Neither we nor Britain encouraged them in this matter. Now that they have decided to leave, they have come to us for support. I no longer feel we should evade them on their entreaty any further."

"Your Excellency, with all due respect, don't enter upon this course of action. It will undoubtedly sever our strong relationship."

"Then if it must, Dayton, it won't be at our choosing."

Dayton was at a loss. "Your Excellency, after the fall of New Orleans, you gave us no indication that France would enter upon such a course of action. Why, all of a sudden, has she shifted her position?"

"It is true, Dayton, that France was hesitant to declare for the South after the fall of New Orleans. But the arrival of William Lytham brought news that Britain would recognize the South if we agreed to do the same; and with the reassurance that New Orleans would be liberated if our support was given, France has returned to her original disposition of wanting to honor the express wishes of the Southern people."

"I am sure, then, that William Lytham will be heading straight back to Richmond to personally inform President Davis of France's decision to jointly recognize the South with Britain," Dayton voiced, hoping Napoleon would reveal some information as to Lytham's future agenda.

"Well, for the present, William is a personal guest of mine, and tomorrow he will be leaving on the *Château* for London," Napoleon said, yet unwilling to say why, "perhaps for a vacation. But, yes, I am sure indeed that when William does return to Richmond, he will personally inform President Davis of France's decision."

Dayton was pleased he found out as much as he did about William's agenda. "Is there any way, Your Excellency, France will reconsider her present course?"

"No, Dayton. I called this meeting to inform you of France's position and for you to inform your president of such. That is all, Dayton, thank you."

Dayton left the Imperial Palace terrified at what might shortly transpire. Arriving at the hotel, he immediately knocked on McKenny's door.

"Darren, it's me, Dayton!"

McKenny opened the door. "Dayton, what is happening?"

"Our entire cause! I just spoke with the emperor and France is on course with Britain to recognize the South."

"Dammit!"

"But both countries have not yet done so. Napoleon stated that William is to travel to London tomorrow. I presume the trip must have something to do with both countries' recognition of rebeldom or else France and Britain would have already declared for the South. So we must get him before he has a chance to set foot on English soil."

"Right."

"He is scheduled to leave on the ship *Château*."

"My men and I will head over to the dock now and purchase tickets for the voyage."

"Actually, the *Château* is a charter ship—only for diplomats. Napoleon is probably sending William on it to ensure his safety. So I'll go over to the dock and purchase the tickets. If you manage to abduct William onboard, use the ship's spare boat and sail to the Isle of Wight. A Union fighter ship is stationed there that you will be able to use to head back to Washington."

"Thanks, Dayton. Sounds good."

"Keep in mind, Darren, that William has bodyguards, and no doubt they are all professionals."

"Fine. But I have a couple of helpers that are good as well, right boys?"

"Right!" Patlin and Topson fervently replied.

"I'm off to purchase the tickets, Darren. I'll be back in about an hour."

"Thanks, Dayton."

Forty-five minutes later, Dayton returned with the tickets.

"Darren, I cannot stress how important it is for William to be apprehended before he arrives in England. If he arrives on the island, his apprehension, and no doubt our cause, will be lost. He will indubitably be placed under the protection of Scotland Yard and will no doubt be given an immediate audience with the queen and the prime minister. Then official recognition by Britain and France will most likely be declared."

"Understood."

"Keep in mind that in order to apprehend him, you will have to address at least two things: one, his protectors, of which I believe he has three, and two, the French soldiers who accompany the *Château* on its voyages."

"Understood, Dayton."

"Good. I am off to send a dispatch to Lincoln, informing him of the dire conversation I had with Napoleon today. Good luck, men. The Union's hope rides with you; get William if it's the last thing you do!"

"We will, Dayton. We will indeed!" McKenny exclaimed as his accomplices nodded in agreement.

Later in the day, Napoleon met with William and John and, after exchanging pleasantries, the emperor informed them of the completion of all the necessary documents.

"Well, I believe everything is set, gentlemen. William, I have the official papers ready for your journey back to England, and I informed Union Ambassador Dayton earlier today of France's new position. These documents state in no uncertain terms that the empire of France agrees to recognize the Confederacy in joint recognition with Great Britain."

"Thank you so much, Your Excellency."

"Oui, Your Excellency. Merci beaucoup," Slidell followed.

"You're most welcome, gentlemen. William, the *Château* leaves Paris for London at ten o'clock tomorrow morning. It has truly been a pleasure, gentlemen. I wish the South all the best in her noble quest for independence. Hopefully, with France and Britain by her side, the South's longing to have a country to call her own will finally become a reality."

"I am sure it will now, Your Excellency!" Lytham exulted.

Chapter Twenty-Four

"Yes, Your Excellency. Without a doubt!" Slidell exclaimed.

"Good! Do keep me apprised, John, of the liberation of New Orleans."

"I will, Your Excellency. I will indeed."

With that, Napoleon smiled and headed off to meet with his military counselors, preparing for a potential war with the United States. William and John, for the remainder of the day, marveled at the realization that their toil for the South's independence was finally starting to pay off. In the evening, after supper, the two made a toast for the South and conversed about William's departure for England.

"I want you to realize, William, that you are carrying valuable information. I do not know the contents of the conversation Napoleon had with Dayton today, but the emperor is one to converse with much pomp. And I know Dayton is a sly fox. Accordingly, I wouldn't be the least bit surprised if he found out that you are leaving for London tomorrow. So be on extra alert for anything suspicious."

"What about the ship? Do you think it will be safe? Do you think I should take another?"

"Well, since the *Château* is only for diplomats, the chances of abduction are probably less than if you boarded a civilian craft. Moreover, with the French soldiers onboard, your safety should be even better secured. Still, be careful. If it was indeed Lincoln who ordered your apprehension in England, then I have no doubt that with the present information you are carrying, he will go to any length to abduct you now."

I ytham contemplated this and became further concerned. "What if the unthinkable occurs and they do succeed, John? Is my apprehension so significant that our recognition by France and Britain would then be lost?"

"I would like to think that wouldn't be the case, William. But in this game of international chess, even the slightest of winds can bring on the fiercest of storms."

25

October 14, 1862, was a beautiful morning indeed. The sun was shining radiantly in the bright blue sky. Not a cloud was in sight. William awoke with hope in his heart. He knew this day he was to land in England with British and French recognition to follow. His heart beat in eager anticipation.

Prior to leaving the Imperial Palace, William thanked Napoleon for all his kindness, hospitality and, most importantly, vital assistance in providing the South with its much sought after recognition.

That same morning, Darren and his accomplices arrived early at the Palace and hid in a nearby bush.

"There he is, men," McKenny pronounced.

"Yes, but he has six soldiers accompanying him, along with his own protectors. It would be far too risky to chance apprehending him here against these odds," Patlin expressed.

"I know. We'll follow at a distance, and when we see him board, we'll do likewise."

As William and his men boarded the *Château*, Darren and his accomplices followed suit. After viewing William for several minutes and seeing that he just had his protectors at his side—as the ship's soldiers were stationed at various locations throughout the *Château*—Darren ordered his men to act. The ship at this time was halfway across the English Channel as a dense fog emerged.

"Well, we're halfway there, men."

"I'll feel a lot better when we are there, William," Sawton responded.

At this time, Theo nonchalantly strolled to where the spare boat was located. The soldier guarding the boat was but a youngster. Patlin was pleased.

"Bonjour, monsieur. *Ca va?*"

"*Pas mal. Vous?*"

"*Mem chose.* Do you have a cigarette?" Patlin asked, hoping he was bilingual.

He was. "Why, yes."

Just as the soldier was retrieving a cigarette from inside his pocket, Patlin came upon him with knife in hand and stabbed him in the heart. The soldier died instantly, without a sound. Theo then stripped him and threw his body overboard with a weight from the deck tied to his foot. Having now donned the soldier's uniform, Patlin approached William and his protectors.

"Excuse me, monsieurs," he said in his convincing French accent, "may I please check your tickets and identification?"

"Of course," replied Retson, not suspecting anything.

"Certainly," followed Letton as Sawton and Lytham also presented their tickets and identification.

Patlin checked them. "Well, apparently there is a problem at the front desk, Monsieurs Retson and Letton. Your names weren't on the list."

"They should be," Lytham interjected, "they are my associates. I am William Lytham, diplomat for the Confederate States of America."

"Yes. I am sure then, Monsieur Lytham, it won't be a problem with your associates being here onboard. If you, monsieurs, could present your identification to the front so that our clerk may record your names."

Letton and Retson looked to Sawton and then to Lytham; Lytham proceeded to look to Sawton. Sawton, not suspecting anything awry, nodded in approval.

"All right, fine," they replied.

As Letton and Retson were led to the front of the ship, Jacob secretly followed. When the men reached an isolated part of the ship, the place where the spare boat was situated, Jacob, from behind, stabbed and killed Retson—who was behind Letton. As Letton turned to engage Jacob, Theo turned on him and delivered a mortal blow with a knife slice to the neck. Theo and Jacob then threw the bodies overboard with a weight tied on each.

Ten minutes later, Patlin returned to Lytham and Sawton.

Chapter Twenty-Five

"I am sorry, monsieurs, but I have just been told by my captain to inform you, Mr. Lytham, that we believe there to be a Union spy onboard seeking your apprehension. As a result, the front clerk has been ordered to go through all the names on the master list to make sure everyone checks out. Until this matter is thoroughly addressed, you and your colleague are to be escorted into one of our holding chambers with full protection. Your other associates are there awaiting you."

As Patlin led the two down the same isolated corridor, Jacob, as before, sneaked up from behind. This time, however, he fumbled his strike upon Sawton, enabling the latter to battle back. As William turned to assist Sawton, Theo knocked William unconscious. Sawton, in his struggle with Jacob, managed to turn the knife on the man and kill him. Yet, before Sawton had time to face Theo, the latter, with knife in hand, slit Sawton's throat. Gasping for breath, he attempted to fight on, but his attempts were rapidly failing. Sawton, now numb, dropped to the floor, and within seconds, Lytham's loyal and faithful protector lay dead.

Seeing the episode unfold, Darren entered the isolated area and, with Theo, threw the dead bodies overboard with a weight attached to each. They then quickly boarded the spare boat and, with William, made out to sea. Since the *Château* was in the midst of the dense fog, they were able to slip away undetected.

Within an hour, William regained consciousness. By this time, however, Darren had burned all the documents William was carrying to Britain. Upon waking, although realizing what was occurring, William was shocked to the core to see his once best friend staring him in the face.

"Darren!"

"Hello, William," McKenny replied with a sinister smile. "William, William, William. It has sure been a while, hasn't it?"

"Yet not at my choosing."

McKenny struck him on the left temple with a baton. "You traitor rebel son of a bitch! I would kill you right now if I had my way."

Lytham was silent as his temple bled.

"Well, at least your cause is down the drain. I burned all the papers you were carrying from France, and you will never see Britain again! I have finally gotten you, William. It has sure been a long, cumbersome struggle, but it has more than paid off."

"What do you mean?"

"This is what I mean." Darren pointed to his right ribs and right arm. "It took me months of recovery in the hospital."

Lytham looked befuddled.

"But at least I managed to slice your arm and leg up pretty good!"

Immediately William realized what Darren was saying. Shock seized him.

"Who'd you think it was? At least I succeeded in killing Jesson and Jedd after crossing the Potomac. That was sweet, especially Jedd. Seeing him die like a pig, squealing for his life, was priceless indeed!"

Chills encompassed William's body.

"I would love to have done the same to you, William, but I guess I just messed up that night. You're one lucky fellow. But not now! I have finally gotten you, and I am going to have a front-row seat when they hang your sorry behind back in Washington." McKenny struck him again with the baton.

Lytham's temple now bled profusely, but he was more energized. "You bastard, Darren. I always knew you were a good-for-nothing Northerner," Lytham countered, yet not really believing such.

"Damn you, William!" shouted McKenny, hitting him even harder. William was now close to unconsciousness as Darren prepared to strike him again.

"Please, Darren, let him alone!"

"Mind your damn business, Theo. I'll do what I want!"

"Fine. When Lincoln hears of this, don't say I didn't try to save you."

The words got through to Darren and he relented.

"You're one lucky man, William. I don't know why the president wants you back alive, but that is the only thing keeping you that way."

26

Having been notified by Napoleon earlier in the week of William Lytham's arrival onboard the *Château*, Queen Victoria sent her personal emissary, Alfred Lytham, along with Scotland Yard, to welcome back England's favorite cousin. Yet, when there was no sign of William onboard, with the spare boat missing and even blood found nearby, Alfred returned straightaway to Buckingham Palace with trepidation.

"Your Majesty! Foul play!" Alfred cried, gasping for breath.

"What? What is it, Alfred? What foul play? Where is William?"

"Gone, Your Majesty. I was awaiting William's exit from the *Château*, and when he didn't appear, I inquired as to his presence. The captain stated that the ship's spare boat during the crossing was taken and that the soldier guarding it is missing. Accordingly, with there being no sign of William or his protectors, with even blood found where the spare boat was located, the captain suspects foul play upon William, his protectors, and the French soldier."

"Oh no! Inform the prime minister of this at once. Tell him I would like an immediate audience."

"Yes, Your Majesty," Alfred replied, leaving.

"Oh, William, I hope you're all right! Oh, South, I'm not sure if you will be now," Victoria sadly sighed.

A short time later at Buckingham Palace, Palmerston met a somber Victoria.

"Good afternoon, Mr. Prime Minister."

"Good afternoon, Your Majesty. Alfred informed me of the news. I am horrified."

"As am I! What are we going to do now?"

"What would you like done, Your Majesty?"

Victoria sighed. "Oh, Palmerston, I just don't know. Although I would like to still declare for the South, perhaps William's abduction illustrates that the Union will go to any length to achieve its goal of defeating the Confederacy. Thus, even with France and Britain by the South's side, the Union may very likely continue to fight on—regardless of the odds."

"Indeed, Your Majesty."

"As a result, perhaps France and Britain's support might not prove fruitful in giving the South its independence. Moreover, we might even lose Canada in the process."

"Indeed, Your Majesty. Perhaps it is better then, for the time being, to await events overseas."

Victoria was saddened, yet resolved. "True, Palmerston, very true. I'll have Alfred send word of this to Napoleon."

The next day, Pierre Charleau, learning of William's plight, immediately informed his emperor. Shocked and horrified, Napoleon inquired as to how it could have happened.

"I don't know, Your Excellency. Not only did we have soldiers onboard, but everyone else was a diplomat."

"Well, something must have gone wrong, Pierre, or William would not have been abducted!"

Charleau was silent.

"I can't believe this! William had all the necessary documents and everything was about to transpire for us and Britain to recognize the South. Now this! Now this!"

"Well, Your Excellency, we can make new documents."

"I don't know anymore, Pierre. I just don't know. I presume the queen and the prime minister are aware of the situation?"

"Yes, Your Excellency. Our ambassador in Britain confirmed their knowledge."

"Presumably, then, they are sending over an emissary to discuss our reaction. At any rate, I want you to cross the Channel and inquire as to Britain's position. If they want to proceed in joint recognition for the South…well, since they did take the initiative on this, tell them that France will still agree. If they ask for our opinion, even suggesting to await events for the time being before declaring for the South, however, inform them France feels the same way. Perhaps the Union's determination in abducting William is but a foretaste of the ominous things they might give us if we sided with the South. I desperately want not to lose my Mexican Empire."

"Yes, Your Excellency." Charleau left.

Arriving on French soil later that day, Alfred was given an immediate audience with the emperor.

"Your Excellency, I bring grave news from the island: namely, the abduction of William Lytham."

"Yes, it is with extreme sadness that I am aware of such."

"As is Britain. Your Excellency, Britain would like to know if France's position has changed with the abduction of William Lytham."

"Actually, France would like to know the same of Britain, Alfred."

"Your Excellency, Britain is committed to honoring its pledge of joint recognition for the Confederacy with France. However, at this present time, we would like to await events across the Atlantic."

"Such is France's position as well, Alfred."

"Then I will inform my government, Your Excellency. Thank you."

"Thank you, Alfred. Give all my best to the island."

"I will, Your Excellency. And the island gives all her best to the empire of France."

Arriving on English soil that same day, Pierre was given an immediate appointment with the queen.

"So, Pierre, how is France?"

"Still grieving from the sinister seizure of William Lytham, Your Majesty."

"As are we, Pierre. As are we. I am truly saddened."

Charleau nodded. "Your Majesty, France is eager to ascertain Britain's position in the wake of William's abduction."

"What is France's position, Pierre?"

"Well, Your Majesty, for the present, France would like to await events overseas before declaring for the South along with Britain."

"Such is Britain's position as well, Pierre. I sent emissary Alfred Lytham to inform the emperor of this very thing."

Charleau nodded in acceptance. "Yes. Well, thank you, Your Majesty, for your audience."

"Thank you for coming, Pierre. Britain gives her best to the empire of France."

"And France gives her best to Great Britain also, Your Majesty."

27

Eventually William regained consciousness, thanks in large part to Theo's care. Patlin continually dressed Lytham's temple, cleaned his face, and set him in as comfortable a position as he could, as McKenny, at the other end of the boat, navigated.

"Thank you," Lytham expressed, waking and seeing Patlin attending to him.

"Don't mention it. It's good to finally meet you, William—though I wish it were under better circumstances." Patlin offered his hand. "The name's Theodore Patlin; I go by Theo."

Lytham shook his hand. "Hi, Theo. Nice to meet you."

"The pleasure is all mine, William. I apologize for Darren's actions."

"Oh, you don't have to. Darren and I go a long way back."

"I know, he told me. He's filled with total hatred for you, William. Yet whenever I ask why he feels this way, he cannot answer. All he says is 'those damn Southerners. They will never let you in.' That is all."

"Darren and I were best friends from when we were children, Theo. In fact, Darren was as much a Southerner as anyone I knew. Perhaps he went out of his way to try and become one because he was originally from the North. Yet, he didn't have to for me. I liked Darren just as he was. He does have a nice side to him, you know—although many times it may be hard to see. I'm sure our last years at Mobile Academy really affected him. In particular, a conversation he overheard between two Southerners questioning his loyalty to the South. Ever since, I think he has believed that all Southerners, including myself, feel the same way."

"Well that would make sense, William, because the hatred he has for Southerners is immense. I myself have much sympathy for the South. I even contemplated joining the Confederacy, even though I am from Indiana. I believe, like many with Southern sympathies, that the Union forced the South into taking the actions that she did. Yet, in the end, being from the North, I believed it would only be right for me to support the Union."

Lytham smiled kindly.

"Anyway, it is good to finally meet you, William Lytham. Your name in Northern circles is well known, though not necessarily for the greatest of reasons."

"Believe me, Theo, I loved and still do love the Union. My decision was hard to the core. Even to this day, I sometimes amaze myself at what I've done. To leave the United States? Truly, many times I have to give my head a shake. Yet, when all the circumstances come into play, I realize why I, and the rest of the South, decided as we did. We truly have developed our own way of life, Theo. One can truly know a Southerner from a Northerner just by meeting him."

"What about slavery, William? Isn't that what this war is all about? The South wants to continue the institution, while the North wants to abolish it?"

"Not for me or for the majority of Southerners, Theo. There is nothing we have wanted to do more than to end slavery. Yet, the North has made our economy captive to slavery, as we are caught in a vicious cycle of having to grow cotton and sugar to be economically viable. If the North would have only offered to help us diversify our economy…" Lytham started to fall into unconsciousness again due to the severe laceration on his left temple.

"Say no more, William." Lytham was now unconscious. "Darren, how much longer? William has fallen into unconsciousness again, and unless we get him to a doctor soon, we may lose him."

"We're almost there," McKenny answered reluctantly.

Theo's conversation with William greatly impressed him. Patlin now realized why Lytham was so cherished by all Southerners. He was the real thing, a true gem. There was nothing sinister or evil about him. He was a thinking man, making a decision only after much deliberation. Theo could see that William honestly believed that he, along with the South, had to make the decision they did. It was not made out of bitterness or disrespect for the Union. Rather it was one made out of great love for all of the United States, but a love that was not reciprocated north of the Mason-Dixon Line. The more Patlin was around Lytham, the more respect he had for him.

At length, the boat reached the Isle of Wight; as Dayton stated, a Federal fighter ship was stationed there. Boarding the vessel, William was taken to the ship's doctor with instructions that he be guarded by at least two soldiers at all times. Examining him, the doctor saw that William was suffering from a badly bruised left temple. Giving him alcohol to numb the pain, he stressed rest for the young man. Accordingly, as the ship sailed for Washington, William was allowed to recover, at least for part of the journey, in relative peace.

During the journey, William was rapidly recovering. Seeing this one day, the two soldiers guarding him instructed another soldier to inform Darren and the doctor of William's improvement. As Darren and the doctor were being informed, the two soldiers guarding William could not help but converse with the Soul of the South. Although Eric Kerr and John Hanton were known to be strong Federalists, they could not help but speak respectfully to the man who was so highly cherished by so many people.

"Good morning, William," Kerr greeted as Lytham awoke feeling his temple.

"Good morning."

"How are you feeling?"

"Better, I guess."

"The name's Kerr, Eric Kerr from Maryland."

Born and raised in the state of Maryland, Eric had strong Southern sympathies, though he rarely showed them. If the South had succeeded in securing Maryland, Kerr would have joined the Confederate side. Yet, since the opposite occurred, Eric believed it best to join the side governing his homeland. Kerr knew of William's fame and, with his Southern sympathies, was inwardly excited about meeting him.

"The name's Hanton. John Hanton."

John Hanton was born and raised in the state of Michigan. To Hanton, Southerners were a bunch of backward, good-for-nothing people; the more damage the Union could inflict upon them, the better. "The only way the South will ever understand the North's superiority is by Northern might," he would say. As a result, speaking respectfully to William was, in fact, a somewhat trying ordeal. The sooner the Soul of the South was hanged in Washington, thought Hanton, the better.

"Nice to meet you," Lytham replied as Darren and the doctor entered the room.

"How do you feel today, William?"

"Fine, Doc."

"Let me take a look. Well, the swelling on your left temple has definitely been healing. Yet, I believe it best that you continue to rest for the next few days until you have more fully recovered."

"Thank you, Doctor," Lytham replied as the doctor left.

"So, how is William Traitor Lytham this morning?"

Lytham was silent.

"I said, how is William Traitor Lytham this morning?"

Kerr, and even Hanton, were embarrassed.

Lytham was still silent.

"Answer me when I talk to you, traitor!" McKenny shouted, striking him with the baton.

"I will not rest until I see you die, Darren. And if God is willing, you will die by my hands."

McKenny struck him even harder. "You will not have that chance, William boy. Although I would love to kill you now, I am prevented from it. Yet, at least I will see you hang in Washington, like the dog you are! Men, continue to watch him. In three days time we are going to give our guest a medieval prison welcome."

William was at a complete loss. *How could my life have taken such a 180-degree turn in just a matter of days?*

Checking William three days later, the doctor deemed him fit for normal prisoner lodging. Yet, he would have been shocked at the type of lodging a prisoner like William received. Immediately, Darren led William to the ship's floor where, in one of the prison cell rooms, there were chains, whips, and cuffs. Fastening William to the floor with the chains and cuffs, Darren proceeded to whip William. "Is this the way you Southerners whip your blacks, William?" McKenny laughed, whipping him even harder. The pain in William was excruciating. After fifty lashes, William was turned over and whipped by Darren on his front side. After another fifty lashes, the man lay near death. While whipping William, Darren decided that if he died in the process, then so be it. He wanted William to suffer, and if he died while suffering, Darren no longer cared. *No president is going to prevent me from inflicting pain upon my mortal enemy*, McKenny resolved.

"I am so sorry, William," Patlin beseeched as he administered cold towels to the young man's body after the beating.

Lytham was near death, in tears. "I know slavery is wrong, Theo. No one should be whipped. When we are sovereign, it will all be ended. I know it will."

"Don't worry, William. Just relax. Everything is going to be all right."

Listening to William's words, Theo at that moment realized what the South was truly all about; that the perception of them being slave-lovers was not the reality. That they were not fighting for slavery, but rather, they were fighting to be free from Northern dictates, so that they, in turn, could free their society—both black and white. Theo was thus now resolved to help William escape. He did not know how, but he knew he would try.

After spending the next several days in the isolated prison cell, William was slowly recovering. He was still, however, sore all over and could barely move.

"Hey, kid, how you feeling today?" Patlin asked, administering to him.

"Hey, Theo. Sore. Extremely sore."

"I'll bet. I didn't believe anyone could survive the hell that Darren put you through."

"Thanks for your help, Theo. I might not have made it without you."

"That no-good son of a…Don't worry, William, Darren will get his! In fact, if I had my way, I would set you free right now to deliver the blow to him personally."

Lytham looked at him in a more focused light. "Really?"

"Absolutely, William!" Patlin declared, willing to reveal his new resolve. "You must be set free to help your people. They need you. Yet, the problem is that we are in the middle of the Atlantic Ocean. Moreover, you are under guard twenty-four hours a day and in the presence of a crew full of Union soldiers."

"What if you or someone you trust were to cross the Potomac River once we get to Washington and alert my president of the situation, telling him you are on the inside willing to help set me free?"

"Sure, William. Anything. But we will talk about this in detail when we arrive on shore. I am sure Darren will continue to have me attend to you. He trusts me totally, William. I think he believes I'm his guardian angel preventing him from killing you, for Lincoln is adamant that you be brought back alive."

Lytham gratefully smiled. "Thank you, Theo. You truly are a godsend to me. What about the others? Are there any other soldiers here willing to help us?"

"We may get Eric Kerr. But I will have to approach the matter delicately. As for anyone else, no. The ship is full of staunch, unwavering Federalists."

"Well at least one, and perhaps two, is better than none."

"True, William."

Lytham, now fully resolved, pondered the conflict. "This war is not over yet, Theo. Some may feel it is, but I sure don't. I, like my fellow countrymen, have given my heart and soul to this struggle, and I won't stop fighting until we are free from Northern tyranny."

"That's the right attitude, William. Never give up!"

Theo continued to attend to William. Realizing the vessel was rapidly approaching Washington, Darren decided to let William be for the remainder of the journey. Although he wanted to inflict more damage upon him, Darren realized how serious Lincoln was about William being brought back alive. At any rate, he was glad he at least had the opportunity to whip his archenemy most viciously.

* * *

In Richmond, Davis was eagerly awaiting the Confederacy's official recognition by Britain and France. When informed by Slidell's dispatcher on what had been accomplished overseas, and that William played a pivotal role in bringing about French and British pending recognition, the Confederate president was overjoyed. *Excellent work, William! I knew sending you overseas was our best move.* After waiting some four weeks with still no declared recognition, Davis became concerned. *What is going on? What is taking them so long? We should have long been recognized by now.* Eventually, another of the Confederates' dispatchers, Hugh Stratton, arrived from Europe and informed Davis of Lytham's abduction and Britain and France's resultant change in policy toward the Confederacy.

"No! You can't be serious."

"Yes, Mr. President. Slidell and Mason told me to inform you, unequivocally, that French and British recognition will now not come about until the battles on land change more to our favor."

"Dammit! What of William? Does anyone know his whereabouts?"

"No, Mr. President, not yet. But Slidell believes he is probably being sent by Union accomplices to Washington to be tried for high treason."

"Damn that Union. Damn them!"

"Would you like something done to Dayton or Seward for what the Union has no doubt done to William, Mr. President?"

"No. That will serve no use. France and Britain will continue their present course regardless of Dayton or Seward's presence. Damn that Union!"

28

News of William's abduction was joyfully received in the North. When informed that Britain and France were no longer interested in declaring for the South, Lincoln was ecstatic. *Well done, Darren. Our cause is saved!*

The president was accordingly in one of the most festive moods he had been in since the outset of the conflict. He felt for certain the outcome of the war was now no longer in doubt, that it was just a matter of time before the Confederacy was no more. Thus Lincoln, at ease, was looking forward to finally meeting the legendary William Lytham.

When the Union fighter ship arrived at shore with news that William Lytham was onboard, hundreds of people assembled to catch a glimpse of the man who, more than any other, personified the South.

Prior to leaving the ship, Darren made it clear to all that he was in charge: "Men, I will lead William to the president and in cuffs and chains. His procession will be a public spectacle wherein all can spit and curse upon him. I want three soldiers to our front, three to our back, and two on each side. I want everyone on high alert! Who knows what rebeldom might do to try to free him."

At that, William was led to the White House. A runner ran ahead to inform Lincoln of Lytham's approach. *So, at last, the time has come. I am to meet William Lytham, the Soul of the South,* Lincoln reflected. Never in his life had the president been nervous or intimidated about meeting anyone. Sure there were people who looked down upon him—believing him to be just a backwoodsman with no sense of gentlemanliness. Yet

Lincoln never allowed himself to be nervous, intimidated, or even bothered by such people. He knew who he was inside and was comfortable therein. He had a wife who loved him tremendously, and he was at peace with his Maker. As a result, nothing really made him nervous. When informed of William's arrival, however, Lincoln felt some unexpected apprehension. All of William's accolades—his illustrious career at Mobile Academy, his success as a spy, his achievement as a diplomat, and, to top it all, his absolute sincerity and passion—were qualities even the most hardened Federalist could not help but admire. Lincoln, perhaps more than any other, realized how cherished William was in the South. All of the thousands of letters sent by Southerners stating that William and the South would defeat him and his Yankees made this crystal clear. In fact, Lincoln knew that William was perhaps the only person who could almost single-handedly bring for the South what he earnestly sought to avoid: a nation to call their own.

Approaching the White House, William himself was nervous. Here he was, about to meet the man who was as much committed to the preservation of the Union as he was to Southern independence. And though he cringed to admit it, William respected the man who, like himself, was so passionate and sincere about his convictions and who, like himself, was willing to see them through to the bitter end. William knew Lincoln was highly respected in the North and that he was, in fact, the president of the United States—a position that for generations was looked upon with reverence not only by his own family, but also by the entire South. William could feel the butterflies in his stomach as he approached the White House.

Leading William, Darren was looking forward to the many boos, spits, and curses he anticipated would be delivered by the large crowd. Yet these did not occur. Unfortunately for Darren, he had failed to take into account the populace's composition. Since William's procession was being conducted in the state of Maryland, a state that had strong Southern sympathies since the outset of the conflict, the crowd, rather than calling for William's head, was calling for him to be released from his chains.

"Take off the chains. What do you think he is, an animal? Take off the chains."

"Take off the chains! Take off the chains! Free the Soul of the South!"

The chant was getting louder, and the people were getting closer. Darren started to worry. He feared that if he didn't free William from his shackles, a mob riot would break out and free him altogether. Having come so far, Darren wanted desperately not to take any chances of losing William now.

"All right, fine. Stand back and I'll take off the chains."

Lincoln could hear the commotion. Unable to hold back, he peered through the window and saw the masses of people gathered and cheering for William. His heart started to beat ever faster.

The entourage had reached the White House. As William entered, the Marylanders could not help but watch in an awed, curious silence.

Greeting the entourage, Secretary Stoddard informed Darren that the president was awaiting a William Lytham without cuffs and alone. Darren suggested it might be better if William was at least accompanied by soldiers to ensure the president's safety. Stoddard, however, said that the president was aware of this but did not feel William posed even the slightest of threats; he knew William to be a true gentleman. Accordingly, Darren, albeit reluctantly, obliged.

Walking to the Oval Office, William's heart beat in even greater earnest.

"Good afternoon, William," Lincoln greeted as Lytham entered.

William did not know how to respond. Should he respond with "Good afternoon," "Good afternoon, sir," "Good afternoon, Mr. Lincoln," or "Good afternoon, Mr. President"—even though Lincoln was no longer the South's, and thus his, president? In the end, William decided to postpone the decision. William was always one to be respectful. As a result, if William believed the occasion called for him to address Lincoln as Mr. President, he would. Yet, if Lincoln said something that burned him inside, William would let him know it by his response to his title.

"Good afternoon, sir."

"Would you like something to drink?"

"Thank you."

"Brandy all right?"

Lytham nodded.

Lincoln poured him one, as well as one for himself.

"Please, have a seat," Lincoln entreated as the two seated themselves. "William, William: the Soul of the South," Lincoln pronounced, pausing, looking in complete amazement and contemplation toward him.

Lytham was humbly quiet.

Each man had an inner respect for the other. Both knew the commitment the other was prepared to make to achieve their goal. Such a determination to see something through to the bitter end, regardless of the consequences, could only be respected—by friend and foe alike. And so, the respect was there.

There was a long silence. The men, at times, looked at each other but, at most times, just stared into the open air. They realized they were the exact opposites on the most important matter in American history, yet they respected the other because of it.

"How is your family in Mobile, William?"

"Actually, I haven't seen them in about two years. I hope they're fine." Lincoln nodded.

"How about yours?"

"Well, my wife is fine, but many of her family and friends back home in Kentucky no longer think too highly of us."

Lytham kindly smiled, realizing why.

Lincoln gave a return smile. "I wish it had never come to this, William."

"You're not the only one, Mr Lincoln. It has been pure hell!"

"Indeed!"

Since both individuals respected the position of the other regarding the conflict, they did not want to bring it up. But, in the end, it was inevitable. Years of sorrow and tragedy could not help but surface.

"Tell me, William, why did you leave the Union and cast your support for a cause that many consider slave-loving—a cause that has resulted in the needless loss of life on both sides of the Mason-Dixon Line. I knew you were against slavery more than any abolitionist ever could be, as you always argued against the institution to Congress and my predecessor. I always believed that you, in the end, would cast your support for the Union and that your support would have influenced the rest of the South to do likewise. I know it is with great joy that they look upon you."

"Mr. President, there was nothing I cherished more before the war than my United States citizenship. And there was nothing I wanted more than for our country to remain united until the end of time. It is true that I deplore slavery. I always have and I always will. It is wrong. Yet the decision we made to secede from the Union was not based on the desire to keep slavery. Southerners are not slave-lovers, Mr. President. The Confederacy is not a slave-loving cause. We for years have wanted to end slavery. If only the North would have offered to help us diversify our economy, slavery would have been ended long ago. Yet they never once offered this gesture. As a result, the South believed itself to be backed into a corner in which secession was the only way it could break free. When the South voted to leave, I, after much deliberation, realized that I had no rational or even honorable choice but to support my fellow people."

"I, like you, William, have always believed that slavery was wrong. Perhaps we could have indeed done more to help the South diversify its economy so that the need for slavery would not have been necessary. Yet, sadly, such is in the past. Right now there is a war on, and as the president of the United States, I will do whatever it takes to keep the Union preserved. I hope after the war, after a period of healing, the North and the South will be kindred again."

Lytham was somber. "I don't know, Mr. President. This war has torn a once-united country harshly asunder. Blood takes a long time to heal. To be honest, I don't know if it will ever heal. My hope is that after the war, the North and the South will be cordial neighbors—each having their own sovereignty."

"Well, I believe the outcome is no longer in doubt, William. Very soon the Confederacy will be no more."

"That is what the North has been saying for the past year and a half, Mr. Lincoln. If one were to believe them every time they stated such, it would be safe to consider such a person a fool."

"This time it is different. They say, William, your ability to perceive is exceptional. Thus I would not be surprised if deep down inside you realize this too. The majority of your ports are closed, and on land, we are increasing our victories."

"I realize things haven't been proceeding as well as we would have liked. Had it not been for the Union's underhanded tricks, such as my illegal apprehension, then I am sure that even you, sir, would have realized the trouble the North would be in."

"That is why we took the action we did, William. To me, any action for the preservation of the Union is justifiable—regardless of who may deem any such action illegal; just as the South has justified its existence even though the Constitution does not allow for individual states to secede."

"Our decision to secede was the result of the will of our people desiring to choose their own destiny—just as the thirteen colonies chose their own destiny against Britain in the 1770s. I am sure the action we took then wasn't considered legal by Britain's constitution either. There is a distinct difference between the so-called illegality of a people's will to choose their own destiny, and acts such as abduction against a person's will."

"William, all of the actions that we have taken as necessary for the preservation of the Union I am fully comfortable with and am at peace with. As the elected president of the United States of America, I deem it my job to make sure the entire nation continues to operate as one unit. I have taken upon this task with all my resources and will continue to do so—regardless of who may deem any particular action illegal."

"I am from the South, Mr. President, and we look upon the Union's invasion and suppression of our aspirations with the same illegality as the Union looks upon our secession. And so, like you, I will continue to give it my all, but for the Confederate States of America—regardless of the consequences."

Lincoln understood what William meant by "regardless of the consequences." Rather than beg for his life, the young man was prepared to pay the ultimate price for his beliefs. Such a man was right after his own heart.

"Do you believe, William, that God created us out of the same mold?"

Lytham was taken aback at the unexpected question. "I don't know, Mr. President."

"Well, I believe he did. Both you and I are determined to see our goal through to the bitter end, and we are prepared to pay the ultimate price to achieve this." Lincoln now contemplated his extreme unpopularity in the South. "In fact, I have a feeling, William, that, in the end, we will both pay the ultimate price for our beliefs."

William was truly taken aback by Lincoln's statement. He realized that he, no doubt, was going to die by hanging in Washington, but for the president to die? *What did he mean?* Although unsure, William did not want to offend.

"Perhaps, Mr. President. Perhaps."

"How is it, then, that God could have created two individuals out of the same mold who are on opposite sides in our dilemma?"

"I don't know, Mr. President. I have always believed that we must follow our hearts in life. Such a following of one's heart, however, may conflict with the following of another's. Yet, in the end, if we are true to ourselves, I believe that we are true to God. So perhaps it is possible then for individuals created with the same demeanor to have such polarizing differences."

Lincoln was impressed. "Perhaps, William. Perhaps." Lincoln now paused, somewhat reluctant. "You know, the actions that you have taken on the part of your beliefs are deemed here as treachery of the worst kind."

"I am aware of that, Mr. President."

"You realize what happens to people guilty of treason in Washington?"

Lytham was nervous but prepared. "Yes, Mr. President. The same penalty as those found guilty of treason in Richmond."

Lincoln gave a slight smile. "I guess there is no way I can persuade you to recant your actions and perhaps incur a less-drastic penalty?"

"No, Mr. President. There is no greater love I have on earth than for the South. I am prepared to face whatever this love brings about."

Lincoln nodded in respect. "I wish your passion and your love were for the same goal as mine, William. There is no telling how far you would have gone."

"My decision, Mr. President, was the toughest decision I have ever made. I believe it was just as tough for the rest of the South. To secede from the nation that dispelled British tyranny, with the North and South fighting side by side, was difficult beyond belief. But I, like the South, embarked upon this course of action only after much deliberation. I have no regrets, as I am sure my fellow countrymen have none either. I love the South more than all the riches and all the glory that any individual in the world can offer. I would rather die in poverty following my heart in life, Mr. President, than live in luxury betraying myself."

"My love for the Union, William, is also greater than all the riches and all the glory any individual in the world can offer. Thus I, like you, will continue to follow my heart in life. And there is nothing my heart wants more than for the United States of America to remain united. Accordingly, I shall do whatever it takes to keep it preserved."

Lytham gave a slight acknowledged smile.

Lincoln ardently wanted to continue to keep William in his company but, in the end, he realized that everything that needed to be said had been said. The time had come to say good-bye.

"Well, it has truly been an honor to have finally met you, William Lytham. I see why the South loves you so much."

"It has also been an honor to have met you, Mr. Lincoln. I realize why the North loves you so much."

"May God have mercy upon your soul, my friend."

"And yours too."

At that, the two shook hands, whereupon William left the Oval Office and was once again put in handcuffs under Darren's watch.

By himself, Lincoln felt a tranquil peace. He had finally met the Soul of the South and all of the accolades attributed to the young man were indeed not without foundation. He was a Lytham through and through. The same Lytham whose family endured excruciating sufferings at the hands of British monarchs for their faith. The same Lytham who served the courts of England and France with the greatest of distinctions. The same Lytham, even in America, who served previous presidents with unwavering loyalty, such as William's great grandfather Henry Lytham, who, along with George Washington, defeated the British at Yorktown, Virginia, in 1781. *Why did it have to come to this?* He sighed. *For me to make a public example of treachery by none other than a Lytham. Moreover, by the man who was deemed, and rightly so, the Soul of the South!* Lincoln believed that although the body may die, the soul is immortal. Thus William's death would not result in a turn for the South to obey the North, but rather cause even more bitterness in Southern eyes as to his presidency. Yet, because the North wanted to see William hang, Lincoln felt compelled to honor the wish of the people who elected him president.

Lincoln informed Stoddard that he would like to see McKenny. Accordingly, placing William under the guard of Theo and the accompanying soldiers, Darren excitedly entered the Oval Office.

"Good work, Darren," Lincoln greeted. "Mission well done."

"Thank you, Mr. President. I only wish I had accomplished the task earlier this year in Richmond."

"Perhaps it is better that you didn't. For if you would have succeeded, it would have most likely resulted in William's death. By apprehending him now, at least I had the opportunity of meeting him. I must admit, I am impressed. He truly is a gem, and I see why the South adores him so."

"Yes, Mr. President. It was William's persona that impressed me while I lived in Mobile; because of it, we were the best of friends, and I became one of the staunchest of Southerners for many years."

"What was it that made you change, Darren—to become one of our most formidable weapons? Was it something he said? I can't imagine William saying anything to make one switch allegiances so."

"Actually, it was what two of his subordinates said, Mr. President. They believed me to be a Northern spy on account of my family being from the North. I accordingly started to suspect that even William felt the same and that, in the end, no matter how much I tried, I would never be accepted as a Southerner."

"Interesting."

McKenny paused, trying to change the subject. "What of William, Mr. President? What would you like done to him?"

"Well, for the time being, have him taken to Old Capitol Prison where he will await execution."

"Yes, Mr. President!"

"Have him guarded under the strictest of security, Darren. No doubt the rebels may try to free him."

"Indeed, Mr. President. Consider it done. William will be guarded as no prisoner has ever been guarded before!"

"Good. Again, job well done, Darren. That is all for now."

Later in the day, Theo conversed with William in his Old Capitol Prison cell.

"Have the inmates in the other cells been rattling you at all?"

"Actually, no. The vast majority of them are Confederate sympathizers."

Patlin smiled.

"So, what of Kerr, Theo?"

"Kerr is on our side."

"Good. What of Lincoln? Do you know what he's planning to do?"

"No. McKenny conversed with him after you, but he has said nothing of the conversation. We do know he is being pressured by the North to have you hanged. However, he knows how unpopular his presidency is in the South, and executing you would only further aggravate the situation. Yet, since the North elected him president, the feeling is that, in the end, Lincoln will appease them."

"Theo, could you arrange for someone to inform President Davis of what is taking place and that in addition to you and Eric, I seek others, perhaps at least two, to assist in my escape?"

"Yes, William. I will do so at once."

"Good!"

"Anything else?"

"Continue to try and gauge Lincoln's deliberations. If he suddenly decides to immediately hang me, we may have to attempt an escape without outside help."

Leaving William's cell, Theo met up with Eric and asked him if he knew of someone who would be willing to embark upon the enterprise. He did. Eric's cousin, Brad Kerr, had always possessed a love for the Confederacy and was even hopeful that William's mission in Europe would succeed in not only granting the seceding states their sovereignty, but also in bringing about Maryland's admittance into the Confederacy. Thus, when Eric asked him if he would be willing to inform President Davis of William's entreaty, Brad was only too happy to oblige.

The following day, Brad set off on his mission. Crossing the Potomac and stating his purpose to the Confederate troopers who came upon him, Kerr was escorted to Richmond to speak with the president.

"Good evening, President Davis," Brad began, with two soldiers at his side. "I am Brad Kerr from Maryland, and I bring important news from Washington: namely, that William Lytham is at Old Capitol Prison awaiting execution and that he has two guards on the inside, one of them being my cousin, Eric Kerr, who are willing to help set him free. William seeks, however, help from the outside to solidify his escape."

"Consider it done! Did he say how many he would need?"

"Yes, Mr. President, at least two."

"Well, I will give him four. Hopefully that should be enough. We desperately need him back!"

29

After the passage of four months, William was still in prison without the opportunity of escape. Although the Confederate accomplices were in place around the prison, Darren's continual presence in front of William's cell thwarted any rescue attempt. In fact, McKenny even made up residence outside his archenemy's lodging to help prevent his worst nightmare from coming true. Yet, Darren could not help but be frustrated at the delay in William's execution. He realized that the longer William was alive, the greater was his potential for flight.

Darren was not the only one who felt this way. The entire North was seething in anger that William had not yet been executed. McDowell, aware of the North's wrathful mood, took it upon himself to be the nation's spokesperson to the president. He fervently wanted to see William hang. The man had destroyed his life, and he wanted him to pay. Perhaps only Darren wanted William dead more. Yet, Lincoln wanted desperately to avoid what the North was demanding. *If they could only meet the man,* he thought, *they would see that he is a true gentleman and that he is only following his heart in life. What crime is it to follow one's heart?* The conversation he had with William impressed him that much. Yet, Lincoln realized why the North wanted William dead. Part of it was retribution for the damage he had inflicted upon the Union cause. Yet, the majority of it was the fear that if he escaped, the potential for the North to win the war would still be in doubt, if not altogether lost. William truly had that ability. He had the talent of bringing about victory, even from the jaws of defeat.

Yet, Lincoln still did not want to see William die. He realized how unpopular he was in the South and was hopeful that if William could just be guarded under the tightest of security and not killed, then perhaps he could gain favor with the Southern people. Moreover, by freeing him after the North triumphed, the South might even accept his presidency. However, Lincoln realized that such hopes of keeping William alive were rapidly failing. The North was increasing in its unrest that William's head had not yet been served on a silver platter. Accordingly, Lincoln felt that he could no longer evade the North in its continual wish.

Such was his disposition when McDowell met with him at the beginning of March 1863.

"Mr. President, the North is anxiously awaiting the execution of William Lytham. It is now March, over four months since William's apprehension, and yet the man is still alive. If William doesn't hang soon, there will be great unrest."

"I know, Irv. I know. I'll be frank with you. I am caught in a precarious situation. The North wants William dead soon and may very well revolt if he isn't, while the South wants William unharmed and will have even more hatred toward me if he is killed."

"Mr. President, if I may speak freely?"

"Of course, what is it?"

"Mr. President, while it would be humane if William's life were spared and thus not offend the South, its people have already been offended by your presidency—so much so that they have been responsible for the deaths of thousands upon thousands of Union boys. The Northern people are the ones who put you in power, Mr. President, and continue to honor your presidency. In fact, they have given their lives to you. It would only be prudent to have their desire appeased—regardless of the South's reaction."

"True. Very true, Irvin. That is why, in the end, I will have William hanged. I've been desperately trying to find a way out of this: to have both the North and the South appeased. Yet, as you suggest, there does not seem to be a way in which this can be brought about. Moreover, in the end, the North is indeed where my support resides. Though I earnestly desire the South to embrace me, I realize that perhaps they never will and that I may need to offend them further in order to appease my constituents."

"Absolutely, Mr. President. I truly believe this is the best and only logical course of action."

"Yes…announce that William is to hang in front of Old Capitol Prison in two weeks, on the morning of the twentieth."

"Yes, Mr. President!"

Learning the news from McDowell, McKenny was ecstatic. *Now, at last, I am going to see the death of my mortal enemy.* Darren immediately informed Patlin, his second in command. Though outwardly receptive to the news, Theo was much concerned; this concern was not lost on William when they met later that day.

"What is it?" Lytham asked.

"Lincoln! He informed McDowell today that you are to hang in front of the prison on the morning of March twentieth. Furthermore, security is going to be increased to prevent any chance of your escape prior to that date."

"It doesn't look good then."

"It definitely could look better."

Lytham was terribly troubled. Death seemed to have a face. He felt for certain the end was near. "If I must die, then I must die, Theo. When I chose the South, I realized it might result in this. Only now it seems to be really hitting home…yet…I am prepared nonetheless. If I am to die for the love I have for the South, then I will die—and do so bravely."

Theo realized William thought his execution was a foregone conclusion. "Don't give up, William. You are not in the ground yet. We still have two weeks. We still have our Confederate helpers on the outside ready, on my command, to proceed."

"True. But with Darren guarding my prison cell with his soldiers twenty-four hours a day, and with this security to be increased until the day of my scheduled execution, my chances of escape are even worse."

"Yes, but remember, William, the mind works best under pressure. Let's think. There must be a time from now until the twentieth when we can attempt an escape under more advantageous circumstances."

Both earnestly thought. "Are there any festive events you know of between now and March twentieth?" Lytham asked.

"Well, there's Saint Patrick's Day, of course. Being of Irish descent, I would never forget that day."

"That's it!"

"What?"

"Darren's of Irish descent! In fact, that is his family's sacred day. He will definitely be out celebrating that night."

"Of course. Darren stated that on the night of the seventeenth there is going to be a huge Saint Patrick's bash at O'Shea's pub in downtown Washington—where he will be a guest speaker from eleven fifteen to eleven forty-five."

"Perfect! We will launch our escape at eleven thirty that night. Theo, do you have the authority to remove me from prison?"

"Only if I believe there to be a plot upon your apprehension and only to the Willard Hotel. I have the documents from Darren stating such."

"What if you and Eric were to remove me from here to the Willard Hotel on the night of the seventeenth, claiming just such a reason? Once I'm outside, our Confederate accomplices could assist us."

"Possibly. The difficulty would lie, however, in the increased security. Darren has ordered that no less than six soldiers are to be in your immediate vicinity at all times. Thus, even if I were to get Kerr scheduled to work with me on that night, that gives us only two. The other four soldiers would never support the plot."

"Are you sure there are no others who will help us, Theo?"

"Absolutely sure, William. There is no one working here, other than Kerr and myself, who even want you to live, let alone escape."

"How prepared are you to help me?"

"To the death, William. When I decided to help you, I embarked upon it knowing full well the consequences of such."

"You don't know what this means to me, Theo. I truly can't thank you enough! What of Kerr? Does he feel the same way?"

"Absolutely, William."

"Good. Perhaps our best course would be for you and Eric, along with my Confederate accomplices, to set upon the four soldiers once outside the prison." William then proposed a plan of action that Theo agreed upon. Theo then told William of Eric's and his desire to cross the Potomac with William and join the Confederacy.

"Certainly, Theo. We would be honored to have you both!"

"Thank you, William. So, Saint Patrick's night at eleven thirty it is then. Although Darren insisted I drop by for at least a drink, I'll leave the pub shortly after eleven."

"If we can pull this off, Theo, I would love to see Darren's face. That man has caused me so much grief."

"Don't worry, William. Good always has a way of overcoming evil. It may not look like it at times. It may even take longer than one expects. But, in the end, good always triumphs. And so you will have your day over Darren—I truly believe it. Maybe your escape will be that day. Or maybe even a greater day is awaiting. I don't know, but I do know that Darren's reign over you won't last."

Lytham was touched and kindly smiled.

"Anyway, I'm off to inform Eric and our Confederate accomplices of the stratagem."

"Theo, a kindly act is rarely forgotten, and your help will be something I'll never forget."

"Just remember, William, not all of us from the North are bad. Many of us are indeed saddened that the South has suffered as much as it has and have much sympathy for you."

That afternoon, Darren triumphantly returned to Old Capitol Prison.

"Good afternoon, men. Soldiers, I bring great news. Our most prized prisoner William Lytham—a.k.a. the Soul of the South—is to be no more come the twentieth of this month!"

"Hurray!" was the enthusiastic reply.

"Come the twentieth, men, William Lytham, by the president's decree, will learn the true price of treason: absolute death by hanging and in front of our prison."

"Hurray!" was the soldiers' even louder cry.

"However, the possibility of an attempted escape is much more likely. As a result, I want this entire prison put on high alert. Starting immediately and lasting until the day of his execution, I want no less than six soldiers guarding the traitor at all times. If the rebels are going to attempt to free him, I want them to know that we are more than prepared to resist. William must not escape!"

Darren proceeded to inspect the entire prison force—making sure everyone was at their assigned post and on high alert.

Yet, as each day passed, Darren became more anxious. *Everything is working too well. Something must be wrong.* As a result, he doubled the number of soldiers guarding the prison to a new number of fifty. In addition, McKenny situated undercover troopers around the prison walls in charge of detaining suspicious persons.

* * *

The night of St. Patrick's Day had arrived, and even Lincoln was celebrating the joyous event by attending the huge bash at O'Shea's.

During the party, although outwardly merry, Darren was a bundle of nerves. In fact, he could neither eat nor drink. He just kept thinking of William and of a potential escape. *What better night to escape than tonight when I am not at the prison?* he thought. Yet, this was the day he and his lineage had celebrated for centuries so that the saint of the Irish would look down upon them with infinite blessings. He had to celebrate this most sacred day.

At 11:07 p.m., Theo left the pub. Arriving at Old Capitol Prison twenty minutes later, he approached the guards outside Lytham's cell.

"Men, I have express orders from Lieutenant McKenny that the traitor prisoner William Lytham is to be taken to the Willard Hotel on account of a believed rebel plot upon his apprehension tonight." Theo showed them the papers stating his authority from Darren to do such.

"Yes, Mr. Patlin," one of the more senior troopers began. "But the lieutenant also stated that the traitor is to be guarded by no less than six soldiers at all times. So, please, select five and we, along with yourself, will accompany the detested prisoner."

"Indeed!" Theo proceeded to choose five, including Eric. "All right, men, follow me!"

Theo and another soldier made up William's front. Two soldiers were stationed on either side, while Eric and the final soldier were situated at the back. Walking past the various checkpoints, each checkpoint soldier was concerned at what was transpiring; yet, in the end, they realized that the papers Theo was carrying were indeed from Darren and that McKenny specifically placed Patlin in charge of Lytham after himself. Thus each checkpoint soldier, after some initial hesitation, allowed the entourage to proceed.

When the entourage left the prison gates, Fred Barner and Trent Lavcrow, undercover troopers in charge of watching the prison for the night, were also taken aback.

"Did Darren tell you of William's movement tonight?" Barner asked.

"No," answered Lavcrow. "I don't know what's going on. But he is being accompanied by six soldiers. So it must be legitimate."

"Let's follow, just in case."

The entourage had now reached a wooded area.

"Oh, my stomach!" Lytham cried, bent over, pretending to be in pain.

"What's wrong, traitor?" Patlin exacted.

"My stomach, my stomach is killing me!"

"See what's wrong with him," Patlin commanded the two troopers at Lytham's side, whereupon they immediately attended to him.

Then, at Theo's call of "Everything is going to be fine, traitor," the Confederate accomplices set upon the entourage. Quickly, Eric administered a mortal knife strike to the throat of the soldier at his side, while Theo did the same to his. William, at this time, just dropped to the ground. The Confederate accomplices were now upon the two soldiers attending to William. Being caught completely off guard, as well as being outnumbered, the Federalists were easy prey for the four Confederates. Hence, in the end, all four Union soldiers lay dead on the ground of the wooded area.

"Quickly, William!" the Confederates appealed.

"Wait, let me get these cuffs off him first," Patlin entreated, removing William's hand and leg cuffs.

William was immediately set on one of the Confederates' horses and, with Theo and Eric on the Confederates' other horses, they made haste to the Potomac River.

Waiting at length for the original group to reappear from the dense interior of the wooded area on their way to the Willard Hotel, Barner and Lavcrow became restless.

"What is going on?"

"I don't know, Fred. I don't know!"

Running to the spot where they saw the men disappear, Barner and Lavcrow saw four soldiers dead, with the hand and legs cuffs of William lying on the ground.

"Dammit! Lytham's escaped. It must have been an inside job. Secure the border! Secure the border!" Barner shouted.

Nearby soldiers, hearing the cry, picked up Barner and made straight to the Potomac; another trooper took Lavcrow on horseback to O'Shea's to inform McKenny. Hearing the news, Darren felt a sharp pain in his heart. "No, it can't be! What happened? What the hell happened?"

Not waiting for an answer, McKenny and McDowell, who was also at the pub, made for the river. At the Potomac's shore, McKenny, McDowell, and their soldiers could faintly see the Confederates crossing to the other side. The soldiers who had arrived prior to McKenny were hesitant to pursue the horses because of a potential Confederate response from across the river.

"After them, men. After them!" screamed McKenny.

Soldiers accordingly pursued, with Darren leading the way. Yet, during the pursuit, the Confederates from across the Potomac opened fire.

"It's no use, Darren," McDowell said. "We'll be slaughtered if we continue."

"No, proceed! William cannot escape!" McKenny cried.

McDowell grabbed him firmly by the arm.

"Listen, McKenny. He's gone. Gone! Accept it. I will not have our men continue in their pursuit and face certain annihilation. It's over."

Hearing these undeniable words from McDowell, McKenny collapsed in the water. The general immediately rescued him, while at the same time he ordered the soldiers to return to shore. Darren, half delirious, could only think that all he had worked for was now gone. It was too much for the young man to take. Returning to shore, McDowell directed soldiers to take the greatly unsettled McKenny to St. Elizabeth's Hospital for much-needed psychological recovery.

Across the Potomac, William was welcomed with open arms.

"William, welcome home!" the Confederates cheered, embracing him.

"It's so good to be home, men!"

"William, welcome!" Johnston greeted, arriving.

"General Johnston! It is so good to see you again also!" Lytham replied as the two embraced. "General, these are my friends who helped me escape: Theo Patlin and Eric Kerr," Lytham continued.

"Good to meet you, men. Thank you for all your help!"

"Our pleasure, General Johnston," Patlin responded. "It was the least we could have done to help correct the injustice of William's apprehension and subsequent treatment."

"Indeed, General," Kerr followed.

Johnston kindly smiled upon them both.

"So, General, how is the situation?"

"Well, we're trying to put the best face on it, William. But it is far from good. So many of our brethren are dead, and so many more believe their fate will be the same. We continue to battle knowing full well we may not see it through alive. Damn that Union! If they would only have honored the wish of our states, then none of this needless loss of life would have happened. The bitterness we have toward the Yankees is extreme indeed."

"I know. Had I only gained French and British recognition…" Lytham sadly expressed.

"Don't blame yourself, William. Had you not been so underhandedly abducted by the enemy, you would have undoubtedly accomplished that very thing."

Lytham smiled, grateful for the kind words. "Would it be too late to travel to Richmond tonight, General?"

"I believe so, William," Johnston answered, seeing Lytham's visible exhaustion. "I cannot even begin to imagine what you went through at the merciless hand of the enemy. It grieves me beyond words. You and your men rest here tonight. Tomorrow, when we are refreshed, we will go to our capital."

"Thank you, General," Lytham gratefully said.

With that, William, Theo, and Eric were shown to their respective lodgings. Wishing Patlin and Kerr a peaceful good night, Lytham entered his room—totally exhausted from his most trying ordeal in Washington. After thanking God and St. Patrick that he had made it through his escape alive, and praying that the South would still be victorious, the young man collapsed on his bed and fell sound asleep.

30

On March 18, Lincoln went to see McKenny at the hospital.

"Good morning, Darren."

"Good morning, Mr. President," McKenny sadly said.

"How are you doing, son?"

"Terrible. I am a total failure. If you wish to have me killed, I will most humbly accept."

"Darren, that is the furthest thing from my mind. You have not failed. Yes, I wanted William to face justice, but just because he escaped does not mean your mission was a failure. It was a success! Had you not apprehended him overseas, I am certain Britain and France would be at war with us, and our goal of unifying the Union would have undoubtedly been lost."

"But still, Mr. President, he escaped! William may very well return to Britain and France and persuade them to recognize the South once again."

"I am sure rebel Davis will have William do no such thing. My Emancipation Proclamation has gone over very well in Britain; so much so that the vast majority of the populace is now firmly on our side. The queen and the prime minister, albeit reluctantly, have accepted this reality, and Davis realizes this. And France will never recognize the South without Britain—especially with New Orleans in our hands. As a result, the only damage William can do now is if he fights alongside the rebels on the battlefield. Yet, the tide is firmly in our favor with our much-greater resources. It is thus only a matter of time before the South is defeated—with or without William's presence."

"If William does fight alongside the rebels on the battlefield, Mr. President, may I still pursue him? I feel as if my mission is only partially complete. I desperately want to finish the job."

"Certainly, Darren," Lincoln consoled.

"Thank you, Mr. President; and thank you for your kind words. Prior to your coming here, I felt like ending my life. I truly needed a friend, and thank you for being that friend—especially at this time, the lowest point in my life."

Lincoln was touched. "You're more than welcome, son."

Later in the day, Barner visited McKenny at the hospital, informing him that he suspected William's escape was the result of an inside job.

"What do you mean, inside job?"

"Exactly as I say, Lieutenant McKenny. My partner Lavcrow and I observed six soldiers leaving Old Capitol Prison last night at approximately eleven forty-five with William Lytham. We thought it unusual that William was being moved at all—let alone at that hour. So we followed them at a distance. As they walked through the dense part of a wooded area, we were expecting them to reappear. When they didn't, we immediately went to investigate. When we arrived, we beheld four dead Union soldiers and the hand and leg cuffs of the prisoner on the ground. The two other soldiers were nowhere to be found."

"Perhaps the rebels took them as hostages."

"Perhaps, Lieutenant, but the soldiers at the prison were presented with papers by Theodore Patlin stating that William was to be moved to the Willard Hotel on account of an impending rebel plot upon his apprehension. We were watching the entire area around the prison that night and did not see even an inkling of anything suspicious, let alone a rebel plot in the works."

"Well, I did give papers to Theo stating that if he suspected a plot to free William, he was to move him to the Willard Hotel."

"If Theo was present to account for his actions, Lieutenant, then his reasons for moving William could perhaps be proved sound. Yet for him not to be among the Union soldiers slain, or even found there alive, suggests that he participated in William's escape."

McKenny grievously conceded such. "Dammit! I trusted Theo—with my life. And he betrayed me!"

* * *

William awoke on March 18 rejuvenated but sad. His beloved South was in trouble and he knew it. He earnestly thought of what he could do next to help the Confederacy. Contemplating, he realized that his best course of action would be to confer with President Davis.

Before setting off for Richmond, William gave a heartfelt good-bye to the soldiers. It was hard for him to say farewell to the troops. Truly, he could see in their countenance the devastating effect the Union momentum was having upon their morale. He encouraged them, however, to not lose hope and to continue to give it their all for the glory of the South—for that was what he was doing.

Entering the Confederate capital, William marveled at its change from the first time his eyes had laid sight on it. Although Richmond was still beautiful, William could see sorrow and concern in the people's faces, as opposed to their previous energy and enthusiasm. Truly, the war was taking a grievous toll upon them. Nonetheless, when seeing him approach, the townsfolk were overjoyed and came out to meet him—giving William many hugs and kisses. William was so happy the South still possessed its Southern hospitality.

Entering into the midst of the city, William's heart joyfully leaped with thoughts of Melanie, while at the same time it exhibited a great sense of regret over his relationship with Nathalie. He knew, however, that before he went to see her, he would first have to see President Davis and discuss the military situation.

Looking out the window, seeing William approach the Confederate White House, Davis was overjoyed. Rather than waiting for William's arrival, Davis ran out of the building and welcomed the young man with open arms.

"William, welcome home, son." Davis embraced him.

"Thank you, Mr. President. And thank you so much for making it possible."

"Our pleasure, William," Davis declared as he led the three into the Confederate White House.

"Mr. President, I would like you to meet Theo Patlin and Eric Kerr—the men who assisted me inside Old Capitol Prison."

"Yes. It is great to meet you, gentlemen," Davis declared, shaking their hands. "Thank you. Thank you for all your help!"

"Our pleasure, Mr. President!" Patlin replied. "After the way the Union apprehended William, and their treatment of him thereafter, it was truly the least we could do. In fact, we would like to join the Confederacy, Mr. President."

"Thank you, gentlemen. We would be most happy to have you."

Lytham saw Davis pause. "Men, would you excuse me for a bit?"

"Absolutely, William," Patlin and Kerr answered.

Lytham and Davis entered the Confederate Oval Office.

"Would you like a drink, William? Scotch perhaps?"

"I would love one, Mr. President. Thank you."

"For the South!" Davis somberly smiled as the glasses clinked and they drank.

"So, how are things, Mr. President?"

"Well they could be better, William. Much better."

Lytham gave a downcast smile.

"You know, I never would have believed it. I knew the Yankees had the advantage over us in terms of resources, but I always believed that somehow, someway, we would see our aspirations through. I still do—though I realize the huge mountain we must climb in order to achieve it. Had we only gained British and French recognition."

"I know, Mr. President. Truly, there was nothing I wanted more than to accomplish that very task. And I had it within my grasp, until…"

"Damn those Yankees! They played the dirtiest of tricks."

"Indeed, Mr. President. Lincoln will do anything, regardless of its illegality, to suppress us."

"Did you converse with the man, William?"

"Yes, Mr. President, and he told me as much."

"What else did he say?"

"That very soon we will be no more."

Davis was downcast. "I fear such, William. I truly do."

"What can I do, Mr. President?" Lytham replied, determined. "Would you like me to go back to Britain and France and seek our recognition again?"

"Actually, things have changed since your abduction, William. Lincoln issued an Emancipation Proclamation, which has turned Britain's willingness to support us upside down."

Lytham was aware of the Proclamation, Theo having showed him a copy in Washington. "But, Mr. President, Lincoln's Proclamation is addressed to areas where he was no power to enforce it, namely the South. Moreover, his Proclamation does not abolish slavery; slave states under his control are not mentioned as being abolished."

"I know, William. But the British populace doesn't seem to acknowledge such; and, as a result, the queen and prime minister feel compelled to honor their subjects in our struggle. They have informed me that the only way we can now gain their recognition is if we achieve notable victories on the battlefield. And unless we gain British recognition, French recognition will not materialize—especially with New Orleans firmly in Yankee hands."

"Then I will join our army, Mr. President, and bring about notable victories!"

"I admire your resolve, William. I truly do. We do need you on the battlefield. Yet, for the present, I must decide where to send you. To put it bluntly, you are needed everywhere. We have incurred many losses in these past months—more than I care to admit. I only hope we can stem the Yankee tide and eventually make an offensive to regain lost territory."

Lytham nodded.

"While I decide, you are welcome to stay at the Spottswood Hotel, as are your friends."

"Thank you, Mr. President. I am most grateful—as Theo and Eric will be. In terms of myself, I may have some other arrangements, if that is all right," he said somewhat elusively.

"That's more than all right, William."

"Thank you, Mr. President."

Davis kindly smiled. "I sure hope we can pull through this crisis. There is no one whom I want to elevate higher in the Confederacy than you, William Lytham."

Lytham was truly touched. "Thank you, Mr. President. I am humbly honored by those high words."

Leaving the Oval Office, William informed Theo and Eric of the arrangement. Both Patlin and Kerr were grateful for the president's kind offer and immediately accepted. Upon bidding them cheerio, William made straight for Melanie's. *I can't wait to see her,* he thought. *Oh, do I ever need my love now.*

William, at that moment, realized how lonely it was to be single. Never before had he worried about his bachelorhood. To William, being a bachelor was the best of all worlds. No commitments, freedom without limitations. *Oh, yes, what a life,* thought William way back when. With the ordeal of the war and all of the heartbreak that ensued, however, William realized, all the more, that he wasn't born to be single. Rather, he was born to be married and have a wonderful family. And William wanted that marriage and that family to be with Melanie. He realized this even more through his relationship with Nathalie. Although Lytham admired the passion of the Latins, he realized he would only be truly happy with one of his own—a woman from the South, a woman after his own heart. And Melanie was that woman. William truly loved her and wanted to marry her.

Yet, will she still receive me? he thought. *It has been many months and things can change in a day. Thus to be many months away, well, that may as well be an eternity!*

Approaching the Wenning abode, William's heart beat ever faster. He knocked on the door. Having purchased twelve long-stem red roses from a florist shop along the way, William was hoping Melanie would be pleased. After one knock, there was no answer. William tried again—each passing second bringing more butterflies to his stomach.

Eventually, a voice from behind the door asked who it was. William could tell the voice belonged to Mrs. Wenning.

"It's me, Mrs. Wenning, William Lytham."

"William, welcome home!" she exclaimed, opening the door and hugging him.

"William!" Melanie exulted, running to William and embracing him.

"How are you, my love?"

"Fine now, William."

"I brought you a little something," he said, giving her the roses. "I hope you like them."

"I love them, love."

"Oh, how I've truly missed you, Melanie."

"And I you, William. I feared the worst when I learned of your abduction by the Yankees."

"William, you are staying for supper, aren't you?" Mrs. Wenning asked.

"I wouldn't miss it for the world, Mrs. Wenning."

"William, let's go for a walk," Melanie entreated.

"Sure, love."

"All right, children, but be on time for supper. We'll be eating at six."

"All right, mother. Let's go, William."

The two strolled to Hollywood Cemetery where they could be in private. Arriving, and seeing they were alone, the two passionately kissed.

"Oh, how I've missed you, William. Every day I feared for your well-being. I prayed to God every night that he would deliver you back to me safely. And he has! My prayers have been answered!" Melanie triumphed, kissing him even more.

Chapter Thirty

William was in a state of euphoria. He previously feared Melanie might not feel the same way she did before he left for overseas. Now, however, his fear was thoroughly dispelled. Melanie still loved him; a love as strong as ever.

"Oh, I love you, Melanie. I am so happy to be with you again. You truly are the love of my life."

"And you truly are mine, William."

William felt the time had come to ask Melanie to marry him. He realized she was the one for him. Yet, before receiving her answer, he wanted Melanie to know what had happened overseas. William had to be totally honest; Melanie deserved to know the truth.

Lytham was now on bended knee. "Melanie, let's get married! Will you marry me? But before you answer, there is something you must know."

Melanie wanted to say yes, but she realized from William's tone that he wanted to tell her something important first. "All right, William, what is it?"

"While I was in France…" Lytham began, grasping for the words.

"Yes, William. Go on."

"Oh, Melanie, this is so hard. I love you so much, and I don't know how to say what I am trying to say."

Melanie suspected what he was trying to say; she was hurt, but her love for him was greater than anything he could say to destroy it. "What, William?"

"While I was in France…I met a woman…and we had a relationship," Lytham revealed as he rushed the ending out.

"What kind of relationship?"

"The kind you might suspect."

Melanie was silent.

"I wanted you to know this before you answered. I love you, Melanie, and I want to be with you always and always be truthful to you. I would never do anything to hurt you. I am a faithful man. Before I left for overseas, although I professed my love to you, I didn't know if it was genuine. So, since we weren't married, I didn't feel my relationship in France was wrong. In fact, the woman helped a great deal in preparing me for my meetings with Napoleon. Yet, being overseas, I realized that it is you I truly love. I want to marry you, Melanie. I will be totally faithful. There is no other whom I want to be with more than you. Being away from you, I realized this all the more. Yet, if your answer is no because of my actions, I'll understand. Know that I love you, Melanie, with my entire heart and soul!"

Melanie gave a somewhat lengthy pause. "I appreciate your honesty, William. You didn't have to tell me this and I probably would have never found out." Melanie pondered such. "You truly are a gem, my love. I know you are a faithful man when you are committed. Are you committed to me now, William Lytham—unconditionally?"

"Absolutely, Melanie! You are the love of my life. You are my destiny. I will never leave you. Please marry me, love. Please say yes."

"Yes, William. Yes, I'll marry you! You are my love forever!"

The couple then kissed with a transcendent love.

"Let's go back home, William. I want to tell Mother the great news!"

Arriving home, Melanie could not contain her excitement.

"Mother. Mother! William asked me to marry him!"

"Yes, Mrs. Wenning. But it is fully contingent upon your approval."

"Oh, William. You have it! Congratulations, my dear! I am overjoyed," Mrs. Wenning exclaimed, embracing her daughter.

"Oh, Mother, I am so happy!"

"Oh, William, welcome to our humble family!"

"Thank you so much, Mrs. Wenning," William said as they embraced.

"Well, it is only four o'clock, children—supper won't be ready for still some time yet."

"That's all right, Mother. We wanted to come home early to bring you the great news!"

"Well, this is great, great news, you two. I am so proud of you both!" Mrs. Wenning proclaimed as all smiled.

"William, let's sit outside on the porch."

"Sure, Melanie."

"Can I get you two some lemonade?"

"That would be delicious, Mother."

"Thank you, Mrs. Wenning."

On the porch, drinking their lemonade, William and Melanie realized the topic of the war had to be brought up. Hitherto, they purposely had avoided it because of its sad nature and because they did not want to spoil their supreme joy. Melanie broke the silence.

"I wish the South's situation was as happy as our present joy, William."

"I know, Melanie," William sadly said.

"How was your mission overseas?"

"Well, we convinced Britain and France to recognize us as a sovereign nation, but before I was able to solidify this from both countries, I was abducted by the Yankees. Shortly thereafter, Britain and France changed their minds. So, here we are, without recognition from the two countries that would have undoubtedly set us free."

"I know, William. It is so sad. I feel as if our cause is lost."

"Well, we must not give up, love. We must fight on—no matter what the odds."

"William, we must be realistic. The Yankees, in a short while, may very well break into Richmond. The talk of the town has been full of such for some time. We can't continue to fight them on our own. They've had a vast military advantage over us right from the start." Melanie was now more vocal. "I don't want you to leave for the battlefield, William! I will not be another Southern widow!" Melanie started to weep.

"Melanie, I must join our army. How else are we to have a chance at winning if we don't give it our all?"

"William, our cause is lost! You gave it your all. We can't stem the Yankee tide. Their numbers and strength increase by the day. We are losing battle after battle, and our ports are virtually closed. Moreover, the Yankees are using every underhanded trick to make sure we lose. Lincoln will not stop until we unconditionally surrender." Melanie was now fully weeping.

Melanie's words struck William to the core. All the facts she stated were correct. The Federalists were getting stronger by the day. The Confederacy was losing battle after battle; all of their ports were indeed virtually closed. The Union continued to use underhanded tricks. Moreover, William had met Lincoln. What Melanie said about him was absolutely true. He would not stop until the South unconditionally surrendered. Thus, without help from overseas, the fate of the Confederacy did seem bleak. Yet William could not, and would not, give up. He had given his entire heart and soul for something he believed in and could not just give up now when the going got tough—regardless of how discouraging the situation looked. Yet, he also loved Melanie infinitely. He wanted desperately to make her happy, not to leave her a widow like so many of the Southern belles in this war. William was at an impasse.

"What would be the alternative, Melanie, if I don't leave for the battlefield? I just escaped execution in Washington. No doubt if the Yankees do win, they will capture and hang me. They are that ruthless!"

Melanie could hear what William was saying. *Yet, there must be a way*, she thought.

221

"We can flee, William. Flee to Mexico and wait till this war is over. Perhaps at that time, the Union will grant an amnesty to Southern fighters and we can then return home together. Or we can even sail to England. I am sure you will be welcomed there. I don't want to lose you, William. I don't. I couldn't bear it. I just couldn't!"

There was a long silence. William did not know what to say. He realized the conversation had to be stopped. Melanie was devastated. He now fully appreciated why they hadn't brought up the conversation earlier. The pain in this conflict was excruciating, and only misery and sadness would come from discussing it—especially between lovers. Yet, William realized he had to go and fight on the battlefield, that this was the only decision he could make. In fact, Melanie, deep down inside, realized this too. That was what perhaps hurt her all the more. She knew William. She knew his unconditional commitment to the South. Perhaps that was what she loved most about him. She knew William would never forsake his people. Moreover, deep down, Melanie didn't want him to either. The South was her home. The men and women were giving their all in the struggle for independence. How could William, considered by all to be the Soul of the South, ever leave his people? It was a contradiction in terms.

"I know how you feel, Melanie. Don't worry; everything will be all right. Tomorrow we will go to Saint Peter's Cathedral to see when Bishop McGill can marry us."

"All right, William. All right, my love," Melanie replied as they affectionately kissed and embraced.

At six o'clock, Mrs. Wenning announced supper was ready. The words were music to William's ears. The man was starved. Moreover, he had not eaten a decent meal for months. William now had not only the opportunity of eating a decent meal, but also a Southern one at that. Mrs. Wenning was also known as perhaps the best cook in all Virginia.

"What are we having, Mrs. Wenning?"

"Fried ham with red-eye gravy and biscuits, William. I hope you'll like it."

Lytham was ecstatic. "Like it? I'll love it."

Mrs. Wenning served the meal, and they all ate with gusto.

"How do you like it, William?"

"It's fabulous, Mrs. Wenning. I love it!"

"Thank you," Mrs. Wenning humbly replied, smiling. "So, William, how is the Confederacy?" she asked, realizing the conversation had to come up.

"Could be better, Mrs. Wenning. I desperately tried to gain our recognition overseas and almost succeeded, had it not been for…"

"I know. It is a miracle you managed to escape from Old Capitol Prison, William."

"Truly. Had I not friends on the inside helping me out, I would have most certainly been executed."

"Those damn Yankees! Oh, they have made life so miserable for us, William. Morale is so low in Richmond, as I imagine it must be in the rest of the South. There is even talk the Union army is building up its forces on the border—preparing for an imminent attack upon us."

"I wouldn't doubt it, Mrs. Wenning. When I crossed the Potomac, I witnessed many more Union soldiers and arsenals than I did the first time I crossed the river over a year ago."

"Do you think we can hold on?"

"I hope so. We have already paid a huge human price in holding on to what we have so far."

"Indeed. All those poor Southern boys who have lost their lives for our safety. It pains my heart!"

Lytham gave a pensive nod.

"What about you, William? What is your next mission?"

"I'm not sure. I conversed with the president earlier today and he is deliberating where I should be next sent. But he did state it will be on the battlefield somewhere," William uttered, glancing at Melanie who, in turn, looked sadly away from him.

There was a long pause by all. Mrs. Wenning, Melanie, and even William realized the danger of fighting on the battlefield. After a time, Mrs. Wenning broke the silence.

"Where will you be staying while he decides?"

"Well, the president has offered me a room at the Spottswood Hotel."

"What about staying here, William?" Melanie asked, looking at her mother to see if it was all right. "Downstairs, of course," Melanie added, still looking at her mother for approval.

Mrs. Wenning now agreed. "Yes, William. Why don't you stay here? We have an extra room downstairs that you are more than welcome to use."

"Please say yes, William," Melanie pleaded.

"Are you sure it is all right, Mrs. Wenning? I don't want to impose."

"No, no, William. It is more than all right!"

Lytham was grateful. "All right, I will. Thank you, Mrs. Wenning!"

"You're most welcome, William!"

"Mother, tomorrow William and I would like to see Bishop McGill about our marriage."

"Have you discussed when you would like to get married? I think the sooner the better."

"We agree, Mother. As soon as possible. Wherever William fights on the battlefield, I want him to fight as my husband."

"Well, I sure look forward to seeing my precious daughter at the altar with you, William Lytham."

Lytham was touched by them both.

After supper, the three leisurely talked about their lives, the lives of their families, and their hopes. It was so relaxing, conserving at ease, without worry. William cherished the moment.

At nine in the evening, the couple made for the nine-thirty showing of Shakespeare's *Romeo and Juliet* at the Marshall Theater. Although invited to watch the play with them, Mrs. Wenning stated that she wanted to get an early night's sleep. Watching the play, Melanie could not help but ask, "William, am I your Juliet?"

"That and so much more, Melanie."

"Well, you are truly my Romeo," Melanie replied as they lovingly kissed.

After enjoying the play, the lovers headed home. Walking, the two marveled at the beautiful Richmond night.

"The stars are sure beautiful, aren't they William?"

"Absolutely, Melanie. It is so nice to be holding your hand in the beauty of the South."

"Oh, William, how I look forward to being your wife."

At that, they embraced and kissed ever so affectionately. Arriving home, William was pleased to see the bedroom downstairs set for him. *Mrs. Wenning is certainly special*, he thought, now realizing her real reason for not accompanying them. Contemplating his present happiness, William felt at peace. He was going to marry the love of his life, and he was back home in his beloved South. With all the hurt suffered by the war and the unknown still to come, William was truly thankful that he had Melanie by his side—the person who could abundantly ease his pain.

31

The next morning, William awoke to see Melanie preparing flapjacks with sorghum syrup.

"Good morning, hon. I've made breakfast. Come and eat."

William kissed her. "You didn't have to do that, love." He tasted the food. "It's delicious, Melanie."

"Well, my mother is an exceptional cook and, well, I've picked up a few things over the years." Melanie smiled.

The two continued to enjoy the breakfast. Since Mrs. Wenning liked sleeping late, Melanie covered her mother's portion so it would still be warm upon her waking. After finishing their breakfast, William and Melanie made for St. Peter's Cathedral to see Bishop John McGill.

McGill was a well-known, pious bishop in Richmond. A man fifty-four years of age, he served the Virginian people with the utmost compassion and love. Bishop McGill looked on all people as images of Christ, and thus his love for them was great. Accordingly, Virginians who had the honor of knowing him truly appreciated the man.

Bishop McGill had heard of the fame of William Lytham. He was pleased to have finally met him some fifteen months ago when William attended mass after escaping from Union hands the first time. William was also impressed with the bishop. McGill's kindness, compassion, and concern for every individual delighted William greatly.

As Melanie and William entered St. Peter's Cathedral, Bishop McGill was praying the Rosary.

While waiting for him to finish, the couple prayed an Our Father and a Hail Mary together in the church and asked God to protect the South and each other. When Father finished reciting the beads, the two respectfully approached him.

"Good morning, William. Good morning, Melanie. What can I do for you two today?"

"Father, Melanie and I would like to get married and would like you to marry us."

"I would be delighted. You two do make a lovely couple. When would you like to get married?"

"As soon as possible, Father. William will very shortly be called to the battlefield. And when he goes, I want him to go as my husband."

McGill smiled. "Well, as you know, church proceedings usually have a waiting period before individuals can marry. This is to make sure they are truly committed to one another."

"Well, William and I are truly committed to each other, Father; and if it weren't for this war, we would not be rushing like this."

"Yes. Well, due to present circumstances, I believe an exception can be made. How about the day after tomorrow, say, eleven in the morning?"

"That would be fantastic, Father. Thank you!" Melanie exclaimed.

"Yes, thank you, Father!" Lytham echoed.

"It is my pleasure."

Arriving home, Melanie rushed into the house.

"Mother!"

"Yes, Melanie? Did the two of you talk to Bishop McGill?"

"Yes, Mother. He said that William and I could be married the day after tomorrow at eleven in the morning."

"Why, that is fantastic! You two will make a great couple."

William and Melanie smiled at each other.

"Well, I must inform our friends of the great news and the time of the wedding."

"Actually, Mother, with the sorrow of the war, we thought it would be best if we had a quiet wedding, with just you in attendance, along with liturgist Joe Kelly as the other witness."

"Well, if that's what you and William want, dear."

"It is, Mother, under the circumstances."

Mrs. Wenning pondered Melanie's request for a quiet wedding. Although she would have liked a grand wedding for her only child, she understood the concern. There was indeed much sorrow in the town, and to have a grand wedding might only serve to remind her friends of something they might never experience for their own children, due to the continual deaths on the battlefield.

On the following day, William awoke especially early to make breakfast for Melanie and Mrs. Wenning.

"Good morning, love."

"William, good morning. You shouldn't have."

"I wanted to, love," Lytham said, kissing her.

"It looks delicious."

"Wait until you taste it."

William had made crepes covered with blackberry jam.

"So what do you think, Melanie?"

"Fantastic, William. You're a great cook!"

Lytham smiled.

"Good morning, children," Mrs. Wenning greeted, entering the kitchen.

"Mother, you're up early this morning."

"Well, it is our big shopping day today!"

William proceeded to serve breakfast.

"This is delicious, William. I didn't know you were a cook."

"Well, I wasn't for the longest time, Mrs. Wenning. But then I learned the art of cuisine from a French chef."

"Well, he taught you well, William. I must say."

"Thank you, Mrs. Wenning," Lytham humbly expressed.

The three continued to enjoy their breakfast. Upon finishing, William insisted that he do the cleaning up in order to enable Melanie and Mrs. Wenning to get themselves ready for the busy day ahead of them. Melanie and Mrs. Wenning, realizing time was of the essence, were most grateful.

Completing the cleaning, William headed over to the barber shop for a trim. During William's hair cut at Barber's Best, Stan Toutly, the shop's barber, surprised him.

"So, tomorrow is your big day, William! Yes, when I got married, it was truly the happiest day of my life."

Lytham was stunned. "How did you know about the wedding, Stan?"

"It's all over town. My family and I are going to be waking especially early tomorrow to get front-row seats."

"How does everyone know? I can't believe it. Melanie and I tried to keep it low-key—you know, with the grief of the war and all. We didn't think it would be appropriate to publicize it."

"William, it is more than appropriate. This city, and indeed the entire South, has been yearning for good news for a long, long while. Your marriage is the talk of Richmond, and I wouldn't be surprised if it is the talk in all the South—word is spreading fast. I believe they will have to build a church a hundred times the size of Saint Peter's Cathedral to get in all the people."

"I am in total shock, Stan. Truly! I never would have believed it. But how? How did they find out?"

"Well, my son told me that his friend, altar boy Jimmy Quinn, overheard you and Melanie converse with Bishop McGill about getting married. Perhaps he was the one who started it."

William now recalled Jimmy near Father McGill at the time. "Yes." Lytham smiled. "Yes, that's probably how it started." Lytham smiled even more. "What a lad!"

Toutly smiled in return and finished William's haircut. "Well, there you go, William. What do you think?"

Lytham looked in the mirror. "I love it, Stan. Just what I needed—a nice trim. How much do I owe?"

"Nothing. It's on me."

"No, really, Stan. How much?"

"No, William," Toutly replied. "You've paid plenty by your presence here already. Have a wonderful day tomorrow, son!"

William left the barber shop thinking about the speed the news was traveling of his marriage. Moreover, he was shocked that so many people were planning to attend. *I must tell Melanie when I get back home*, he thought. *She will be amazed.*

William proceeded to Chrisham's Clothing Store. Entering the store, he was again met by his school professor.

"We thought you'd show—you know, with your wedding tomorrow and all."

Lytham smiled. "My, how news travels."

"Sure, when it's about you, William. Richmond is electric. The city is so looking forward to tomorrow."

Lytham humbly smiled. "Well, Professor, as you know, I need a suit. Do you think your grandson can help me out in that regard again?"

Robert, within hearing distance, entered. "Absolutely, William! We set one aside for you as soon as we found out about the wedding."

Robert had selected black wool trousers, a white silk shirt with gold buttons, a black silk double-breasted vest, a double-breasted black wool tailcoat with silk lining, a white silk bow tie with matching silk handkerchief; and for William's footwear, smooth black leather lace-up shoes. "So, what do you think, William? Do you like it?" Robert asked, after William left the change room. He looked absolutely fabulous.

"I love it, Robert."

Robert smiled. "We'd thought you would. It's yours. On the house."

"No, really, I must pay."

"No, William," Professor Chrisham interjected. "Tomorrow is your special day. The city is ecstatic. Your wedding has brought great joy to a grieving people. This is the least we can do for the Soul of the South," Chrisham smiled. "Nothing but the best, at the best price, for you, son."

Lytham realized that it was hopeless to continue his entreaty. "Thank you so much. I am abundantly grateful!"

It was not just William who was amazed by the unfolding events. Wherever Melanie and Mrs. Wenning went, the townsfolk treated them like gold, not charging them for anything. "You are going to marry the Soul of the South tomorrow," they trumpeted to Melanie. "Our Melanie Wenning, the princess of Richmond, is going to marry the pride and joy of our entire nation!"

William arrived home first and began preparing supper. Yet, ten minutes into his cooking, Melanie and Mrs. Wenning burst through the door.

"William! I have incredible news."

Lytham smiled. "I bet I can guess."

"The town is electric! Can you believe it, William? Everywhere we went, we were treated like royalty. I see why you don't want to flee. The South loves you! You are their pride and joy. I am so proud you are going to be my husband!" Melanie exclaimed, embracing and kissing him.

"This is truly going to be a joyous occasion," Mrs. Wenning declared. "Well, so much for our quiet wedding."

William and Melanie smiled.

"I'll go get supper ready."

"Actually, Mrs. Wenning, I've started cooking potato-topped casserole."

"That's perfect then, William," Melanie followed. "We'll all finish the cooking together."

"So, do you two have butterflies in your stomachs yet?" Mrs. Wenning asked as they leisurely conversed after supper.

"I sure do."

"Me too, Mrs. Wenning."

"Well, it's only to be expected. I know when I married your father, Melanie, I was nervous beyond belief. Marriage is a big step; it is ideally a continual commitment until the day you die. It is only natural, then, that one should have butterflies in the stomach before such an event."

William and Melanie could only smile.

32

The following morning, March 21, 1863, William, Melanie, and Mrs. Wenning all awoke early, earnestly getting ready for the big day. Approximately fifteen minutes before they were to leave for St. Peter's Cathedral, with Mrs. Wenning's somewhat run-down carriage as the means of transportation, someone knocked on the door, and Mrs. Wenning answered it.

"It's Walter Adams, Mrs. Wenning, President Davis' chauffeur. I am to take you all to the cathedral—compliments of the president."

Mrs. Wenning stood in shock as Adams removed his cap. Melanie and William joined them.

"Melanie, William, this is Walter Adams—President Davis' chauffeur. He is going to take us to the church!" Mrs. Wenning said, amazed.

"Thank you, Walter. We are abundantly grateful for the president's kindness!"

"You are all most welcome, William. President Davis said this was the least he could do."

"Is the president going to be there?"

"He and the entire congress!" Adams answered as William was truly taken aback.

Upon leaving the Wenning residence, William, Melanie, and Mrs. Wenning beheld a carriage with beautiful trimmings and vibrant young horses awaiting them. The weather itself was delightful: a splendid shining sun, a bright blue sky, and a caressing balmy breeze. Even the birds seemed to be chirping louder and happier than usual. *Truly, this is meant to be,* William thought.

Journeying in the carriage, William looked at his bride-to-be with the brightest of smiles. Melanie looked absolutely gorgeous. Her beautiful bright white moiré wedding gown with Venetian lace embroidered with orange blossoms and a bodice lined with muslin, her lovely long blond hair done up with curled ringlets flowing ever so carefree in the warm soothing breeze, and her beautiful blue eyes sparkling alight had William awestruck. *What a joyous event,* he thought. *I am truly blessed.*

During the carriage procession, crowds quickly formed alongside the road.

"Hurray, William! Hurry, Melanie! God bless you both! We love you!"

Crowds of thousands had formed. Everyone wanted to be part of the event. The populace was overjoyed—full of cheer and merriment. Truly, the procession was like a royal wedding in England. William and Melanie were completely taken aback. Something that was supposed to be conducted with as little fanfare as possible had turned out to be a gallant event—perhaps the most gallant ever seen in Richmond.

Arriving at St. Peter's Cathedral, William, Melanie, and Mrs. Wenning witnessed throngs of people gathered around the church's front entrance. The church was packed to the hilt, and those unable to get in wanted at least to see William and Melanie enter.

Entering the cathedral, William was led to the altar while Melanie and Mrs. Wenning were directed to the back in order to make their dramatic walk down the aisle. Approaching the altar, William noticed a man standing there waiting for him. Advancing closer, young William could not believe his eyes.

"President Davis!"

"Good morning, William. I heard you didn't have a best man, so I thought I would be the one—if you don't mind, of course."

After about ten minutes, the organ began playing, and Mrs. Wenning led her daughter down the aisle. All eyes were on the beautiful twenty-three-year-old bride, radiant and graceful. William's heart beat in earnest as he saw his angel approach. *I must be in heaven,* he thought. *God is truly good.*

Now at the altar, with Mrs. Wenning by Melanie's side and the president by William's, the two were married by Bishop McGill. When they exchanged their vows to love each other in good times and in bad, the crowd was joyful to tears. When Bishop McGill said, "I now pronounce you man and wife. William, you may kiss the bride," the crowd cheered ecstatically as William kissed his love.

As the newlyweds walked to the exit, the townsfolk festively tossed confetti upon the two. Addressing the populace as they assembled outside St. Peter's Cathedral, Davis proclaimed a reception for William and Melanie at the Richmond Roar.

"Reception, Mr. President?"

"Yes, William. Your wedding has given us joy in a time of much sorrow. It is the least I can do. In addition, you and your lovely wife," Davis continued, smiling at Melanie, "are welcome to stay at the Spottswood Hotel grand suite for the next seven days as a honeymoon present. The arrangements have already been made."

They were almost speechless, though they managed to stutter thanks as Davis looked on amused.

The reception was a fantastic gala. The newlyweds, along with Mrs. Wenning, were seated at the premiere table along with the president and his wife. The young couple danced the night away, and whenever the spoons clamored upon the plates, they happily answered the call by sharing a kiss. After the reception, William and Melanie were escorted by the hotel's senior butler, George Chapson, to their room.

The grand suite was fully furnished and equipped with the latest in luxury. As the newlyweds entered, they beheld a bottle of champagne, chilled on ice, with glasses situated therein—"Compliments of the President," the accompanying card read.

"I hope you like the room, Mr. and Mrs. Lytham," Chapson said. "If you want anything, please, just call."

After he left, Melanie turned to her husband. "It's perfect, William. Everything is perfect! This has been the best day of my life—by far. And now for our honeymoon…" Melanie continued with a radiant smile. "Which I know will make it even better."

With that, the two made love. Their passion was even greater than their anticipation. At last they were united. Not just in soul, but now in body; they were husband and wife—and the happiest pair in the world. If ever two people were made for each other, it was truly William and Melanie.

Throughout their stay in the grand suite, the newlyweds continued to savor each other's company—realizing in the process how dedicated they were to each other. On the sixth day of their honeymoon, William and Melanie were invited by the president and the first lady to attend Verdi's *Rigoletto* at the Metropolitan Hall. Entering the hall, the two were escorted to the auditorium's main seats, where Davis and his wife were awaiting them.

"Welcome," Davis said. "I hope you both enjoy tonight's performance."

"I'm sure we will, Mr. President. Actually, this is my wife's and my first time at the opera."

"It is? Splendid! Then I have no doubt you will both enjoy it. I find operas very soothing and relaxing. They seem to take one away from the worries of the present. As you might imagine, I am starting to attend operas more and more these days," Davis pronounced with a partial smile.

William gave a partial smile in return.

"So, are you two enjoying the grand suite?" Davis asked, smiling.

"Very much so, Mr. President," William answered. "We are having the time of our lives!"

Melanie blushed.

"I didn't know if you two were ever going to come up for air." Davis chuckled.

"Now, now," said Mrs. Davis.

The opera was a gallant affair. The host even went out of his way to pay tribute to Mr. and Mrs. Lytham in attendance. At that, the audience gave the newlyweds a most boisterous, cheering welcome.

At the opera's conclusion, Davis was eager to discover William's reaction to it.

"So, what did you think, William?"

"Truly fantastic, Mr. President. I see why the opera is so popular."

After a pause, Davis grew serious. "William, I don't mean to bring this up but…I was wondering if you could see me tomorrow morning, say around eight o'clock?"

"Of course, Mr. President," William answered.

Davis and his wife went on to wish William and Melanie a lovely evening and thanked them once again for coming, to which the newlyweds happily returned the good tidings. The two then had the complimentary carriage, which had brought them to the hall, take them back to the grand suite.

"So, what did you think, love? Do you like the opera?" William asked during the return carriage ride home.

"Oh yes, William. Immensely! The music was moving, the costumes were amazingly colorful, and the storyline was quite stirring."

"Indeed...Melanie?"

"Yes, William?"

"Melanie, the president asked me if I could see him tomorrow morning."

Melanie paused with apprehension but was resolved in what William had to do. "Well, I would have been a fool if I never expected such a time to come about. Oh, William, I don't want you to go on the battlefield. Yet, I know you must. The South loves you. These past days have made me realize this all the more. But, William, there is no one on earth who loves you more than I. If you must fight..." Melanie continued with a painful pause, "please, please be careful!" Melanie beseeched, kissing and embracing him.

"I will, Melanie. I will. You know you are my everything. You are my soul!"

Arriving home, the two made love. In fact, it was greater than all of the other times they had been together. The thought of separation made everything more intense, as did the thought of losing each other.

Walking to the Confederate White House the following morning, William was torn. He had made love to his wife the night before and it was wonderful. There was nothing he wanted more than to be with his wife and make love to her again. Yet, at the same time, he realized Davis probably now knew where he wanted him to go on the battlefield; thus he would soon be away from her. William was at least grateful that Melanie had accepted this reality.

Seeing William approach the Confederate Oval Office, Davis greeted him.

"So, how was your evening after the opera last night?" Davis asked, his eyes twinkling.

"Most fine, Mr. President," Lytham answered, smiling back. "Honeymoon time has to be the best time in a person's life."

"Indeed, William. Indeed," Davis agreed as he now pondered. "I remember when I was a newlywed. I'm not sure if I enjoyed being alive any more than at that time. Loving a woman, and being loved by her, has to be the greatest feeling in all the world."

"Now if we could only solidify our independence, my life would be complete."

"Mine too, William. And that is why I have called you here this morning. I've decided where to send you."

"Yes, Mr. President?"

"William, I've been debating whether to send you to Vicksburg—to help defend one of our last major ports from the Yankees and thus prevent their control of the Mississippi River—or to Fredericksburg—to assist General Lee in the defense of Richmond. I've decided upon the latter. Vicksburg is a long way from Richmond. As a result, it would take you a while to get there—perhaps too long for your services to be of major use. In addition, although Yankee General Grant will no doubt try his utmost to reduce Vicksburg, the town is situated in a heavily fortified location and, as such, should withstand all of Grant's assaults. Consequently, I believe that it would be better to send you to General Lee at Fredericksburg. I've been informed that there is a Yankee army not far off under the direction of General Hooker; an army that is increasing by the day—no doubt preparing for an imminent attack upon us. Since Fredericksburg is closer to Richmond, it won't take you as long to get there. Moreover, our capital must not fall, William. If Richmond falls, I fear our cause will too."

"Yes, Mr. President. I will go to Fredericksburg then. When would you like me to depart?"

"The sooner the better, William. You will assume your former title of officer but now in the Confederate army. General Lee has already been informed of your title and pending arrival."

"Thank you, Mr. President. I am honored. Can Theo and Eric accompany me?"

"Absolutely, William."

"Thank you, Mr. President."

"Good luck and Godspeed!"

Traveling back to the hotel, William thought of his eventual meeting with General Lee. Like William, Lee deplored slavery. Furthermore, like William, the general turned down the opportunity of serving with distinction in the Federal army to instead serve a greater post: the heart. They were Southerners and, as such, they realized they had no honorable, or even rational, choice but to support their fellow people. Finally, Lee, as Lytham had at Mobile Academy, had that ability to bring about victory on the battlefield, even from the jaws of defeat—time after time. It was thus not surprising that William eagerly looked forward to meeting the Confederate general who was so much like himself and who was also so loved and cherished by the Southern people.

"The president wants you to leave today for the battlefield, doesn't he?" Melanie asked as William entered.

William was somewhat quiet. "Yes."

"Then give it your all, William, and defeat those Yankees!"

William was taken by complete surprise.

"I love you, William, and I feel so honored to be your wife. You are my husband and there is no love I have greater on earth than for you. But I realize how much the South loves you too. So when you fight, give it your all. Don't worry about me. Don't allow any distractions to enter your mind. You must be totally focused," Melanie said with conviction.

With that, the two made love. It gave William a renewed determination to fight for his beloved homeland. With his wife lying by his side, William understood the words his father spoke some ten years ago: "Having a wife supporting you, William, is the best feeling in all the world."

After their union and then their heartfelt separation, William met up with Theo and Eric. After informing them of the mission awaiting them, the three, on horseback, headed to Fredericksburg.

"So, how was your honeymoon, William?" Patlin asked as they rode.

"Far too short, Theo."

"I'll bet," Kerr followed. "But I am sure you had the taste of love, William."

"These past few days with Melanie have been the best days of my life—by far!" he paused. "So, are you two soldiers ready to cause havoc on the Yankee army like I am?"

"Indeed, William!" the two answered.

After a cumbersome, lengthy ride to Fredericksburg, the three, on April 5, were within sight of the town. Seeing the massive display of Confederate troops, William could not help but reveal his emotion.

"There they are, men. Look at the sight. It is truly magnificent!"

"It certainly is, William! I desperately look forward to joining them, to give the Yankees all the hell they have given the South, including my Maryland!" Kerr declared.

Coming within fifty yards of the town, one of Lee's scouts, Greg Stillwin, approached.

"Who goes there?" Stillwin inquired.

"William Lytham and his accompanying soldiers," Lytham answered.

Stillwin's heart earnestly beat. "William Lytham? Please, come forth."

At that, the three advanced to Stillwin. Seeing William and now recognizing him, Greg removed his hat.

"It is a pleasure to meet you, Mr. Lytham. My name is Greg Stillwin, a scout for General Lee. Welcome to General Lee's army! The general is anxiously awaiting you. Please, please follow me."

As the trio were led to Lee's camp, the Army of Northern Virginia could not help but gaze upon the individual immediately following Stillwin; for word was spreading that the man was, in fact, the legendary William Lytham.

Paul Shen, who served with William at Mobile Academy, enthusiastically called out to his friend.

"Welcome, William!" Shen embraced him. "Welcome." The army cheered.

"I am truly glad to be here, men," Lytham responded. "Paul, I would like you to meet Theo Patlin and Eric Kerr. Without them I would still be in Old Capitol Prison—or worse."

"It's good to meet you both," Shen said.

Lytham smiled to the men around him. "So, how is the situation?"

"Much better now that you're here, William," answered a soldier. "We believe General Hooker is about to attack. Our scouts have reported their numbers are twice that of ours. But we have supreme confidence in General Lee and General Jackson. And now with you here, our victory is assured!" All the soldiers smiled.

Lytham smiled back. "Well, I guess it's best that I meet up with them, men."

"Indeed, William," Shen replied as the troops nodded.

At that, Stillwin continued to lead William, Theo, and Eric to Lee's camp.

"General Lee, William Lytham has arrived from Richmond," Stillwin announced, introducing him.

"William, William Lytham. It is so good to finally meet you. Welcome."

"The honor is mine, General Lee," Lytham replied as they shook hands.

"And this, of course, is General Jackson."

"It is truly an honor to meet you, General Jackson." Lytham humbly shook his hand. "Your legend is well known in the South, as is yours, General Lee. It is truly an honor to meet you both." Then he turned to his men.

"Generals, I would like to introduce Theo Patlin from Indiana, and Eric Kerr from Maryland—two men who played a pivotal role in freeing me from Old Capitol Prison and have asked to join our army here."

"Well, all of you have come just in time," said Lee. "We believe General Hooker will very shortly launch a strike against us."

"Well, we are ready to serve you in any capacity, General Lee," Lytham replied.

"Well, Theo and Eric, I have a division of soldiers comprised from the border states who have offered their services for our cause. Would you two be willing to join them?"

They were pleased at the offer to join such a division. "Yes, General Lee!"

"Good. Consider yourselves in that division then, men. William, I was thinking of placing you in charge of two divisions from Alabama. I know you are from there, and I thought you would do well at leading your fellow Alabamans."

"Indeed, General. Thank you!"

Lee continued. "Any news from the president, William?"

"Well, he is concerned about the safety of Richmond, as well as the preservation of Vicksburg on the Mississippi River, General."

"Well, holding Vicksburg is important, as is defeating Hooker here if we are to keep Richmond secure."

"Indeed, General."

"Come, William, let me show you to your divisions."

As William was led to his fellow Alabamans, Theo and Eric were taken by General Jackson to their division.

"Men, I would like you to meet one of your own, Officer William Lytham, who will be leading you in battle against Hooker."

"William!" the soldiers cheered, embracing him.

Lee smiled. "William, if you could rendezvous with me and General Jackson at around seven this evening, we need to familiarize you on the particulars here."

"Yes, General," Lytham replied as Lee returned to his camp.

William and his divisions talked at length about home and the war. And in his divisions were men William knew as a small boy, as well as others whom he led at Mobile Academy. One such solider from Mobile Academy was Jonathan Samton.

"We're so glad to see you, William. Many of us, prior to your arrival, believed we were doomed. The Yankees have far more soldiers than we. In fact, our scouts have stated they have up to twice our number," Samton said as the troops nodded.

"Don't worry, men. The Yankees know we are a determined people, that we are fighters to the end. We will emerge victorious in this battle. Believe me, it will happen!"

33

Toward the end of April, the Union army located just outside Fredericksburg became aware of William Lytham's arrival. Learning the news from Private Matthew Yonning on April 29, Hooker was much distressed.

"You must be joking, Yonning, and it is a most cruel joke at that."

"I wish I were, General, but I am not."

"No, dammit! How many of the soldiers know?"

"Most of the men, General. Word is spreading like wild fire. There is some panic in the ranks. Some of the generals are attempting to allay the fears of the soldiers, but without success. There is no one the troops want to face less on the battlefield than the legendary Officer William Lytham of Mobile Academy!"

"They are not alone. I still can't get over his escape from prison. We should have executed him. Immediately!"

"What should I tell the troops, General? They need cheering up. As of right now, there is nothing but bedlam."

"Tell the troops that I will speak to them within the hour."

Immediately Yonning exited, leaving Hooker to himself. After three quarters of an hour, having drunk in excess of five shots of whisky to appease his newfound grief, Hooker felt much better. Drinking was one of his favorite remedies to heal his ills. Thus, in much greater spirits, Hooker used this disposition to instill courage in his men, whom he addressed ten minutes later.

"Men, no doubt you are all aware that William Lytham has arrived in the rebel camp. You needn't be discouraged, however. Lytham is only one man. We are winning this war! We are on the verge of rebel annihilation. Moreover, in this upcoming battle, we have twice the number of the enemy. Not even Lytham can change that fact. We will continue to follow our course of action, attacking very soon. Don't be afraid, men. This is your finest hour. You have the opportunity to accomplish what no one has accomplished before: to defeat and even kill William Lytham on the battlefield. Do not shrink from this opportunity, men. Cherish it! Be thankful for it. You soldiers will become famous as the army that defeated William Lytham, the Soul of the South. Once the South's soul is defeated, victory over the rebels will be assured. God is on our side, men. We have nothing to fear. So renew your hopes, renew your courage, renew your passion, and very soon we will send the rebel army, with Lytham leading the way, straight to hell!"

A thunderous hurray filled the air. Hooker had done it. He had accomplished what he believed could not be done: to prepare the Army of the Potomac with a determined battle resolve after their learning of William Lytham's arrival. Sobering up and recalling his actual speech, Hooker impressed even himself. *Perhaps liquor is my valor syrup after all?*

Later that day, he summoned Generals Sedgwick and Stoneman and planned strategy.

"Sedgwick, I want your fifty thousand troops to strike just beneath Fredericksburg—to Lee's right. Stoneman, I want your ten thousand cavalry to strike to the rear of Lee's force—to break up his route of communication with Richmond. As for myself, I am going to catch Lee off guard. Since the rebel general will undoubtedly think our main attack will come from your advance, Sedgwick, I will lead my seventy thousand troops nine miles to the west of Fredericksburg, then cross the Rappahannock River and therein surprise Lee with a strike from the direction of Chancellorsville."

"Sound thinking, General," Sedgwick affirmed, "but what of William?"

"No doubt William will be fighting by Lee's side. So when we surprise Lee, we will surprise William."

"Yes, General," Stoneman concurred. "Sound strategy. To the battlefield!"

The following two days, April 30 and May 1, the Confederates witnessed the Federalists on the move. Hooker had now reached Chancellorsville, while Sedgwick had advanced just below Fredericksburg.

Realizing an imminent Union offensive was in the works, Lee held an emergency meeting with Jackson and Lytham in the late evening of May 1.

"Men, I believe Hooker is trying to convince us that his attack is aimed at Fredericksburg. Yet, I am not convinced. My scouts informed me that the bulk of his army is located about seven miles to the west of Fredericksburg, in an area surrounded by trees and heavy bush. No doubt he is hoping that by hiding behind such a terrain he will go undetected by us."

Jackson and Lytham nodded.

Lee contemplated strategy. "Jackson, take your force of thirty thousand and travel twelve miles around the Union army to its most vulnerable spot and attack. William, you and I, with our fifteen thousand troops, will keep Hooker in check."

"Yes, General," Jackson and Lytham answered.

The next morning, May 2, Lee and Jackson each gave an impassioned speech to the troops to prepare them for battle. After both speeches, the soldiers were filled with a renewed determination to gain victory over the Union. Yet, the men wanted more. They wanted William to speak. They wanted the man who had already given the South so much to be thankful for, to instill in them an even greater determination to defeat the Federalists.

"William! William! William!" they chanted.

Lee and Jackson could not help but oblige.

"William, would you say a few words?"

Lytham nodded. "My fellow people, this day will go down in history as one of our finest hours. Generations of Southerners will look upon this day as a day of pride, glory, and honor: the day their forefathers defended their homeland from the tyranny of the North." The Confederates gave a loud cheer. "Cherish this moment, men. This day we will become famous. We will be compared to the best armies of all time. And rightly so! The Union has twice our number, but they don't have our hearts!" The men listened breathlessly. "Our hearts are twice the size of theirs and they know it. We are fighting for our homeland, they are fighting to invade it. We are fighting to escape Northern tyranny, they are fighting to preserve it. Our cause is just. Our victory here will prove this to the entire world!" The cheers increased. "We will win, men! God is truly on our side. So, don't be discouraged, no, not for one second. Fight to the end! Never give up! We will redeem the blood of our brethren who have gone before us. We will show to the world that their deaths were not in vain." Louder cheers were heard throughout the Confederate ranks. "This is the hour we were born for, men. This is our destiny, and we will not shrink from it." The tension in the air was thick. "So, fight like tigers. Fight to the end. Never give up! We will never surrender!"

The crowd erupted. The men were ready, ready to crush the Federalists. Even Lee and Jackson marveled at the fervor that William had brought about. *Truly, this man is the Soul of the South,* they thought.

The cheers were so loud that the Union soldiers heard them. *It is William,* they thought. *William Lytham preparing them for battle!* Hooker was devastated. He had gone to great lengths to motivate his troops, and now the zeal of the Confederates was there to dispel his enterprise.

He deemed that the sooner they attacked, the better. The longer his troops had to ponder upon what William had said, the worse it would be. So Hooker emerged from his tent and urged the battle forward.

The Confederates, however, were ready. Jackson, on Lee's signal, marched his force around the Union army to search for the most vulnerable point of attack.

Jackson's march, however, was spotted early on by a Union scout.

"General Hooker, rebel Jackson and his soldiers are marching around our army," the scout reported.

"This is great news, son. They have come to their senses and are retreating. They realize they are greatly outnumbered, and not even William's presence can change that reality. This will undoubtedly make our crushing of Lee's army even easier."

Ever the wise owl, Jackson, in his uncontested march, reached Chancellorsville and found the Union's most vulnerable spot: namely, Hooker's separated right under the command of General Howard. Seeing Howard's force at camp leisurely relaxing, even playing cards, the Confederate General seized the moment.

"Attack, men! Attack! Destroy the enemy. Destroy them all!" Jackson exclaimed.

The fighting was horrific. Blood, wailing, and complete savagery were the calls of the day; Jackson's soldiers, having the advantage of surprise, thoroughly crushed the Federalists.

Meanwhile, Lee and William's troops were engaging Hooker's superior number and were even inflicting mighty damage upon them. William's exhortation prior to battle, and his leadership on the field, was having its intended effect.

"What the hell is going on?" Hooker cried.

"We are being thoroughly destroyed, General," Yonning answered. "The rebels are fighting like tigers out there. We are being overwhelmed!"

"I can't believe it. We vastly outnumber them," Hooker moaned.

Cries of sorrow and wailing could be heard throughout the Union divisions.

"We're dying like dogs out here, General Hooker," bemoaned a dying Federal soldier. "Help us!"

Yet, there was nothing Hooker could do. His bluff that the main force of his attack was aimed at Fredericksburg had not fooled Confederate General Lee for one second. Moreover, Jackson's troops were now marching to the headquarters of Hooker himself. Although his reserves prevented Jackson's soldiers from destroying his camp, those same reserves were needed in combating William's and Lee's divisions. Thus, without having reserves to battle on both fronts, Hooker's soldiers became helpless prey as William's and Lee's troops commenced a smashing rout.

"Fight on, men. We have them! Fight on. Destroy them all," Lytham exhorted.

The Confederates charged again. Seeing his divisions being penetrated, Hooker ordered an immediate retreat across the Rappahannock River.

"Cross the Rappahannock, men. At once! We must withdraw."

The Union retreat, solidifying the Confederate victory, was euphorically received by the Confederate soldiers. Yet their thorough victory at Chancellorsville was not without a price. General Jackson had died in the battle, as did William's friends Theo Patlin and Eric Kerr.

Hearing the news, William was bereft. This was his first real taste of war on the battlefield, and he now realized the true terror of it—as death always stares one in the face. Contemplating the deaths of Theo and Eric, William made a silent prayer, asking God to look after his friends in the afterlife who so courageously looked after him in the present one. Regarding General Jackson, William realized they had lost a brilliant leader—perhaps the best after General Lee; a man who had that great ability of succeeding in battle after battle, time after time.

The loss of General Jackson greatly affected the Confederates. Not only was Jackson a superb leader, but he was also a loving one. Never one to tell a trooper what to do unless he himself was willing to do it, General Jackson was truly loved by his fellow Southerners. Seeing the soldiers' visible sorrow, Lee, who after giving deep condolences to William on the plight of his friends, addressed the Army of Northern Virginia.

"Men, we have lost a great, patriotic fighter today," Lee began. "General Jackson will go down in history as one of God's chosen leaders. Truly, Southerners will always remember the valor of General Jackson on this day, the day the South proved to the world that their cause is just." Tears flowed from the men; Lee was visibly moved. "Don't worry, brethren, General Jackson's life has shown that fighting for the South is truly noble. We must continue his successful legacy, and we will!"

* * *

With the Union defeat at Chancellorsville, Hooker was beside himself. "I am ruined. Ruined, Yonning. Lincoln will have my head."

"Tell the president you had to contend with William Lytham."

"Do you really think that will appease him? Although Lincoln knows of William's success at Mobile Academy, we had twice as many troops. There is no way he'll understand this defeat. I am a dead man."

"General, what would you like me to do?"

Hooker realized his duty, but he was reluctant to act. "Head to Washington, Yonning, and inform the president of the battle's outcome. Also inform him that it was in large part due to the fighting and inspiration of William Lytham."

"Yes, General," Yonning answered and left.

"I am ruined!" Hooker cried to himself. "McDowell, I am only now starting to understand the complete sorrow you have been through as a result of William Lytham. Oh, woe is me!"

Hooker spent the next few days in a drunken stupor attempting to alleviate his pain. The defeat of his army by a vastly inferior number, led by the legendary William Lytham, was too much for the general to take.

Yonning quickly reached the White House.

"Good morning, Mr. President."

"Good morning, Matthew. What news from the border? Has General Hooker proven his worth?" Lincoln inquired, confident Hooker was victorious. "You know, Matt, I should have had him in charge of our troops long ago. If I had done so, I am sure we would have suppressed rebeldom by now."

"Mr. President…I desperately wish the news were good."

"What?"

"Mr. President…" Yonning paused, trying to find the words.

Chapter Thirty-Three

"No. No. No."

"Yes, Mr. President. We were thoroughly crushed at Chancellorsville."

"My God! My God! What will the country say? What will the country say? We had vastly superior numbers. I was informed we had as many as twice their number. How? How? I don't understand."

"Nor do we, Mr. President. Yet, William Lytham was instrumental in our defeat."

"My God! He has resurfaced! Yet, we had twice their men. We should never have lost. I know William is a successful military leader, but to bring about victory with half our number? It should never have happened!"

"If it is any consolation, Mr. President, General Hooker is taking the defeat terribly."

"How else should he react? He made a terrible mistake. Immense! William or no William, I put the nation's hope in Hooker's success."

"Would you like me to impart any instructions to him, Mr. President?"

"Yes. Where are we situated?"

"On our side of the Rappahannock. Lee's army is on the other side."

"What of our present numbers? Do we have enough to be comparable with Lee's?"

"Yes, Mr. President. We have about the same number as Lee's now."

"Then inform General Hooker that the Army of the Potomac is to act as a buffer between Lee's army and Washington. The capital must not fall!"

"Yes, Mr. President. Consider it done! What of William, Mr. President?"

"Well, if it was indeed William who played a major role in our defeat, perhaps we can even the odds a bit. For the time being, Yonning, I want you to remain outside my office. I will send you back to General Hooker soon, but not without another. Perhaps there is someone, after all, who can stop William. I should have everything in place shortly."

"Yes, Mr. President."

Lincoln had Secretary Stoddard summon Darren McKenny from his temporary residence at the Willard Hotel.

"Darren, your partially completed mission has the opportunity to be fully achieved."

"Mr. President?"

"William Lytham has returned. He has joined the rebel army, and they have just crushed General Hooker's Army of the Potomac at Chancellorsville with only half our number. Suffice it to say, I am infuriated."

247

"What would you like me to do, Mr. President?"

"Darren, I want you to join General Hooker and what's left of his army and stop William when we next engage the rebels. We currently have enough soldiers there to be at least on an even keel with them; though that is not much of a consolation, considering we had twice their number only days ago."

McKenny nodded. "Then I will leave at once, Mr. President, and complete my mission."

"Good. You will be accompanied by Private Matthew Yonning, General Hooker's dispatcher."

"Yes, Mr. President."

"Again, Darren, William must be stopped. I cannot stress this enough. If he is not stopped, our goal of winning this conflict is again put in jeopardy. If the man can bring about victory in an army against one double its number, ultimate victory by us truly cannot be assured. I cannot believe it! I knew William was a proven military leader at Mobile Academy, but I never thought he possessed the ability to help orchestrate a victory of this magnitude. We had twice their number!"

"Serving with William at Mobile Academy, Mr. President, I witnessed time and again his ability to bring about victory—even against overwhelming odds."

"Who is this William Lytham? Who is on his side?" questioned Lincoln, thinking of divine providence. "I shiver to guess."

"I will get the man! Consider it a foregone conclusion, Mr. President. Would you like him brought back alive?"

Lincoln paused, reluctant yet resolved. "It doesn't matter anymore, Darren. I want William stopped. Do what you must."

34

Savoring their huge victory, Lee and William conversed with relish and deliberation.

"Great work, William. You led your troops like a seasoned commander out there, and they fought with the utmost of courage and fortitude."

"Thank you, General. We gave it our all and, thanks to your sound strategy, we are now victorious."

Lee gave a humble smile. "What do you think we should do next?"

"I think we should follow up on this victory, General, and take the war to them."

"To them?"

"Yes, General. I believe we should invade Yankee territory."

"What would be the advantage of such?"

"Firstly, we will rejuvenate the spirits of our soldiers—as they'll see that we are just as able to invade the North as the North is able to invade us. Furthermore, if we can defeat the Yankees on their own soil, and therein threaten Washington, an end to the war that is acceptable to us may indeed transpire—because the North will realize that not only are we not going to be defeated, but also that we may even conquer them. Finally, a victory on their soil, with our forces firmly there planted, may even gain us our much-desired European recognition—Britain and France will see that we are more than holding our own and thus we should be recognized as a sovereign nation."

"Sound thinking, William. Sound thinking indeed. Where in Yankee territory should we invade?"

"Well, to threaten Washington, General, perhaps our best course would be to march west into the Blue Ridge Mountains in Virginia and then travel north until we reach Pennsylvania. Not only would we then be within Washington's vicinity, but we would also be situated in the fruitful farmlands of the Cumberland Valley to accumulate provisions for our troops."

"I like your thinking, William. Very sound. Let's do it, then. I will send dispatcher Hanney to gain the president's approval."

As Hanney arrived in Richmond, the thirty-three-year-old was greeted by the populace. A Richmonder himself, Henry was a key player in Virginia's secession. The cry "Freedom not tyranny," which played such a receptive note upon the ears of the Virginians, was his coined phrase. Thus, when the townsfolk saw him approach, they immediately welcomed their beloved son and, aware that he was Lee's main dispatcher, earnestly asked him of events at the border.

"Welcome, Henry," the crowd greeted.

"Henry, did we crush 'em Yankees?" a Richmonder entreated.

"That and much more! With William Lytham we crushed a number twice our size," Hanney proclaimed.

"Hurray! Hurray! Hurray!" the Richmonders exulted.

Viewing these events from his Oval Office window, Davis concluded that Hanney had brought good news from the border.

"Good afternoon, Mr. President," Hanney greeted, entering the Oval Office.

"Good afternoon, Henry. What news from the front? Gauging the town's reaction, I deem it most certainly good."

"Indeed, Mr. President. Indeed! We thoroughly defeated General Hooker's Army of the Potomac; an army that was originally double our size. William Lytham, General Lee, and General Jackson proved that we are the most determined fighters in all the world, Mr. President!"

"This is splendid news, Henry. Splendid! Our nation is materializing right before our very eyes!"

"Indeed, Mr. President! Moreover, General Lee and William deem it best to follow up on this victory by marching right into tyranny."

"They want to march into Yankee territory?"

"Yes, Mr. President. They believe that if we can be firmly there planted, and therein pose a formidable threat to Washington, we will be in a strong position to negotiate a peace treaty acceptable to us."

"Fantastic thinking. I like it. No, I love it!"

"They were hoping you would, sir. They sent me to gain your approval."

"Tell them they have it, Henry. In addition, inform them that I'll send Vice President Stephens north to negotiate an end to the war in our favor."

"Yes, Mr. President, I will. On a more somber note, sir, our victory was not without a price."

"What?"

"Mr. President, we lost General Jackson."

"How?"

"He was accidentally killed by his own troops. They believed him to be a Yankee as he approached from a distance. He died shortly thereafter."

"Terrible. Absolutely terrible! We will dearly miss him. He was an example for all of us to follow. General Jackson will go down in history as one of our best men."

"Indeed."

"How is William doing, Henry?"

"Fantastic. He has instilled enormous morale in our men and was most instrumental in our victory."

"Good! Give my best to the army, then, and defeat those damn Yankees in tyranny."

"Yes, Mr. President. We will!"

With Hanney's exit, Davis pondered recent events. He was truly saddened that they had lost such a fine commander in General Jackson, and to have lost him at the hands of his own men. On the converse side was their huge morale-boosting victory at Chancellorsville and their strategy of taking the war onto Northern soil. Davis was elated that the South was showing the world that though they might have less in terms of military resources, their ability to win, notwithstanding, was an undeniable sign that they deserved to be recognized as a sovereign nation.

Hanney, on his part, made straight to the Army of Northern Virginia.

"General Lee. William. I bring good news from the president."

"Did he agree, Henry?" Lee asked.

"Most abundantly, General. We are to proceed with our resolve. In addition, the president is going to send Vice President Stephens north to negotiate an end to the war in our favor."

"The pendulum is finally starting to swing in our favor!" said Lytham. "I sure look forward to giving the Yankees all the hell they have given us on our soil."

* * *

Having returned to the front, Yonning immediately met up with Hooker. "Good afternoon, General."

"I sure hope it is, Yonning. What news from Lincoln?"

"He wants your troops to act as a buffer between Lee's army and Washington. The capital must not fall, General. The president is adamant about that!"

"Fine. It will be done."

"General, I would like you to meet Lieutenant Darren McKenny," Yonning continued as Hooker and McKenny shook hands. "The president has sent Darren to apprehend or eliminate William Lytham. Darren has known William since they were children. Moreover, it was Darren who seized William overseas."

"Excellent. Well, it is good to meet you, Darren. I am sure you are aware that William was instrumental in our defeat at Chancellorsville."

"Yes, General. I have made it my mission to get that man. And I will. And this time it will be for good!"

"Great. Matthew, how did the president take our defeat?"

"Terribly, General. Most terribly."

"Am I still in charge?"

"Nothing was said to the contrary."

Hooker was relieved, believing Lincoln still had faith in him. "Yonning, go back to Washington and ask the president for reinforcements."

"Reinforcements, General?"

"Yes, we took a tremendous hit at Chancellorsville. We need more men."

"May I speak freely?"

"Of course. What is it?"

"General, the president was furious at our defeat, especially being defeated by a force half our size. If you were to ask him for reinforcements, having as many men as you once did, I fear he will say no."

"Yonning, I, like the rest of us, wish we had not suffered to the extent we did. The simple fact is that we did and, as a result, we need more men. Go and tell Lincoln this."

"Yes, General."

Chapter Thirty-Four

Matthew made his way back to the White House, while Hooker's men acted as a buffer between Lee's army and Washington. Throughout this time, the Union troops were trepid about having to face William Lytham on the battlefield again. They wanted desperately not to do so. In fact, after Chancellorsville, many of Hooker's soldiers deserted him, while those who did stay lost all confidence in his ability to lead. As a result, a great sense of hopelessness permeated the Army of the Potomac.

Seeing his troops in such a low countenance, Hooker realized something had to be done. Accordingly, he ordered a halt to the march.

"Men, I would like you to meet Lieutenant Darren McKenny—the man who successfully seized William Lytham overseas."

The soldiers became ecstatic. Finally, there was someone, and that someone was in their midst, who could contend with William Lytham.

"It is so great to meet you, Lieutenant McKenny," they said, shaking his hand and embracing him.

Overcome with emotion and beseeched to speak, Darren could not help but oblige.

"Thank you. Thank you, my fellow Americans. There is nothing I want more than to defeat the Soul of the South. Don't worry, men, we'll get him. Heed my words! It will come to pass. Moreover, by defeating William, we will also defeat and expel the rebel army presently in our homeland. Then your families and your land will be forever safe from rebel anarchy. The Army of the Potomac will soon show the world that the Southerner is nothing but a no-good, backward villain, one that will never, ever match the superior Northerner."

"Hurray! Hurray! Hurray!" was the deafening uniform response. They had changed from utmost despair to joy. Hooker had done it. By introducing McKenny, the general had replaced his soldiers' hopelessness with confidence in victory. The troops, to a man, believed they would crush William and the Confederates the next time they faced them.

At the White House, Yonning was given an immediate audience with Lincoln.

"Matthew, good afternoon. I didn't expect you back so soon. Is everything all right?"

"Mr. President, General Hooker would like more troops."

"More troops? He had twice as many as Lee only days ago, and now he has the gall to ask me for more troops? What does he want, to have ten times as many soldiers as the rebels? Does he feel that such a number would then solidify victory? This is outrageous!"

"Sir, the general has stated that because of our hit at Chancellorsville, we need more men."

"No. Absolutely not. You tell Hooker that he will get none. I am sure he will understand the meaning of my answer," Lincoln pronounced, thoroughly annoyed.

"Yes, Mr. President."

Matthew returned to the Army of the Potomac and informed Hooker of Lincoln's answer. Even Hooker, a man known for naivety, understood what the answer meant.

"Then it is over. I am defeated. That William Lytham has added me to his trophy of defeated generals! First he defeated McDowell as a spy, and now he's defeating me as a soldier on the battlefield. I am destroyed. I am completely destroyed!"

"It's all right, General…"

"It's not all right, dammit! Don't you understand? I am nothing now. I will forever be remembered as the general who was smashed by the rebels with half my number, and all at the hands of the Soul of the South! Why me? Why me?"

Yonning was silent. Although he felt bad for Hooker, he was not surprised at Lincoln's response. He had even tried to warn Hooker of such a reply. Yet, Hooker would have none of it.

"So be it, then. I realize what the president is saying, and as a soldier I will obey my commander in chief—I shall resign."

Hooker bid the troops farewell. To be honest, they were relieved he was going to be replaced. The general had led them into a dreadful slaughter, which generations of Northerners would look upon as a day of great shame.

With Hooker's resignation, Lincoln once again replaced the Union's premiere general. This time he elevated General Meade to the position.

Although the Army of the Potomac would rather have had General McClellan as Hooker's replacement, they were at least contented that Meade was a cognizant, committed, and courageous fighter. In fact, at Chancellorsville, Meade was the only Union leader whose troops put up any type of effective resistance against the Confederates. Accordingly, with Meade at the helm to devise strategy, and McKenny in their midst to boost morale, the Union soldiers firmly believed that victory was nigh.

35

Approaching Gettysburg, Pennsylvania, Lee's advance unit under General Heth surveyed the town for Union soldiers. Spotting Federal cavalry, he asked his superior, General Hill, for approval to take them out on the following day before they continued their march farther into Pennsylvania—as the current day, June 30, was almost over.

"Is it a large force, Heth?"

"No, General, my unit alone will be able to clear them out."

"All right, come tomorrow morning, clear them out!"

Accordingly, on the morning of July 1, 1863, Heth's unit advanced to the town of Gettysburg to eliminate the Union presence. As they approached, Heth noticed that the Federal cavalry, led under General Buford, was unmounted.

"Look, men. There they are: the detested Yankee cavalry. And look, they are unmounted! We have the advantage. Fire upon them, men, with all your might. Take them down, all of them, like the dogs they are!" Heth exhorted.

Heth's force fired upon the unmounted cavalry with deadly accuracy. The Union soldiers, unprepared for the attack, fell like flies.

"General Buford, help!" a Federalist cried. "We are being overwhelmed. We need reinforcements."

"Don't worry, I'll get them. Hold your ground," Buford frantically answered.

Buford immediately sent dispatcher Roy Brickson to inform the closest force, led under General Reynolds, that reinforcements were desperately needed.

"General Reynolds, the rebels are smashing our cavalry at Gettysburg. While coming here, I informed your advance units of the crisis. They themselves made haste to assist General Buford. Yet, we desperately need additional reinforcements, General. No doubt more rebels are on their way."

"Tell Buford we will join them, Brickson," Reynolds said. "Men, there is a war at hand!" he proclaimed to his soldiers. "This is our opportunity to redeem the blood of our slain at Chancellorsville. Away!"

Seeing the onset of Reynolds' advance units, Heth immediately sent dispatcher Paul Witton to General Hill to inform him of the need for reinforcements. Witton made haste.

"General Hill, General Heth desperately requires reinforcements at Gettysburg."

"Why? He informed me that his unit alone would be able to clear the Yankee cavalry."

"Yes, General, we have been. But the Yankees are sending in reinforcements. Thus we need reinforcements also. It is urgent, General Hill!"

"Consider it done!"

As Hill's corps set off to reinforce Heth's unit, Hill's dispatcher Dan Pallet made haste to inform General Lee of the growing battle.

"General, General Heth and General Hill's forces are engaging Yankee detachments at Gettysburg. No doubt the entire Army of the Potomac will soon enter upon the scene."

"Gettysburg? I did not expect to face the Yankees so soon, and especially there of all places," said Lee. "Inform General Hill that we are on our way."

"Yes, General!" Pallet quickly left.

"Men, glory awaits us," Lee declared to his soldiers. "Now is the time to gain our much sought after independence. Let's go!"

At that came a thunderous roar, as the troops zealously set forth to battle.

During this time, Heth and Hill's forces were overpowering Buford's cavalry and Reynolds' advance units, as Reynolds and his main force had yet to arrive.

Accordingly, seeing the Union soldiers about to be overwhelmed, Buford commanded them to make for Gettysburg's high ground—in the hopes the Confederates would not pursue against such a terrain. Yet Hill, smelling blood, ordered the Confederates to attack them even on the ridge. Buford, seeing the potential end in sight, urged the Federalists on.

"Fight on, men! Never surrender. Fight to the death. To the death!"

The Confederates, however, were still pressing and would not be denied.

"Fight on, men!" Hill exhorted. "We have them. Crush them. Crush them all!"

Just when it looked as if the Union was about to lose the ridge, as well as be thoroughly destroyed in the process, General Reynolds and his main force arrived.

"Thank God you're here, Reynolds!" Buford exclaimed.

Realizing the strategic importance of the high ground, Reynolds ordered his main force to immediately fortify the terrain's vulnerable areas.

Seeing this, Hill was angry beyond belief.

"Dammit! It's Reynolds. His force is securing the ridge. Take down that Reynolds. Take him down now!" Hill commanded to a sharpshooter at his side.

The Confederate sharpshooter, now perfectly positioned, fired with deadly precision upon Reynolds, striking him in the heart. Reynolds died instantly.

"General Buford," a Federalist cried, "General Reynolds has been shot and killed!"

"Bloody hell," Buford moaned. "Continue to hold your positions, men. We will not relinquish our ground. Fight on!"

And fight on they did. Unfortunately for the Confederates, the Federal flanks did not falter with Reynolds' death, as the Union was still in possession of Gettysburg's high ground.

Arriving within sight of the battle, Lee and William surveyed the situation.

"What do you think, William?"

"Well, to be honest, I wish we were the ones in control of the ridge, General."

"What if we were to attack to gain the ridge, William—as the full Army of the Potomac has not yet arrived?"

"Such an enterprise would take many men, General, with the outcome in doubt—since their defense from the strategic position may very well be able to withstand our assault, even with their lesser number."

"True, William." Lee contemplated. "The Yankees do have the advantageous position, and for us to acquire it would take a momentous effort. Yet, coming off our triumph at Chancellorsville, I believe we should still attack to gain the high ground prior to their army's full arrival. No doubt the Yankees are still in a state of despair from their thorough defeat, while our troops are at their highest levels of confidence. We can't risk the pendulum swinging to the Union's favor, William, by not doing battle."

"Yet what of Jeb Stuart's cavalry? They are supposed to inform us on the whereabouts of the Union army. If the Army of the Potomac is close to arriving, perhaps it would indeed be best not to challenge the Yankees under these conditions."

"True. Well, I am still awaiting Stuart's return."

Just then, Confederate General Longstreet emerged.

"General Lee! William!"

"Yes, Longstreet. What is it?" Lee inquired.

"General, this is Mr. Harrison—one of my spies who claims to know where the Army of the Potomac is located, as well as other important information."

"General, the Army of the Potomac is heading north to confront our troops here at Gettysburg. However, they are still a ways off and shouldn't arrive before midnight."

"Good. We still have time then."

"In addition, Lincoln has replaced Hooker with General Meade as commander of the Potomac."

Lee pondered. "Meade, yes, I know the man. I served with him in the Mexican War. A fine soldier, but not one that can't be overcome."

"There's more, General." Harrison looked at William. "Lincoln has sent a man by the name of Darren McKenny to assist the Army of the Potomac."

William looked shocked.

"William? What's wrong? You look as if you've seen a ghost," asked Lee.

"General, may I converse with you in private?"

"Of course. Harrison, continue to keep us apprised."

Chapter Thirty-Five

"Yes, sir," Harrison said as he left.

"General, Darren McKenny is the man who apprehended me overseas. I fear that Darren's presence in the Army of the Potomac is serving to boost their morale."

Lee nodded in agreement.

"With McKenny in their midst, the Yankees are no doubt reinvigorated. As a result, our momentum from Chancellorsville may no longer be in place. Moreover, to engage a revitalized Union army with them possessing the strategic high ground might be suicidal. For myself, I have no problem facing the man. I have a score to settle against him that I eagerly seek to fulfil. What concerns me, however, is the morale-boosting effect Darren is most certainly having upon the Army of the Potomac. If the Yankees have a renewed vigor to fight to the end, as our troops possess, then I fear that our victory over them—with them in possession of the high ground—may not come about."

"Well, Harrison did inform us that the Army of the Potomac shouldn't arrive anytime before midnight. In addition, perhaps their advance units are unaware of Darren's arrival. And even if they are, our men's intrepidness as a result of your presence and of our victory at Chancellorsville is at least the same as theirs, if not greater, wouldn't you say?"

"I would, General."

"With such being the case, I believe we should still attack to gain the ridge; for a victory will enable us to control the strategic position when Meade's army does arrive."

At that, the two made straight to the battle with the full force of the Army of Northern Virginia.

The arrival of Reynolds' main detachment was shortly followed by the arrival of Union General Hancock's corps.

"Secure the hills, men," Hancock shouted, arriving. "Assist your fellow brethren against the rebel assault. Hold the ground at all costs," Hancock beseeched as his soldiers further secured Gettysburg's ridge.

Facing these overwhelmingly odds, Hill and Heth's forces still bravely fought on; yet their defeat was, by this time, a foregone conclusion.

Seeing Lee and William approach, Hill immediately reported to them the situation.

"General Lee, William, the Yankees have reinforced Gettysburg's ridge with the recent arrival of General Reynolds and General Hancock's forces, making it virtually impossible for our forces to overtake them—even though we eliminated Reynolds in the hope that his soldiers would break ranks and flee."

"Do you think we can overtake them, Hill, and seize the high ground before the Army of the Potomac arrives at midnight?"

"Yes, General, absolutely."

"What do you think, William?" Lee continued.

"I think we can then too, General."

"Let's do it, then. Soldiers, join your brethren and seize the ridge. Fight! Attack!"

The battle was fierce. Blood, sorrow, and death were the calls of the day—on both sides. William led the Alabama divisions as he had at Chancellorsville. Knowing what was expected of him, as well as what was most necessary for victory, William led his soldiers into the fray.

"Fight, men. The battle is ours!" Lytham beseeched.

William instilled the utmost of bravery and courage in his troops. In fact, they were fighting like soldiers possessed. Believing the high ground absolutely secure, Hancock was shocked as Lytham and his divisions began a rout upon the Federalists.

"Fight on, men. We have the enemy on the run. Take them down! Take them all down," Lytham exhorted.

William was fighting like a lion. He was fighting like his ancestor Thomas Lytham under Alfred the Great. Fighting like his forefather John Lytham under Henry V in France. Even fighting like his great grandfather Henry Lytham under George Washington at Yorktown, Virginia. All who saw the battle unfold, on both sides, were amazed. William's passion instilled in his men the same demeanor. The divisions were fighting like ten of their size.

"Retreat, men. Withdraw. Withdraw into Gettysburg!" Buford cried, seeing the Union break down.

As the Federalists reeled back from the high ground at Gettysburg, Lee ordered General Ewell to secure the strategic position. Yet, just when it looked as if the Confederates would finally gain the coveted position, Ewell's follow-up was nowhere to be found, enabling the Union to maintain a hold upon the same.

"What the hell is going on? Where are Ewell and his men?" Lee exacted.

"General," Ewell's dispatcher commenced, "General Ewell interpreted your order to follow up our success 'if he found it practical' as being given the choice of either securing the hills or giving his soldiers time to rest. Since his troops were exhausted from the fighting, he chose the latter."

"I can't believe this! Ewell knows that is how I speak. Damn that Ewell. If I still had Stonewall Jackson, he would have followed up our success and completely routed the enemy."

Accordingly, as the day ended, the Union soldiers miraculously—or rather, due to Ewell's error—continued to maintain possession of Gettysburg's high ground.

Yet, Buford was far from content. If Meade's army did not arrive soon, the Federal troops would most certainly be crushed by Lee's Army of Northern Virginia on the following day.

Pacing to and fro, Buford could take the anxiety no longer.

"Where the hell is Meade? His men should have arrived by now!" Buford vented to General Doubleday.

"Look, General, there they are," Doubleday declared, spotting them. "General Meade. General Meade. Over here."

"General—thank God you've arrived!" Buford followed.

"What's the situation, Buford?"

"We narrowly escaped the dagger, General. William Lytham and General Lee led the bulk of the rebel army against us this past day. We were overwhelmed. We were forced to commence a retreat to the low ground of Gettysburg. Had they followed up their attack, we would have undoubtedly lost this high ground—as well as been annihilated in the process."

"Well, the Army of the Potomac is arriving, even as we speak. By daybreak, we'll all be ready to battle. Men, I would like you to meet Lieutenant Darren McKenny. Darren, this is General Buford and General Doubleday."

Buford and Doubleday had already been informed of Darren's previous success upon William and of his recent entry into the Army of the Potomac.

"Nice to meet you, Darren," Buford said. "We're so glad that you're here."

"Indeed, Darren!" Doubleday followed. "William Lytham led his troops like soldiers possessed. In fact, it was because of William and his divisions that we almost lost our high ground."

"Dammit then! I wish I were here but one day earlier, so that I could have faced and destroyed that Lytham!" McKenny said, full of discouragement and frustration.

"Don't fret, Darren. Tomorrow you'll get your chance," Meade consoled.

"Yes, General," McKenny replied, better collected.

"Men, reinforce the ridge," Meade commanded to his arriving soldiers. "Assume the position of an inverted J three miles along the hills."

That same night, Lee and William learned of Meade's arrival and of his army's assuming position.

"What are you thinking, son?" Lee asked, seeing William pensive.

"General, the situation is now difficult, if not impossible. The Army of the Potomac is securing the ridge. Unfortunately, we will have to postpone our campaign—until a time when we ourselves control the strategic position."

"William, I believe we can still take them."

"General?"

"The way we fought out there today, I have no doubt that, come the morning, we will crush even the entire Army of the Potomac—regardless of their possession of Gettysburg's ridge!" Lee pronounced.

Although aware of the difficulty in accomplishing such a task, faithful William embraced his general's resolve and mentally prepared himself for battle. During his preparation, William thought of his eventual showdown against Darren McKenny on the battlefield. Most likely he was going to face him tomorrow sometime. *Yes*, he thought, *God has provided me with the opportunity to settle the score against that degenerate. You better be ready when we clash, Darren, because I certainly will be.*

36

On the humid, overcast morning of July 2, Lee prepared the attack.

"Longstreet, I want you to take your soldiers and storm the Yankees' left flank. Ewell, I want you and your troops to engage the Yankees' right flank. William, I want you, with your divisions, to attack the outermost boundary of the Yankee line."

"Would it not be better, General, if we all sweep around the Yankees' left flank and thus, by placing ourselves between the Army of the Potomac and Washington, force Meade to evacuate the high ground to engage us?"

"No, Longstreet, that would be impractical. We don't know for certain that Meade would evacuate the ridge with that course. And if he doesn't, we run the risk of losing our hard-won momentum gained at Chancellorsville."

Longstreet nodded, yet would rather have employed his own suggestion.

"Any questions, gentlemen?" Lee asked.

There were none.

"So, let's do it, then," Lee commanded.

Witnessing the Confederate advance, Meade passionately addressed each of his generals.

"Sickles, Longstreet is marching his soldiers to attack yours. Defend the left flank at all costs! "

"Yes, General."

"Slocum, Ewell and his troops are ascending upon your position. Defend that right flank at all costs. To the death, I say! To the death!"

"Yes, General."

"What of William, General?" McKenny asked. "Where is he?"

Although Meade earnestly searched the battlefield for William's whereabouts, all efforts proved fruitless. This was because William, ever the crafty leader, advanced his force to the extreme end of the Union line under cover of Longstreet's divisions.

Not being able to locate the legendary William Lytham, Meade was angry beyond belief.

"Dammit! I don't know, Darren." Meade proceeded to address two of his scouts. "Men, find out where Lytham is. Now!"

Meanwhile, William and his Alabamans had reached the extreme end of the Union line and found it vulnerable.

"There it is, men. The Union's outer boundary and vulnerable. Let's take it down. Fire, men! Fire!" Lytham exhorted.

The Alabamans opened fire with deadly precision. The Union soldiers, all from the state of Maine under the command of Colonel Chamberlain, were caught completely off guard and fell like rain.

"That's it, men," Lytham continued. "Keep it up! Fire on!"

And fire on they did. Blood and wailing consumed the Maine ranks.

"William, we are doing it! We are destroying the foe. They are even now out of ammunition. Once we penetrate their ground, we will be able to pour in behind the Yankee lines and destroy the Army of the Potomac once and for all!" a Confederate exclaimed.

Yet, William was concerned. Realizing Chamberlain's troops were out of ammunition and about to be crushed if they did not retreat, Lytham was astonished to see that not only were they not retreating, but they were also preparing themselves for a last measure of attack with their remaining carrying weapon—their bayonets.

"Get ready, men. They are making a bayonet charge. On my command!"

As the Federalists were at their most vulnerable point in their charge, Lytham did not hesitate.

"Fire, men! Fire!"

And fire the Confederates did. Nearly all of Chamberlain's soldiers lay dead, but not without preventing William's advance. For during the Colonel's charge, massive Union reinforcements had arrived.

Chapter Thirty-Six

With the virtual impossibility of now breeching the Federalists' outer boundary, Lee directed William instead to have his force join Longstreet's divisions in their attack upon Sickles' and now Hancock's units.

Yet, after an intense day of fighting, which saw the Confederates battle ever so valiantly, the Union still maintained possession of Gettysburg's ridge.

That night, Lee held a battle-of-war meeting.

"We did well out there today, men. Our soldiers fought most effectively. And tomorrow the toils of our labor will yield abundant fruit. Tomorrow, men, we will attack the Yankees right up the center with the full force of our army, destroying them all in the process."

"General, why don't we concentrate our attack on Meade's left flank, positioning ourselves between their army and Washington?" Longstreet beseeched. "I have no doubt that if we do so, they will evacuate the high ground to engage us. They undoubtedly fear us attacking Washington, and would do whatever it takes against whatever odds to prevent this."

"Trust me, Longstreet, sending the entire Army of Northern Virginia upon the Yankee center will break it and send Meade's army in flight. I know it will. And then our hard sought after victory on Yankee soil will be accomplished."

With the conclusion of the meeting, William, prior to falling asleep for the night, could not help but contemplate the heroic stand made by Chamberlain and his Maine troops earlier that day. Though almost all of them died in the process, their deaths saved the Union army from being routed. *Truly this is a sad war*, Lytham sighed. *We were once united Americans, occupants of the greatest nation on earth with the best fighters in the world; now we are being torn asunder, with each killing the best of the other…I wish it were all a bad dream.* Tears started to flow. He knew neither side would stop, regardless of the odds, until their goal was achieved. The young man was utterly shaken. "Oh, blessed God," William prayed, "please forgive us all!"

37

On the morning of July 3, Lee launched the Army of Northern Virginia upon the Army of the Potomac's center. With the attack in full progress, wailing and sorrow of the wounded and screams and shouts of those still fighting, filled the air as the two armies were giving their all upon the other. In the engagement, William and his Alabama divisions were steering the Confederate attack deep into the Union center.

"Fight on, men! Fight on!" Lytham exhorted.

The battle raged with a fierceness never before seen on North American soil.

"General Meade, William and his troops are infiltrating our center. Please help. We are losing fast!" a Federalist cried.

"Darren!" Meade called. "Lead the reserves to assist our center. William is there." Meade grabbed McKenny's right arm, looking him straight in the eyes. "Now is your time for glory, son. Do your country proud!"

"Yes, General Meade!"

As Darren led the Federal reserves into battle, the rivals spotted each other. The moment had finally arrived. Both knew what was at stake: not only the battle between the two great armies, which might very well decide the fate of the war, but also the showdown between them. Confederate and Federalist alike looked upon their respective leaders with a sense of this realization. The air was beyond electric.

"Men, I am sure you realize who is leading the Yankee reinforcements against us now."

"Yes, William," the Confederates answered, seeing Lytham's eyes focused squarely on McKenny.

"The time has come, brethren, to show the North the strength of the South's will!"

The Confederates were fully ready for their greatest battle.

"Charge, men. Charge!"

With William's command, the Confederates unleashed a fury even they did not know they possessed. They fired, charged, and fought with incredible determination.

Seeing the Confederate advance, with the rebel yell screaming at its highest pitch, Darren exhorted his troops.

"Charge upon William and his soldiers, men. Destroy the Soul of the South. Glory is come to us! Charge, men. Charge!"

At that, the Federalists stormed the Confederates with the same unyielding fury.

The battle waged with unparalleled savagery and resilience. Federalists and Confederates were fighting like soldiers possessed, like supernatural beings. The ground they were fighting on seemed to shake. The end of the world seemed at hand. The fighting and bloodshed continued relentlessly for hours on end. William was destroying every Federalist he came upon, as Darren, conversely, was doing likewise.

Now, within fifteen yards with nothing but air between the two, Lytham charged on horseback, while Darren returned the call. At last they clashed. Both out of ammunition, William leaped from his horse upon Darren, and both fell to the ground. William got up first and pounded Darren with a fist blow to the face. Darren, with left cheek severely gashed, took out his bayonet and thrust it toward William, grazing his right shoulder. Lytham, whose bayonet was dislodged from his leap upon McKenny, immediately seized the latter's, with each now fighting for its possession. To gain control of the bayonet, Darren head-butted William away from him, and then charged upon him with bayonet fully drawn. Although weary from the head blow, William managed to see Darren just in time to sidestep him and kick him in the ribs as he went by. Immediately Darren's right ribs, which had been broken by William in Richmond, rebroke. The pain in McKenny was excruciating. Yet the adrenalin and primal rage filling his body prevented him from dwelling on it. Quickly, Darren turned and knocked William to the ground with the shaft of his bayonet. With blood flowing freely above Lytham's left eye as he lay helplessly upon the ground, McKenny came upon his mortal enemy. Standing over the Soul of the South, Darren could not help but revel in his triumph.

"Now you are dead, William Lytham. My mission in life is fulfilled. The Soul of the South destroyed, and by my hands!" McKenny lifted his bayonet. "See you in hell!"

Just as Darren was about to bring his bayonet crashing down, William noticed a bayonet from one of the dead soldiers immediately to his side. Quickly he rolled, seized the bayonet, and sent it straight into McKenny's stomach. Caught completely off guard, Darren froze with eyes wide open and crashed upon the ground.

"William...I am dying."

William was filled with both pleasure and sadness. Darren was, after all, his best friend prior to the war. To see him dying before his very eyes and by his very hands, regardless of what he did to him since their parting of ways, visibly affected Wiiliam.

"Oh, Darren, I wish it had never come to this."

"Oh, William, as much as I sought to kill you after Mobile Academy, my rage always hid a profound love and respect for you. I wanted to be like you, William. I wanted the South to love me as much as they love you." Tears flowed from his eyes. "I tried so hard to have them love me, William." McKenny was coughing up blood. "Oh, William, I have done you wrong!"

Oh God, William sighed, *why was I born in this time?*

Lytham clasped McKenny's hand, which was outstretched for him.

Within seconds, Darren breathed his last. Complete rage consumed William. The war had damaged him so that he was beyond wrath.

"Soldiers, what is the situation?"

"We are penetrating the Yankee line, William. We are succeeding!"

"Fight on, brethren. We will never surrender!" William pressed the attack upon the Union with an even greater vigor—instilling in his soldiers an even greater determination.

The Federalists, seeing William leading the Confederates and Darren lying dead, were consumed with panic and fear. Consequently, all of a sudden, the Union line collapsed. It was three in the afternoon, and William, with Confederate General Pickett and fifteen thousand Confederate soldiers, now possessed the high ground on Seminary

Ridge—only one mile away from the main thrust of the Union army on Cemetery Ridge.

"There they are, men!" Lytham declared. "Those detested Yankees on Cemetery Ridge. Let's go and take them all down."

At William's exhortation, the Confederates pressed dauntlessly on.

During this time, Confederate artillery had been firing upon the Union position, while the Union artillery was returning fire. The noise was deafening.

William, Pickett, and the Confederates had now reached the base of Cemetery Ridge. Believing the Federal artillery had been effectively silenced, Pickett ordered a cessation from the South's firing to enable the Confederates to march up Cemetery Ridge. Yet William, always wary of a trap, had doubts about the supposed silenced Federal artillery and told Pickett as much.

"General, should we not continue our bombardment upon them until we know for certain that their artillery has been silenced? Their present silence may just be a ploy on their part to lure us into climbing the hill, whereupon they would again unleash their artillery. We would then be totally exposed."

"Trust me, William, we have silenced their artillery. Their cannon fire has stopped because they are out of ammunition. We thus have an easy march up Cemetery Ridge with the subsequent annihilation of the enemy. Victory is ours," Pickett confidently proclaimed.

William earnestly hoped Pickett's assessment of the situation was correct. Advancing up Cemetery Ridge, however, William's dire concern came true. Just as he believed, the Federalists were tricking the Confederates into thinking that their artillery had been silenced. Meade, who had just been informed of Lytham's victory over McKenny, was savoring even more watching William and the Confederates taking his bait. *That's it, William. Climb, climb, climb you son of a...I will be the one who will achieve immortal fame by killing the Soul of the South and his rebels.*

As the Confederates became fully and helplessly exposed upon Cemetery Ridge, Meade gave the command.

"Fire, men. Fire with all your might!"

The Federalists unleashed the full force of their artillery upon the most vulnerable Confederates, firing with deadly precision. Dying cries were heard throughout the Confederate ranks.

The Union continued its relentless battery with unprecedented fury. It was a horrific sight. Yet, Pickett urged his troops on.

The Confederates continued to march. The Federalists, now out of ammunition, began firing cans made out of tin, stuffed with iron balls. One such can struck William on the left shoulder, making him crash to the ground.

"William, William," a Confederate cried.

"Attend to him," Pickett commanded to the soldier, Keith Pinetree. "Keep marching, men," he said to the others. "We're almost there!"

Seeing William fall, however, the Confederates were greatly shaken. The South's pride and joy had fallen. What omen was this?

The slaughter of the Southern soldiers continued.

"William, are you all right?" Pinetree asked, though he saw that Lytham was unconscious. Immediately, Keith set William on his shoulder and made haste to Lee's camp.

Having only a fraction of the soldiers they originally possessed prior to climbing Cemetery Ridge, Pickett and the Confederates finally reached the top.

"We have made it, men. Continue the attack!"

The Confederates, ever the professionals, followed Pickett's orders— yet with much less vigor than they had only minutes before. They succeeded in making the Federal defenders break ranks and flee. But when the Federalists were forced to go back and fight, due to their officers' bayonets drawn upon them, the Confederate advance into the heart of the Union center was at last stopped. Moreover, Pickett and the remaining Confederates were captured.

"General Lee...William's been shot and needs immediate help," Pinetree cried, arriving at Lee's camp.

"Doctor. See to William at once!"

"Yes, General Lee," the doctor answered, rushing to William as Lee followed with two soldiers.

"How is he, Doc?" Lee frantically asked. "Will he live?"

"He still has a pulse, General, but it is faint, and he's lost lots of blood from his shattered left shoulder. He should immediately be taken to my tent."

"Quickly, men, at once," Lee commanded his two soldiers. "Pinetree, what is the situation?"

"We are being slaughtered, General. As we advanced up Cemetery Ridge to engage Meade's army, the Yankee artillery opened fire. We thought their artillery was silenced. Oh, General, there is wailing, bloodshed, and death everywhere!"

Later that day, Hanney arrived from the battle.

"Sir, General Pickett and his men have been captured. We have lost staggering numbers. The Yankees still hold Cemetery Ridge and seem to be preparing for a follow-up."

"Men! Pack your bags. Prepare to withdraw," Lee exhorted.

Seeing the Confederates formulating a retreat, Hancock beseeched Meade to pursue them.

"That's all right, Hancock. Our goal was to be victorious, and we have succeeded."

"Yes, General, but we should still pursue Lee and destroy the Army of Northern Virginia once and for all."

"Hancock, we have many wounded that need attention. It is best, then, that we attend to them first before embarking upon another battle with that rebel general."

Accordingly, the Confederates crossed safely into Virginia, much to Lee's relief. He feared that a Union follow-up would have destroyed the remnants of his beleaguered force, with the aspirations of the Confederacy in tow. At least his men now had a chance to nurse their wounds, including, of course, the South's pride and joy.

In Virginia, William was slowly recovering. Once again, he had escaped death by the narrowest of margins. Had the iron ball in the tin can landed only inches lower, striking his heart, he would have died instantly. When Lee believed William fit to carry a conversation, he immediately conversed with him.

"How are you today, son?"

"Getting better, General," Lytham answered in great pain. "How did we fare?"

"Not well...not well at all."

Lytham was downcast.

"I'm so sorry, William. Perhaps we should not have confronted Meade's army while they possessed Gettysburg's high ground. I thought coming off our triumph at Chancellorsville that our momentum would have seen us through."

Chapter Thirty-Seven

There was now a long silence. Both were contemplating the fate of the Confederacy. Truly, the situation did not look good. The South had been severely beaten in a major battle; they no longer posed a threat to Washington; and they were even driven from Federal soil. The chances for international recognition and a negotiated end to the war favorable to them now seemed impossible. One could see this deliberation upon their faces as they gazed sadly into the open air.

"What of Darren McKenny, William? Did the two of you meet?"

"Indeed, General. Darren is no more."

"Good. Perhaps we have some consolation from Gettysburg after all."

"Perhaps, General…perhaps."

"Anyway, I've sent Hanney to inform the president of the outcome. In addition, I am going to have a company leave for Richmond tomorrow to take our wounded…and I would like you to join them."

"But, General, really, I am fine," Lytham replied, yet knowing that he really wasn't. "I should stay."

"No, William. You must go back to recover. Don't worry, when you've healed, we'll fight side by side again," Lee smiled. "You fought most heroically during those three days at Gettysburg, William. I can see why you were so highly praised at Mobile Academy!"

Lytham smiled humbly in return.

"Anyway, the entourage will be leaving at eight tomorrow morning. Don't worry about us here; we are in the advantageous position and on familiar terrain. If the Yankees do attempt to enter Virginia, we will be more than ready."

* * *

News of the Union victory reached Lincoln via Meade's dispatcher Doug Wiley.

"Mr. President, I bring great news from the front!"

Lincoln was most anxious. "What is it?"

"Mr. President, we were thoroughly victorious at Gettysburg!"

"Great news indeed! So, the rebel army is now no more?"

"Mr. President, the rebel army is no longer a threat to Washington and, in fact, no longer a threat to any part of Federal territory. And all in thanks to the bravery and resilience of our General Meade and his Army of the Potomac."

"Good, but what of the rebel army?"

"Well, they retreated into Virginia, Mr. President. But General Meade instructed me to inform you that we have cast 'from our soil every vestige of the presence of the intruder.'"

"My God, is that all?"

Wiley was taken aback.

"I wanted the breaking of Lee's army!"

"Mr. President, the general desperately wanted to follow up his victory but felt it would be best to attend to the wounds of his troops first—for we also suffered many casualties. If it is any consolation, we did manage to shoot William Lytham—though we are unsure if he is dead."

"What of Darren McKenny?"

"Dead, Mr. President. And at the detested hands of William Lytham."

"Oh, poor Darren," Lincoln lamented. "You served our country most well, my son…you were a true patriot. May God have mercy upon your immortal soul, my friend."

Wiley bowed his head a moment.

"I am extremely upset, Doug. General Meade should have followed up on his victory—regardless! If he had done so, this conflict would be over. Instead, Lee has been allowed to regroup and this war is needlessly prolonged—with many more casualties to come."

38

Arriving in Richmond, Hanney made straight to the Confederate White House.

"Good afternoon, Mr. President," Hanney sadly greeted.

"What news from the Army of Northern Virginia, Henry?" Davis asked, fearing the message behind Hanney's greeting.

"Mr. President, once we reached the town of Gettysburg, Pennsylvania, an initial skirmish soon soared into a three-day all-out war. While we succeeded many times in penetrating the Yankee line, in the end, with them having the advantage of the high ground, they always managed to regroup to repel us. Our entire army would undoubtedly have been destroyed had not General Lee ordered an immediate withdrawal into Virginia."

"Dammit! This is terrible news, Hanney. We were counting on victory!"

Hanney was silent.

"What of casualties?"

"There are many, Mr. President. General Lee blames the entire tragedy on himself."

"I don't understand. Why did he confront the Army of the Potomac at Gettysburg with them in possession of the high ground?"

"He believed that with coming off our major victory at Chancellorsville, we would be able to ride the wave of our momentum and defeat the Yankee army."

Davis shook his head. "I fear great unrest throughout the South will ensue from this news."

Hanney sadly nodded.

"What of the wounded? Are they being attended to?"

"Yes, Mr. President. In fact, General Lee is sending the more seriously wounded here to recover…and William Lytham is a member of this company."

"William? Is he all right? What happened?"

"As we were advancing up Cemetery Ridge on the third day to engage the Yankees, we did so believing their artillery had been silenced. But we were wrong. As we proceeded up the hill, the Yankees opened fire. It was a deadly slaughter. In fact, General Pickett lost seventy-five percent of his force. William Lytham was among these casualties, hit by a Yankee iron ball, which shattered his left shoulder."

Davis gave a long, pensive pause, contemplating the battle's horror. "How did we fight?"

"Like true warriors, Mr. President. We fought most valiantly against overwhelming odds: for not only did the Yankees possess the ridge, but they also had some thirteen thousand more men than we did. William Lytham, in particular, was a sight to see. He fought like a lion out there and instilled in us the greatest of resolve."

Davis was impressed at William and the Confederates' valor. "How is the situation at the border?"

"Secure, Mr. President. We are on familiar terrain and in possession of the strategic ground."

"Good. Inform General Lee to carry on in his protection of Richmond."

Two days later, William, along with the rest of the wounded, arrived at the Confederate capital. Quickly, throngs of people gathered around the injured soldiers as they progressed up Cary Street toward Winder Hospital.

"William. It's William Lytham!" a Richmonder exclaimed, spotting him among the wounded.

At that, the crowd rushed to William's side.

"William. Welcome home!" they cried.

William warmly smiled and asked them to inform his wife and mother-in-law of his return.

Arriving at Winder Hospital, William and the troops were immediately placed in the vacant cots. Although there were enough spaces, there were not enough physicians. The city's doctor was truly a busy man, with over two thousand patients to care for. Fortunately for William, all that his shoulder required was rest.

Later that day, Davis arrived at the hospital.

"President Davis! President Davis!" the soldiers called out.

Davis was moved. "Hello, brave men!" He proceeded to visit them all. Approaching William's bed, the president was overcome with great emotion.

"William, it is so good to see you again—though I wish the circumstances were far different."

"It is so good to see you again too, Mr. President. I'm so sorry with what happened…we should have won!"

"Hanney told me you men fought like true warriors. I am so proud of you all. Truly, the South possesses the most courageous and bravest fighters. How are you feeling, son?"

"Well, my left shoulder is in great pain. Soon, though, I will be ready to fight again."

Davis smiled at Lytham's resilience. "You truly are the Soul of the South, William Lytham. I pray to God every day that he preserve you. You give us all reason to fight on."

Lytham humbly smiled.

"I spoke to the doctor, and he says that rest is all you need to recover. So, at my request, he'll allow you to recover at the Wenning abode—if you so wish, of course."

"Absolutely, Mr, President. Thank you so much."

About an hour after Davis' departure, Melanie entered Winder Hospital, rushing through the door.

"Where is my husband? Where is he?" she demanded from the doctor.

"Please, Mrs. Lytham. It's all right. William is over there," the doctor answered, indicating where.

"William! William!"

"Melanie!" William exulted as they embraced.

Melanie saw his shattered left shoulder wrapped in a sling. "Oh, William, how's your shoulder? The president informed us of the disastrous events at Gettysburg and of your injury. William, this is so terrible."

"Oh, Melanie. We lost so many men! We were being shot down at the will of the enemy," William lamented. "As for my shoulder, it is extremely painful, but, fortunately, I'm getting better each day. In fact, the doctor said all I need is rest to recover."

"Oh, William. Please promise me you won't fight anymore!" Melanie cried.

William embraced his love. "It's all right, Melanie. Please, it's all right. Everything is going to be all right. Melanie, the doctor said I can recover at home," William pronounced, desperately trying to change the subject.

"Then let's go, William. I want you home now!"

At that, the Southern belle left the hospital with her love as they proceeded home in the family carriage. During the carriage ride, Melanie had her own news to share.

"William…I'm pregnant!"

"Pregnant? You are?"

"Yes, William, you are going to be a father and I a mother."

"Oh, Melanie, this is terrific!" William exclaimed, kissing her hand. "What shall we name the child, love?"

"Well, if it's a boy, I like Matthew—after my father."

"Sure, William. But if it's a girl, well, I like the name Stephanie—after my mother."

"Sure, love. Oh, Melanie, I am so happy!"

"Me too, William!"

"Where's your mother, love? At home?"

"Actually, she's gone to try and reconcile with Father. She didn't want to go at first, but, after his letters begging her to meet with him in Washington, she finally agreed to do so. Oh, William, I hope they get back together. My father truly loves my mother, and I know that my mother, at least inwardly, still very much loves him."

"I hope they get back together too then, Melanie."

* * *

Weeks passed, and William got better by the day. Each day saw more strength return to his left shoulder; by the third week in his recovery, the doctor had given him clearance to resume military action. Accordingly, Davis' dispatcher Luke Embleton informed William that the president would like to see him on the following morning. Although Melanie longed for him to stay, she realized he had to go. It was William's soul. It would not rest while his nation was at war. Thus, although reluctant, Melanie gave way as her husband went to see Davis on the following day.

Davis saw William approach the Oval Office. "How are you feeling, son?"

"Fine, Mr. President. I am ready to serve our beloved South again. The doctor visited me yesterday agreeing to that very thing."

"Excellent. We desperately need you, William."

"How is the situation, Mr. President?"

Davis was downcast. "Worse by the day, son. I put so much hope in a victory on Northern soil. In fact, I believed such a victory would have brought about an end to the war favorable to us. Yet, with our loss, Lincoln, as I feared, no longer wants to negotiate—stating that our request to do such is 'inadmissible.' Unbelievable!"

"Has there been any change on the European front, Mr. President?"

"Unfortunately not, William. In fact, it's only gotten worse. The Emancipation Proclamation, followed by key Union victories, has only hardened French and British opinion against us."

"Mr. President, if I may speak freely?"

"Absolutely, William. I wouldn't want it any other way."

"Mr. President, I believe and have always believed slavery to be wrong. Slavery is not why I embraced the South. In fact, I believed that in fighting for the South we could in turn end slavery altogether through our independence—as we would no longer be held hostage to the economic dictates of the North, which has resulted in this subjugation of human beings."

"You and I are of the same mind and heart, William. In fact, the South would never have left the Union if she agreed with the slavery status quo. Our fight is not about slavery. The North is no doubt promoting that perception, but it is indeed not the reality."

"Agreed, Mr. President. So we must also address European misperceptions by informing Britain and France that we will immediately end slavery rather than wait until we are sovereign—as you have accurately stated that the Emancipation Proclamation is dissolving the two countries' support for us."

"We must truly be of the same disposition, William, for I have been deliberating upon that very thing; I have come to the conclusion that such must indeed be done. Accordingly, I am going to send a congressman from New Orleans, Duncan Kenner, on a mission to Europe to declare that very thing."

"Excellent, sir. If we can destroy the prevailing perception, which Lincoln created with his Emancipation Proclamation, it will surely help our quest in getting Britain and France on our side."

"Truly, William. Yet, at the same time, successes on the battlefield will also assist our entreaty in Europe. And we desperately need your services on the battlefield again to help change the Yankee momentum."

"Well, here I am, Mr. President. Would you like me to return to the border and rejoin General Lee's army?"

"Actually, William, dispatcher Hanney informed me that the border is presently secure. Where we need you, however, is in Georgia. Apparently, the Yankees are planning to attack Chickamauga. As a result, I would like you there to assist General Bragg."

"Yes, Mr. President. Consider it done."

"Thank you, William. In fact, I think you will enjoy Chickamauga."

"Mr. President?"

"Your brother is there."

"James?"

"Yes. He enlisted in our cause soon after you."

Lytham was astounded. "Well, I definitely look forward to defending our homeland in Georgia from those detested Yankees, Mr. President!"

At the Wenning abode, Melanie was in tears. She could no longer bear the thought of her husband on the battlefield. *Perhaps this time he will be killed, and then I will never see the love of my life again.* Such were her distressing thoughts as her husband entered.

"Hi, Melanie," William greeted, then saw her devastated. "Melanie! What's wrong?"

"I can no longer bear the thought of you out there, William. I will not let you go!" she declared, standing in front of the door, weeping.

William himself was close to tears. He realized if he did leave for the battlefield, he might not make it through this time. Then Melanie would be a widow, and their child would be without a father. A long silence ensued. Yet William would not continue the conversation. If this was, in fact, the last time he would see his wife, he did not want it to end like this. Melanie was William's soul mate and, as such, he would not leave his soul mate in this grievous state. He would wait for Melanie to continue the conversation; for as much as she did not want her husband to go and fight on the battlefield, William knew there was another part of her that respected and even admired his resolve to defend his homeland, regardless of the strength of the enemy. Perhaps that is what attracted Melanie to William more than anything else—his absolute love and commitment to the South. Melanie, deep down, was as much a Southern patriot as anyone could be, and William knew it. Consequently, William believed Melanie would eventually accept what he had to do. Yet William waited and waited.

Eventually, he went over to his love and embraced her. Finally, with the two sitting on the couch, Melanie in William's arms, she broke the silence. Melanie resolved that it was William's destiny to go and fight on the battlefield. She appreciated his kindness in not leaving with their conflict at its highest level. The Southern belle realized how much William truly loved her.

"Where does Davis want you to go this time?" she asked, purposely not calling him "president" to make William fully aware of the extremity of her discontent.

"To Georgia. Apparently the Yankees are going to attack Chickamauga."

"Oh, William, the Yankees are attacking everywhere and winning!"

"Actually, love, I'll be joining your brother-in-law there."

"James?"

"Yes, the president informed me that James is serving our cause in Georgia."

"Oh, William, please, please be careful. You have a child. Don't leave me a widow, and the child without a father."

"I won't, Melanie. I promise."

With that, the two embraced tearfully. Truly, a large part of William did not want to go. William loved Melanie infinitely, beyond description. Only this war could have prevented him from being with her. No other circumstance would have done so. He truly loved his wife; yet he also loved the South.

After packing his belongings and giving his wife yet another emotional, lengthy embrace, William took her leave and boarded the next train to Chickamauga.

39

When notified that William would be assisting the South in Georgia, General Bragg was ecstatic and immediately informed his troops. A uniform "hurray" filled the soldiers' vocal cords. The troops, like Bragg, knew of William's success as a spy, as a diplomat, and most recently as a soldier. Word of William's success, in even his most recent enterprises, had spread fast. Accordingly, when one of Bragg's scouts spotted William on September 10 heading toward the general's camp, he could not help but reveal his elation.

"William. William Lytham!"

"Hello, friend."

Quickly learning of William's approach, nearby soldiers rushed to meet him.

"William, welcome!" they exclaimed.

"Your brother is here," stated one of the soldiers, who called out, "James."

James, within hearing distance, spotted his brother. "William!"

"James!"

Now within reaching distance of each other, the two clasped in a great, soul-embracing hug.

"How are you, little brother?"

"Fine now, William. I was overjoyed when General Bragg informed us you would be coming. How are you?"

"I am definitely glad to be here and with you," William replied, smiling from ear to ear. "It has sure been a long two and a half years, little brother."

"It has felt like much longer, William."

"Indeed. How are Ma, Pa, and Tara?"

"Worried, very worried about the war and of our safety."

"No doubt. This has truly been a terrible time."

"In fact, Pa has even contemplated coming out of retirement and fighting by our side. Fortunately, Ma has convinced him otherwise. The man is now sixty years old, William. I would greatly fear for his safety."

"Me too. That was extremely wise of Ma."

"They are praying for us and the South every day, William."

William appreciatively smiled. "Good. We definitely need divine intervention in this horrible conflict. James, did you know that I am a married man?"

"Yes. Congratulations, big brother! News of your marriage spread like wild fire. The family is so happy. We only wished we would have been able to attend; yet we understood that because of the war…"

"Of course, James! If it weren't for this detested war, Melanie and I would not have rushed like this but would have waited until all of you were in attendance."

James smiled. "Melanie, what a nice name. Is she pretty, William? I hear she is. In fact, they say she is the princess of Richmond!"

"That and much more, James. Oh, James, she is beautiful and kind, as well as endeared by all the Richmonders. In fact, our wedding was celebrated by the whole city."

"That is amazing, William."

"Not only that, James, but you are soon to be an uncle."

"An uncle? William, good going!" James exclaimed, embracing his brother. "Men, my brother is going to be a father and I an uncle."

"Congratulations, William! Congratulations, James!" the troops cheered, shaking the hands of William and James.

After numerous felicitations, James and the soldiers took William to General Bragg.

"General Bragg, I would like you to meet my brother, William Lytham," James proudly proclaimed.

"William," Bragg greeted, embracing him. "It is so good to finally meet you."

"Well, I am certainly glad to be here, General. I am honored to serve our nation here in beautiful Georgia."

"We are all honored to have you, William," Bragg declared, now smiling at James. "Your brother is truly a fine soldier, William, fully giving glory to the Lytham name."

"I knew that he would be, General. James truly loves the South, and I am honored to be his brother!"

"You joined us just in time, William. We recently lost Chattanooga to the foreigners, and they have been pressing us ever since. I believe a battle here in Chickamauga will transpire very shortly. I only hope General Longstreet and his men arrive in time."

"General Longstreet?"

"Yes. General Lee informed the president that Longstreet and his divisions could be safely detached from the Army of Northern Virginia for our assistance."

"That's very good news. I served with General Longstreet at Gettysburg. He is both a fine soldier and leader."

"I agree, William. Those Yankees will soon know the taste of defeat."

Bragg proceeded to introduce William to the rest of the army. When James revealed that William was a father-to-be, the general proclaimed a toast: "To William Lytham and his lovely wife on the arrival of their beautiful child! Cheers!"

"Cheers!" The troops clanged their water cantons and drank. The atmosphere was festive. With William Lytham in their midst, new hope entered the soldiers' hearts.

When Longstreet and his divisions arrived later in the week, belief in absolute victory amongst the men was now the norm rather than the exception.

* * *

Shortly after the middle of September, Bragg decided to initiate the engagement against the Union Army of the Cumberland. Accordingly, on the night of September 18, he held his council of war meeting and prepared strategy.

"Men, tomorrow we will engage the enemy in full force. Longstreet, I want your troops to search for a weak spot in the Yankees' right flank, which is under the command of General Rosecrans. The general is a resilient fighter but is well known to leave openings. Once you find such an opening, attack it with all your might and penetrate the Union line. I, meanwhile, will attack Yankee General Thomas head on."

"Yes, General," Longstreet replied.

"William, I am going to have you and your brother join Longstreet in his search for a weak spot in the enemy's right."

"Yes, General," William answered, enthusiastic that he would be fighting alongside his brother.

The next day, September 19, the battle began.

Meticulously scanning for a weak spot in Rosecrans' right flank, William eventually found one.

"There it is, General," William exclaimed.

"Attack, men! Attack!" Longstreet accordingly ordered.

With the screaming of the rebel yell, the Confederates struck and penetrated the Union weak spot, and then followed up their success.

"William, take one of my divisions and attack General McCook while I set mine against General Crittenden," Longstreet said.

"Yes, General," Lytham answered, then addressed the division. "Men, we have McCook's soldiers on the run. Let's take them down. Charge!"

And charge they did, inflicting mighty damage upon General McCook's troops.

"General McCook, it's William Lytham and his force. We are being overwhelmed. Please, help us," a wounded Union soldier cried out.

"Retreat, men, retreat!" McCook ordered, panicking.

"Men, the enemy is retreating. Pursue them!" William exhorted as the Confederates commenced a smashing rout upon McCook's soldiers.

Meanwhile, Longstreet's force was pressing the attack upon General Crittenden's troops.

"Fight on, men. Destroy them all!" Longstreet beseeched.

"General, please, we are being annihilated by Longstreet's divisions. Please do something!" a Federalist said.

"Retreat, men, retreat," Crittenden cried, seeing his troops about to be wiped out.

"The enemy is fleeing, men. Pursue them!" said Longstreet.

Seeing his subordinates McCook and Crittenden being driven from the field, Rosecrans ordered what remained of his right flank to make an immediate withdrawal back to Chattanooga. Bragg, at this time, was attacking and penetrating the main body of Thomas' force.

Chapter Thirty-Nine

"Fight on, men. Destroy the invader. We are succeeding!" Bragg exclaimed.

"General Thomas, we are being overwhelmed. Please, we can't go on," begged a Union soldier.

"We must and we will! Fight on, men! Never surrender!" Thomas shouted.

Thomas' troops fought on with unyielding resilience; and, by holding their ground, they prevented the Union army at Chickamauga from being fully destroyed. Yet, that night, when informed of McCook and Crittenden's defeat and Rosecrans' retreat to Chattanooga, Thomas realized he had no rational choice but to follow Rosecrans' lead—and accordingly did so.

The Union defeat at Chickamauga was highly celebrated by the Confederate soldiers. Yet, although there was much euphoria, the cost of victory was high. Not only the North, but also the South—especially Bragg's divisions—suffered many casualties. Yet, it was a victory for the Confederates nonetheless, and Bragg was determined to ride the crest of this momentous wave.

"Way to fight, Longstreet. Way to fight, William. We did it, men! We sure showed it to 'em Yankees," Bragg proclaimed.

"We sure did, General."

"Men, we are going to follow up our victory by laying siege upon the retreating Yankees at Chattanooga."

"Would it not be best to engage them now, General, before they reach Chattanooga?" William asked. "By doing so, they will be unable to set up a defensive position around the city."

"I agree with William, General. We should engage them now," Longstreet concurred.

"Yes, but men, we have suffered—especially to my units—many casualties. It is thus best to first attend to them. Moreover, it would be better to lay siege upon them at Chattanooga rather than pursue them now in battle; for it will still accomplish our goal of a follow-up but with less loss of life."

Accordingly, the Confederates first attended to their wounded, and then marched to Chattanooga—in the hope of starving the remnants of the Army of the Cumberland into submission or, at the very least, evacuation.

During the march, William and James had the opportunity to converse about many things—life back home, family, and friends. When the topic came to America, both revealed their extreme dismay at the way the war was unfolding for the South.

"I never believed it would be this tough, William. I thought that as soon as we declared our independence, we would have incurred only a verbal rebuke or, at the very most, a few skirmishes on the border states, but that's it. I never believed the Yankees would set their entire arsenal upon our independence. Even President Buchanan declared that although the states do not have the prerogative to leave, the Union does not have the prerogative to prevent it."

"If it was anyone other than Lincoln, little brother, we would have our sovereignty by now, most definitely. I met the man. He is just as determined to keep the Union together as we are to have a country of our own. Thus, these polarizing differences have become abundantly manifest in this terrible, bloody war."

James nodded. "How is Lincoln anyway, William? What is he like?"

"I tell you, James, when I was face-to-face with him, I could not help but admire the man. Although he may look uncultured, he is elegant and sincere. He will tell you where he stands, and he will make no bones about defending such a position. It is truly a shame our disagreements have come to this. Another time, another era, and many things would be different. May God have mercy on us all."

40

Arriving at Chattanooga, Bragg ordered the Confederates to lay siege to the city. The men went upon their task diligently and effectively; by the middle of October, the Army of the Cumberland was practically starving to death. Yet Thomas, informed that relief was on its way, encouraged the Union troops to hold fast.

"Don't give up, men. I have just been informed that General Grant and General Sherman are on their way, even as I speak."

Immediately the Union soldiers' spirits revived, especially upon learning of Grant's pending arrival. All of them knew of the legendary general. His ability to conduct war was nothing short of remarkable. Accordingly, the Federalists were determined more than ever to hold on regardless of their present plight—because very soon the North's champion general would arrive to relieve them.

Bragg, however, remained fully confident in his siege strategy.

"We are doing it, men. The Yankees will not be able to hold out for much longer."

William responded with only a slight smile.

"What's wrong, William? Don't you think so?"

"Well, I would have predicted they would surrender long ago, General. I am starting to suspect they believe relief is on its way."

"Well, even if it is, we are in firm control of the high ground in and around Chattanooga, namely Missionary Ridge and Lookout Mountain. In addition, we have units in strategic positions all along the Tennessee River preventing Union navigation. As a result, even if the Yankees do attempt to relieve their brethren, we will spot them way ahead of time and, with our advantageous positioning, thoroughly destroy them."

"Well, we shouldn't have allowed the Army of the Cumberland to ever reach Chattanooga, General!" Longstreet snapped. "If we would have engaged them immediately after Chickamauga, they would now be vanquished, and we wouldn't have to be concerned about their potential relief."

"Longstreet, the decision I made was sound! Our wounded troops needed to be attended to before anything else, and we have yet to lose any lives by my strategy. Meanwhile the enemy is on its last legs," Bragg retorted, leaving in disgust.

"William, I am convinced that nothing but the hand of God can help us as long as we have our present commander. I have even stated as much to our secretary of war. He must be removed."

Learning of the rift between Longstreet and Bragg, Davis made the trek to Chattanooga to resolve the matter.

"Good afternoon, Mr. President," Longstreet humbly said, aware of why Davis was present.

"Good afternoon. So, what's wrong, Longstreet?"

"Mr. President, General Bragg and I just don't get along. He has bungled our entire operation upon the Army of the Cumberland."

"What do you mean? He resoundingly defeated them at Chickamauga and has followed up his victory here at Chattanooga. Such is the proper course of action upon a retreating force."

"Yes, Mr. President, but our follow-up should have been an engagement against the Yankees immediately after our success upon them at Chickamauga. If we had done so, we would be victorious by now. Instead, here we are, still laying siege upon them—with rumors of General Grant and General Sherman's imminent arrival to relieve them."

"Longstreet, I have no doubt that the Army of the Cumberland will soon evacuate the town, if not surrender altogether. They are starving! They cannot, and will not, hold out for much longer."

"I so much want to believe that, Mr. President, but I just don't. With talk of Grant and Sherman's approach, Thomas is undoubtedly using such to motivate his troops to remain steadfast."

"Well, even if Grant and Sherman do arrive, we are the ones who hold possession of the strategic ground in and around Chattanooga. There is no possibility they will even get close to relieving Thomas."

"I hope you're right, Mr. President, but it should have never come to this. I fear with Bragg in charge, even assured victory is compromised."

"Listen, Longstreet, Bragg is a victorious commander, and while he remains such, he will continue to lead. I hereby mark this the end of your dispute with him. Do I make myself clear?"

"Yes, Mr. President."

Returning to Richmond, Davis was not totally convinced of Longstreet's reconciliation with Bragg's leadership. As a result, he offered him the opportunity to take his force to Knoxville to confront Union General Burnside's army. Longstreet willingly accepted, then informed Bragg and William.

"Well, if that's what the president has offered, Longstreet, you are perfectly free to go," Bragg said.

"With all due respect, generals, I am in complete shock!" William declared. "Longstreet, you have command of one-third of our entire force here at Chattanooga. Why are you to leave, especially when you are most needed? Grant and Sherman have been spotted. No doubt a battle will shortly ensue. We need you here, now!"

"Well, the president believes me necessary elsewhere also, William, and I am sure it is not without foundation," Longstreet casually answered.

But William knew the real reason behind Longstreet's leave. With Longstreet and his divisions' departure, William immediately met up with his brother.

"There's trouble, James. Lots of trouble!"

"What do you mean?"

"You know Longstreet and Bragg's dispute."

"Yes."

"Well, apparently the president has settled the matter by allowing Longstreet and his divisions to leave for Knoxville to battle Burnside's army."

"But Longstreet possesses a third of our force!"

"Exactly. And Grant and Sherman have been spotted."

"Oh my God, William."

"Stay by my side, little brother."

"I will."

* * *

When news of Longstreet's withdrawal reached Grant and Sherman's forces, cheers rang out throughout the Union divisions. Yet Grant, the general in charge of lifting the siege at Chattanooga, exhorted the Federal troops to remain focused on the task at hand.

"Remember, men, they still have William Lytham. The man has yet to be conquered. He has brought more success to rebeldom than anyone else. Just because Longstreet has withdrawn does not mean that we are guaranteed victory. We must continue to work hard and give it our all. They still have many troops, and even with some soldiers under William's command, there is no such thing as a sure thing. Do I make myself clear?"

"Yes, General."

On the night of November 22, Grant held a council-of-war meeting with his generals.

"Men, tomorrow will be the day when we not only commence our full-scale attack upon the rebels and relieve our brethren, but it will also be the day when we once and for all smash William Lytham!"

"Exactly, General," Hooker affirmed. "That William has destroyed my life! I have a score to settle with that one."

"Precisely! All right, men, listen. Tomorrow I will strike the main body of Bragg's army on Missionary Ridge. Sherman, I want you to cross the Tennessee River at the Brown's Ferry juncture and then proceed to the east end of Chattanooga. Once you are there, I want you to attack the rebel right flank on Missionary Ridge's north side. Hooker, I want you to storm the opposite end position of the rebels on Lookout Mountain and take from them this high ground. Any questions, generals?" Grant asked.

There were none.

The next morning, Grant's battle plan began. The fighting was fierce. Although Grant was having some success, the Confederates, under Bragg, were holding firm.

"Don't let them penetrate, men. Fight to the end!" Bragg exhorted.

The battle continued to rage on with a most deadly ferocity.

The Confederates' outer flank on Lookout Mountain was also facing a horrific assault. Yet Hooker's divisions, although greatly outnumbering the Confederates, were also facing incredible resistance. In the end, however, Hooker's larger force prevailed, and the Federalists seized Lookout Mountain's high ground.

Having succeeded to Missionary Ridge's north side, Sherman ordered his troops to engage William Lytham and the Confederates' right flank.

"There are the rebels, men. And William Lytham is in charge. Now is the time to dispel once and for all the legend of that man. Attack them, men, attack!"

The Union soldiers, although nervous about having to face William, had the utmost of confidence in their general and, as a result, pressed the attack forward with incredible determination.

Seeing the Federalists fierily charging, William instilled in the two brigades he was given to command by Bragg the greatest of resolves.

"Here come the detested Yankees, men. Coming to us here, in our home of Tennessee. No one, and I mean no one, comes into our home and conquers us! Engage them, brethren, and destroy them all."

At that, the Confederates engaged the Federalists with the utmost of resolve, such that they were smashing Sherman's superior number.

Sherman, baffled by the battle's course, was filled with rage.

"What is going on? We should have defeated them by now!"

"General, it's William Lytham," a Union soldier cried. "He and his men are repelling and even destroying us. Please, General, we are losing staggering numbers. Please, we can't go on!"

"We can and we will. I will not go back to Grant and tell him that I failed. We will take this ground, or we will all die in the attempt!"

The battle was being fought with a wrath that could only compare with Gettysburg. The savage fighting continued not only for the remainder of the twenty-third, but also for the entire day of the twenty-fourth; by the twenty-fifth, William and his troops were still in possession of Missionary Ridge's north side. On the morning of the twenty-fifth, Sherman was informed by Grant that in no uncertain terms he was to either succeed that day or face demotion.

"Dammit! I can't believe this," Sherman said to himself. "How is it possible? I see why Hooker and McDowell feel as if their lives have been destroyed, and all at the hands of that William Lytham. How does he do it? How can he time and again thwart the best-laid plans and do so even with a much-smaller force? If I don't gain this north side today, I'm history."

Sherman's dire urgency was not lost on his troops.

"Men, I realize we have been unsuccessful in expelling William and his rebels from the north side of the ridge. Though we have lost many in the process, we have, in fact, been fighting most valiantly. And today our hard work will pay off. Today we will succeed…we bloody better succeed! We will not stop until we are victorious—even if it takes us all day and all night. It is either victory today or death. Do I make myself abundantly clear?"

"Yes, General," was the enthusiastic yet nervous response.

Prior to the impending battle, William also addressed his troops.

"Men, I am so proud of you all. We are showing the Yankees that no one comes into our home and conquers us!" Lytham exclaimed as cheering could be heard throughout the Confederate brigades. "No doubt, Sherman will send his force upon us again today. No doubt, he does not want to go back to Grant and tell him that he has failed. But he will fail. And the more he tries, the greater his failure will be." Even louder cheering occurred. "We are Southerners. This is our home. The Yankee yoke is not welcome!" Confederate cheering increased. "Today, men, we are going to breach Sherman's force and destroy them all." The rebel yell was now at its highest pitch.

William's men were ready. Full of passion and increased fervor, the Confederates could not wait to crush Sherman's charge and his interior thereafter.

Seeing his soldiers ready for the battle of their lives, Sherman ordered the attack.

Both sides engaged, yet this time the Confederates with seemingly supernatural strength. The Federalists were falling like flies. *Oh my God, what is happening? My worst nightmare is coming true!* Sherman cried inside.

The Confederates were taking the battle deep into Sherman's interior. Realizing the urgency of the moment, Sherman sucked in his pride and sent a dispatch to Thomas—begging for help from the Army of the Cumberland.

Thomas immediately sent two of his divisions, one under General Sheridan and the other under General Wood, to assist Sherman's force. Fortunately for Sherman and his soldiers, Thomas' divisions arrived just in time.

"Thank God you're here," Sherman said. "Sheridan, Wood, have your men overtake the rebel rifle fortifications at the bottom of Missionary Ridge. They are shooting us down like dogs."

After intense, fierce fighting, the Federalists overtook the Confederate rifle fortifications. Then Sheridan and Wood's soldiers, in the heat of the battle, decided to climb the rugged mountain to the top of Missionary Ridge in the hope of surprising the Confederates.

"We must do this, men," a Union soldier exclaimed. "There is no time for orders. Climb the ridge and surprise the enemy!"

Immediately, the soldiers climbed the jagged mountain. Pressing the assault upon Sherman's force, William was unaware of the Federal climb.

While William and his brigades were in the midst of a rout upon Sherman's unit, the Army of the Cumberland troops had reached the top of Missionary Ridge—catching the Confederates completely off guard. Accordingly, the Army of the Cumberland troops easily overcame their now-fleeing enemy. Consequently, William and his brigades became trapped between Sherman's soldiers on the one side and troops from the Army of the Cumberland on the other.

Bragg, who was fighting Grant on the other side of Missionary Ridge, was being overwhelmed.

"We must retreat, General. Grant's army is penetrating our lines!" a Confederate pleaded.

But Bragg did not want to leave William without support. "Where is William?"

"We're not sure," the Confederate answered as Grant's force advanced even closer. "Please, General!"

"Retreat, men, retreat," Bragg reluctantly ordered.

Still unaware that to his back was the approach of Sheridan and Wood's troops, William continued the attack upon Sherman.

"William, look, Sherman's men are fleeing! We've got those Yankees now once and for all," James exulted.

Yet, just when William and his brigades were about to rout Sherman's force, fire came upon them from behind.

William turned around. "What the…?"

Immediately, a bullet struck James in the back.

"William!" James called as he fell to the ground.

"Oh my God. James!" William cried as he then addressed one of his brigades. "Men, to our back side. Forget about Sherman, defend our back." William then called his dispatcher Peter Gratton. "Peter, find out what's going on."

Immediately, William's brigades reorganized themselves to confront the Federalists on both sides. Thus, no longer being pursued by the same volume, Sherman ordered his men to not only cease from their retreat, but also to advance.

During this time, William was at James' side. "Don't worry, little brother, you're going to be fine."

He did not know that the bullet had entered James' left shoulder blade and exited just above his heart.

"Oh God, William!" James cried. "I'm so cold."

William then saw the bullet wound with blood flowing from it. "Be strong, James. Please, please, little brother, you're going to make it!" William uttered, weeping, trying to stop the blood flow.

"I love you, William…and I am honored to be your brother…"

"You're going to be fine, James!" William encouraged but realized his flesh and blood was close to death.

"Oh, William…please tell Ma and the family that I love them so much."

William was crushed and could not help but continue to weep.

"May I ask a favor?" James struggled out.

"Anything."

"If your child's a boy, would you name him after me? Perhaps then my life will not have been in vain," James cried.

"It was never in vain, James! Of course. Your request is granted!" William was totally destroyed as he saw his brother close to death. "I love you, James." William embraced him as James died.

"Oh God, William!" Gratton cried, returning and seeing James dead as William wept over his brother's body.

"What news, Peter?"

"Terrible, William. Soldiers from the Army of the Cumberland have climbed Missionary Ridge. It is they who are engaging us from the back. Moreover, General Bragg's army has withdrawn. We are now all alone."

Realizing the only rational option was to follow Bragg's lead, Lytham called to his brigades.

"Men, we must withdraw. Follow me."

William led his brigades through an opening on Sherman's left and the Army of the Cumberland's right and, accordingly, completed the Confederates' evacuation from Missionary Ridge.

After almost two hours, William and his brigades caught up with Bragg and his force.

"General, what happened?"

"We were overwhelmed by Grant's army, William. We had no choice but to withdraw."

Lytham was downcast.

"Where's James, William?"

Lytham gave a lengthy pause. "Dead, General."

"I am so sorry, William."

William was trying hard to suppress his melancholy. As a soldier, he believed sadness was a sign of weakness. Yet, he could overcome his sorrow no longer. Bragg immediately embraced the South's pride and joy, while the other soldiers could not help but bow their heads, mourning William's loss.

"It's all right, son. It's all right. James' death was not in vain. He will now be fighting with us in heaven—an even more formidable force," Bragg consoled as Lytham mourned. Bragg's thoughts turned to the debacle at Chattanooga. "Oh, William, I fear that both the president and I erred in the conclusion for me to retain command here. You and Longstreet were right, and I should have indeed heeded your strategy. I am even going to write to the president stating such. I am so sorry, William. I truly let us down."

"No, General; if Longstreet had remained, your strategy might very well have worked."

"Perhaps, William. But I feel bad nonetheless—especially for our men, including your brother. They all fought so valiantly against incredible odds."

What Bragg said was correct. And to lose, at such a high human cost, when victory had seemed so near, was extremely difficult for William.

William remained in Bragg's army for the remainder of 1863 and early into 1864. During this time, he wrote to his family—though it was hard to do. William wanted desperately to tell them of James' death in person but knew that, because of the war, it was impossible. As a result, in the most affectionate way conceivable, William informed them of his brother's death and of James' love for them. Similarly, William wrote to Melanie of the tragic event and asked her if they could honor James' dying request of naming their child, if it was a boy, after him. William's letters to his family and wife were filled with affectionate phrases and an expressed hope that very soon they would be united.

At the end of January 1864, William received the news he was anxiously awaiting: his beautiful wife had given birth to a beautiful baby boy. Melanie's letter informing her husband of the blessed December 22 event was filled with good news that their child was healthy and honorably named James, but it was tinged with sadness that William was not with them but rather far away. Melanie, throughout her letter, professed undying love for William, with heartfelt supplications that he make it home alive. William immediately wrote back to his wife reassuring her that everything was going to be all right; that he was determined to make it home to his beloved.

William told his fellow soldiers of the joyful news. The Confederates, to a man, hailed William's divine blessing and celebrated the event with toasts and merriment. Hence, while the situation looked bleak for Bragg's army and the Confederacy in general, the joyful news visited to their champion energized the troops to remember that life was indeed good. With perseverance, this war would come to an end, and they, too, would enjoy the beauty life had to offer.

At the beginning of April 1864, Davis informed William to rejoin Lee on the Virginia border, as Grant and his forces were closing in on the Army of Northern Virginia. After thanking Bragg and his troops for having him and beseeching them to remain resilient, William took the train to the border of Virginia.

Arriving at the border near the end of April, William was enthusiastically welcomed by Lee and his army. Additionally, the Confederates expressed to William both their deep sorrow on the death of his only brother, and their joyful happiness on the birth of his newly born son. William graciously accepted, and truly appreciated, their loving kindness toward him on both these matters. Later that day, William and Lee conversed in private.

"So, how is the situation, General?"

"Unfortunately, not good, William. As you know, Grant has arrived, and his movements suggest that he will soon launch a strike at us."

Lytham paused. "Yes, I'm not surprised. We faced that determined general in Chattanooga. Unfortunately, he is a very clever man. His fame, I'm sure, is well deserved."

"Indeed, William. You know, I served with Grant in the Mexican War. Yet, no one believed he would become the person he has become: the Union and its president's hope. Yet, looking back, I do remember that determination in him and his willingness to fight at all costs. Yes, he did have that fire in his eyes. However, I never believed such a fire would have resulted in a bon fire! Truly, this war has been good for Grant. He has climbed to the pinnacle in such a short time...I guess war has that ability, William."

Lytham gave a slight smile.

"Anyway, I guess I don't need to stress the importance of holding our position. To put it bluntly, the future of our nation rests on it."

"Well, if that is what it must come down to, General, I am more than prepared to hold our position—at all costs."

Lee gave a respectful, contemplative smile. "You truly are a fine soldier, William Lytham. Had America not been torn asunder, you would have undoubtedly one day commanded her entire army."

Lytham was moved. "Coming from a man who was offered that command, General, I am honored by those high words."

Lee looked thoughtful. "I believe we are very much alike, William. We could have had so much had we only embraced another allegiance; yet we realized that the only true allegiance in life is the love for one's home."

With that, Lee patted William on the shoulder and walked off by himself in quiet contemplation. *What a man,* thought William. *What an honorable man! "Do your duty in all things" Lee once said. "You cannot do more. You should never wish to do less." And truly the general was personifying his doctrine. What greater duty than charity; and charity begins at home.* William realized that of all people in the conflict, General Lee truly stood head and shoulders above them all. He was a kind man, relinquishing all power and glory the world offered him for a love greater than all material possessions: a love for his home. Thinking these thoughts, William became even more resolved to fight to the end—regardless of what the end might entail. He prayed at the outset of the conflict for God to give him the guidance to make the right decision. And the decision William embraced, in the end, was the one he made while in earnest prayer at St. Mary's On-the-Hill. Right then, with Lee in view, William realized that his life was not in vain; neither was his brother's life, nor any of the other Confederate soldiers' lives, alive or dead. Instead, their lives were noble, a nobility future generations of Southerners would realize.

41

At the beginning of May 1864, Grant, with his 118,000 troops, was preparing to crush, once and for all, Lee's 66,000 soldiers and the Confederacy with it.

"Men, we have before us but one final task," Grant began, "namely, the defeat of the Army of Northern Virginia. Our success in this endeavor will enable us to march right into the rebellion and therein destroy rebeldom. But the Army of Northern Virginia has two leaders in much repute, namely General Lee and William Lytham. Don't let their names or past success, however, consume you. They are only human. Moreover, we possess greater numbers, far greater than the enemy. As a result, with God's grace, victory awaits us and therein an end to this needless war once and for all. Are you with me, men?"

"Yes, General!" was their energetic response.

"Good. The hour is about to approach, and the hour will be yours. Fight like the true men you are. Do your nation proud. You are all the true heroes of this war. History will treat you well."

On May 3, Grant began the march into the heart of Confederate territory by leading the Army of the Potomac across the Rapidan River. Learning of the move via his scouts, Lee addressed his troops.

"Men, the Army of the Potomac has crossed the Rapidan and is on the march near Fredericksburg. But we are ready, ready to repel the Yankee invader. We will show the Yankees yet again that we will never allow a foreign power to invade our home. Are you ready, men?"

"Ready, General!" was the enthusiastic reply.

"Then let's charge!" Lee commanded.

Cries of the rebel yell were heard miles away.

Having crossed the Rapidan, Grant and his army became stuck in the dense woods just outside Fredericksburg. Lee and William, arriving and seeing Grant's force trapped in the terrain, took complete advantage as the Confederates fired relentlessly upon the Federalists.

Ever the determined fighter, Grant urged his force to engage the Confederates with the same severity. But the Union soldiers were sitting ducks, and Lee and William made the most of it.

Grant, however, refused to retreat, and even pressed the battle farther into Confederate territory toward Cold Harbor. Complete savagery and bloodshed ensued, with the Federalists experiencing the brunt of the horror.

At an enormous human price, the Army of the Potomac reached Cold Harbor on June 1. Facing them, the Confederates situated themselves behind formidable fortifications. Yet William, who had studied Grant's campaigns in the West, believed the Union Commander would not be deterred by them and accordingly informed Lee.

"Impossible, William! Grant would never send his army against our fortified terrain. His men would be completely exposed to our fire."

"I believe he will, General. When Grant attacked Bragg on Missionary Ridge, it was against our advantageous position."

"Yes, but Grant did so while having his other divisions, namely those of Sherman and Hooker, assault our other units in the surrounding vicinity. In any case, I'll inform the troops to be on high alert. Let's hope you're right. If you are, we will score a huge victory at Cold Harbor."

And William was right. Never one to be dictated by terrain, and supremely confidant in his ability to succeed, Grant ordered his soldiers forward.

The Confederates, seeing the Union charge, were ready. "Time to get you, Grant," William said aloud. When the Federalists were within perfect range to be fired upon, William, at Lee's signal, gave the order.

"Fire, men! Fire with all your might!"

And fire they did. In fact, blood, death, and despair consumed the Army of the Potomac for the full three days of Grant's Cold Harbor campaign.

By the third day, Meade felt compelled to confront Grant on his seemingly suicidal strategy.

"General, our men are falling like rain. Please, we must cease this approach. The enemy is fully fortified. We haven't penetrated an inch in these last three days, and we have lost thousands in the attempt! Please, we must stop!"

Realizing the truth of Meade's words, Grant heeded the advice—though reluctantly—and called for a withdrawal.

Accordingly, the battle-wounded Army of the Potomac withdrew. Their human cost was ghastly: over twelve thousand casualties at Cold Harbor, and, since their crossing of the Rapidan River, over fifty-five thousand men lost—almost the total number of troops in Lee's army.

With the Confederate victory at Cold Harbor, Lee could not help but reveal his elation.

"That's the way to fight out there, men! We made Grant retreat, and we did it against a much larger force. You are truly doing your nation proud." The troops cheered.

Lee turned to William. "You did a most fine job leading, son. In addition, your insight on what Grant was planning helped prepare us. We were sure ready for him!"

"Thank you, General," Lytham humbly replied. "Sir, shouldn't we pursue Grant now, and finish them off once and for all?"

Lee smiled a bit sadly.

"William, although we were victorious against Grant, we also lost many men. While the Union can continue to mobilize more soldiers, our supply is limited to the point of exhaustion. We cannot match the North with its manpower and machinery. In sum, hope of vanquishing the Yankee army is virtually gone. Our only chance now is to continue to hold our ground and hope that heavy war weariness will set in on the Yankee side—resulting in Lincoln's defeat in this year's Union election and a negotiated end to the war on terms at least tolerable to us."

"Is it that bad, General?" Lytham asked. He realized that the chances for an electorate to replace a sitting president in the midst of a full-scale war, having now the decisive advantage, would be slim if not nil.

"Indeed it is, William," Lee said.

* * *

In the Union camp, Grant was licking his wounds.

"General, we lost so many men!" Meade addressed a downcast Grant. "Sending our troops against those rebel fortifications was pure suicide."

"I did what I thought was right, Meade. I realize now, however, that my course was far from sound."

"What are we to do now, General? Lee and William are still strongly fortified. Thus our goal of defeating them here and marching straight into Richmond is hampered."

"Perhaps there is another way."

"General?"

"Attack them from another angle."

Meade looked puzzled.

"What if we were to transfer our army south of the James River? We would then be in a position to move upon Richmond from the back. This would force Lee and William to evacuate their fortifications to engage us."

"Yes, General, but both the James River and the Chickahominy River—which we would have to cross first—are rivers without bridges. Not only would such crossings involve complicated engineering on our part, but we would be exposed to rebel attacks in the process. And this is not even including our vulnerability in the boggy terrain surrounding these rivers, without personnel or even maps to help guide us."

"I realize it would be a cumbersome and formidable enterprise, Meade, but sometimes extraordinary accomplishments require extraordinary measures. Our strategy of attacking the rebels north of Richmond, as you continually remind me, has been a disaster. So we must try something new!"

"All right, General."

On June 12, Grant and his army commenced the new strategy.

During this second week of June, William was concerned about Grant's Cold Harbor inactivity.

"General, what do you think Grant is up to? It has been over a week since we last fully engaged the Yankees at Cold Harbor. I know inactivity is far from that man's character."

"True, William. Yet, I believe his thrashing has made him reconsider his restless nature."

"I don't know, General. For Grant to change his temperament, one that has given him so many victories in the past, seems unlikely to me."

"Yes, William, but remember, Grant gained those victories in the West—not in the East. Moreover, when he employed his restless nature here, look what happened to him—he was resoundingly defeated! I'm sure he's adopted the strategy his predecessors have employed against us; namely, retiring for a period of time after an assault, awaiting our response in the process, and then mounting another offensive."

William, however, was still concerned. Knowing Grant's industriousness, William believed he was up to something else.

His anxiety was justified on June 16 when news reached Lee that Grant had completed his army's crossing of the James River. He was now leading them to Petersburg, Virginia, to assist General Butler's force in their assault upon Beauregard's soldiers guarding the city. Realizing there was no time to do anything but address the issue at hand, Lee summoned his troops.

"Men, Grant and his army have just crossed the James River and are on their way to Petersburg. We must leave at once to defend our city. Time is of the essence. Let's go men, away!"

The Army of Northern Virginia made straight to the town. Prior to Grant and Lee's arrival, Beauregard's units were, incredibly, repelling Butler's far-numerous force.

Grant arrived on June 17 and, aware that Lee's army was trailing, commanded his troops accordingly.

"Men, Lee's army is yet to arrive. We have the advantage. Join Butler's men and reduce the city. All of it! Advance, men! Advance!"

Seeing Grant's army joining in on the assault, Beauregard exhorted his troops with all his passion.

"Keep fighting, men! Don't give up! Lee and William are on their way. Show to the enemy that we will never surrender."

With that, Beauregard instilled an even greater determination in his already valiantly fighting force. Accordingly, and astoundingly, the Confederates were now repelling Butler's and Grant's combined assault— with less than a third of their number. Yet, Beauregard knew his soldiers could not hold out for much longer against these odds. If the Army of Northern Virginia did not arrive soon, Petersburg would be lost.

Just as Beauregard was contemplating these somber thoughts, Lee's army appeared.

Lee surveyed the situation. "William, take one of my divisions to the southwest side of the city." Lee directed his remaining divisions to Petersburg's other vulnerable areas.

Heavy fighting continued to ensue.

Seeing William and his division fortifying Petersburg's southwest side, Hancock was irate.

"Dammit! Men, it's William Lytham and his rebels preventing our march into Petersburg. No one, and I mean no one, is going to prevent our advance! Onward, men."

Hancock's soldiers charged the Confederates with an unyielding fury.

"Here they come, men. On my command!" Lytham exhorted. "Fire, men! Fire!"

And fire the Confederates did. The Union soldiers fell like rain.

Not only at William's location, but at Petersburg's other locations as well, full unbridled savagery prevailed. While the Union continued its full-scale attack upon the city, the resilience of the Southerners was prevailing.

By June 18, Grant realized the bloodshed and sorrow of the Petersburg campaign was falling primarily upon the Federal forces. Learning from Cold Harbor, he called off the attack and deliberated upon another course of action. As a result, Petersburg remained Confederate. Lee was overjoyed.

"That's the way to fight out there, men! We did it. We overcame superior numbers once again. We have saved our town!"

The Confederates, although much fatigued, were elated at their hard-earned victory.

During this time, William conversed enjoyably with Beauregard and his good friend Officer John Childs. It had been a long time since they had last seen one another, and many things had changed. Yet, as soon as they were reunited, their lengthy absence seemed to disappear and with it, the sadness of the present.

In the Union camp, Grant was livid. Although he realized that a withdrawal from Petersburg had to be made, he was not one accustomed to losing.

"Bloody hell! We lost again. We continue to have superior numbers, and yet we continue to lose. This does not make sense!"

"No, it doesn't, General," Butler humbly concurred.

"Dammit, Butler! You greatly outnumbered Beauregard's force prior to Lee's arrival, or even my own for that matter. Petersburg should have been reduced long before I even got here."

Grant was like a man possessed. He angrily walked off as he continued to contemplate strategy. The defeat of the Confederacy was always on his mind. Grant realized that a triumph over the Confederacy would accomplish his goal of going down in history as one of the world's best military leaders. Consequently, every defeat he incurred by William and Lee made him more wrathful. *I will get you, William and Lee; you just wait! I will not be denied my destiny! I will not!*

After much deliberation, Grant recalled his experience at Vicksburg. *Yes*, he thought, *we'll employ the same strategy here.* Immediately, Grant made his way back to his generals to confer on them his new resolve.

"Men, obviously we have not had much success against the rebels here in hand-to-hand combat. At Vicksburg, I experienced somewhat the same thing. As a result, I laid siege to the city and starved the enemy into submission. I believe such should be done here. By laying siege to Petersburg, we will not only save lives, but also, no doubt, finally bring the Army of Northern Virginia into complete surrender."

Although many of the generals did not want to employ a siege-waiting plan but rather continue the military attack, they realized Grant's strategy might indeed have a better chance at success than the combat alternative and ultimately save lives in the process. As a result, without any vocal disagreements, the plan was laid. Thus began the siege of Petersburg.

42

By late June, with the siege barely a week old, General Burnside became impatient. Burnside, the general who inwardly dissented the most from Grant's siege strategy, wanted to immediately engage the Confederates in any way possible. Accordingly, when Colonel Pleasants suggested the idea of building a large mine that could be detonated under the Confederate fortifications at Petersburg, Burnside embraced the idea and immediately conferred with Grant.

"I don't know, Burnside. Why risk error with such an enterprise? The mine might go off too soon, with us losing even more numbers; whereas, with time, our siege will no doubt work and with little loss of life." Cognizant of the staggering numbers lost since his Eastern campaign, Grant was extremely concerned about further casualties.

"Trust me, General, we won't lose any men with this enterprise. Colonel Pleasants, a coal mine engineer, brought the idea to my attention and, with his engineering expertise, we have no need to worry about error."

"All right, then, send Pleasants upon it!" Grant said as his restless disposition only needed a nudge to surface.

With that, the development of a massive underground mine began; when completed at the end of July, its length was no less than five hundred feet long with eight thousand pounds of powder amassed for its explosion.

On July 30, at 3:15 a.m., Burnside ordered the mine to be ignited. After forty-five minutes, the mine had yet to explode.

"What the hell is going on? I thought the mine was ready, Pleasants."

"It is, General! The fuse must have burnt out. It needs to be relit."

Hearing this, two soldiers immediately volunteered. "We'll relight it, General."

"Go to it then, men. The longer we take, the longer rebeldom lives!"

Within minutes of the fuse being relit, a huge explosion occurred, and tons of earth was hurdled high into the air—coming down upon an entire Confederate unit, killing them instantly.

"There it is, men—the breach we've been waiting for. Charge! Charge upon the enemy!" Burnside exhorted.

Yet, as the Federalists advanced, they became stuck in the large hole created by the mine's explosion. William and Lee, arriving on the scene and seeing the Union soldiers trapped, took full advantage of the situation.

"There they are, men," Lytham exclaimed, "stuck like animals in quicksand! Take them down. All of them!"

The Confederates fired upon the trapped Federalists. Vicious hand-to-hand fighting ensued. But, having the territorial advantage, the Confederates were smashing their foe.

"Retreat, men! Retreat!" Burnside cried, realizing the Union catastrophe.

News promptly reached Grant of Burnside's debacle and of the resulting casualties. Grant was enraged.

"Burnside!" he screamed, seeing him approach. "Damn you, Burnside. You've lost us four thousand men—for nothing! This was a stupendous failure."

"General, the enterprise worked, but we were unable to climb the crater that the mine had left after its explosion."

"Then the enterprise did not work. Its desired result did not come about!" Grant was fuming. "This is the saddest affair I have witnessed in this war. Get back to your post, Burnside, before I lose it and strangle you in my midst!"

"Yes, General." Burnside left quickly, completely humiliated at his failure.

In the Confederate camp, although the soldiers were much pleased at having repulsed the Federalists yet again, Grant's siege upon them was being effectively applied. As a result, anxiety as to their eventual fate consumed their minds, with an increase in such as each day passed—since no relief was expected.

Chapter Forty-Two

In November, the Army of Northern Virginia, still under siege at Petersburg, sadly learned of Lincoln's reelection to the Union presidency. Lee was all the more distressed.

"I fear the worst now, William. I was hoping our resistance against the Yankees, and the great number of lives they have lost in trying to overcome us, would have resulted in Lincoln's defeat with a more conciliatory successor. Yet, the North has again elected him president; and you, as much as I, realize that he will not stop his war upon us until we unconditionally surrender. Currently, we are under siege, and although our provisions will last for some time, eventually they will run out and we will have to leave. But where can we go? We will be pursued. Moreover, the Yankee army gets stronger by the day. I don't know any more, William. I just don't know."

"What is the alternative, General? To give up and have the deaths of those who have gone before us be in vain?" Lytham asked, exceedingly troubled.

"Perhaps soon, William, we may have to surrender. Believe me, I would rather die a thousand deaths than surrender to Grant, but there may come a time when we have to. We already have lost so many men. If we continue to fight on, when the outcome no longer seems in doubt, I would be hard pressed to send more of my brethren to the grave."

"Oh, General," Lytham sighed, "like the rest of us, I have dedicated my life to the South. Like you, I have turned down glory for our home. I don't know if I could ever surrender."

"Nor do I, William; but for the sake of the lives of our troops, we may have to do that very thing."

William was greatly disturbed and left. Lee was shocked at Lytham's abrupt exit, yet he was not surprised. William was one after his own heart. The young man had given everything to the South, and to even ponder surrender, after all that he and his nation had gone through, was torture enough. *All of that bloodshed, all of those widowed wives, all of those fatherless children, all of that devastated land, and all at the hands of Yankees; and seemingly all for naught,* Lee sadly sighed. Truly, the plight was terrible. Lee, realizing Lytham desperately needed consolation, went over to give hope to the man who gave more hope to the South than anyone else.

"William, my son," Lee embraced him. "Please, please don't fret. It's not over yet. We still possess Richmond. We still are holding the Union forces at bay." Lee paused. "Our soldiers look up to us. They need us to remain positive, or they themselves will lose hope. That is why when I am with them, I give them a brave countenance. It is only with you, William, that I impart my soul. That is because our circumstances are much alike."

"Yes, General." Lytham appreciated his remarks. "Sir, you truly are the best general in all of America—both in the Confederate States and in the United States."

"And you are the best soldier, William. You truly are the Soul of the South. Come, William, let's go see our men."

At that, Lee and William met up with their compatriots, equipped with a renewed, vigorous disposition.

43

By March 1865, the siege by Grant upon the city of Petersburg was in its tenth month—strong as ever, with no apparent end in sight. As a result, Lee decided to take the initiative by imploring Lincoln to negotiate a peace to the conflict—a peace the Confederacy could at least tolerate. Lincoln, however, confident that the end of the Confederacy was near, would have nothing to do with Lee's overtures and informed him of such.

"Well, what we thought was right, William: Lincoln does not want to negotiate unless we unconditionally surrender."

"That was the response we expected anyway, General. It was worth a try, however. We must simply keep fighting on, that's all."

Lee was troubled. "Indeed…you know, William, our food rations are running short. It has been a long ten months, and we can't remain here forever. We might very soon have to withdraw."

"True, General, but if we withdraw, we leave the Yankees with a clear march right into Richmond."

"Yes, William, but our supplies are quickly running out, while the Yankees increase in their size around us. Sherman's force has arrived, and the enemy is now more than double our size."

Lytham nodded.

"I am thinking of informing the president to move the government out of the capital."

William immediately thought of his wife's presence in Richmond. *Melanie! What will the Yankees do to her and to the rest of the women of the city?*

"General, I fear that if the Yankees enter the capital, they will treat the women the same way as they treated the women of New Orleans. I have a wife there, General."

"Don't worry, William, as much as Grant is a bastard as a warrior, as a human being he is kind. He is not like Butler. He will do no harm to the female population, nor even to the civilian population for that matter."

Lytham, pondering such, acknowledged with a nod.

"Yet, before we evacuate Petersburg, we will await events and see what transpires. There is no sense taking this drastic action unless it is our last and only resort."

"Yes, General."

* * *

During March 27 and 28, Lincoln visited the Federal forces amassed just outside Petersburg at City Point to boost morale. Personally meeting and shaking hands with the troops, while exhorting them to remain steadfast in their campaign, Lincoln went on to confer with Grant, Sherman, and Admiral David D. Porter on the task remaining.

"Generals and Admiral, you have all done an outstanding job. The end is near—I can certainly feel it!"

"So can we, Mr. President," Grant enthusiastically responded. "Our siege upon the Army of Northern Virginia is proving most effective. They are no doubt almost out of provisions. Moreover, with the arrival of Sherman's force, we outnumber the rebels better than two to one. It is only a matter of time before they either starve into submission or attempt a suicidal escape against our superior numbers."

"Good! Well, now that we have them firmly where we want them, I want this conflict over with soon and with mindful regard to human life. I have been bombarded with complaints over the length of this war and of the incredible number of lives we have lost in the process. Many hold me primarily responsible. And who can blame them? If I were in their shoes and had lost a family member in this seemingly endless conflict, I would be angry with my president too. In fact, although I won my re-election with a convincing number of electoral seats, it was only with less than half a million votes over my opponent. As a result, the anger the nation has toward me is still there, and I want to avoid further wrath. So defeat the last vestiges of rebeldom posthaste but with careful concern for human life."

"Yes, Mr. President," the men humbly answered, Grant in particular. He realized Lincoln's address was largely to him on his baneful Eastern campaign.

On the last day of March, Grant believed the opportunity had arrived to crush the Army of Northern Virginia once and for all. The Confederate line of defense in and around Petersburg, due to the increased Union presence, was vulnerably thin. Moreover, at Five Forks, Virginia, the Confederate line of defense was at the breaking point. Thus, not wanting to miss this moment, Grant conferred with his generals on his new plan.

"Tomorrow, men, we will attack the enemy, and in particular at Five Forks. The rebel line at that location is at the breaking point. We will attack their positions in and around Petersburg, while Sheridan's force will concentrate on Five Forks. With our concerted effort, we should be able to break the Five Forks line and therein penetrate into the heart of Petersburg."

The generals agreed with Grant's resolve, pleased that their commander was finally going to engage the Confederates after months of relative inactivity.

Lee and William were well aware of their lessening hold of Petersburg, especially at Five Forks, but were powerless to address it. They were determined, nevertheless, to confront the Union at any location— regardless of the odds.

The next day, April 1, Grant launched the full-scale Federal attack.

With the Union assault in progress, Lee sent William along with one division—all that he could afford to send—to confront Sheridan's force; they had just routed the Confederates at Five Forks and were now advancing into Petersburg.

"Here they come, men. Hold your ground! We will never give up," Lytham exhorted.

The Confederates were battling incredibly, such that, against numbers better than two to one, they were preventing Sheridan's advance. Other parts of the city's surroundings, however, were not faring as well for the Confederates. The Federalists were attacking on all fronts, upon all Confederate lines of defense; the Union army, with its vastly superior numbers, was achieving the bulk of the success.

Seeing the situation speedily deteriorate, Lee conferred with William on his reluctant resolve.

"William, we must move out. We can't defend Petersburg any longer."

Lytham was sadly aware of such. "Yes, General."

Hence on the afternoon of April 2, Lee ordered an evacuation of the city; the troops left that very evening. They marched westward—in an attempt to find a way around Grant's army and to join General Johnston's force in North Carolina. Yet by vacating Petersburg, the town was left open to the Federalists, with Richmond not far behind. The next day, April 3, Grant's army moved into Petersburg uncontested. Grant appeared jubilant when he greeted Lincoln, who had arrived for the occasion, but inwardly he was beside himself. Lee's army had escaped and with virtually all of its artillery. Grant correctly feared that Lee was heading west to rendezvous with General Johnston in North Carolina, with the result that the war would be, to him, frustratingly prolonged. Accordingly, after exchanging pleasantries with Lincoln, Grant summoned his men and, under forced march, headed west.

On the night of April 5, he finally caught up with Lee near Sayler's Creek, Virginia. Once and for all, Grant wanted complete victory over his unconquered foe.

"This is our finest hour, men. Petersburg has fallen, and Richmond is in our hands! All that remains is the destruction of their forces at large. And tomorrow we will crush one of these insubordinate forces, namely, the Army of Northern Virginia. They have escaped our grasp for far too long. Yet, come tomorrow, their escape from justice will finally end. Tomorrow we will engage this rebel army and destroy it—thoroughly. This is our hour, men. This ending battle against rebellion will bring us immortality! Now is our destiny at hand! Are you with me, men?"

With that came a thunderous "Yes, General!" The Federalists were ready, ready to once and for all eliminate their ever-elusive foe.

That same night, Lee and William conversed. Both realized the superior number of the Army of the Potomac had caught up with them; their hope of joining Johnston's force prior to another engagement with Grant was thwarted.

Lee was somber. "Tomorrow may be our last fight, William."

"Yes," Lytham sighed.

"Whatever happens, I want you to know that I have loved you like a son," Lee said. "Oh God, William, you have done so much for our cause."

Tears formed in Lee's eyes. "It should never have come down to this, William. You deserved a better fate!"

A long pause ensued. Both realized the end seemed near, that their chances of victory against Grant were slim. With the defeat of the Army of Northern Virginia—the main Confederate defense against the Union nation—there would be no question that the Confederacy would be no more. In addition, what were their fates going to be? Lee wanted to convince William that they should surrender. Yet Lee realized that William, and even he himself, were not prepared to do such a thing. Both men fed off the other, such that the strength in one increased the strength in the other. For William, it seemed not only near the end of the Confederacy, but also the end of his own life. William then recalled Lincoln's dire words: "I have a feeling, William, that, in the end, we will both pay the ultimate price for our beliefs."

Perhaps this is the time for me? Lytham thought. *Perhaps this is the end.*

"I am not sure what tomorrow will bring, General, but if it is defeat, it will only be defeat in the flesh and not in the spirit. We know, at least, that we can hold our heads high; that we gave our entire hearts and souls to something we truly believed was right. Our goal was noble. Our goal was just. We were defending our homeland, and such a defense can only bring victory—regardless of what the world might say."

"Indeed my son. Indeed," Lee affirmed as tears flowed from his eyes.

With that, the two embraced. Each realized it might be the last time they would see and converse with the other.

44

The following morning, April 6, 1865, Grant organized his men into attack formation.

Witnessing the Union's movements, Lee and William realized the hour had come. As was the case at Chancellorsville, Lee exhorted his men to fight bravely. Again they entreated William to speak. The troops, to a man, realized this might indeed be the final clash between their army, their country, and the Union nation. As a result, they wanted the man who had led them as a spy, who had led them as a diplomat, and now who led them as a soldier, to speak this one last time. Realizing this might truly be his final hour, William embraced the request; not just to address the soldiers there assembled, but also for his words to somehow address his entire beloved South—both in the present and in the years to come.

"My fellow Southerners, the hour is upon us; Grant's army will not stop until we surrender. But I would rather be destroyed than surrender to Grant and his Yankee race! They have tried to defeat us over and over again since our decision to have a country to call our own. Yet we, our nation, the Souls of the South, have continually defeated the Yankee invader of our homeland!" The troops cheered. "And if I were to do it all over again, I wouldn't change a thing. The South is my home; the South is your home; and we have loved our home with all our might, and we always will. It is not a crime. It is a noble act. And we have showed this noble act to the Yankees time and time again, and we always will!" Even louder cheers permeated the air. "We, our nation, will never surrender. Not even in death. The blood of those who have gone before us cries out in love for our land. Their lives, our lives, all our people's lives are not in vain. Rather all our lives are noble, the noblest!" Tears entered Lytham's eyes. "I am so proud of you all. We are the true victors in this struggle. And today we will show this to the Yankees yet again!"

Cheers of "Yes, William!" rose throughout the Confederate divisions. The men were ready, ready to defend the South once again against their invader. Witnessing the episode, Lee could not help but join in on the abundant cheer. *What a soldier*, thought the general. *What a human being!*

Hearing the fervor and seeing the Confederates forming defensive positions, Grant ordered the attack.

"The hour is now upon us, men. Bring glory to yourselves and to your country. Attack and destroy the Army of Northern Virginia. Charge!"

Grant's army advanced upon the Confederates with all their might. The Confederates, however, were ready.

"Hold your ground, men," Lee beseeched. "Fight to the end! Never surrender!"

Lee seemed to possess supernatural strength. He was not only engaging the Federalists with all his resources, but he was even fighting at the front of his army—facing the brunt of the Union scourge.

Grant continued to unleash the full fury of his army. Everywhere the Army of Northern Virginia was attacked and assaulted. Yet, facing much greater numbers, the Southerners were not giving in.

Lytham was still leading that same division under his command at Petersburg. "Keep holding your position, men. Never give up! We will prove victorious once again!" Like Lee, William seemed to possess supernatural strength—stationing himself at the front of his division, facing the thrust of the Union brawn with all his power.

The battle waged on with ever-increasing savagery. Both armies seemed to realize this was perhaps the last campaign they would fight against the other, and that one side was going to lose. Thus every bit of vigor left in the battle-wounded, fatigued armies was drawn upon by the men in this last-ditch attempt to once and for all defeat their foe.

As combat raged in earnest, Confederate General Anderson's battalion became rooted at Sayler's Creek—creating a huge gap in the South's line of defense. Immediately, William rushed with his soldiers into the opening to fill the gap. Unbeknownst to them, however, Sheridan and his troops were waiting in the wings, hiding behind dense thickets. Accordingly, just as William and his division were patching up the

Confederate line of defense, Sheridan and his soldiers emerged from behind their camouflage.

"Fire, men, fire! They are vulnerable! Shoot them down, all of them," Sheridan commanded.

The Federalists assaulted the startled Confederates with a relentless aggression.

"Men—to our backs! Regroup!" Lytham exhorted.

Suddenly, a bullet struck William directly above his heart, and he fell on the ground in excruciating pain.

"William!" Childs cried.

Sheridan was astonished when he heard that William had been shot and wounded. Sheridan's adrenalin was now pumping at maximum speed. "Men, it is William Lytham and his division who are in front of us. And William is wounded. Wounded, I say! Now is our glory at hand. Charge, men! Destroy them all. Charge!"

Sheridan's troops charged upon the Confederates with an even greater fury. They all realized what, in fact, was taking place: the Soul of the South, at their hands, was about to fall and his men along with him. Yet, William's exhortation to regroup had its intended effect: the Confederates were putting up incredible resistance against Sheridan's overwhelming numbers.

Lytham saw blood flow from his chest; tears were in his eyes.

"Oh, William, I have to get you out of here!"

"Oh, Childs...I'm dying." Lytham forced himself to maintain his composure, yet he was unable to stop his great sorrow. "Oh, John, tell my wife that I love her. Tell her that I'm sorry. That I'm so, so sorry." Lytham wept.

Just then, a Union soldier emerged. The man had succeeded in penetrating the regrouped Confederate line and was rushing upon William to kill him. Childs, however, managed to get between Lytham and the onrushing soldier and was now battling the Federalist.

"Oh God. Oh Mary. Please, please not now! Please...oh, Melanie...my sweet Melanie!" Tears now flowed from Lytham's eyes as he was unable to quell his total devastation. "Oh Lord, my life's been in vain!"

Just then, a radiant light shone exceedingly bright through the overcast sky upon William. The young man felt a sudden warmth of happiness inside, and his pain from the bullet vanished. Moreover, the voice William recognized in that bright light made him all the happier: "It was never in vain, William."

"James!" William now saw him.

James smiled. "Thank you for naming your son after me, big brother."

"Oh, James, I love you so much!"

"And I you, William! That is why I have come: to be here for the man who has always been there for me and for his beloved home."

"How is it, little brother?" William asked, contemplating heaven. "Beautiful?"

"Completely beautiful, William. Beauty beyond belief!" James proclaimed, smiling.

William smiled in joy, but then remembered his present situation. "Oh God, James, not yet, please?"

"Not yet, William; but soon…very soon."

The radiant light vanished; departing as fast as it appeared. William was back in his body and again in much physical pain. Yet the kind, restoring gesture from heaven refocused the Soul of the South. He now knew beyond any doubt that his life was not in vain, that he had indeed made the correct choice in choosing to love and defend his home with all his heart and soul.

Lee emerged and, seeing the assault upon William's division, immediately led some of his own into the fray. Yet, due to Grant's attack from all angles, Lee had to dissipate the majority of his force accordingly—leaving him with only two divisions at his disposal. And such were not enough; not even with William's force. Sheridan had no less than five divisions, and it was a miracle that William and his troops were holding on for as long as they were. With Lee's entry, however, the Confederates were able to stem the Union tide for a while longer. During this time, Lee desperately searched for William's whereabouts. Yet, because of the mass assembly of men fighting at close range, with dead bodies being piled upon one another, it was difficult for Lee to locate him.

Childs was now victorious over the Federal soldier. "William."

Lytham saw his troops in need; he looked at his chest and realized the end was indeed near. "Set me on my horse, Childs. I have one last battle to fight."

Childs tearfully abided.

Lytham saw the bright light again. "Keep fighting, men! Keep fighting!"

Sheridan's divisions, however, were starting to advance. Seeing this, William summoned up what remaining strength he had left and successfully fired upon the advancing Federalists, such that they were being thwarted from their forward progression. William was fighting on pure spirit; his flesh had already given way.

"William…"

Lytham was physically unable to turn, yet he recognized the voice. "General Lee."

"William, we must withdraw. We are being overwhelmed!"

"All right, General. Men, follow General Lee! I'll provide your cover."

"No, William—get someone else!" Childs vehemently insisted.

Lytham tearfully smiled. "No, John. Take the others and follow the general. Thank you for everything. You've truly been a great friend!"

"I love you, William!" Childs was unable to stop his sorrowful pain. "I will tell Melanie what you asked of me!" Childs now addressed the troops, ever reluctantly. "Let's go men, away!"

As the Confederates withdrew from Sayler's Creek, the Union barrage came upon William.

"For the South!" Lytham exclaimed, firing his remaining ammunition.

"William!" Lee called out.

Just then, with William holding the Sayler's Creek line as the withdrawing Confederates had escaped to safety, a Union soldier fired the deadly shot, and his rifle's bullet pierced Lytham's heart. Falling from the blow, William landed in the creek, and with tears of reassurance in his eyes that his life was indeed not in vain, the Soul of the South breathed his last.

At that, soldiers from both sides ceased from fighting and gave a moment of silence—in absolute respect to the North's worthy opponent and to the South's pride and joy.

The next day, April 7, Grant expressed to Lee his absolute remorse and sense of loss at the death of William Lytham, and in turn entreated the Confederate commander to surrender in order to prevent further loss of life. Although resistant to surrender, Lee realized the time had come to concede. Accordingly, on April 9, 1865, Lee officially surrendered the Army of Northern Virginia to Grant, closing the greatest chapter of the greatest conflict in America's history.

Less than a week later, Lincoln's prophecy became fulfilled as he himself paid the ultimate price for his beliefs—assassinated by John Wilkes Booth at Ford's Theater on April 14.

* * *

"Mr. President, welcome!"

"William!"

"You were truly correct: we both paid the ultimate price for our beliefs."

"True, William. And yet I have no regrets!"

"Nor I, Mr. President. Nor I!"

Acknowledgments

I would like to thank my parents and grandparents who have always been by my side in a loving, supportive manner. I would also like to thank my editor, Gayla Mills, whose knowledge and expertise in editing made this book the best it could be.

About the Author

Mike Witham is a high school teacher in Ontario, Canada. He has a bachelor of education from the University of Ottawa and a specialist degree in English and History from the University of Toronto. He has always had a love for writing and history and enjoys bringing history alive.

Soul of the South is his first novel. While writing the book, the work took on a life of its own and challenged his previously held thoughts on the American Civil War. It made Witham realize the agonizing dilemma Southerners had to face, as they became caught in a conflict where love for home and love for country became two divergent roads in which only one path could be taken. He hopes that the book will elicit understanding, and even admiration, for the noble individuals who fought in America's bloodiest conflict regardless of the side they fought on.